# Books by Michael C. Grumley

BREAKTHROUGH

LEAP

CATALYST

AMID THE SHADOWS

THROUGH THE FOG

THE UNEXPECTED HERO

*To Andrea. My wife and partner in everything. Including writing. If people only knew what my stories look like before she gets a hold of them.*

# ACKNOWLEDGEMENTS

Special thanks to Autumn, Julie, Liz, Richele, Susan, Tony, Frank, Bojan, Rob, Luke, and Shawn, for their expert advice and proofing help.

And to Jill Weinstein, a great proofreader and editor if there ever was one (easyedits@outlook.com).

# 1

"I THINK YOU'D BETTER get down here. We've got company."

Her eyes opened wide with the phone receiver still gripped tightly in her hand. She immediately hung up and jumped out of her chair, rounding the desk and running for the door. After flinging it open and sprinting down the carpeted hallway, she approached the wide stairs and descended as quickly as she could without tripping.

The layout of the new building was strikingly similar to the old one, but here the air conditioning system was barely able to stave off Puerto Rico's brutal humidity. By the time she'd made it to the large double doors, the familiar flush through her body told her that her sweat glands were kicking into gear. She lowered her head and leaned into the doors, pushing them both open.

The familiar computerized voice sounded almost immediately. *Hello Alison.*

Alison smiled broadly toward the giant seawater tank. "Hello, Sally," she replied, partially out of breath. "You're back."

Sally wiggled her tail happily. *We back.*

Alison raised an eyebrow, scanning the rest of the tank's bright blue water. "Where's Dirk?"

Before she could answer, Dirk plunged into the top of the tank with a giant splash and performed a barrel roll as he skirted past Sally.

Alison laughed. He loved making a grand entrance. Of course, they really needed to change the part of the tank that allowed him to do that.

Dirk continued to the bottom where he swung up and around before coasting in next to Sally. *Hello Alison. Hello Chris.*

Alison smirked and tilted her head slightly. "Hello, Dirk."

*We happy see you.*

"We're happy to see you too." Chris Ramirez joined Alison in front of the tank, holding his perpetual cup of coffee. How he could drink coffee all day in this heat, she would never know.

Their new facility was smaller than the aquarium in Miami, but this one was strictly a research center, which meant fewer unplanned distractions. Gutted from an old cannery, the building was refurbished and expanded to include a large indoor-outdoor tank for Dirk and Sally. Now they could come and go as they pleased. No more bars.

It was, of course, the least she and the team could do after what they'd all been through. And true to their word, the dolphins returned regularly. It also helped that Dirk was fed like a king.

Behind Alison and Chris, and against the far wall, stood an immense computer system with hundreds of blinking lights. IMIS, short for Inter Mammal Interpretive System, was the same system that made their first communications with Dirk and Sally possible. But now IMIS was over twice its original size. After her team relocated to Puerto Rico and closer to the dolphins' natural breeding ground, the IMIS system had gone through a major upgrade. It was almost quaint to think about its abilities before, compared to its computing power now. It made Lee Kenwood, their head of technology, absolutely giddy. In fact, Alison and Chris had both joked to Lee that it looked as though he were trying to show up the engineers at NASA.

Alison didn't fully understand the specifications of the newly upgraded IMIS, but she did know it had a lot to do with what Lee called *teraflops*. But to her, it was simply bigger and faster. And even though it had doubled in size, Lee claimed it was almost eight times more powerful. The amount of data that IMIS could process before in a day, it could now do in a couple hours.

Sally swam close to the underwater microphone. *How you Alison?*

"I am very well," she smiled. "How are you?"

*We good. You ready now.*

"Not yet, but soon."

Smiling, Chris took a sip from his cup. "I guess we have some calls to make."

"We sure do."

*Food now.*

Alison glanced back at Dirk as he thrust his tail up and down, excitedly. She folded her arms in front and shook her head.

If the world had been surprised at their breakthrough before, this time they were going to be absolutely stunned.

## 2

"THE CRADLE OF Naval Aviation" was the unofficial name of the Naval Air Base near Pensacola, Florida. It was built as the country's first Naval Air Station and remained so even well into the First World War. In present day, it was known for being the primary training facility for all Navy, Marine, and Coast Guard aviators and flight officers. It was also home to the Blue Angels, the Navy's famed flight demonstration squadron.

Spanning an area of well over eight thousand acres, the Pensacola Naval Complex employed twenty-three thousand military and seventy-four hundred civilians. Not surprisingly, it was a major hub for modern hi-tech naval research and testing.

It was also where Commanders John Clay and Steve Caesare, from Naval Investigations, had been living for the past two weeks.

Both men briskly made their way down the long, polished hallway of the Naval Education and Training Command building's third floor. When they reached the end, the pair stopped before a large white door. John Clay knocked and the door was promptly opened from the inside. Stepping into the room, Clay and Caesare recognized Rear Admiral David Einhorn, the commander of the NETC. Einhorn was sitting behind his desk with his Force Master Chief standing next to him, both of whom ceased their conversation and looked up expectantly when Clay and Caesare entered. Almost unnoticed, the lieutenant who had opened the door then silently stepped out behind them and closed it again.

Einhorn nodded. "Gentlemen, I understand you have something for me."

"Yes, sir," replied Clay. They both approached the desk, but Clay took an extra step forward and handed Admiral Einhorn a thin folder. "We've finished the investigation, sir. Here is the signed report."

Einhorn took the folder and flipped it open, glancing over the first page. "A power failure? Are you kidding?"

Clay shook his head. "No, sir."

"How the hell does a power failure cause a drone to go rogue?"

They'd been expecting this reaction, especially from Einhorn. After all, they'd already uploaded their report online and forwarded copies to both Einhorn and their own boss, Admiral Langford, a half hour ago. Their hand delivered copy was merely a formality. Judging from his reaction, Einhorn had read the online version already.

Einhorn hadn't wanted them there from the beginning. The failure with the drone was a fluke as far as he was concerned. Hell, as far as his entire staff was concerned. But it did happen. A new drone lost connection with its remote pilot for twelve seconds. It may not have seemed like a big deal to everyone else, especially since the connection was reestablished successfully, but it required an investigation. Not because the Navy necessarily worried about the connection, but because of what might have happened during those twelve seconds.

A few years before, a Predator Drone had been captured in Iran by blocking the aircraft's satellite connection back to its remote pilot in Arizona. Worse, Iran never had to hack the drone. They only had to keep the connection blocked long enough to force it into an emergency mode, which compelled the drone to get itself to the ground safely. It was a bug in the software: a mistake.

Nevertheless, having the world watch their televisions and see Iranian soldiers dancing up and down on one of the Unites States' four million dollar secret weapons was not something the Pentagon was willing to endure again.

Clay cleared his throat and answered Einhorn. "Well, sir, the failure was caused by a power fluctuation on one of the drone's motherboards. It's the same board that controls the transceivers and antennas. We think it's a design flaw with the hardware since we've been able to reproduce the problem several times."

Einhorn dropped the file on his desk and leaned back in his chair, clearly irritated. "So, was it hacked?"

"No, sir."

"I didn't think so," the Admiral scoffed. "I told them they were sending you boys out for nothing."

This time Clay and Caesare looked at each other. "Well," replied Caesare, "it doesn't necessarily mean that it *couldn't* be hacked...sir."

Einhorn furrowed his brow at Caesare. He didn't care for either one of them. He had a department to run, one of the most important in the Navy, and he didn't like these guys from investigations poking their noses wherever they liked. Yet, while Einhorn was not happy, he certainly wasn't stupid either.

It wasn't clear why, but he knew both of the commanders standing before him reported directly to Admiral Langford, the President's new Chairman of the Joint Chiefs of Staff. Langford had replaced General Griffith, who moved to fill the role of National Security Advisor after that position was unexpectedly vacated. Now Langford had the President's ear, so Einhorn wasn't about to do or say anything stupid.

"So, what's your recommendation then?" asked Einhorn, with heavy sarcasm.

Clay paid no attention to the Admiral's tone. "A full analysis, which includes an audit of the hardware design and software computer code."

"And how long will that take?"

"I'm not sure, sir. It would depend on the resources available." Clay knew Einhorn wasn't going to like any estimate he offered, so he simply left it at that.

Einhorn grunted and picked up the folder again. "Well, I trust Langford will let us know how to proceed. I suppose that's all, gentlemen. Thank you for your time."

Clay and Caesare both gave slight nods and spun around. They walked back to the door and exited without a sound.

After Caesare pulled the door closed behind him, he looked at Clay. "Have we ever discussed how thankless this job is?"

"Almost weekly," smiled Clay. He turned to fall into step with Caesare when his cell phone rang. Stopping, he pulled it out of his pocket and looked at the displayed number. "It's Langford."

He held the phone to his ear. "This is Clay." After a long pause, he replied with a simple, "Yes, sir."

Caesare raised his eyebrows, curiously. "That was quick."

"We need to find a conference room."

* * *

Truth be told, Admiral Langford never wanted the chairman job. But in the end, he was an officer and the President asked him to do it. And frankly, he was leery of who else would have been asked had he declined. Although he originally had his doubts, Langford decided that Carr actually had the fortitude and ethics to be a solid President. And that was something most military leaders longed for.

Langford's weathered face appeared on the video screen in front of Clay and Caesare. "I see you've uploaded your report on the drone. Have you talked to Einhorn yet?"

"Yes, sir," Clay nodded. "We just dropped off the signed hard copy."

"How'd he take it?"

Caesare smiled. "He loved it!"

"I bet." Langford couldn't decide whether to scoff or roll his eyes. "I guess as long as he didn't physically throw you out of his office, we can consider it a success. You're probably aware that he's not a big fan of Investigations."

"We picked up on that."

"Good," Langford continued, glancing at his watch. "I'm sure I'll be hearing from him shortly." He looked back into the camera. "In the meantime, I'm sending a plane for you. I need you on it ASAP."

"Where are we going?"

"Brazil. We have a bit of a situation. Call it a surprise."

"I hate surprises," Caesare chortled.

Clay looked at Caesare. "That's true, sir. His second marriage was largely a surprise."

The corner of Langford's lip curled at the joke. "Relax. It's not an engagement party. It appears we are the proud owners of a new sub."

Clay and Caesare peered with anticipation at the screen.

"Last night the Brazilian Navy captured a submarine off the coast of French Giana. It's Russian. November class."

Both men's expressions changed from curious to confused. "November class? I thought those were decommissioned."

"So did we." The admiral leaned forward onto his elbows. "It appears at least one was not. It was first detected three days ago and a Brazilian Tikuna was dispatched."

"And they *captured* it?" Clay asked. A single submarine catching another was quite a feat.

Langford smiled, reading Clay's face. "Well, they asked for a little help. We had two of our boats behind the Tikuna. Unofficially, of course."

"What's a November doing in Brazilian waters?" asked Caesare. "Something that old wouldn't simply be out on patrol."

"No, it wouldn't. Unfortunately, we don't know why. The crew isn't talking. All twenty-seven of them."

"Twenty-seven?"

"A skeleton crew," confirmed Langford.

Caesare raised an eyebrow. "Is that even possible?"

"Evidently."

"What did the Russians say?"

"We haven't asked them yet," Langford replied, with a smile.

"You're not suggesting *we* talk to the crew, sir?"

"No, I want you two to get down there and take a look at that Russian sub. The pictures we got back suggest it has something important on board, and we want to know what it is."

## 3

LEE KENWOOD WAS thrilled with their new lab. Finally able to separate their systems from the main observation area, it gave him some much needed elbow room to work on the hardware for their next project. And it was a doozy.

He also appreciated the extra help from Juan Diaz, a Puerto Rican native and computer engineer, just a few years out of college. He was a fast study and incredibly sharp.

Lee and Juan both looked up from a large table they were standing over as Alison opened the door, letting in a loud roar from the yelling children behind her.

"Hi, Ali," they said, in tandem. Lee punched a button on his keyboard and watched the results appear across the screen. Juan was carefully holding still a large device with a thin computer cable attached.

"Hello." Alison let the door close behind her and crossed the room. "How are things looking?"

"Pretty good. We've got most of it uploaded and tested. I think we should be ready by Thursday morning." He looked up from his screen. "I take it Dirk and Sally are back?"

"How can you tell?"

"Sounds like a zoo out there."

The 'zoo' was approximately forty screaming, very excited children. During their big move to Puerto Rico, Alison and her team somehow managed to become local celebrities with all of the press. Earlier in the year, her team had officially revealed the amazing breakthrough of their IMIS translation system in a demonstration for several news crews. Not surprisingly, the news went global and people from everywhere quickly descended upon the aquarium to see for themselves. Their communications with the dolphins was deemed the 'Achievement of a Lifetime' by several magazines, and for the next two months, she and her staff were invited on hundreds of television and radio interviews. It was overwhelming, but it initially provided a welcome change of pace after what they'd been through. However, in the end, the attention and visits never seemed to let up, so their move off the mainland wasn't just for their research; it was also for their sanity.

Of course, no matter where they went, they were going to garner a lot of attention, and Puerto Rico was no different. In fact, the entire island went wild when they found out that one of their old buildings on the south side of the island, just outside of Ponce, would be converted into a new research center for the famous

'Dirk and Sally.' What *was* a surprise was the reaction of the kids in Puerto Rico.

In the States, during their early stages of research, Alison and her team played host to countless children on field trips, coming to visit the dolphins. Many of the kids were genuinely excited, but many others were not. Instead, they sat off to the side, glued to their cell phone screens. Alison had thought it odd at first, but after seeing the same thing class after class, it became downright depressing.

However, she did remember a very special fifth grade class from Hedrick Elementary in Lewisville, Texas, and the Puerto Rican children reminded her of them a lot. In Puerto Rico, all the children were absolutely *thrilled* to come. Every face remained pressed against the thick glass the entire time. They couldn't get enough, and, as a result, it couldn't help but bring back some of that early excitement for Alison and her team. So, in exchange, they decided to do something special for the kids.

Alison had an idea one day and talked to Lee and Juan about it. It took a while, but they managed to set up a smaller translation server for visitors. It had a much shorter vocabulary than the giant IMIS system and couldn't translate new words, but it allowed the children to do something astounding: actually stand in front of the tank and talk with a real-life dolphin.

Alison remembered watching the children type on the keyboard for the first time, thinking some of the kids might actually pop from the excitement. It was contagious. She had never seen Dirk and Sally so excited either. They would stay and talk to the children for hours until the very last one had left.

Of course, Dirk and Sally were free now and they came and went as they pleased. So, when they did arrive, Alison and her team would promptly call the nearby schools to arrange some visits. And neither the children, nor Dirk and Sally, ever showed any signs of tiring. It was indeed a 'zoo' and she loved it.

"By the way," Lee interrupted, standing behind her. "Did DeeAnn find you? She was looking for you earlier. Something about helping with her research this afternoon."

"No. I'll head over."

Lee nodded and turned back to Juan, who was showing him something on his monitor. As Alison turned to leave, her phone rang. She looked at the screen and answered immediately.

"Hey there," she said, smiling sheepishly.

"Hi," replied a deep voice on the other end.

"How are *you*?"

She instinctively turned away from Lee and Juan, who both chuckled at her. Lee playfully cupped his hands over his mouth. "Tell him we said, 'hi.'"

She made a shushing gesture with her hand and turned further around. "Sorry."

John Clay chuckled himself. "I'm fine. How are you?"

"Oh, pretty good. I was just standing here giving Lee and Juan some tips on computers."

Clay laughed. "I bet that's some advice."

"Hey," she said, half pretending to be hurt. "I have a toaster. I know how this stuff works! So, where are you?"

"Um, I'm on a plane."

Alison glanced at her watch. "Already? I thought your flight wasn't until this evening."

"Yeah, about that…unfortunately, something's come up and I'm not going to be able to make it."

Alison looked dejected. "That's too bad. I was looking forward to seeing you."

"I know. I'm sorry. So was I. Hopefully, it won't be too long."

"Where are you going?"

"Brazil," Clay answered. "Not too far. Just on the other side of you."

"Can you say what for?"

"I'm afraid I can't. Let's just pretend I'm scouting romantic vacation spots."

"You know it's going to be one year pretty soon."

"Yes, I know."

*Of course he did,* she thought. The man didn't forget anything. He had a mind like a steel trap. He was actually kind of amazing that way. He not only knew how to *listen*, but he actually remembered what she said for more than ten seconds.

Alison had to admit, he was nothing like she had expected when they first met. He worked for the Navy, a branch of the military she loathed. Of course, to be truthful, she hated all military branches. But as it turned out, John Clay wasn't just some Marine jarhead. In fact, he was not only a man; he was a bona fide anomaly. He was smart, considerate, and devastatingly handsome. And those shoulders!

"I'm really sorry, Alison." Clay swayed side to side in his seat as his plane turned and bounced onto the runway. "I'll call you in the next day or two, okay?"

"Okay," Alison said, still wearing a trace of a frown. "Be safe."

"Always."

"Bye." She ended the call and remained staring at the phone.

"I take it he's not coming," Lee said behind her.

She sighed and dropped her hand, sliding the phone back into her pocket. "No."

* * *

The plane was a C-20 Gulfstream III, which had arrived less than thirty minutes after their video call with Langford. Clay powered off his phone and closed his eyes, pressing his head gently into the leather headrest. He regretted hearing the disappointment in Alison's voice.

After a long moment and from the table between them, Clay picked up the folder containing his copy of the report on the Russian sub and flipped it open again. He remained quiet, thinking.

"So, what I can't figure out," Caesare said, speaking first, "is what the hell kind of interest Brazil would hold for a Russian sub, and an old one at that?"

"I've been wondering the same thing. Russia has a pretty good relationship with Brazil, so why the secrecy?"

"Because that's what you do when you're *hiding*."

"But what were they hiding from?" Clay pondered. "And why a fifty-year-old submarine everyone else in the world thought had been decommissioned?"

"Maybe it was *because* everyone thought it had been decommissioned," Caesare said, with a touch of sarcasm. He raised his bottle of beer and took a swig. "But if I was

Russia and wanted to go stealth, I sure as hell wouldn't do it in a November class sub. They're noisy."

Clay tilted his head back and absently examined the ceiling. "Brazil has the second largest navy in the Americas. Their entire fleet and infrastructure are well known. What could the Russians be trying to find out?"

"It's also odd that they haven't said anything."

"Agreed. If there really was some secret to hide, wouldn't they want to get their crew out quickly?"

"Unless speaking up makes it worse." Caesare tilted his bottle, examining it. "Even if it did, why not just make up some PR story or misdirection? Governments do that all the time."

"True. But it means we're still asking the same question. What do they want to know about Brazil?"

Caesare placed the bottle in a cup holder and leaned his seat back. "Maybe there's a simpler explanation."

Clay raised an eyebrow, waiting.

"Maybe their navigator's just an idiot."

Clay laughed. Outside, the dual engines of the Gulfstream reached maximum thrust, and the plane abruptly began to roll forward as the pilot released the brakes. The aircraft sped down the runway, building speed until it lifted smoothly into the air.

As he watched the ground quickly fall away, Clay tried to relax, but couldn't seem to dismiss something. It was a nagging question that should have been answered in the report, but wasn't.

# 4

AFTER ALISON LEFT the guys in the lab, she headed back downstairs. She was disappointed at not being able to see John, but a small side of her actually felt relieved. They'd been dating for a year but given their jobs, and her move off the mainland, they hadn't spent much time together lately. Their relationship was moving slowly and Alison had to admit, she was beginning to feel a tad insecure. It was why she was both excited and nervous to see him. She had finally mustered the courage to broach the topic of 'exclusivity.'

But it didn't matter now. She decided she was relieved to get a reprieve and gladly pushed it to the back of her mind.

She reached the bottom of the stairs and continued down the building's new stone hallway, past the giant saltwater tank. As she strode by, she grinned and stopped to watch the dozens of children surrounding the tank. Chris was standing next to them, giving each child a turn at the keyboard, typing something out to Dirk and Sally. Above them, an oversized monitor displayed each question for everyone to see. The little boy now standing in front of the keyboard and typing away looked to be about eight. Alison smiled when she read his question overhead; *how high can you jump in the air?*

That was a dare if she'd ever heard one. She watched as Dirk heard the message and immediately darted off, swimming around the tank and shooting to the top of the water. He then jumped high into the air above. The kids went absolutely crazy.

Alison grinned and continued walking. She passed the enormous wall of humming servers, which made up the new IMIS distributed computer system. All of the machines were contained within dozens of large climate controlled, glass cabinets.

Turning a corner, she headed for the other half of the complex. The second hallway was longer and darker but led into a bright, open area, lined with glass walls along the right side. Unlike the dolphin's tank, these walls were much taller and wrapped around part of the wild habitat area. The rest of the perimeter continued around the habitat in the form of equally high walls, but made out of concrete. In the middle was a wide, man-made hill sloping downward and covered in dense foliage, including Rosewood and Tabernanthe trees of varying sizes. The ground was covered with hundreds of different types of thick bushes and shrubs with a small, artificial brook running down through the uneven hillside. High above was a wide roof of thick netting, covering the entire jungle habitat. It was a perfect, or *near* perfect, half-acre replica of an African rainforest.

All along the top of the walled perimeter, separated about every hundred feet, were all-weather, high-definition, motion-detecting cameras. Collectively, they captured video of nearly every square foot of the enclosed habitat and recorded a live feed around the clock. The data was then sent in digital form through the thick cable and back into the heart of the building, where it was fed into IMIS.

Alison peered through one of the giant walls of clear glass and spotted who she was looking for inside. Dee-Ann Draper, an older woman with dark hair and dressed in light khaki clothes, was squatting next to a young female gorilla.

Alison looked up at the nearest camera as it automatically zoomed in and focused on the two playing in the shade beneath one of the taller Rosewood trees. As they played, every movement, facial expression, sound, or gesture, was recorded and broken into individual frames. It was then saved to IMIS's enormous data drives.

The data gathering was not all that different from how they had originally done it with Dirk and Sally. Although, some differences required an overhaul of certain pieces of IMIS's computer code, since communication with primates was significantly different than ocean mammals. First and foremost was the sound. Contrary to popular belief, gorillas were a very quiet species. They used only a limited number of verbal sounds. The vast majority of communication happened instead through gestures and complex facial expressions. It presented very different requirements for capturing language.

DeeAnn was the real expert. Even though Alison was in charge at the Center and of her dolphins, DeeAnn Draper was every bit her equal when it came to primate research and gorillas. Alison loved having DeeAnn on the team.

Inside the habitat, DeeAnn sat next to Dulce, wearing a thin black vest over her khaki shirt. The name *Dulce* was Spanish for 'sweet' and the small three-year-old gorilla fit her name perfectly. With light brown eyes and dark, protruding lips, which constantly smiled, Dulce sat playfully on the ground pointing at DeeAnn. She made a short chuckling sound and tilted her head.

Since the habitat was far too large to make traditional speakers practical, the speaker receiving the translation was much smaller and integrated directly into the special vest that DeeAnn wore. Dulce's words came out in the tone of IMIS' mechanical voice. *I like play.*

DeeAnn smiled, copying Dulce's movement. "I like play too." It took less than a second for IMIS to translate DeeAnn's words into a similar sound for Dulce, which again emanated from the vest.

Dulce pursed her lips and grunted softly, waving her lanky arm over her head. *I want play chase.*

When DeeAnn heard the translation, she smiled wearily. "Again?"

Dulce nodded her head vigorously and spread her lips into a wide, toothy grin. She could read the look in DeeAnn's eyes as she tried to change the subject.

"Let's play count."

Dulce shook her body playfully and spoke again. *You silly.*

DeeAnn smiled. She wasn't silly; she was tired. It was almost one hundred degrees in the habitat. She could only run around so much before Dulce would think she was playing dead. "Let's play count," she repeated. She held up her hand as the small speaker on her chest vibrated and spit out the gorilla version of the sentence. Displaying four fingers, DeeAnn asked, "How many is this?"

Dulce's grin turned into a wide smile, and she barely looked at DeeAnn's hand before replying with a purr followed by low squeals. *Four. Play chase now.*

DeeAnn sighed and looked around, spotting Alison with relief, who was standing on the other side of the glass, watching them. She pointed through the glass. "Who's that, Dulce?"

Dulce turned and followed DeeAnn's finger. Her excitement was immediate. *Alison!* Dulce sprang from her position and ran forward on her fists, covering the distance to the wall quickly. She put her dark hand on the glass and patted it playfully. That was how she greeted people on the other side.

Alison smiled back at Dulce and leaned forward, patting back against the glass. She waited until DeeAnn and her vest had reached them before Alison replied. "Good morning, Dulce."

"Hey, Ali," DeeAnn said.

"Morning. Lee said you were looking for me."

Before DeeAnn could reply, the speaker on her vest emitted a loud tone, signifying the last sentence was not translated successfully. She instinctively pushed a small button, pausing the system.

"Yeah, I wanted to steal Kelly from you this afternoon to work on some more group translations with us. Lee said he fixed part of yesterday's problem, so I wanted to give it another try."

"Sure," Alison glanced at her watch. "I think she's going to feed Dirk and Sally in about thirty minutes or so. I'll send her over after that."

"Thanks," DeeAnn gave Alison a devious smile. "You want to come in and do some laps with Dulce?"

Alison laughed. "I would if I could, but I need to make sure everything is ready for Thursday. It's a big day," she added, with a wink.

"Gotcha, have fun." DeeAnn waved and stepped back from the glass, pushing the button again on her vest. She looked down at Dulce, who was smiling up at her. "Okay, one more chase."

* * *

Alison watched DeeAnn run away after Dulce, hopelessly outmatched. She still marveled at what Lee and Juan had done, with help from IBM, of course. The mobile unit was amazing, providing it stayed within wireless range of the IMIS system. But as incredible as the vest was, it almost seemed trite compared to what Lee and Juan were working on now: an improved vest that was also *waterproof*.

# 5

DULCE SAT ON the ground, across from DeeAnn, studying the large board in front of her. Her small brown legs bowed in front of her as she reached down with her thick fingers and spun the wooden dial on the board. It was a game that DeeAnn had built to teach colors and shapes.

The oversized dial stopped turning above a large red triangle, which made Dulce clap her hands. She loved the triangles. Excitedly, Dulce stood up and swung her arm over the board. She grasped her piece in her dark hands and moved it to the next red triangle spot. She immediately raised her head and grinned happily from ear to ear.

"Very good, Dulce," DeeAnn clapped along with her.

Still standing, Dulce examined the board again and then pointed at DeeAnn.

*You turn you turn.* The words emanated from the built-in speaker on the vest.

DeeAnn laughed and leaned forward. "I know. I know." She reached down and brushed the dial with her hand. When it landed on a black circle, Dulce suddenly stopped and shook her head.

*Not good.*

DeeAnn opened her mouth, pretending to be offended, causing Dulce to promptly begin laughing with another toothy grin. When DeeAnn could no longer hold her smile in, Dulce jumped over the board and into her lap.

Dulce squealed and wrapped her arms around her. *Me love Mommy.*

DeeAnn hugged her back and gently touched her forehead to Dulce's. "I love you too."

Dulce was, of course, smart enough to understand she wasn't human, but DeeAnn was the only mother figure Dulce had ever known. Or at least remembered.

DeeAnn was already caring for Dulce when they traveled to Puerto Rico to join Alison and her team. In fact, Dulce was just under a year and one-half old when DeeAnn had found her. Now almost two years later, they were as close as ever. It seemed as though Dulce had forgotten the terrible trauma before DeeAnn came along and had managed to become trusting again, as proven through her physical affection. Most gorillas were much less affectionate, or downright dangerous, if they got too close. But Dulce was different. She was naturally strong for her size, but she also had a soft side which made her more human than DeeAnn had ever seen.

DeeAnn Draper would know. She had spent several

years working with the famed female gorilla Koko, in southern California, whose ability to learn sign language had made news around the world in the mid-1990s. Koko was an exciting step forward when it came to communication between primates. But if Koko was a step forward, then Dulce was a giant leap.

Sign language was an amazing accomplishment, but IMIS changed all that. DeeAnn came to the research center to prove the Koko skeptics wrong. Yet even after witnessing a real exchange between Alison and Sally, she never imagined that IMIS would ultimately be able to reinvent how she communicated with Dulce.

But it did. It took several months, but when IMIS broke the language barrier, it did so in a big way.

DeeAnn let her go and watched Dulce scramble back to the other side of the board and point at the wooden pointer again. *Me turn me turn.*

"I know," she conceded. "It's your turn."

* * *

Kelly Carlson arrived less than an hour later, carrying a large box containing several pounds of lettuce, celery, and kale, for Dulce's lunch. She punched her code into the console on the opposite wall and waited for the large glass door of the habitat to click open behind her. She then backed up, pushing it open with her backside, and wiggled through, letting the door close hard behind her.

Of all the staff Alison had hired, Kelly was one of the most dynamic. Attractive, with a slender figure and long blonde hair, Carlson was, among other things, a former scuba instructor, boat captain, private chef, and tour guide. She'd grown up in the tropics of the Caribbean and unlike many people who eventually got island fever, she showed no signs of wanting to leave. She was a sunshine addict and as sharp as a whip.

Kelly winked at DeeAnn as she approached and then turned to Dulce, who was already on her feet rocking back and forth excitedly. She seized the top of the box and nearly tore it from Kelly's hands by accident.

"Easy, honey." Kelly smiled and dropped the box gently onto the ground. She watched Dulce tear into it, before turning to DeeAnn. "Ali said you were ready to do some more group play."

"Thanks, yes. Maybe in thirty minutes?"

"Sure," Kelly nodded. "I'll be back in a few. I've got to check a few things on the boat."

DeeAnn propped herself up onto her knees in the soft dirt, watching Dulce eat her lunch. With a sudden, playful push, she forced Dulce's small forty-pound frame off her feet, causing her to roll onto her hindquarters. Behind her, DeeAnn quickly snuck a piece of celery from the box and took a bite. Dulce pulled her own stalk from her mouth and stared back questioningly until she watched DeeAnn take another bite and make a funny face. Dulce snorted at her and laughed.

* * *

Not far away, inside the lab, Lee was watching them on his monitor. He and Juan had completed the diagnostics on the new vest and were now waiting for the data to finish uploading.

He wasn't watching DeeAnn and Dulce live. Instead Lee was studying previous video segments that IMIS had recorded. But Lee had a problem. A big one.

Along with the current video segment, the right side of his screen displayed a window with detailed system log information. As he clicked on various log entries, the corresponding video and set of changing pixels would be highlighted, showing the area IMIS had zoomed in on while recording.

Lee put his hand over his mouth and tapped his cheek, struggling to understand what was causing the problem. Some of the logs and video sequences appeared to be out of sync, and he couldn't find a reason for it. In other words, it was happening so infrequently that he was unable to predict it, let alone recreate it, which meant troubleshooting was extraordinarily difficult. And if he couldn't isolate the cause or at least a reliable pointer, he could not even begin to fix it.

Because of this, his anxiety was silently growing. It was looking more and more likely that something was seriously wrong with the new computer code on IMIS. Like the original system, IBM had helped program the code for the entire system, including the artificial intelligence based algorithms. However, when they added the complication of studying a primate, in addition to dolphins, part of the system needed to be reprogrammed.

Primates were much more expressive and the vast majority of their communication happened on a much more subtle level. Facial expressions alone were something IMIS never had to track with Dirk and Sally. Dolphins simply didn't have the myriad muscles in their faces as humans and primates did. Instead, IMIS tracked everything else such as whistles, clicks, and even physical movements. And even those took years to record and process. Yet in the end, from a technological standpoint, the original efforts to translate the dolphin language were in some ways *simpler* than primates.

But now all of the progress IMIS had made with Dulce was suspect, and Lee knew it. If the accuracy was compromised, even as little as ten percentage points, it meant that many more words may be misinterpreted due to their cross-relationships. Scientific methods were very strict, and, in this case, the size of the possible breach seemed to be growing.

Lee watched another red error scroll by in the log file and leaned back in his chair, shaking his head nervously.

## 6

THE FLIGHT TO Belem in Para, Brazil took five and a half hours. The late day sun had just under two hours before its final descent behind the lush but distant mountains far to the west.

Founded in 1616 as the first European colony on the Amazon River, the multicolored buildings of Belem glowed brightly below as the jet banked to the right and prepared its approach. From his seat, Clay gazed out across the dense, green tropical landscape, extending as far as he could see. It was so lush it was almost glowing. Somewhere in his memory, Clay remembered reading that the forests of South America were responsible for creating more than twenty percent of the world's oxygen. From the incredible view through his side window, he believed it.

The fourth largest continent by landmass, South

America was home to some of the most exotic life and incredible features on the planet, including both the world's largest rainforest and the tallest waterfall in the world. It was a vast and mystical place, remaining almost entirely unexplored until well into the early twentieth century. Legends claimed that many of its hidden mysteries were still waiting to be discovered. The one that Clay and Caesare had come to see was man-made. Floating silently in the Val-de-Cães naval yard, it rested just several hundred feet below them.

The sub had been under heavy guard since being escorted into port, where the Russian crew was quickly isolated for questioning. And according to Langford, they weren't very talkative.

Next to Clay, Caesare's snoring was interrupted by a loud snort as he startled himself awake. Caesare blinked and rubbed his eyes with his hands, then remained still for a moment feeling the descent of the aircraft. "Well, that was quick."

Clay smirked, finally turning away from the window, and gathered his papers from the small table. He stood the papers on end to straighten them before sliding them back into the folder, tucking the stack neatly into his pack.

With a yawn, Caesare leaned forward, letting the back of his leather seat follow him up into its upright position. He glanced at his watch. "Four-thirty. We'd better hustle."

"You know, this report doesn't have much on the capture of this boat."

"Yeah, I noticed that."

"We don't know who was involved, what was used, or whether there was any communication established."

"Right," Caesare answered. "My guess is sonobuoys, but knowing whether they were active or passive would be a big help."

"And whose buoys they were," Clay added.

Caesare raised an eyebrow. "You don't think they were Brazilian?"

"I don't know. Brazil uses a lot of the older MADs. The buoys could be theirs, but it also seems like our boats got here awfully fast."

"As in...they were already here."

"Maybe, maybe not. Either they were already here or they took a couple days to get here. Which makes me wonder..."

Caesare finished his thought. "How long did they know about the Russian sub?"

* * *

The summer heat and humidity enveloped both men the moment they exited the craft, making it feel as though they were sweating. Together, they walked briskly across the hot tarmac, each pulling a suitcase behind him with a pack slung over an outside shoulder.

The airport was small by most U.S. standards, with an old metal-and-glass framed terminal building standing alone on the very far side of the tarmac. As Clay and Caesare approached, a dark green Humvee suddenly rounded the corner of the building and sped toward them, almost skidding to a stop.

A young ensign jumped out and ran toward them with an apologetic look on his face.

"Commanders," he said, addressing them in a thick Portuguese accent, "I'm very sorry to be late now." He stopped abruptly in front of them with an awkward expression, wondering if he was supposed to salute. Caesare was closest and smiled at him, extending his hand. Relieved, the ensign relaxed and shook Caesare's hand first, then Clay's. "I am Ensign Costa. I've been sent to accept you. May I assist you with your bags?"

"Pleased to meet you, Ensign Costa," Caesare smiled and shook his head. "Nah, we're fine."

Costa nodded back and promptly turned to the car, trotting several steps ahead of them and opening the back tailgate. The two men approached, tossing their bags and packs in without losing a beat. Clay climbed into the front passenger seat and Caesare slid in behind him. They were happy to find the air conditioning already on high.

Costa opened the driver's door and reached in, handing each man a bottle of water. Clay thanked him and Caesare whistled. "Look at that. It's like we're important."

The ensign nodded and climbed in next to Clay. He closed the door and immediately dropped the vehicle into drive. "Your flight was good, yes?" He turned them around, heading back past the old terminal.

"Fine, thank you," Clay answered, peering out the windows. The base looked older than he was expecting. If not older, then certainly more run down. Another jet was landing further away on another runway and looked to be a commercial flight. The place was apparently still being used. They bounced high in their seats as Costa crossed over a rough section of asphalt and out onto the main road.

"I'll take you to the submarine first, yes? Before the hotel."

"How long has it been here?" Caesare asked, from the back seat.

"Uh…two days," replied Costa, changing lanes. He looked back through his rearview mirror. "It is very secret. You are the only Americans to come."

"Why so secret?" Clay prodded. He already knew the answer. "What if people see it in the water?"

Costa grinned as they crested the top of a wide overpass, crossing above one of the wide tributaries feeding into the largest section of the Amazon River. "Yes, people could see it very easy, and ask questions. If it was still *here*."

Clay glanced back over his shoulder to Caesare who raised his eyebrows curiously. "So Costa," he said, changing the subject. "How long have you been in the Navy?"

"I am in the Navy nine years. My father and grandfather were sailors too, both on battleships, and my great grandfather was a hero in the Revoltas da Armada. We are..." he paused to think of the right phrase, "a military family."

Clay nodded warmly. "Your family must be proud of you."

Costa nodded and almost chuckled. "Yes, they are proud of their Enrique."

* * *

The sub was not nearby. It was now being held roughly thirty minutes north, up a smaller river, and tied up at a very old and seemingly abandoned cannery. The place looked much worse than the base at which they'd just landed, and the rundown buildings along the cannery's dock looked rusted through as if ready to fall down at any moment.

Costa drove over an old wooden bridge, which groaned as they passed over and was guarded by two armed soldiers. Once on the other side, they came around past the dock and slowed near one of the last structures. Here, Costa finally stopped the Humvee and pushed the transmission back into park.

As they climbed out, Caesare bumped Clay on the arm and motioned to the canopy of Brazil nut trees above them. Dozens of the tall, dark green trees rose up well over a hundred feet with dense crowns of branches spreading out and surrounding both sides of the dock. "Nice place for blocking satellite pictures."

"Very convenient."

They followed Costa down a crumbling concrete path between two buildings, opening up into a wide area where several military vehicles were parked. Several soldiers in their Brazilian fatigues were milling around the Russian submarine, sitting motionless in the water.

When Clay and Caesare finally got a full view of the vessel, they stopped dead in their tracks. Costa noticed their halt and turned with a quizzical expression.

Clay and Caesare looked at each other quietly. After a long moment, Clay turned back to Costa. "We need to make a phone call."

# 7

ADMIRAL LANGFORD WAS at his desk when his secretary rang on a special phone line, prompting him to end his other call.

"Yes," he answered, switching over.

"Sir, I have a call for you from John Clay."

Langford glanced at his watch then leaned forward onto his wide desktop. "Put him through." He waited for the familiar "click" in the line before speaking. "Clay?"

"Hello, Admiral."

"You and Caesare onsite?"

"Yes, sir, a bit north of Belem. We've just arrived."

"Good. Do you have an ID on that November?"

"Well, sir," Clay said, staring out at the submarine. "It's definitely a Soviet class, but it's not nuclear…and it's not a *November*."

"Not a November?"

"No, sir. It's a Beluga class."

Langford froze on the other end of the phone. "Did you say Beluga?"

"That is correct, sir. As in the Forel."

"The *Forel?!* Are you sure, Clay?"

Clay turned to Caesare, who was watching three men standing on top of the sub. "I am. And, sir, it's painted blue."

"Christ." Langford took a deep breath and leaned back into his chair. "Listen to me, Clay, carefully. I just got off a call with the State Department. It seems the Brazilian government has decided it no longer wants our help. They're putting up obstacles left and right which means I don't think I can get anyone else in there except you two. More importantly, I think it's just a matter of time before the higher ups realize you've arrived, escort you both back to the airport, and send you off with a couple of nice Brazilian tarp hats."

Clay looked at Costa, patiently waiting about ten feet away. "I see."

"If that boat is the Forel," continued Langford, "you'd better get a look at it fast, before whoever is in charge there gets a call."

"Understood."

Langford leaned forward again, gripping the receiver. "There's something about that sub they don't want us to see. So get aboard quick and get as much intel as you can!"

"Yes, sir." Clay abruptly hung up and lowered the satellite phone from his ear. He folded down the bulky antennae and stuffed the unit back into his pack. Standing back up, he took a casual step closer to Caesare and whispered.

"We've got to hurry."

Caesare gave a knowing nod. He then spoke loudly to Costa. "All right, Ensign, we're all set. Show us the way."

Costa smiled graciously and turned back toward the sub, motioning them to follow.

* * *

Unlike the Soviet November class nuclear submarines with their more compact but noisier power generators, the Beluga was very different. It was a prototype diesel-electric, originally designed to test new propulsion technologies and hull properties. However, the project was thought to have been scrapped in 2002. The S-553 Forel was the only known Beluga class submarine built, and it hadn't been seen since 1997. Until now.

Langford sat silently in his chair, thinking. *So the Forel was still in operation. But what for? And what in the hell was it doing in Brazil?* He knew one thing for certain. There was only one reason to paint a submarine blue: for hiding in shallow water.

* * *

Like all subs, the Forel's interior was spotless and metal gray, yet Brazil's warm, moist jungle air gave the compartments of the Russian sub a subtle dank smell.

Once aboard, Clay and Caesare quickly made their way aft. They stopped and examined the giant diesel generators, taking several pictures. The generators were modernized with a more compact design but after some inspection, nothing appeared unusual. However, what did surprise them was what they found in the engine room.

Against the wall were two large metal racks filled with computer and audio equipment. From the racks, very thick, black cables ran up the steel wall, branching off into dozens of slightly smaller cables. They all spread around the engine room, terminating at the giant electric motor in the tail.

"What do you make of this?" Clay stepped forward and curiously ran his fingers over the cables. Caesare continued taking pictures behind him.

"Dunno." After taking pictures of the computer racks, Caesare flipped the tiny digital camera into video mode and proceeded to record. He carefully turned and covered the entire room.

Clay turned back to the rack. All modern subs were computer-controlled these days, but he'd never seen any with computers like these. "Look at this," he said to Caesare.

Caesare stepped in next to him and peered at the large devices on top. "What are those, amplifiers?"

"I'm not sure."

Suddenly they heard footsteps approaching quickly from a forward compartment, along the metal floor. Caesare turned off the camera and dropped it into his pocket just moments before Costa appeared at the hatch. His face bore a look of confused urgency.

"Commanders," he said, "I'm sorry, but I am informed that you need to leave this submarine immediately."

## 8

WILL BORGER WAS sitting in his office, studying his computer monitor, when the phone rang. He didn't acknowledge it at first as he scrolled down a window filled with complex computer code, examining it carefully. After the phone's third ring, he finally glanced at the number and opened his eyes wide. He immediately reached out and picked up the receiver. "Yes, sir."

"Borger," barked Langford's voice, "I need you up here right away."

"Now?"

"Yes, now!"

"Uh, yes, sir," he repeated. "I'll be right there."

Borger scrambled to hang up the phone then closed the window on the computer to save his work. He grabbed his half-empty can of Jolt and finished it off before finally looking down and straightening his shirt.

He turned to leave. As an afterthought, Borger reached back and grabbed his laptop, quickly unplugging its cables and tucking it under his arm.

Will Borger was what Admiral Langford liked to refer to as his secret weapon. He worked in the Department of Naval Investigations with Clay and Caesare and was arguably the smartest geek in the Pentagon. Even after Langford's promotion, he kept a few "key" personnel reporting directly to him and Borger was one of them.

Although Borger was technically a contractor, it never made a difference to Langford. Which was why, even being forty pounds overweight, Borger was now running for the Admiral's office.

When he arrived, Langford's secretary was waiting for him and opened the door. Upon seeing him, Langford waved Borger in and motioned to one of the chairs in front of his desk.

"Good, hold on. I've got Borger here too. Let me put you on speaker."

Langford pushed a button on his phone set and replaced the receiver back on its cradle. "You there?"

"Yes, sir," answered Clay.

"Did you get on board the Forel?"

"Briefly, but you were right. Someone got the word

down fast. We received a first class escort off the boat, but apparently we can't leave yet as our plane requires some emergency maintenance. I presume that was your doing."

"It was," grumbled Langford. "We needed to buy you some time there, so our pilot found something important that needed fixing. Where are you now?"

"We're at a hotel. They dropped us off with instructions to leave as soon as possible."

Langford nodded. "They want us out, but they're certainly not going to risk ruffling feathers. Did you get anything from the sub?"

"We did." Clay looked at Caesare, who was reviewing the video on the camera. "It's got a pretty advanced computer system on it, along with what looks to be some strange audio equipment. The video is hi-def but trying to send it over the sat phone is going to take a while. It might be easier to find a hotspot somewhere if we want to forego security."

Langford looked up and across his desk at Borger, who shrugged. "Doubtful anyone would be watching for it."

"Okay, send it," Langford followed. "I want to find out what we're looking at before you and Caesare are airborne. Any idea what this is?"

"No, sir. Not yet." Clay glanced at the video over Caesare's shoulder. "How much longer can we keep our plane grounded?"

Langford frowned and shook his head. "Not long. They're pushing hard. We probably have about twelve hours before they get rude about it. The Brazilians have clearly decided there's something on that sub they can benefit from, and I'm assuming it has to do with the equipment you found."

"Agreed," replied Clay. "Will, we'll send the files over for you to take a look at. In the meantime, Steve and I will try to find out more."

"Alright. Keep me posted." With that, he ended the call. Langford sat staring at the phone. This was feeling damn peculiar. That sub obviously had something the Brazilian government wanted badly. But what was it? Normally he wouldn't have been all that concerned. Countries were always coming up with new prototype ideas but most never made it even close to production. In this case, there were two facts about the Forel that bothered him. One was its mysterious rise from the dead. The other was that, even with their best sonobuoys, this particular sub had been *damn* hard to find.

* * *

Their hotel was located on the colonial side of the city and was one of the oldest in Belem. With its traditional blue tiles, it looked more like a historic building than a hotel. And judging from a few patches of peeling paint and old furniture, it seemed that their complimentary bottle of water in the Humvee had been the peak of their special treatment.

Costa had dropped them off with another round of apologies. It was obvious he had no idea why Clay and Caesare were being evicted. Even though he was following orders, one trait that most citizens of South American countries all shared, even the soldiers, was a healthy skepticism of their governments.

When he dropped them off, Costa mentioned that

his cousin worked at the hotel's reception desk should they need anything. And if she was like most people in a country with a struggling economy, she was no doubt just as helpful.

Shortly after hanging up with Langford, the men made their way downstairs to find Costa's cousin, Mariana. They spotted her across the tiled lobby, standing behind the long, faded reception counter and typing on a computer probably half her age.

Caesare approached and gave her his award-winning smile. "Olá, Mariana." She smiled back warmly.

"Olá," she replied in a light Portuguese accent. "What can I do for you gentlemen?"

Caesare leaned casually on the counter. "Enrique said you might be able to help us with something." With that, he withdrew a hundred dollar bill and placed it in front of her.

Mariana stared at him for a moment as her expression turned dubious. "What exactly are you looking for?"

Clay peeked around from behind his friend and laughed, watching Caesare realize the girl had misunderstood his request. Caesare shook his head, embarrassed. "No, no." He turned and shot Clay a sarcastic frown, only to find him still grinning.

"That's not what I meant. I'm wondering if you know someone who can rent us some scuba equipment."

Mariana smiled again, relieved. "Oh, yes, you would like to go on a boat? I have someone pick you up in the morning."

"Actually, we don't need a boat, just the tanks. And we were hoping to go out tonight."

"Tonight?"

Caesare whispered and motioned back to Clay. "What can I tell you…my friend's a little weird."

Mariana glanced at Clay and thought a moment. "Um, yes, I know someone. I will call him. He is to meet you here?"

"That'd be swell."

Mariana picked up her phone, but Clay stepped forward before she could dial and laid another bill on the counter. "One other thing. We need an internet connection."

"We have one here, senhor,".

"Better yet," Clay replied, lowering his voice, "is there another hotel and internet connection nearby? Perhaps one you know the password to?"

* * *

After transferring the files to Borger, Clay and Caesare returned to the hotel. Mariana was waiting in the lobby with a young man who looked a few years older than she.

"Misters," she started, when spotting them, "this is my brother, Lucas. He is come with your scubas."

Caesare smiled and shook the young man's hand, as did Clay. Lucas nodded toward the door and led them out and around the side of the building. Another young man was waiting next to a darkly painted car, smoking a cigarette. As they approached, he tossed it to the ground and walked to the back of the car, opening the trunk.

They rounded the rear of the Chevy Malibu, which looked older than it probably was, and peered into the trunk. Inside were two scuba units, complete with buoyancy control devices or BCDs, regulators, and tanks.

Clay and Caesare looked at each other, amused when they saw the words "Hilton Belem" painted on the side of each tank.

The large mesh bag next to the rest of the gear held snorkels, masks, fins, and two dive lights.

"Did you bring suits?"

"Yes," nodded Lucas. He reached under one of the tanks and pulled out a fold of neoprene to show them. When Lucas straightened back up, he gave them a slight grin. "My sister says you're swimming tonight?"

Caesare frowned sarcastically. "Why would you think that?"

Lucas' grin turned into a smile as he reached up and quietly closed the trunk. "You must be here about the submarine, yes?"

Caesare retrieved his wallet and opened it. "You know about the submarine?"

"I know about many things."

"I bet." Caesare counted out the rest of the money before looking to Clay with raised eyebrows. "How much you got?"

Clay reached for his own wallet and motioned to the Chevy. "We need the car, too."

* * *

With some extra direction from Lucas, they managed to find the old dirt road that put them just over a quarter mile past the Forel's location. Caesare's shorter, more muscular frame stretched his wetsuit to the limit and made Clay chuckle, never having seen a wetsuit without any creases in it. Yet, Clay's was only slightly better, being more than two sizes too large.

After locating a footpath toward the beach, it took them nearly forty-five minutes to reach the water and start swimming south. Progress was slow to avoid making any unnecessary ripples or noises in the water. Once they reached the crumbling walls of the old channel, they floated inward, now barely moving their fins behind them.

Several vehicles were still parked along the dock, sitting idly in the darkness. The rest of the men they had seen earlier appeared to be gone, save for some soldiers guarding the bridge on the far side of the Forel.

Clay, slightly in front, put his hand up and signaled to stop. Together they floated motionlessly for a few minutes, listening. Nothing.

They continued forward, closing in on the top of the Forel's giant vertical tailplane.

When they were within a hundred yards, Clay nodded to Caesare a few feet away and inserted his black regulator into his mouth. He gave a thumbs up before donning his mask and releasing some of the air out of his vest, causing him to sink gradually below the surface.

Once well below the surface, they both turned on their modified dive lights. The red colored T-shirt they had torn up and banded over the top of each light presented a subtle glow as they reached the hull.

What they found was puzzling. Small depressions in the metal ringed the rear of the hull, just above the propeller. The rings were successive and traveled consistently down the hull to the base of the lower stern plane, where they ended. Inside the holes appeared to be a thick, metal mesh painted the same color as the sub.

The indentations were large but very subtle and probably impossible to spot unless within inches of the hull.

Clay made a rough measurement of the depressions with his fingers and pushed himself back to get a closer look at the prop. Nothing else seemed out of the ordinary.

After several minutes, Caesare joined him and shook his head from side to side, motioning that he hadn't found anything else further up. Clay nodded and pointed back the way they came. Together, both men descended further and proceeded to head back out toward the sea.

At 6:31 a.m., when the bright orange sunrise broke over the horizon of the Atlantic Ocean, Clay, Caesare, and their Gulfstream jet were gone.

## 9

ALISON WAS EXCITED and propped herself on the edge of the giant tank and let her legs dangle into the warm water. She adjusted the thick weight belt around her waist for comfort before looking up over her shoulder.

Lee and Juan stood over her, each holding one side of the vest. When Alison nodded, they both lowered it so she could wrap her arms through the wide straps. Once in place, Alison moved her shoulders from side to side to make sure it was comfortable enough.

She nodded and then both men hoisted the scuba gear off the ground and held it lightly against her back, allowing her to wiggle her arms through the second set of straps. Lee and Juan had measured the dimensions of the scuba vest and designed their own vest to hug her below the BCD. It was a perfect fit.

Alison brought the Velcro sides of the BCD in tight and overlapped one on top of the other, creating a snug fit. She could feel the weight of the tanks pulling her back and leaned forward to compensate.

The yellow scuba shell on her back was a CCR, or "closed circuit rebreather." Unlike the older, traditional scuba systems, modern *rebreathers* had some distinct advantages. Old scuba systems were "open circuit'" and disposed of the air the diver breathed out by blowing it out from the mouthpiece and into the water in the form of bubbles. It was a very inefficient process since exhaled air still retained a large percentage of valuable oxygen. That oxygen was then discarded, along with the carbon dioxide as bubbles, and the remaining air in the tank determined the amount of time a diver could remain underwater. Rebreathers, however, captured that exhaled air and removed the carbon dioxide, allowing the system to reuse the valuable oxygen instead of wasting it. This radically prolonged the diver's time underwater. On top of that, the efficiency grew even more dramatic as the diver descended and the pressure grew. Just as importantly, rebreathers were virtually silent, which made the translation process easier.

Alison shifted slightly under the weight of the unit. She grabbed the full-face mask and held it briefly in place, testing the airflow.

She nodded and looked up to Lee. "I've got air."

He knelt down next to her. "Remember, we're only staying down for a few minutes this first time to test the unit and the wireless connection to the server." He took her mask and turned it around, pointing to a small rubber circle at the bottom. "This is the microphone and camera, so you must be facing them when you speak or IMIS won't be able to capture and translate correctly." He motioned to her vest. "And I showed you where the speaker is, right here in the middle."

"Right." Alison tapped the round speaker on the vest.

Juan handed the special earplugs to Lee, who passed them to Alison. After she had inserted both, Lee brought the mask to his lips and spoke softly into its microphone. "Can you hear me?"

Alison nodded.

He couldn't help but smile at her petite frame under all that equipment.

Alison looked at the water in front of her and smiled, spotting both Dirk and Sally with their heads above the surface, watching.

"Does everything feel okay?" Lee asked.

Alison nodded again. She pulled the mask up and over the top of her thick hair and fitted it in place.

She peered down through the water. "Can you hear me, Chris?"

Chris was below in their observation area, standing in front of the tank and next to a large server. "Yes," he replied through his headset. "I read you loud and clear."

"Okay. Here I go." She gave Lee and Juan a thumbs up and abruptly pushed forward off the ledge.

The warm salt water enveloped her as she sank below the surface, pulled gently down by her weight belt. Dirk and Sally dipped back down below the surface and swam after her as she descended. They slowly circled her, watching intently as she calmly pressed the small button on her scuba vest and added a touch of air to increase her buoyancy. She kicked her fins slowly to keep herself in place.

Alison peered in at Sally through the glass mask. "Hello, Sally." Inside her waterproof vest, the miniature computer recorded the sound from her mask and sent it back to IMIS over a wireless connection. Seconds later, she could hear her own greeting through the speaker as a familiar set of clicks.

Sally didn't respond immediately. Instead, she drifted in for a closer look at Alison and her vest. After getting within just inches, she excitedly shot past and around Alison in a tight circle. *Hello Alison.*

Alison heard her perfectly through the earplugs and grinned. She kicked forward and reached out, running a hand along Sally's slick body. She then turned to Dirk.

"Hello, Dirk."

Dirk was equally excited. *Alison, you swim and talk.*

"Yes. I can swim and talk with you now." She looked down through the clear wall and waved to Chris. He smiled and waved back.

Dirk spoke again. *You make metal for swim and talk.*

Alison shrugged. "Lee and Juan made the metal for us to swim and talk."

*They make good,* Dirk answered.

*They sure did*, she thought to herself. She looked up and around the tank, raising her arms and letting her body float in place. She could see the rough, wavy images of Lee and Juan above them, still standing at the edge and staring down into the water. She turned back to Dirk just in time to see him speak and rush below her. *We play now.*

Alison had just begun to reply when she suddenly felt Dirk's nose underneath her, lifting and pushing her forward along with him.

"Whoa!" Alison gasped and tried to steady herself against the powerful surge of water. Dirk effortlessly began to circle the tank, but Alison leaned and rolled herself to one side and off his nose. "No, no, Dirk!" She almost chuckled. "I'm not a *ball!*"

Dirk made a strange sound, which Alison knew well, but never translated. He was laughing.

*Very funny*, she thought and kicked her legs hard, propelling herself toward Sally, who was watching quietly.

*Dirk like play,* Sally said, as Alison neared.

"Yes, he does."

*Alison, you like us.*

This time Alison did chuckle. "Well, for a little while." She began to say something else when she heard the familiar buzzer in her ear, signifying that something did not translate correctly. She turned to find Dirk closing his mouth, having just spoken. She realized the camera in her mask had not been facing him.

"Did you say something, Dirk?"

*Yes, we like you swim and talk.* Dirk floated forward again, this time more slowly, and held out one of his flippers. Alison reached down and gave it a playful tug before he kicked forward with his powerful tail and circled under her.

*You come now*, Sally said.

Alison knew that was a question. "Not yet, we must

test the metal more." The buzzer went off again in her ears. "We use metal more," she rephrased.

*How more long use metal.*

"Just a few more days."

## 10

IT WAS A huge success! The new system worked, and it worked well. Lee and Juan huddled around the custom vest, running diagnostics to see if there were any problems. The unit's processor in the waterproof compartment didn't have enough power to do faster live translation, but it had no problem offloading that piece to the IMIS supercomputer.

The diagnostics looked clean. No glitches, no wireless drops, no sign of voltage issues or leaks. It was better than they had hoped for. But it didn't mean those problems *wouldn't* happen. They still had a few more days of testing before they could do what everyone was so eagerly waiting for: to take the vest out into the open ocean.

* * *

Downstairs, Alison and Chris stood in front of the tank, grinning from ear to ear. It was a marine biologist's dream come true. To really communicate with another species was incredible enough. Now to be able to do it "out there," in their native habitat, was a huge leap in oceanography research. They couldn't imagine what they were going to learn outside of the tank.

They stood in a daze, gleefully watching Dirk and

Sally being fed by Kelly up above, when someone spoke up behind them. "Are we too late for the big event?"

Alison recognized the voice immediately and turned breathlessly with a grin that managed to get even wider.

John Clay was standing behind her, along with Steve Caesare. Clay was smiling back at her.

"I thought you were in Brazil?"

Clay gave her a hug. "We left early, and Borger is working on something at the moment." He glanced at his watch regretfully. "We're due back in D.C. in five hours."

Alison tried to hide her disappointment. "Well, I'm glad you made a stopover."

"It's the least I could do." Clay squeezed her tight and looked up over her shoulder. "Hi, Chris."

"Hello, John. How are you?"

"A little tired, but good, thank you."

Chris was closest to Caesare and he reached out a hand to him. "Mr. Caesare. It's nice to see you again."

Caesare shook Chris' hand and almost scoffed. "Come on Chris, I'm not that old yet." He winked. "Clay makes me seem older."

"Well, well, look what the cat dragged in." They all turned to see DeeAnn looking at Caesare as she entered the room. She had met him several times before. The two had instantly fallen into a friendly but rather sarcastic relationship. "How did we get so *lucky*?"

Caesare raised an eyebrow at her. "Ah, Dr. Draper. What a pleasure. You're looking...*older*."

After what seemed like a long moment, they smiled at each other playfully and laughed. DeeAnn flicked his thick, muscular arm as she passed. She turned warmly to Clay. "Nice to see you again, John."

"Good morning, DeeAnn," Clay said. "How are things going with Dulce?"

"We're making excellent progress, thank you. In fact, the translations are coming faster and faster. Your girl here," she said, with a wink at Alison, "runs quite a ship."

Clay didn't see the nervous look Alison gave DeeAnn after being referred to as John's "girl."

"So," Clay said. "I take it the test went well, judging by the look on everyone's face."

"It was flawless," Alison beamed. "Lee and Juan are upstairs checking things out. It was only for about five minutes, but it worked perfectly."

"I'm not surprised," Clay nodded. "I guess that means it's a "go" for your big trip."

"Hopefully. We still have more testing to do, but assuming we don't have any major problems, we're set to leave in a few days. So cross your fingers. I think Dirk and Sally are getting impatient."

"This is very cool, Alison," Caesare said, folding his arms. "Translation out in open water is exciting stuff." He flashed her a devilish grin. "Come to think of it, maybe you could use some help from a couple old 'sea dogs.'"

Clay laughed. He could imagine Langford's reaction.

Caesare held up a hand in an innocent gesture. "Hey, let's not forget Alison's got some pull with the Admiral."

Alison remained close to Clay, smiling, but said nothing. It was true, she still had a few favors to call in, but that wasn't something you did lightly with Admiral Langford. No, she was saving her favors for a very rainy day. Not one involving Caesare lounging around on her boat and soaking up the sun with a beer in his hand. She liked Steve Caesare a lot. He was both tough and smart, but from what she'd heard, parties had a habit of finding him.

She turned and looked up at Clay. "So, how much time do you have before you have to leave for D.C.?"

"Probably a couple of hours."

Caesare watched her frown with a look of mild disappointment. He rolled his eyes. "Oh, for crying out loud. Why don't you two get out of here? I'll hang out with my pal DeeAnn." He gave her a wink. "Besides, I want to have a look at this new portable unit the boys have created."

Clay looked down at her with raised eyebrows. "What do you say to an early lunch?"

"I would love that."

"Just make sure you have him back on time."

Clay nodded to Caesare, waved to the others, and grabbed Alison's hand. "I'm all yours."

Wasting no time, they headed for the outside door. She flung it open and pulled him outside into the bright sunshine. She paused for a few moments, letting the large metal door close behind them with a loud "click." Before Clay could say anything, Alison pulled him close and kissed him.

# 11

CAESARE FOLLOWED DEEANN back through the hallway to the habitat. She punched her code in and pushed the door open, then held it a moment for Caesare. As the two stepped up onto a gentle mound, they spotted Dulce sitting on the ground, playing with a large wooden game board. She promptly looked up and stared at Caesare.

"There's my girl!" he called out.

Ecstatic, Dulce jumped up and covered the distance quickly, leaping into his big arms.

Caesare hugged her, then reached up and gently rubbed her head. "How's my sweetheart?"

*Steve here, Steve here,* Dulce said, the words coming from DeeAnn's computerized vest. *Me miss you.*

He matched her wide smile. "And I missed you." He hugged her again and then leaned back and stared at the adorable gorilla in his arms. "You want to race?"

* * *

An hour later, Caesare was staring down at Lee and Juan's new toy, lying on the table. "That's pretty impressive, fellas."

"Thanks," Lee replied. "We got a little help with production, but the design is pretty close to what we drew up. The board is under here." He touched an outside section of the vest's material. "There's obviously some processing needed locally but we tried to keep it to a minimum, pushing the rest to IMIS for translation. Unfortunately, even with the barest operating system, and a load of flash memory, it still sucks up a lot of energy. Especially with the constant, high-speed wireless connection." Lee reached down and peeled the thick rubber seal away, releasing the plastic door to the battery compartment. "Less than five minutes underwater still used up quite a bit of power. Which means usage is going to be limited in open water."

Caesare nodded and looked curiously at the large rectangular battery. He fingered it and gently pulled it out of its socket. "This lithium?"

"Yep."

Caesare turned it over, noting the connection points. "You know, the Navy's got a team working on a new battery prototype for some drones. They're using a special nickel coated polymer which gives them a much higher storage density. I may be able to get you a few."

"Really?" Lee and Juan looked at each other excitedly.

"Really. They even have one that's a similar size. I might be able to get some overnighted. You may just have time to work it in before the trip."

"That would be amazing!"

Caesare shrugged. "Don't mention it. As a matter of fact, if you print up the schematics for your board and the processor, including the frequency you're using, Clay and I can take a look and see if there are any other areas where we can help reduce electrical draw. Our Electronics and Signaling group back in D.C. does this all the time. Between some frequency modifications and the prototype batteries, I bet you could increase your operating time quite a bit."

"That would be fantastic." Lee turned back to

Juan, who was already at the computer looking for the schematics.

"So, I presume you guys are taking a server when you go out, to handle the translation."

"Three, as a matter of fact," Lee said. "IMIS does the heavy lifting, but we can offload the basics onto some smaller servers. Very much like we did last year on the Pathfinder with Mr. Clay. Of course, the vocabulary is more advanced now and we have the wireless bit."

"And a more reliable boat," Caesare teased.

Lee laughed. "Yes, definitely a more reliable boat."

"Cool, I'm looking forward to hearing how things go. This is pretty exciting."

"Oh, yeah, very! It's too bad you can't come with us."

Caesare smiled, thinking of his joke earlier to Alison. "Unfortunately we're in the middle of something." He reinserted the battery and laid the corner of the vest back down, now thinking of the Forel sub and the reason they had to get back. He hoped Borger had a little insight into the data they had sent him from Belem.

He was about to find out that Borger had much more than that.

# 12

CLAY STARED THROUGH the side window and watched the Mercedita runway fall away as they climbed over the south end of the island, banking to the left. The late sun reflected brightly over the crystal blue Caribbean water, and Clay gazed down wistfully at the dozens of sailboats below them.

He'd loved the ocean since the first day his father took him out on the boat. It was just a small daysailer, but he loved every minute of it. From then on, it was something they did religiously, every time he visited his father in Florida. Ultimately, it was that very same relationship with the ocean behind his enlistment in the Navy. Now he looked forward to the day he could cast off for good, traveling the globe through the blue water with nothing but a sturdy boat, stars in the sky…and of course, a woman to share it with.

Clay leaned his head back and thought of Alison, letting his lips crack into a smile. She seemed as happy to see him as he was to see her. After a few minutes, he took a deep breath and reached down for his pack on the floor.

Caesare sat across from him, studying the schematics Juan had printed out. He noticed Clay pull a shiny object from his bag. Caesare glanced up to see a small silver brick, reflecting brightly from the incoming sunlight. It was about the size of a deck of cards and Clay sat gazing at it curiously.

"You still carrying that souvenir around with you?"

Clay didn't look up. He simply nodded and flipped it over, rubbing it gently with his thumb.

"Any idea how it works yet?"

"Not exactly."

He'd had the device for over a year, since a harrowing event which nearly ended in a global catastrophe. In the end, few people knew what really happened. That was the way it always was when the government was involved.

Clay turned the object over again in his hand. "Borger and I put it under an electron microscope but couldn't determine what it was made from. It's plated in silicon and its core is deuterium. But the rest is made out of elements that we can't identify."

"Well, you already know it's a fusion device," replied Caesare. "Maybe you're not supposed to know how it works."

Clay looked up at Caesare thoughtfully. "Then why would he let me keep it?"

"Clearly, it was to drive you insane."

Clay smirked. "Clearly."

Caesare watched Clay quietly examine the object. They had worked together for over twenty years, beginning with their service as Navy SEALs. Eventually moving out into Investigations once their aging bodies began to object to the constant physical punishment. There were also the questionable missions that the teams were increasingly instructed to carry out, which ultimately left some of the SEALs wondering just which side of the fight they were really on.

Caesare had seen his friend in a number of binds, even some in combat. He'd come to know the man inside and out. Through it all, he had learned one unswerving fact about John Clay; the man never gave up. No matter what the predicament, Clay's mind simply never stopped working. He would continue studying that silver object, chipping away at logic until he figured something out. The question really was just how long it was going to take.

He mused and gave Clay a minute before changing the subject. "So listen, I've been looking at the design of that new vest Alison's team developed. It's pretty impressive. Tighter than I was expecting."

"Yeah, IBM helped them with it."

"There are a few things we can help them with too, particularly around the wireless. There are better frequencies they could be using, but it would probably mean testing another prototype." He reached out and handed the sheet to Clay.

Clay reluctantly dropped the silver block back into his bag and studied the sheet, holding it up to the window for a better look. "You know, with a thicker design, I bet they could make this thing self-contained."

* * *

Will Borger stole a look at his watch and looked back to the screen. He wasn't going to make it.

The program he'd written was still crunching through the data, and the meeting with Admiral Langford was in fifteen minutes. In fact, the job was barely halfway done.

Behind him, his office in the Pentagon's basement was crowded with enough computer and signaling equipment to put the displays at the Smithsonian to shame. To him, technology wasn't just a job, it was an obsession, and Langford was happy to oblige him. Especially lately.

Borger jumped when the door opened behind him and the overhead lights suddenly came on.

"You really need to get an office with some sunlight," Caesare announced. "We all need a little vitamin D once in a while."

Borger swiveled in his chair, arms still folded over his stomach, which was protruding a bit from under his loud, orange Hawaiian shirt. "I take pills for that."

Caesare raised his eyebrows. "Really?"

"No, but I should." Borger looked to Clay, who had just closed the door behind them. "Hey, Clay. How was Brazil?"

"Who ever said getting thrown out of a country wasn't exciting? How goes it, Will?"

"Pretty good." Borger swung back toward his monitor. "Langford asked me to do something for him, but it won't be done for quite a while yet."

Caesare sat backwards in a small metal chair and rolled it up next to Borger. "What do we have here?"

"A deep scan of the North Atlantic, pixel by pixel."

Clay and Caesare both raised their eyebrows curiously. "Pixel by pixel?"

"Just about. I got the last three months' worth of data from the NSA, recorded by the ARGUS reconnaissance satellite." Both Clay and Caesare were familiar with the government's newest bird. They were also both familiar with the term *reconnaissance* when referring to a satellite. It was the preferred term over the more accurate label "spy satellite." The ARGUS had recently been launched under the generic name of 'NROL-39' and was the first with *real-time* capability. All other previous spy satellites had the ability to take increasingly sharper pictures and at frame speeds faster than video. However, what they still lacked was bandwidth and the ability to send their ultra-high definition pictures back to Earth quickly enough for a real-time experience.

That limitation had finally been rectified in ARGUS.

With most of the new system's design focused squarely on transmission capacity, the ARGUS was literally able to stream live, ultra-high definition video back to Earth, where it was recorded twenty-four hours a day. And all with a field of view that was unprecedented. It was a huge technological advance for a "reconnaissance" satellite and a capability that few countries, including allies, were even aware of.

Nevertheless, a pixel-by-pixel scan was an enormous undertaking. It was the digital equivalent of examining every grain of sand on a given beach.

Caesare leaned in closer to Borger's monitor. "What on earth would you need three months of pixel data for?"

"For the Forel," Clay murmured, peering over Caesare's shoulder.

"That's right." Borger began typing on his computer again and brought up another window. He then used his mouse to drag the new window onto a second monitor. With a few clicks, the new window instantly filled with a blue frame of the Atlantic Ocean, detailed enough to easily make out several small white caps on top of one of the swells.

Clay and Caesare could see the computer making a thin white line as it zoomed horizontally across the image, one tiny pixel at a time. It finished scanning the frame in less than five seconds and started another. "How far along is it?"

"Maybe halfway."

"You must be looking for a periscope," Caesare said.

"Or the exhaust."

"Correct again. It's a long way from Russia to Brazil, especially for a diesel-electric, which means they would have had to surface many times to expel their stale exhaust and recharge their batteries. I've got almost a thousand servers backtracking through images for a three hundred square mile area, looking in both visible and infrared."

"Find anything yet?"

"Nope." Borger frowned and shook his head from side to side. He swiveled his chair back to them and smiled. "But that's the bad news."

"There's good news?"

"The good news is I think I know what that equipment is for aboard the Forel." He moved to yet another screen and brought up the video that Caesare had taken before they were thrown off the sub. Borger played the video until Caesare's camera focused on the rack of equipment. He froze the image. "I spent some time going over this with several engineers in Pensacola, and we all agree that these devices are indeed amplifiers. And you see this?" He pointed to the bottom edge of the screen. "These appear to be power cables. These other cables," he traced up the side of the still picture, "carry the audio."

"Audio for what?"

"Ah..." Borger clasped his hands. "That's the million dollar question."

Caesare smirked. "Something tells me you have a million dollar answer."

"Why, yes, I do." He paused, staring at them but saying nothing.

"And what is it?"

Borger grinned and held his hands up for dramatic effect. "Active Noise Control!"

Both Clay and Caesare sat motionlessly. Not because

they didn't understand; they did. Instead, they remained quiet, considering the possibilities.

Clay looked back at Borger's screen and mumbled, almost to himself, "Noise cancellation."

"Bingo!"

Borger leaned back in his chair. "Navies have been trying to perfect ANC in their subs for years, but so far it's been unattainable. If you ask me, I think they've found a way to do it with the Forel: not just *reduce* their noise but eliminate it altogether."

"Wow. Does Langford know about this yet?"

Borger shook his head again. "Not yet."

Clay remained quiet, thinking. Borger's assessment suddenly raised a number of other questions. Finally, he turned his wrist and checked his watch. "It's time."

## 13

TO THEIR SURPRISE, Admiral Langford and Stan Griffith, the National Security Advisor, were already waiting in the conference room when Clay, Caesare, and Borger arrived. Langford broke off his conversation and motioned the three inside to the chairs on the other side of the wide table. The new Secretary of State, Douglas Bartman entered and closed the door just moments behind them.

"Gentlemen," Langford began, "I'd like you to meet John Clay, Steve Caesare, and Will Borger. They came with me from Investigations." Silent nods were exchanged while Langford continued. "Clay and Caesare were onsite to examine the Forel. Mr. Borger is our computer expert, trying to figure out exactly what we're looking at here. Clay, want to start us off?"

"Yes, sir," Clay spoke up. He quickly recounted their trip to Belem and time aboard the Forel submarine, leading to their abrupt expulsion. He also described their dive beneath the sub in the middle of the night, including what they saw around its tail section.

"Okay, Will, you have the data they sent. Any idea what we're looking at here?"

"Yes, sir," nodded Borger. "It looks like we may be looking at an operational Active Noise Control system."

"What?"

"ANC, sir," repeated Borger. "It's only a guess without being able to put my hands on it, but I'm pretty sure that's what it is."

"I'll be damned."

Bartman looked back and forth between them. "What's Active Noise Control?"

"Noise cancellation," answered Langford. "A way to render a submarine silent underwater. No wonder the Forel was so damn hard to find."

Borger continued. "From what Clay and Caesare described, there are sensor and actuator rings around the entire tail section, which mimics some of the test designs other countries have tried, including our own."

"So it's completely silent?" asked Bartman.

"Well, not completely, but very close."

Bartman pondered the Admiral's reply. "But we still don't know what the Russians were after."

"Correct, but we now know what Brazil's government is after. And why we got kicked off the sub so fast.

My guess is that this is a working prototype of the technology used in Russia's new stealth submarines. And I think the Brazilian Navy may have just realized the same thing." Langford turned to Borger. "Anything on our other project?"

"The image scans? No, sir. Not yet."

"Sir," Clay spoke up. "Have the Russian's asked for their crew back yet?"

They all looked to Bartman, who shook his head. "No, no communication yet."

"That's peculiar."

"Very," agreed Langford.

"Sir," Clay continued. "The initial report we received on the Forel was lacking a few details. For example, information on the actual capture itself. Was there a reason for that?"

Langford looked at Stan Griffith, who in turn exchanged a knowing expression with Bartman before speaking. "What would you like to know, Commander?"

It seemed the omission from the report was intentional. "Who exactly located the Forel?" Clay asked.

"The Brazilian Government. We don't know who exactly."

"They knew where it was?"

"Yes."

Clay frowned, confused. "Brazil has five submarines, all much closer than we are. If they already knew where the Forel was, why did they need our help with the capture?"

"It was a favor," Griffith sighed and continued looking at Clay. "The relationship between the United States and Brazil has been slowly eroding for some time. As a major emerging market, they have voiced their displeasure over a number of recent political and economic decisions of ours, which has put our relationship on delicate footing." He shrugged. "It was a simple political favor, nothing more."

"So we kept quiet to give Brazil credit over the Forel's capture," stated Caesare matter-of-factly.

"Something like that."

"And to avoid souring our relationship with the Russians at the same time."

Griffith reluctantly nodded.

"Except we didn't know what was on it," Clay picked up where Caesare left off. "The Admiral indicated that it was harder than usual to locate the Forel. Exactly how hard was it?"

"Four attempts."

Clay and Caesare were both surprised. "Four attempts? Even after Brazil told us where to look?"

"That's right."

"So, it took four sonobuoys to find it?"

"That must be some damn effective noise cancellation," Caesare mused.

Clay turned back to Griffith and Bartman, asking the question that everyone was now thinking. "So, if it took *us* four tries to find that sub, and our sonobuoys are better than the MADs that Brazil uses...do we actually know *how* Brazil knew about the Forel?"

After a long pause, Bartman shook his head. "We thought it better not to ask."

The expression on Langford's face told Clay that something in that discussion was a surprise, even to him. But the look was only momentary. "Okay," Langford began, "so we have what appears to be a prototype of a new Russian technology. Their crew is obviously well-trained on it, and Russia still hasn't made a sound." He shot Bartman a subtle but dubious glance. "So either they're afraid to say something, or they've already quietly spoken to the Brazilian government. And if that's true, it means the Russian crew may be about to disappear on a first-class flight home." He looked at the others. "Any other possibilities?"

Clay was chewing absent-mindedly on his lip when he looked up. "Well, there is one other possibility, sir. The simplest and most obvious." He shrugged at Langford. "What if the Russians don't even know it's been captured?

## 14

AFTER UNLOCKING TWO deadbolts, Clay pushed open the door and stepped into the still darkness of his apartment. Flicking the light switch revealed a large, sparsely decorated living room that looked as though it hadn't been used in months. It hadn't.

In the bedroom, he parked his suitcase near the bed and dropped his bag onto the blue and grey striped comforter. He was looking forward to a good night's sleep, and had a feeling he was going to need it.

* * *

Unfortunately, Clay's sleep only lasted until 4:10 a.m.

when his cell phone rang. He picked it up off the nearby nightstand and squinted at the bright screen.

He answered and sat up, groaning. "Will, do you *ever* sleep?"

Borger chuckled on the other end. "Probably more than you do. Sorry to wake you up, but it's important."

"What do you have?"

"I found something with my pixel scanning. I think it's significant." Borger switched the phone to his other hand and used his mouse to enlarge the picture on his screen. "It's not what we were expecting."

"Have you called Langford?"

"Yes. He should be online in a few minutes. He told me to get you and Steve on too."

* * *

Seven minutes later, Clay sat hunched in a dining room chair, staring at his laptop screen. Langford and Caesare were doing the same on theirs. They were all looking at the display Borger was sharing from his own monitor. He enlarged a picture of the Atlantic Ocean so everyone could see it.

"I came back to my lab last night after our meeting," Borger began. "Clay's comment about the simplest answer got me thinking. What if what we were looking for was more obvious? We've been scanning data from thousands of miles of ocean looking for the signs of the Forel. It would have taken the sub weeks to get here. And knowing that the longer they were out, the higher the chances of somehow being discovered, probably means a direct route." Borger zoomed out to a larger picture, highlighting the area he was scanning. "But what if we were approaching this from the wrong angle, or more specifically, the wrong direction? The Forel was captured here." A bright circle appeared off the northern coast of Brazil. "From there, pretty much anywhere south has a higher chance of being patrolled by the Brazilian Navy. So I decided to take a look to the north."

Borger double-clicked his mouse. Again, the picture zoomed in, but this time closer to the northeastern coastline of South America. The next countries north of Brazil were the small countries of French Guiana, Suriname, and Guyana, lastly followed by the larger Venezuela at the top of his picture.

"I managed to commandeer more servers to run another search and went north instead. And this is what the program found." He typed something on his keyboard and his map zoomed in even further, down to the individual wave level where a tiny red cloud appeared.

All three of the others stared at their own screens, studying the red image. "That's it," said Langford.

"Yes, sir," answered Borger. "The Forel's exhaust plume. Or at least the heat from it. But that's not the best part. Look at *where* I found it." He zoomed out yet again and the other three on the line fell silent.

"Guyana?"

"Guyana," repeated Borger.

Caesare tilted his head curiously at the image. "What on earth was it doing in Guyana?"

"That's where it gets weird." Borger leaned forward again in his chair and resumed typing. "It's not just that the Forel was submerged off the coast of that country. "It's *how long* it was submerged for."

"How long?"

"Two months!"

"Two months?!" cried Langford. "Are you sure?"

"Yes, sir. Once I found it, I downloaded another two months of data and started going backward. The exact location varies a little, but not much. That Russian sub had been sitting there for exactly two months and four days."

The conference line fell silent again as the three digested the information. Modern submarines could, of course, remain stationary for a long period of time. Although no one really ever did it for that long, outside of running drills.

"What the hell were they doing?"

Clay spoke up. "Will, can you tell in which direction they were pointed?"

"I certainly can!" Borger smiled. Clay was one sharp cookie. "Because subs need to approach the surface to discard their exhaust, I was able to identify the outline of the sub pretty easily. We can see that the sub's direction was almost always pointed toward the city it was nearest to, which was Guyana's only major city: Georgetown."

Clay was interested in the direction the Forel was pointing for one reason. Aligning either the bow or stern with a target gave a submarine the smallest possible profile.

"So, it didn't want to be seen by the city of Georgetown?"

"Not the city," corrected Borger. "Something *in* the city."

Borger continued typing and the picture on their screens scrolled slightly south, traveling through the wide mouth of the Demerara River where it met the

Atlantic Ocean. Approximately two miles upriver sat an unmistakable shape.

"This is why I woke you all up," said Borger.

The others were quiet yet again, this time studying the crystal clear image of a ship. It appeared to be anchored near the only bridge crossing the Demerara from Georgetown.

"It's big," Caesare offered. "Do we know whose it is?"

"The Chinese," answered Langford solemnly.

"What do the Chinese have a ship in Guyana for?"

Langford's voice was slow and deliberate as he continued studying the picture. "This came across my desk a few weeks ago. It wasn't a priority. The word the CIA picked up was that it was there for minor repairs. They had been caught in a storm."

Clay spoke up. "What kind of ship, Admiral?"

"A warship. A Corvette Class."

"So is it just me," Caesare said, "or is anyone else wondering what a Chinese warship is doing in the Atlantic?"

The Admiral said nothing, still staring into the eerie glow of his laptop screen.

"Will," Clay changed the subject. "Any idea how long the Corvette has been there?"

"I only have three months of data. But it's been there the whole time."

"Can you zoom out again so we can see them both on the screen?"

Borger complied, zooming out until both vessels were visible as two large dots inside of the same shot.

Clay held up a piece of paper to his screen and angled it slightly. "Line of sight."

"Ideal observation through a periscope," Caesare added. "And pointing directly at it not only gives the Forel its smallest profile, but would also allow it to fire right up the mouth of that river. Potentially before that ship could even make it out."

After a long pause, Admiral Langford cleared his throat. "I need to make some phone calls."

# 15

ALISON AWOKE AND rolled toward the illuminated clock on her desk.

5:24 a.m.

She pressed her eyelids shut, hoping to drift off again, but eventually she gave up. It was no use. Her mind was already racing.

She lay in the darkness for several more minutes before sitting up on the edge of the firm couch. She used it often, especially when Dirk and Sally were there. With a sigh, Alison stood up and turned on the light, briefly blinding herself. She waited a moment before taking her hand away from her eyes and double-checked the time using her wristwatch.

Quietly opening the door, she walked down the dark hallway, feeling her way along the wall. She took the stairs down slowly and walked the length of the hallway until she spotted the wide door under a pale reflection from the moon outside. She opened it softly and stepped in.

The water in the huge tank was lapping softly.

Near the surface of the tank, Alison could see the darkened shapes of Dirk and Sally, floating motionless as they slept.

Sleep was a very different experience for water-born mammals such as dolphins and whales. The ocean was teeming with danger, which made the practice of completely shutting down the brain during sleep, the way humans did, a dangerous prospect. Instead, the mammals slept by shutting down only half of their brain at a time. This allowed them to remain in a semi-conscious state for protection, yet still garner the eight hours of rest they needed.

Alison approached the tank, watching them sleep. Sally's eyes suddenly opened. After a brief pause, she used a very soft sway of her tail to move down and forward. Sally stared through the glass at Alison but said nothing. Instead, she turned and looked at the microphone.

Alison took the hint and turned on the computer screen atop Lee's desk. She then opened the window, which allowed her to turn down the volume of the speakers. When it was done, she leaned into the microphone and whispered, "Good morning, Sally."

Sally moved in close to the microphone. *Good morning Alison. You no sleep.*

She shook her head at Sally's question. She hadn't been sleeping much at all lately. "Not much tonight."

*Why you no sleep.*

"Too much work." Interestingly, one of the several words IMIS seemed to have trouble translating was 'work.' It appeared dolphins didn't have a precise equivalent in their language. As a result, when Alison said "work," the dolphins heard something more akin to their sound for "effort." Nevertheless, Sally seemed to understand.

*You work much Alison.*

"I know I do." She smiled at her own next thought. *You know it's a problem when it's not just your mother saying you work too much, but the dolphins too.*

Alison continued watching her float in place until Sally spoke again.

*You no happy Alison.*

"What?"

*You no happy.*

Alison frowned. "I am happy, Sally. I'm just tired."

Sally emitted a very soft set of clicks and whistles for Dirk's sake, as he was still sleeping near the surface. The external speaker on Lee's desk emitted more of the translated words. *Me happy. Me with Dirk.*

Alison was about to reply when Sally's next statement cut her off. *Where you friend.*

She meant John Clay. Sally had picked up on Alison's relationship with Clay from the beginning. "He's working too."

*He work much too.*

Alison shyly nodded.

*Why humans work much.* Sally asked.

Alison took a deep breath. It was a simple question, but hardly a simple answer. She thought it over and finally shrugged. "To make the world good, I guess."

Sally was quiet for a moment, as if considering her reply. *World good now.*

Alison smiled. "Maybe to make things better then."

*What better.*

"Better is making things more good."

Sally was quiet again. She remained floating in the water, looking at Alison and barely moving. *World more good before.*

She stood still, staring at Sally. Alison was overcome by a frightening thought. *They were making the world better, weren't they?* To change the world; that was the point of the whole project. It was what she told herself year after year, working eighteen-hour days and having to overcome obstacle after obstacle. *They wanted to change the world. But had they?*

The initial breakthrough they made with IMIS shocked the world. There was no doubt. But through it all, what surprised her the most wasn't the overwhelming press, the interviews, and torrent of visitors. It was the critics. She would never have imagined how strong the backlash from them would be. Skeptics in the scientific community were to be expected, but the nastiness from people in so many other fields was surprising.

The number of articles attacking the validity of their data was tremendous. Many of them were written by people who knew far less about dolphins or marine biology. She and her team initially thought it was just the conservatives, but a significant number turned out to be liberals too. Some claimed it was a hoax for more attention, or more funding. One talk show host insinuated that it was a simple "trick" using sophisticated software, never meant to do anything but fool the public. *For what? What on earth did she stand to gain by fooling the world?* It was then she realized that being under the scrutiny of public opinion had a very dark side. Yet fortunately, for every doubter, there were many more believers. *But had they really changed anything?*

Alison remained motionless, staring at her own reflection in the thick glass. It was true. They had gotten an awful lot of people excited, but was the world fundamentally any different or better? She thought about what Sally had said. Was the world better, or could it really be worse?

The United States was arguably the epicenter of recent technological advancements, on virtually every level. The computer changed everything, and then the internet came along and accelerated it all again. Everyone now had phones that were more powerful than the first space shuttles. Televisions were almost the size of an entire wall, and video games made real life look downright boring to most kids. And to top it off, diseases like heart disease and obesity were at record highs.

What exactly *was* she working for? In many ways, the world was getting worse. She dropped her head, struck by a wave of shame, but immediately pulled herself out of it. She knew the answer. Now she was working to prove the critics wrong. To prove the communication was genuine. That it was real. That was the whole reason for the vest; to be able to travel out into the wild, where she could show and immerse herself in the real world of dolphins, and to do so out from under the shadow of a man-made tank and any supposed tricks.

Nevertheless, Sally's remark had caused Alison to step back abruptly and consider whether what they were doing now was truly for the science…or for her.

*Go sleep Alison. Rest,* Sally said softly.

Alison shook herself out of her trance and managed to grin.

Sally studied Alison through the thick glass, standing in the darkness. *Tomorrow we show you.* Sally continued. *Tomorrow we show you world is beautiful.*

She sighed, with just a little of the smile still remaining, and gently reached out for the tank, pushing her palm against the clear glass.

Slowly, Sally floated forward and touched her bottlenose to Alison's palm, separated only by the thick pane of glass.

* * *

Alison sat behind her desk. She stared out the window and watched the sun rise into the morning sky over the bright green hills of Puerto Rico. The scattered, white clouds crawled across the endless expanse of blue. Behind her, the sun's warm rays slowly crept across the wall of her office.

Her laptop sat on the desk in front of her, displaying a detailed budget sheet. She hated running everything. All right, hate was a strong word. Resentment, perhaps. Deep down she resented having to do it, but the old director was gone, and no one else knew as much about the project details as she did. She had been the lead since the very beginning. The driving force.

Now it was all on her: the vision, execution, details, budgeting, everything. The truth was that it was too much. The difference between being the lead researcher and actually running the place was huge. She was constantly bogged down in administrative minutia, and it was keeping her from doing the one thing she wanted most: to be free. Alison yearned to be back on the front line doing nothing but pure research. Instead, she was stuck in her office much of the day, making sure that everything else was done. She'd thought about stepping down, but she was deathly afraid of what bureaucrat would replace her.

She tilted her head, listening to the loud murmur of children downstairs. It was the last class visit before the big trip tomorrow. Alison smiled at the thought of the small, excited faces pressed up against the glass.

A moment later, there was a knock on the door. Her administrative assistant, Bruna, opened it and poked her head in.

"Alison?"

"Good morning, Bruna."

The assistant smiled. "There's someone here to see you. He said he doesn't have an appointment."

Alison rolled her eyes. "I'm not in the mood for solicitations. Whatever it is, just tell him I'm not interested."

Bruna blinked. "Um...actually, he said he's here to ask for your help. In fact, he asked to see DeeAnn too."

"Help with what?"

"I don't know. But he sure doesn't look like a solicitor."

Alison raised an eyebrow. "What do you mean?"

"Well, he's old. And he's dressed in the nicest suit I've ever seen."

* * *

DeeAnn had just joined Alison in her office when Bruna escorted the old man in. He entered with the help of a cane and a young female assistant attentively at his side. His hair was completely white, combed straight back and neat. His face bore a deep tan highlighted by his crème-colored dress shirt, which he wore beneath a dark blue, and very expensive, Kiton suit. His cane looked to be made of ivory.

The man smiled sincerely at Alison and then DeeAnn. With a brief nod, he staggered eagerly across the room toward them.

"Ah, Ms. Shaw and Ms. Draper, it is an honor to make your acquaintance." His accent was noticeable but subtle. "I very much appreciate you meeting me without an appointment. I'm afraid there is a certain urgency to my trip."

He reached them and held out his hand. "My name is Mateus Alves."

Alison shook his hand politely. His aged skin was soft and cool. Standing next to her, DeeAnn did the same. "What can we do for you, Mr. Alves?"

"Please," Alves waved his hand humorously, "call me Mateus. Being called by my first name may be the only thing left that helps me feel young." He motioned to his aide next to him. "This is Carolina, my assistant. Please excuse her silence. She knows very little English."

Both ladies smiled politely at Carolina.

Alison motioned to one of the chairs in front of her desk. "May I offer you a chair?"

"Wonderful, thank you," Alves replied. He turned around and fell gently into the seat with a welcomed sigh. "Please excuse our abruptness. I hope I haven't intruded too much."

"Not at all." Alison relaxed and watched the man curiously. "We were just doing some planning for a trip."

Alves raised his cane and nonchalantly propped it up in front of him, resting on it. "I'll be as brief as I can. I know you are very busy. I've come to see you both, as I am a follower of your work. And a big fan, I might add. I'm a businessman in Rio de Janeiro. I own a number of hotels and, as you might guess, have done rather well." He made a humble gesture at his clothing. "As you can also see, I am an old man. And as such, I have spent a number of my later years trying to give something back."

Alison and DeeAnn glanced at each other. "That's very kind of you, Mr. Alves." Alison caught herself. "I mean, Mateus. But we're not actually in need of additional funding at this time. We have a number of-"

"Forgive me, Ms. Shaw," he interrupted. "That's not what I meant. My visit is of a different nature entirely."

A flash of embarrassment passed between the women. Alison motioned for him to continue.

"You are correct. I am somewhat of a philanthropist, but my efforts reside more around my home country than outside. In fact, it is one of those endeavors that brought me to you." He glanced up at Carolina as he went on. "I have spent a number of years building a wildlife preserve for the indigenous animals of South America. I'm sad to say many are now threatened. I've spent all my life in South America, and wanted to build something that would help preserve the beauty of our continent well into the future, both flora and fauna."

Alves stopped briefly and caught his breath. "And I wanted to make it big. Our *preserve*," he announced, with a hint of pride, "is approximately the size of eighty thousand of your acres." He watched their expressions change with some amusement. "It's the least I could do for a country that has given me so much."

Alison watched Alves lean back in his chair. "And you need some help with your preserve?"

He grinned. "Of a sort, yes. But probably not what you are guessing. You see, I have hired a great number of people, not just to build this ecological oasis, but to run and maintain it. Many people, including botanists, agriculturalists, and even animal behaviorists like yourself."

DeeAnn, still standing next to Alison, tilted her head questioningly. "Where did you say your reserve was located?"

Alves turned. "Ah, I didn't, Ms. Draper. My reserve is called 'O Nosso Mundo' and is located a few hundred miles north of São Luis. It was an ideal location for several reasons of which I won't bore you with. But we have since acquired a great many indigenous animals, including snakes, macaws, jaguars, as well as a number of primates. All now part of our growing preserve."

Alison was watching Alves with a slight look of confusion, still waiting to understand the significance of his visit. Although what she didn't notice was the color slowly draining from DeeAnn's face.

Nor did she notice the subtle shift of Alves' attention toward DeeAnn as he continued. "In fact, our lead researcher is a strong follower of your research here. He is fascinated with the dolphins and especially your young gorilla."

Alison finally nodded. "Oh, I see. He must be doing similar research, I presume."

Alves glanced back to Alison. "Yes, very much so. He's been working with Capuchin Monkeys, which are native to South America. And as you probably know, are the most intelligent of the New World primates."

Alison turned to DeeAnn and opened her mouth to

speak but suddenly stopped when she saw the expression on her face.

Alves paused and took a deep breath. He was staring at DeeAnn again. "Unfortunately, something has happened to our researcher, and he's now missing."

DeeAnn finally spoke, in a low whisper. "What's his name?"

Alves didn't answer immediately. Instead, he glanced up at Carolina, then back to the two women.

"What's his name?" DeeAnn repeated, louder.

"Luke...Luke Greenwood."

Alison watched DeeAnn begin to waver in place then stumble back a step. Her face was now completely white. She reached out and grabbed her arm. "Dee?!"

DeeAnn blinked and reached for Alison at the same time. A split second later, she fell back against the edge of the desk.

Alarmed, Alison looked back and forth between the two. "What is it? What's going on?"

DeeAnn interrupted. "What...happened to him?

Alves took another deep breath. This was the part he had been dreading. He thought a moment, trying to find the right words. "Please know that South America is a most beautiful place, but it's also very...volatile. I am the first to admit this. And while I have become very wealthy as a businessman, it has not come without its share of controversy." A look of guilt began to appear on Alves' face. "I'm sorry to say I have developed many political enemies over the years, and I fear that Mr. Greenwood is now the victim of such."

Alves dropped his gaze to the floor and gently shook his head. "Recently our preserve was attacked. A large portion of our new complex was destroyed and many of the animals slaughtered. Mr. Greenwood was the only one there that night. He has now been missing for two weeks, and I fear the worst."

DeeAnn closed her eyes and began to cry.

Alison squeezed her hand. "Oh Dee, do you know him?"

DeeAnn pulled her hands up and placed them over her face. Her cries quickly turned into sobs.

Alves answered for her. "Ms. Shaw, the reason I've come to talk to you is because I believe Ms. Draper knows Mr. Greenwood very well."

# 16

DEEANN THREW OPEN the double doors to the lab and rushed in, letting them close loudly behind her. She immediately fell against the wall to the right and slid down to the floor, sobbing.

At the far end, Lee poked his head out from a small room, wondering what the noise was. He stood up and spotted DeeAnn huddled on the floor. With a concerned look on his face, Lee started to approach her. He then saw Alison ease one of the doors open and look around. She waved him off and he nodded, quickly retreating and leaving through another door in the opposite corner.

Alison let the door close, knelt down in front of DeeAnn, and put a hand on her shoulder. She said nothing. She just waited.

After several minutes, DeeAnn's crying finally slowed. She used the back of her hands to wipe the tears away and sniffed loudly. She let her head fall back against the wall and opened her blurry eyes at Alison, who moved her hands down to DeeAnn's bent knees. "Are you okay?"

DeeAnn sniffed again and rolled her head from side to side against the wall. "No."

"Do you want to talk about it?"

"Not really."

"Okay."

After a long silence, DeeAnn angled her head and looked up at the ceiling, absently following the dozens of support beams connecting one wall to another. "I've been friends with Luke Greenwood for a long time. Almost twenty years. But I haven't seen him in a while." She exhaled slowly. "We were both working on our doctorates when we met at grad school. He was a few years older." DeeAnn dropped her eyes back to Alison. "He was also further along than I was, but our interests couldn't have been more aligned, and he became my mentor. In fact, we worked together for several years even after we got our PhDs. Until I went to work with Koko." She stared off to the side as the memories came flooding back. "He's really brilliant."

Alison adjusted her position and sat down cross-legged. She leaned forward, listening.

After a moment, DeeAnn turned back to her. "Do you remember what I told you about how I came to have Dulce?"

"You said you rescued her in Mexico."

"That's right. It was a testing facility, used by the

pharmaceuticals. It was outside of U.S. regulations and barely one step away from a slaughterhouse. What they were doing with those animals was horrific. It was torture in every sense of the word."

Alison nodded. "I remember that part."

"That was right after I left working with Koko and the Gorilla Foundation. I told you I left the Foundation because I wanted to make a bigger difference. A difference in the lives of these poor animals. Dulce being one of them. But I didn't tell you what inspired a change at that point in my life." She leveled her eyes at Alison. "It was Luke Greenwood who got me to leave."

Alison raised her eyebrows curiously.

"I hadn't seen him in years, but one day he showed up at the Foundation. He told me he was forming a group to track and save captive and abused animals. And he wanted me to join him."

DeeAnn closed her eyes for a long moment, before opening them again. "Luke always made it impossible to say no. He was so passionate. Seeing animals being tortured made him angrier than anything."

"So you went with him."

DeeAnn nodded. "By the time I left, I was as angry as he was. And you know what?" she asked.

Alison shrugged.

"We saved a *lot*." She breathed in deeply. "From places all over the world. And then we learned about the facility in Mexico. All funded, built, and run by pharmaceutical money. And they didn't care who knew about it. It's like they were flaunting it. So with help from others, we found the place and watched, planning. And then late one night, we raided it."

Alison frowned. “That sounds dangerous.”

“It was. They even had a few armed guards, but we caught them with their pants down and disarmed them.” A smile spread across DeeAnn’s face. “It was glorious!”

“And that’s where you found Dulce?”

“Yes. We saved hundreds of animals that night. Many were able to survive in the local ecosystem so we set them free. The rest we took out of there. By morning, we’d made it to the border where we had a team from San Diego waiting, along with some government officials who supported us. It was a major blow to those drug companies, both economically and politically. We’d also taken video of the factory. One of the companies got so much negative press and came under so much scrutiny that they abandoned their animal testing completely. We broke their back. And it was all thanks to Luke.”

“So what happened to him?”

“After we rescued the animals, I discovered that Dulce was far more intelligent than I expected. So I started working with her, trying to provide whatever possible therapy I could. I was hoping we could return her to the wild someday, but she never wanted to leave. At the same time, I was making progress communicating with her even faster than we had with Koko. I just fell in love with her. But Luke wasn’t done. He said he wouldn’t stop until he’d broken the back of every drug company. I didn’t think it was practical and tried to tell him, but he wouldn’t listen. We parted ways, and I’m afraid not under the best of terms. Something I’ve always regretted.”

“When did that happen?”

“About a year and a half ago. The last I’d heard,

he was working with someone in South America. On a preserve."

Alison opened her eyes wide. "I had no idea."

"How could you?" DeeAnn shrugged, then thought about something. "Unfortunately there's one more thing. Dulce calls me mommy for obvious reasons. But if she considers me her mother, then Luke would undoubtedly be considered her *father.*"

* * *

"I'm terribly sorry, Ms. Draper. My intention was not to cause distress. I should have been more delicate about the news over Mr. Greenwood. Please accept my apology."

DeeAnn forced a polite smile. "It's all right. I've never been one for tip-toeing." Her eyes were dry but still red. She and Alison had returned to the office and now sat facing Alves and his assistant. "I assume there is more to your visit."

Alves nodded gratefully. "Indeed. Perhaps it might help if you could tell me the last time you saw Luke."

"About a year and a half ago."

Alves thought for a moment. "Right. I met him shortly after that. Shortly after he arrived in South America. He approached my organization in an effort to raise funds. I almost dismissed him at first, but then I realized exactly why he was there; to rescue animals which had been captured and were being sold for medical testing."

DeeAnn smirked. "Medical testing is too kind a term."

"Yes, I suppose you're right," Alves nodded. "I'm afraid South America has a dark side to our beautiful jungle landscape. It's very easy to hide things you don't want seen. And like other economically strapped countries, ours is also subject to a great many humanitarian abuses. Which is why Luke wanted to go straight to the source."

DeeAnn turned to Alison, "Poaching."

"Correct. The animals trapped in test labs first need to be captured. Luke called them 'torture labs,' and while South America does not have many of these facilities, we do have a large number of poachers who are happy to provide the supply, unfortunately. Men travel deep into our jungles and capture a variety of different animals to sell cheaply on the black market. And with Brazil being the largest country in this region, we have the disgrace of carrying out more of these crimes than anyone else." He turned to his assistant who shamefully dropped her head. She obviously understood enough English to know what Alves was referring to.

"So, Luke went after the poachers."

"More or less, yes. But he didn't go alone. You see, when Luke came to us and explained what he needed the money for, it became obvious that we had a rather symbiotic relationship. He wanted to save wild animals, and I wanted to keep them within the safety of my preserve. It seemed an ideal solution." Alves shrugged subtly. "So he joined my employ."

"And you funded his raids?"

"Well, the word 'raid' may be a tad extreme, but yes, I funded him. I also provided him with protection: a team from my own security service accompanied him and helped plan the rescues. And I dare say we were rather successful. Over the course of ten months, we freed hundreds of captured animals that were being prepared for shipment. Many of those animals joined my preserve, where they currently live a safe and happy life in the wild."

DeeAnn frowned. "So, what happened?"

Alves leaned back in his chair. "Dexter happened."

DeeAnn and Alison raised their eyebrows and spoke almost in unison. "Dexter?"

Alves' lips broke into a smile. "Dexter was one of our rescues. He's a capuchin monkey, rescued in our last mission." His face became serious again. "That mission was the deepest into the Amazon rainforest to date. What they found was a big operation and a rescue that was, well, quite surprising."

Both women were listening intently as he leaned forward, obviously getting more excited. "Luke and his team always went in at night. It was much easier. Normally, they would observe the camp for several days first to assess the situation."

"However, on this trip, they saw something rather extraordinary. These particular poachers had rounded up hundreds of capuchin monkeys and were preparing to truck them back down to the coast, where they would meet a cargo ship and make the transfer. The capuchins would not be caged until loaded onto the ship since the space requirements were far too prohibitive for using individual cages in the mountains. Instead, they were gathered and kept in giant nets.

"You can imagine some of the problems involved in keeping them in these large nets. And it was while Luke was observing the camp that he spotted Dexter."

"Spotted him in a net?" Alison asked.

"Not exactly." Alves now smiled, almost humorously. "Dexter hadn't been captured. At least not yet. He was outside the net, which was bound by a strong rope." Alves paused for effect. "You see, Dexter was trying to free the other monkeys. More specifically, he was trying to untie the knot in the rope."

Both women's eyes suddenly shot open. "What?" DeeAnn gasped. "He was trying to untie the knot?!"

Alves was smiling wider now and nodded. "That's right. But that's not the best part." He leaned forward even more. "Dexter was not only trying to untie the knot, but he almost did it! One of the poachers spotted him and netted him, but he didn't realize what Dexter was trying to do. When Luke told me the story, he said that when he examined the net himself, Dexter had managed to get most of it undone!"

DeeAnn was speechless. The story had not been wasted on Alison either. She was no expert on primates, but even she knew how incredible that was. The look on DeeAnn's face confirmed it.

Alves gave DeeAnn a knowing look. "From what I understand, Luke Greenwood had a very similar reaction."

She just stared at him, shaking her head silently in utter disbelief. Finally, she put her hand against her cheek. "Luke told you that story?"

"Nearly word for word."

"That's…amazing. And in the wild. My God."

"Luke was equally shocked," said Alves. "But he was also excited. In fact, he was so enthralled that he stopped his missions and began working with Dexter. He knew what you were doing with Koko and then here with Ms.

Shaw. He was planning to contact you. I'm surprised he hadn't already."

"He never did." DeeAnn's excitement quickly faded to disappointment.

Alves noticed Alison staring at him with a raised eyebrow and turned back to her.

"I'm afraid you still haven't told us what you need help with," Alison reminded him.

He looked at her, impressed. "You're both very sharp. The reason I'm here is that while I understand that he did not have Ms. Draper's experience, Luke was able to make quite a bit of progress communicating with Dexter. I believe this was why he was following your work here with such interest." The pleasantness in Alves' face seemed to fall away and was replaced with grief. "But, eventually came the attack on our complex."

"And the animals were killed."

"Yes. And Luke disappeared." Alves sat up straight. "But there may be a silver lining. We believe Dexter survived and escaped back out into the preserve. I've come to get your help in finding him."

## 17

"EXCUSE ME?"

"Ms. Shaw, I know this may sound a bit presumptuous, but I'd like you to help us find Dexter." Alves' expression was serious. "We still don't know who attacked us, or where Luke might be. Even though we haven't received any communication, we are still hopeful. But more than that, I believe Dexter saw what happened that night, and he may just be smart enough to give us vital information about it. How many were involved? What they were wearing? If we can just get an idea of who did it, I promise you, I will spare no expense tracking them down and finding Luke."

"I don't-" Alison started, then turned to DeeAnn, who remained silently thinking.

Finally, DeeAnn looked back at him curiously. "This isn't just about finding the monkey. This is about *talking* to him."

Alves nodded. "That's correct."

"Is that even possible?" Alison asked.

DeeAnn rubbed her finger softly against her lip. "It's feasible…maybe."

"I thought IMIS was programmed specifically for gorillas. Is this monkey similar to a gorilla?"

"No," DeeAnn answered. "Not even close."

"Could IMIS talk to it?"

DeeAnn shook her head. "Doubtful. But…"

"But what?"

"But there's another possibility. Dulce may be able to talk to a capuchin."

"Are you kidding?"

"No." She paused to think again before continuing. "I'm not sure, but I think it's possible. When I worked with Koko at the Gorilla Foundation, there was a researcher by the name of Joanne Tanner. She was brilliant and had worked there for years." DeeAnn's speech began to speed up, with a trace of excitement. "She spent ten years filming gorillas at the San Francisco Zoo and discovered something startling. The gorillas there had never been taught to sign like Koko, but she found that they used *gestures*. She documented almost thirty common, instinctive gestures used by the gorillas. It was a major discovery in primate studies, demonstrating what some of us had already suspected. There is a lot more to their communication than we know. More importantly, she found those common gestures spanned multiple species. And I believe one of them was capuchin monkeys."

"You mean like some kind of sign language?"

"Yes, exactly. And with Dulce and this Dexter monkey both being highly intelligent, it's conceivable that they could actually speak to one another. I don't know how likely it is, but it's certainly possible. Joanne was sure there were many more gestures yet to be identified."

Alves was smiling broadly, excited at DeeAnn's explanation.

"But transporting a gorilla is a production," she continued, thinking about the logistics. "It would have to be as fast as possible so she didn't become too anxious or nervous. She would also need to be in a cage, just in case. Dulce is young, but she's still strong. Too strong for us if she became frightened. It would definitely have to be by plane."

"I can provide whatever you need."

"Whoa, hold on!" Alison interrupted, holding up a hand. She looked at their visitors. "Would you mind if we excused ourselves for a minute?"

"Of course," Alves replied.

With that, Alison stood up and motioned for DeeAnn to follow her. They crossed the room and opened the door, stepping out into the hallway. After it clicked shut, Alison wasted no time.

"Okay, hold up. What exactly are we thinking here?"

"A trip," answered DeeAnn.

"A trip," repeated Alison. "Just like that?"

DeeAnn folded her arms. "I don't think we have much choice, Ali. Or time."

"Okay," Alison said calmly. "I know you're worried about Luke. I understand that. But we just met this man. We know nothing about him."

"That's true, although we should be able to check him out pretty easily. I mean, the man sounds like some kind of billionaire mogul. I doubt we'd have much difficulty finding out."

"Okay, fine. Let's assume everything he says is true. We'd be heading off into the jungle in some unknown country-"

"You mean *I* would be."

"Wait, what? Alison looked confused.

"I would be heading off into the jungle."

"*You* would be? What about me?"

"Because you, Alison, have a very big day tomorrow. You can't miss this."

"Are you kidding?" Alison raised her voice. "You think I'm going to just ship off while you and Dulce get on a plane bound for God knows where?"

"Yes," replied DeeAnn, with her face forming a determined look. "Because everything is ready now. Including Dirk and Sally."

Alison froze with her mouth open, working on her rebuttal. But she had none.

"Listen, Ali. I don't want to argue. Do I think this is a brilliant idea? No. But we also don't have a lot of time. If there is any chance Luke is still alive and we can help find him, then I have to try." Her dark eyes softened. "He would do it for me."

Alison glanced at her, then off to the side, finally closing her mouth. She sighed in resignation. "Okay. What are the risks?"

DeeAnn thought about the question. "Something happens to me…or Dulce."

"Exactly!"

"I see what you're doing. Could something happen to me or Dulce? Yes. It's a possibility, but probably not a very likely one. Listen, Ali, something has *already* happened to Luke. We'd be talking about a low probability against one that's already occurred. It's not a terribly hard decision."

"Dee, there's a lot more involved than that and you know it."

"I do, but when it's all boiled down, it still comes down to whether we try to help. And I think we both know each other well enough to know what that answer is."

Alison stared at her in silence. Her head began to shake back and forth. DeeAnn was right. As long as Alves and his security team checked out, it wasn't a huge risk. It was really more about the logistics. And it was not as though they wouldn't be coming back. "Well, I don't like the idea of both of us being gone at the same time. It doesn't seem smart."

"We can stay in touch by phone. You have the satellite phone on the boat."

Alison sighed again and covered her face with her right hand. Something about this didn't feel quite right. It was too rushed. In reality, they still knew very little.

The only reason to throw things together so haphazardly was because they didn't know whether Luke was alive and, if so, for how much longer.

"Assuming Alves can provide what's needed," DeeAnn said, "there's really only one thing left."

They looked at each other and then both slowly turned around. The one thing was an awfully big '*if*.'

## 18

"YOU WANT US to make another vest?!" Lee Kenwood was leaning over his metal workbench. Juan Diaz was on the opposite side, disconnecting wires.

Both Alison and DeeAnn stood at the end of the workbench, watching them. "Is it possible?"

Lee stopped and looked at them. "You mean when we get back from the open water testing?"

Alison glanced nervously at DeeAnn. "No, before we leave."

Both Lee and Juan stopped what they were doing. "*Before* we leave?"

Alison eked out a small grin. "Possible?"

The two engineers turned their gazes back to each other, considering. Juan shrugged first. "There's always V2."

Lee took a deep breath, still thinking.

"What's V2? DeeAnn asked.

Reluctantly, Lee replied. "It's the backup."

"The backup what?"

"The backup waterproof vest."

Both women's eyes opened wide. "We have a second *vest*?"

"Well, 'second' might be a stretch. It's a second unit primarily for spare parts. We were planning to take it with us on the boat."

"Does it work?"

Again, Lee and Juan exchanged looks. "It could work. But I'm not sure how quickly. We'd have to do a data dump and then go through testing, which takes longer than anything else. More importantly, the translations would be very slow without a separate server. The processor in the vest is small which is why we offload the bulk of the work to other servers. When are you and Dulce supposed to leave?"

"How about tomorrow?"

Lee rolled his eyes. "I don't think we can make that. The data dump would take almost that long, leaving us virtually no time to test. Could you leave on Saturday?"

DeeAnn frowned. "I have a friend in trouble."

"And you need an IMIS system to help?"

"Yes. And Dulce too."

Lee was still pondering when Juan spoke. "We could probably put it together in time, but with only minimal testing. If it didn't work, it would be a wasted trip. It also means we have no backup or spare if we have problems during the open water test. And speaking from a technical standpoint, having no backup is a *really* bad idea."

"Have you had any problems so far with the first vest?" Alison asked.

"Not yet."

"Well, that sounds encouraging."

"We're still in a controlled environment. Sending the second vest off without thorough testing, especially if you need it so badly, scares the hell out of me."

"Well," DeeAnn interjected, with her hand resting over her mouth. "Maybe we can test on the way." They all turned and looked at DeeAnn, who smiled at Juan. "Ever been to South America, Juan?"

Juan returned the smile. "I can be packed in ten minutes."

DeeAnn looked at Alison playfully. "I hate that about men."

"Hold on," Lee said. With a sigh, he ran his hand over his face. "There's something else." Lee circled the other end of the workbench and headed for his computer. "Something I need to show you both."

He fell into his black chair and rolled forward, placing his hands on an extra wide keyboard. "We have another problem." He opened a window that filled the entire screen, displaying another frame of video footage. The long list of system log entries appeared alongside of the video. The frequency of red colored errors in the log was increasing. "I've been trying to track it down, but I can't seem to find it."

"Track what down?"

"This." He pointed to the list of errors on the screen. "This is the main system log for IMIS' translation process. This is where identification and translation happens. And these red entries are indicating problems."

Alison leaned in closer, staring at the text. "What kind of problems?"

"Problems with the translations…as in *mistakes*."

Both of the women's eyes widened. "Mistakes?"

"Yes." Lee sighed again, turning around to face them. "There's a lot involved in what IMIS does. It starts with converting the analog wavelengths of our voice into digital data. It then parses that data into chunks that can be matched against spelling and grammatical rules looking for errors. Then it applies dozens of-" he suddenly stopped when he noticed their eyes beginning to glaze over.

"Okay," he continued. "So that's basically how it works…but here's the problem: the communication is increasingly becoming *less* systematic. In other words, it's unraveling." Lee swung back around to his screen. He grabbed the mouse and scrolled up through the log until the entries displayed the time and date from four days ago. "Look at this. Not as many errors as today." He then scrolled up further. "And even less last week."

"So they're increasing?"

"Exactly."

"So what are the errors saying?" asked DeeAnn.

"What they seem to be indicating is that an increasing number of language translations are no longer matching. The time synchronizations are off. Which means the data is being received and transmitted out of order."

Alison stood up straight. "So what does that mean? We're not really talking to Dirk and Sally, or Dulce?"

"No, that's the weird part. There aren't any errors for Dirk and Sally's translations, just Dulce's. And, yes, we are really talking to her, for now." He scrolled back down his log entries. "But the errors are clearly increasing, and we're already close to one error out of every twenty translations. It's getting worse, fast."

DeeAnn shot Alison a worried look. "And you have no idea what the problem is?"

Lee shook his head sheepishly. "I don't. I've been trying to figure it out, but haven't been able to yet. If I had to guess, I would say there's something wrong with one or more of the logic sequences we developed for Dulce. Those that are primate specific. Or, perhaps a flaw in one of the algorithms itself. Either way, it indicates this to be a deep problem and not something we can fix quickly, or easily."

DeeAnn took a deep breath and exhaled loudly. "So what you're saying is even if we build another vest for me to take, it may not work regardless."

"I'm afraid so. I agree with Juan. We could assemble a vest in time and make it work, even if he went with you and did the testing on the plane. But at some point, your communication with Dulce is going to become less and less accurate until you reach a point that you can't even understand her."

"How long do you think I'd have?"

"Hard to say," Lee shrugged. "Judging from the speed the errors are increasing, I'd guess three or four days."

Alison folded her arms. "And you think this will take some time to fix."

"Eventually, yes. We haven't even identified where the problem is, let alone begun working on a fix."

Alison turned to her left and stared at DeeAnn. "Well, I guess it's now or never!"

# 19

WILL BORGER PEERED through the side window of the blue-gray SH-60F "Oceanhawk" helicopter and watched the blur of the blue Caribbean waters passing beneath them. His white knuckles gripped the top of his bag, which was secured tightly between his knees as he kept his eyes closed and tried to fight off a budding sense of nausea.

Borger didn't like to fly, especially in helicopters. He understood all the physics involved. He understood the properties of air pressure and lift. He even understood the dynamics behind autorotation for emergency landings but none of that helped. In the end, his respect for the simple, yet "terminal", role of gravity ultimately won out.

Borger checked his watch again, anxiously. He recounted the steps in his apparent mistake at waking up Admiral Langford to give him the news about the Chinese ship. He hadn't expected to be included on a plane flight with Clay and Caesare, now headed south. Nor was he expecting the Oceanhawk, which had been waiting in Grenada to fly them out to sea, to drop onto one of the Navy's research ships already en route to Guyana.

Borger heard something through his bulky headset and turned away from the window. He leaned forward and peered past Clay, who was seated in the middle. Steve Caesare was slumped quietly against the wall on his side of the narrow cabin. Borger shook his head in amazement. Watching Caesare sleep, despite the thunderous blades of the helicopter, was bad enough. Having to listen to him snore blissfully through the headset was just plain ridiculous.

The blur of the water below them slowed and the helicopter began to bank to the left. As it came around, Borger glimpsed part of the ship below them. Finally, they had arrived.

The USNS Bowditch was one of the Navy's Oceanographic Survey Ships, performing research for acoustical, biological, physical, and geophysical ocean surveys. At an impressive 328 feet, with a stark white painted hull, it was one of six "Special Mission" ships in the Navy's Military Sealift Command.

Once the helicopter dropped softly onto the pad, the sliding door next to Borger was pulled open. The face of a petty officer appeared in helmet and goggles. Powerful rotors could be heard winding down above them while the three stooped and climbed down the short set of steps.

Borger, still hunching forward, followed Clay and Caesare across the gray deck and up the two flights of stairs to the ship's bridge.

A tall and lean Captain Krogstad nodded to all three men as they stepped inside.

"Gentlemen, welcome aboard the Bowditch."

"Thank you," they said, almost in unison. Clay stepped forward and extended his hand. "We appreciate the lift, Captain."

Krogstad eyed Clay as he shook his hand. "I have my orders."

Clay hoped that was Krogstad's version of a joke. He knew the Captain was actually longtime friends with

Admiral Langford, and had effectively "retired" to a research ship simply to stay off the "hard."

The fact of the matter was that Krogstad had seen his share of naval incursions over the last thirty years, both official and unofficial. Like many hardened senior officers, he had decided combat was rarely the answer to most problems; something politicians never seemed to figure out. Krogstad had also long since given himself to the sea and, frankly, had no intention of giving up an active command. Not until they took it from him.

The captain turned to the young female officer standing next to him, dressed sharply in a white shirt and skirt. "This is Commander Neely Lawton, our technical officer. She will show you to your quarters and help you with anything you need. Once the chopper's buttoned up, we can get underway again." He glanced at his watch. "We should make landfall by tomorrow morning."

They thanked the captain again and nodded to Commander Lawton. "Welcome, gentlemen," she said. "If you'll come with me, please." With that, she stepped past them and pulled open the door they'd just come through.

The three followed her down another set of stairs to the mid-deck, then along a catwalk to the foredeck. She led them through a series of hallways until they reached an end with doors to each of their cabins.

Lawton motioned to the doors. "Feel free to settle in, gentlemen. Have you been on a Pathfinder class ship before?"

Steve Caesare flashed his winning Italian smile from under his dark mustache. "We sure have."

Lawton was turning away but stopped and did a double take at his smile. Almost imperceptibly, she furrowed her brow and continued. "Then I assume you know the layout of the ships. I'll be in the science lab for most of the afternoon. If you're hungry, please feel free to stop by the cafeteria. Our cook should be there for another couple hours and would be happy to make you something."

The men thanked her and watched Lawton turn and walk back down the narrow passage. After she disappeared from view, Clay frowned and looked at Caesare.

"Not the reaction you were looking for, eh?" He slapped him on the back. "Maybe your smile is losing its charm."

Caesare scoffed. "Impossible!"

* * *

After an early lunch, the men visited the lab, which was located near the center of the ship and one of the largest sections on the mid-deck. The room, brightly lit from dozens of fluorescent lights overhead, had only a few small windows. The walls were painted in the ship's familiar light gray, covered with glass-door shelving. The tables were full of science equipment and computers.

Commander Lawton was on the far side of the room, standing over two seated researchers. All three of them studied a huge computer monitor mounted securely above the table. On the screen was a three-dimensional topological map of the ocean floor, with bright orange dots spread uniformly across the picture.

Caesare crossed the light-colored tile floor and stopped next to her, joining them to examine the monitor. "And what do we have here?"

Lawton did not take her eyes off the screen. "It's part of a new array we've been deploying in the eastern

Caribbean. Similar to the old hydrophones, but these are based on active sonar technology. More sensitive with a much better range."

"How many have you deployed?" asked Clay.

She straightened and turned around. "Several thousand square miles so far. We're still running tests and fine-tuning, but within a few years, we'll be able to monitor everything larger than a life raft in this area."

Caesare looked wryly at Clay and Borger. "Could have used that with the Forel."

"Is that the Russian sub you found near Brazil?" she asked.

"Correct."

"Any chance you know what direction it came from?" asked Lawton.

"It's debatable," Caesare grinned.

"I don't think it came through your array if that's what you're asking." Clay suddenly had a thought about the Forel. "Although it would be interesting to see what happened if it did. We found it carrying a powerful active noise reduction system on board, which we assumed was used to silence its propulsion system. But now I'm wondering whether it could do something similar with the sound waves from sonar."

Borger's eyes lit up. "Oh, wow. I hadn't thought about that. If those speakers run the length of the sub... that could be big."

Caesare eyed the two biosafety cabinets behind them, used for providing ultra-sterile testing environments. "So, Commander Lawton, what is your background, if you don't mind my asking?"

"Biology. Systems Biology, to be exact. DNA, proteins, complexes...that sort of thing. We have two other biologists onboard, both biochemists. The rest of our science team is comprised of geologists, oceanographers, and marine ecologists. The technical team covers electronics, sounding and imaging, and a few other areas. All in all, we have a pretty well-rounded group."

"It certainly sounds like it."

"Speaking of which, your arrival has us all a little curious. Why exactly are we headed for Guyana if the sub is reportedly in Brazil?"

"You don't know?" Clay asked, with raised eyebrows.

Her blonde hair pulled back into a bun, Lawton shook her head with a serious expression. "No. All we know is that we were ordered to pull out in the middle of our project, without much explanation. We were told to prepare to receive you and head straight for Guyana. We were assuming you would fill us in."

Clay looked at Caesare. "We have a Chinese corvette class warship sitting in the middle of Guyana, which has been idle for some time. It appears we're not the only ones interested in finding out what it's doing there."

"Corvette class?" Lawton exclaimed. "What's a corvette doing in the Atlantic?"

Caesare shrugged. "Beats us. They're new, with a pretty stealthy hull design to boot. Yet this one was being spied upon by the Russian sub."

"How long has it been there?"

Borger spoke up. "At least a few months from what we can see from the ARGUS."

Lawton's looked at him with surprise. "You have access to the ARGUS?"

"We do."

"I'm impressed. Do you have the data with you?"

Borger smiled at her. "I sure do. Shall I fire it up?"

"Please."

Once logged in, Borger accessed the data on his external drive and brought up some of the detailed overhead shots he had shown the guys during their call with Langford.

They were examining an overhead shot of the corvette when Lawton leaned closer to the wide screen that Borger was borrowing. "How close can you zoom in?"

"Pretty close." He used his mouse as they zoomed in, stopping to reposition the frame so that it came in on the middle of the ship. The extreme detail was incredible. They could see the anti-ship armament almost as clearly as if they were standing on the ship itself.

"Wow," she mumbled.

"The ARGUS is pretty impressive."

"You're telling me." Lawton tilted her head to compensate for the rotation of the picture. She glanced at the bottom right corner where the time and date were displayed. "Midday," she said. "Where is everyone?"

"Good question. I haven't had time to run a detailed scan yet, but so far I haven't seen anyone topside."

"It supposedly came in for repairs." Caesare straightened up and folded his arms. "So far, we can't see any damage or repair equipment."

Next to Caesare, Neely Lawton straightened as well. "It's not there for repairs."

Clay and Caesare looked at each other, then back to her.

"Guyana doesn't have facilities for repairing a ship that size. I've been there. If anything, its capital, Georgetown, is more of a retail and administrative center. Its biggest claim to fame is having the CARICOM headquarters there."

"So, it's there for something else," mused Caesare. "What are Guyana's primary resources?"

"Rice and sugar exports," replied Clay, dryly.

"Rice and sugar?"

"And a little timber and gold. But if that's what the Chinese were after, they would have come with a freighter, not a warship. Which means…"

"They're probably *guarding* something," finished Caesare.

"Without anyone being on the ship?" Borger leaned forward, rotating through the same images taken on different days. Each picture looked the same, with only a few obscured by the cloud cover. They all watched Borger continue further back. He looked up over his shoulder. "Could it be abandoned?"

Clay shook his head. "Not with a ship like this."

Lawton watched, thoughtfully. "Can we bring it back to present day?"

"Sure." Borger complied until he was back at the most recent image.

"Now let's roll back again at, say, an hour a minute."

After a few mouse clicks, the video began to advance at an accelerated pace. The brightness of the hull dimmed several times from patches of clouds. As they stood, watching silently for several minutes, there was still no sign of anyone. They could then see the resolution begin to darken across the frame as evening approached.

Less than a minute later, the picture had grown almost completely dark. The only exception was the faint lights from the modest city of Georgetown, illuminating one by one.

"This *is* strange," said Lawton. "I guess I can see why you hijacked our ship."

Caesare grinned. "Now you know almost as much as we do."

Borger spun his chair around to face them. "I'll see if I can get more data from the ARGUS and go back even further. If we can zoom in from the beginning, when it first arrived, we should be able to find out what happened to everyone."

"And where the Forel came from."

"Right."

"I'm assuming the Forel arrived after the corvette. Something strange is going..." Borger suddenly fell silent as he noticed the expression on Clay and Caesare's faces change. Their eyes were wide open, as was Neely Lawton's. All three were staring at the screen behind him. When Borger whipped back around to the monitor, his eyes grew wider than anyone's. "Whoa!"

The video was still advancing and had elapsed through the first two hours of darkness, as viewed from the satellite. That's when things changed. At just a couple of hours after darkness, the area around the mysterious warship suddenly lit up like a Christmas tree.

# 20

"SHE'S DOING WHAT?!" Chris Ramirez' jaw dropped open as he sat on one of the boat's padded bench seats.

Alison took a deep breath and shrugged. "She's going."

Kelly Carlson was leaning against the skipper's chair with a similar look of surprise.

The boat was a forty-eight foot Prowler catamaran. Alison still wasn't a huge fan of the government, but their generous funding certainly helped. It also meant that Alison's team had been able to replace their old boat with a larger model: one with more range and less mechanical problems. The extra room also meant they were able to stay out in the ocean longer without the team feeling like sardines.

"And you're just going to let her go?" Chris asked, appallingly.

"Well, I can't exactly stop her now, can I?"

"Ali," Chris said, with concern. "I've been to South America. I spent almost three years in Paraguay with the Peace Corps."

"I know."

"I'm telling you, South America is a dangerous place. Unless you're in a large city, it can be *very* dangerous!"

Alison didn't say anything. She remembered the stories Chris had told her when they'd met. Especially the one night when their camps were raided, a few people in Chris' group were nearly kidnapped, and a young woman in another group had been raped by two of Paraguay's soldiers. It still made her sick to even think about it.

Kelly crossed her arms and raised one of her feet, resting it on the rung around the bottom of the chair. "How much do we know about this billionaire guy?"

"He checks out. And he certainly seems genuine."

"This is nuts," Chris muttered, shaking his head. He knew how strong-willed DeeAnn was and decided to take a different tack: one of practicality. "How is she even going to talk to Dulce?"

"Lee and Juan are putting together a special vest. One that's self-contained."

"Really." Chris rolled his eyes. "This, from the guys who have to test everything a thousand times?"

"They're still going to test it…but it will have to be done on the way down."

"How the hell are they going to do that?"

Alison bit her lip. "Juan is going with her."

"What?!"

"He's going with her. He's going to make sure the vest works. Hopefully, they won't be gone long."

"And we're still going out with Dirk and Sally?"

"Yes, but we'll go Friday instead."

Chris turned and looked incredulously at Kelly, who frowned but said nothing. "Well, I hate to be a downer here," Chris began, "but you and I both need to go. Kelly is the captain, so without her we can't even leave, and Lee is the technical expert. So…who exactly is staying behind and watching the place?"

"Bruna."

"Bruna? She's part time."

"She said she can come in every day. And she can

always call on the maintenance crew if there's a problem." Alison was expecting this reaction from Chris. For months, he and Kelly had worked hard on the details of their groundbreaking trip with Dirk and Sally. They'd covered everything, and last minute changes could present all kinds of issues. The most obvious was that the building, not to mention IMIS, would be almost completely unattended. And without Juan, there would be no one to check and rotate the backup tapes: an important task that had saved their bacon not too long ago. Juan was also supposed to be on standby in case they had any serious problems out on the open ocean.

Chris shook his head again. "This could be a real problem, Ali."

Alison put her hands on her hips. "Yeah, well what would you have me do then? Put an ankle monitor on her and forbid her to go? Maybe I can just get her arrested!" She stood, glaring at him. "There is nothing I can do. Christ, there's nothing I would *want* to do! DeeAnn is afraid for her friend, Chris. She's desperately hoping she can help him before it's too late. Are any of us seriously suggesting she shouldn't do that?"

He frowned and dropped his eyes to the floor, embarrassed. "No. Of course not. We'd all do the same." He looked back up at her. "I'm sorry." After a moment, he stood up. "DeeAnn needs our support. Let's help her, and then we'll figure out the logistics."

Alison finally exhaled with relief. "Thank you."

Built atop old sugarcane fields, the Mercedita Airport in Puerto Rico was located just three miles outside Ponce, and less than ten miles from the research center. The airport, after expansion during the Second World War, now served over one hundred thousand passengers annually.

Mateus Alves' Gulfstream G550 rested motionlessly under the bright sun, taking up almost a third of the wide lot reserved on the north side of the airport. The door remained open, with a short set of stairs in place, as Alves arrived in an expensive, black sedan. The driver exited quickly and opened the back door. He stood, waiting while Alves and his assistant Carolina stepped out into the heat.

They immediately made their way across the concrete lot to the stairs. Alves climbed up and stepped into the Gulfstream's plush, air-conditioned cabin just as his cell phone rang.

He stepped in front of one of the cool vents and retrieved the small phone from his pocket. "Hello?"

"Mr. Alves," said the voice on the other end. "This is DeeAnn Draper. I wanted to let you know that we've decided to join you."

"That's wonderful, Ms. Draper," he replied, enthusiastically. "I'm very happy to hear that. How long will you need to prepare?"

"We can be there tomorrow morning."

If Alves was surprised, he didn't show it. "I'm very grateful to you and your colleagues. What can I do to provide assistance? Perhaps send a car?"

"We should be fine getting there. But yes, we will need a few things. First and foremost, we'll need about forty pounds of food. All vegetables. Mostly green leaves, but as much kale and celery as you can find. And lots of berries."

"Of course," Alves answered. "Is there anything else?"

"Yes. We'll need a large cage. Gorillas can become very excitable in strange environments. Dulce will need a cage to travel in, with something soft to sit on inside. And I need to be able to sit next to her."

Alves nodded. "Yes, yes, of course. We'll find a way to make it happen. We'll be ready for you both."

"Actually there will be three of us. One of our engineers is coming too."

"Excellent. We're happy to have him. We will be ready for all three of you then. Please do not hesitate to call if you require anything else."

"I think that will do it," DeeAnn replied. "I suspect you'll have your hands full with that cage."

Alves chuckled. "All right then, Ms. Draper. We shall see you soon. Thank you again."

He hung up the phone and slipped it back into his pocket. He glanced at Carolina before looking past a set of white leather seats and couch to the square object at the rear of the cabin.

A large cage had already been installed.

## 21

"WHAT IN THE hell is that?"

Everyone was staring at the screen, puzzled by what they were seeing. The Chinese corvette ship was suddenly illuminated, bathed in bright lights. Figures could be seen appearing from below deck and quickly lowering a long gangplank to the dock.

Yet, what was really perplexing was the stream of lights that appeared from out of the dense jungle less than a mile from shore. It was a stream of…headlights.

Borger zoomed in as far as he could. Each set of headlights shone brightly against the vehicles in front of them. Trucks.

Several more from Neely Lawton's research team had joined them on the far side of the room now and stood observing over their shoulders as everyone watched the trucks back up against the gangplank. One by one, the men from the ship retrieved dozens of crates from the trucks and carried them below deck.

"What are they doing?"

"Unloading *something*," Clay said, hesitatingly.

After less than fifteen minutes, it was over. The transfer of crates was complete and the bright lights abruptly disappeared. The only lights left were those of the half dozen trucks, which appeared to refuel before heading back into the blackness of the jungle.

Clay and Caesare exchanged looks again. "Well, that's not normal."

Clay turned to Borger. "Will, we need to find out how long this has been happening." He turned back to Caesare. "And *we* need to call Langford."

* * *

Given everything Admiral Langford had seen during his career, he didn't surprise easily. However, Clay and Caesare managed to accomplish that more often than he liked.

"You've got to be kidding?" Langford leaned forward onto his desk, the phone pressed to his ear.

"No, sir," replied Clay.

"Any idea what was in the crates?"

Clay shook his head on the other end. "None, sir. Borger might be able to enhance the image, but the crates looked sealed so I doubt it will show much more."

"And how many were there?"

"Forty-eight."

"So, let me get this straight. We have a warship sitting in downtown Georgetown which does nothing all day, but it mysteriously receives and loads *something* onboard in the middle of the night, from out of the jungle."

"Yes, sir. That's about it. Borger's working through it now to get us a timeline. We're going to have to get another dump from the ARGUS data first, which is going to take a while. As far as we can tell, both the corvette and the Forel sub have been here a while."

Langford leaned back again, thinking. "This is becoming damn peculiar."

"We agree, sir."

"Okay, go through everything as quickly as you can. Call me back by oh-seven-hundred and give me an update. I need to bring this up in tomorrow's security briefing. Something tells me we're not going to like what we find out."

"Yes, sir. We should be nearing Guyana by sunrise."

"Good," nodded Langford. "Make sure you and Caesare are ready to go ashore. I want to know what that ship is taking onboard."

# 22

CHRIS AND ALISON stopped the large van in front of the Gulfstream jet and saw Mateus Alves in the doorway. Excitedly, he began to descend the stairs with his assistant close behind.

Alison climbed out and then stepped back to pull the large side door open, sliding it smoothly backward. A moment later, DeeAnn's head emerged from the inside and she stepped down onto the ground. In her hand was a chain, which revealed itself to be attached to Dulce's collar when the gorilla curiously peeked outside. DeeAnn promptly reached in and picked Dulce up into her arms, then turned to look at the airplane.

Unfortunately, she had no way to communicate since she'd left her original translation vest back at the facility. After explaining to Dulce where they were going, the small gorilla became very excited. She wanted to help, but she was equally excited at the prospect of making a new friend. Dulce had known other primates, including monkeys, but it was in Mexico under horrendous living conditions. There was no telling what kind of trauma or cognitive associations she still carried with her. Animals in a panic, especially gorillas, were very unpredictable. Dulce had seemed relatively calm during the preparations. Now watching Dulce's eyes nervously examine the large plane, she wondered if she was making a mistake. Especially when she felt Dulce's arms tighten around her.

Behind her, Juan climbed out carrying a medium-sized cardboard box with the newly designed vest inside.

In his other hand, he carried a large suitcase filled with computer equipment, as well as his clothes.

Leaving the driver's seat, Chris circled the back of the van and came up behind the others, grabbing two more suitcases for DeeAnn.

Alves and Carolina had stopped at the bottom of the stairs, waiting politely. Alison turned to DeeAnn.

"You're sure about this."

"Yes," DeeAnn replied, peering over Dulce's small, furry head. "We'll be back before you know it."

Alison smiled but didn't reply.

"Don't worry, Ali. We're not staying long. Our home is here now."

Alison maintained her smile and reached out, gently rubbing Dulce's head. The small gorilla purred and said something, but it went unanswered. She looked at Dee-Ann and stepped forward, wrapping her arms around both of them.

"You have the number for the boat's satellite phone, right?"

"I sure do."

Chris stepped up beside them, pulling the two bags. "Everybody ready?"

All eyes turned to DeeAnn, who in turn looked down at Dulce. The two then walked across the small tarmac.

As they neared the plane, a male crewmember emerged and quickly climbed down the stairs, waiting to take their bags.

Mateus Alves smiled warmly as they approached, glancing down at Dulce. "Welcome, Ms. Draper. We are very grateful for your assistance. We have accommodated all your requests and hope you will be comfortable."

"I'm sure we will be," she agreed. "May I introduce Juan Diaz, one of our computer whizzes."

Alves smiled again, revealing a perfect set of teeth. "Welcome, Mr. Diaz. We are very happy to have you join us."

"It's my pleasure, sir. Anything for Ms. Draper."

Alves laughed. "Indeed." He then turned to Alison. "Ms. Shaw, thank you again for allowing this brief interruption to your team's work. You are very generous."

Alison smiled and shook his hand. He probably didn't realize that she had no choice.

The crewmember took the bags from Chris and promptly returned up the stairs, disappearing inside the plane.

Alves clasped his hands together. "Are you ready to depart?"

"We are." DeeAnn turned, winked once more at Alison, and followed Carolina up the stairs. Juan stepped in behind them, leaving Alves standing with Alison and Chris.

"We'll have her back soon, Ms. Shaw. You have my word."

Alves climbed up the stairs after them, with noticeable difficulty. With one final wave, the white metal door was pulled closed.

* * *

DeeAnn was pleasantly surprised to see the size of the cage. It was larger than usual, which provided a much more comfortable place for Dulce during the flight. After takeoff, DeeAnn immediately slid over onto the couch and gingerly reached in through the bars. Dulce quickly placed her dark hand inside DeeAnn's.

Alves sat in one of the nearby leather seats, observing the connection between the two. "She loves you."

DeeAnn smiled without looking away. "It's mutual."

"It's quite obvious." Alves leaned forward. "I must apologize, Ms. Draper. I'm afraid I don't know as much about your program as Luke did." He suddenly caught and corrected himself. "I mean, as much as Luke *does*."

DeeAnn displayed no reaction to the mistake. "I hadn't been aware he was following our work."

"Well, forgive me if I sound improper, but I suspect he's been following *you* as much as your work."

DeeAnn looked up abruptly at Alves, considering his words before letting her eyes drop. "I wasn't even sure where he was."

Alves shrugged, in a supportive gesture. "I obviously don't know about your history, but I sense he cares a great deal about you. Of that, I am sure."

"You do know this is a long shot, right?" DeeAnn said, motioning to Dulce. "I'll be honest, even if we can find your capuchin monkey, I'm having a hard time imagining what information he might have that would make a difference."

Alves' eyes softened. "I suppose I should be candid as well. I've never had any children, Ms. Draper. And I've become quite fond of Luke. His passion and the righteousness he feels for protecting others, especially animals, made me come to feel for him as I would for a son. I've never seen that level of compassion in a young man before. Many of his beliefs reminded me of why I decided to establish the preserve in the first place. You've known Luke much longer than I have, but our goal is the same. I will do nearly anything to find him, even if it's a long shot."

"That makes two of us."

After a momentary silence, they both turned around and watched as Juan laid the new vest on a small table in front of his seat. He proceeded to attach two cables to the vest, plugging the other end of one into a power outlet. The other cable went into his laptop. After a short wait, he focused on the small screen and began typing.

Lee and Juan had given DeeAnn a rundown on the vest before they headed to the airport. It was larger than her old model, and heavier. It was unavoidable since more equipment had to be built in. The majority of the hardware was distributed carefully around the waist area, very similar to the waterproof version they had designed for Alison.

The difference with DeeAnn's new vest, though, was the batteries. It had more than four times the number of batteries to allow it to work as a completely self-contained unit, thanks to Steve Caesare. The prototype batteries he had sent over had a much higher energy capacity than the lithium variety. Another benefit was avoiding the need for any wireless transmission, reducing energy consumption even further. Instead, the smaller, slower processor would do all the work to communicate directly with Dulce, using the existing translation data that IMIS had already identified back in their lab.

One major limitation that both vests suffered from was line of sight. There was not only a microphone and speaker on the front of DeeAnn's vest, but a small camera as well. Both vests had to "see" to translate. Whether observing dolphins or gorillas, it was the only way to allow the computers inside the vests to correctly identify and translate their expressions and words. Alison had already seen this challenge when testing the underwater unit. It would prove to be just as limiting for DeeAnn and Dulce.

Juan studied his screen and continued typing. Neither Lee nor Juan wanted to alarm Alison and DeeAnn, but their concern over those translation errors was growing.

Juan leaned back in his plush chair and continued watching the information scroll down his screen. So far, so good. He glanced up and noticed the others watching him.

"A couple more hours and we can do some tests," he said to DeeAnn.

DeeAnn smiled and tried to remain calm. She realized at that moment the terrible mistake she'd made with Dulce. The IMIS system had been so astonishingly effective at translating between herself and Dulce, far better than any other technique. Because of it, DeeAnn hadn't taught Dulce more than a few words in sign language. And without the vest, she couldn't speak with Dulce, even at a basic level. She was completely paralyzed.

To make matters worse, Dulce was beginning to look very nervous inside her cage.

# 23

ADMIRAL LANGFORD SAT at one end of a large, polished conference room table, joined by Secretary of Defense Merl Miller, Secretary of State Douglas Bartman, and Stan Griffith, the National Security Advisor. A large monitor behind Langford displayed a frozen satellite image that he'd received from Borger.

"How the hell did we miss this?" Miller was the first to speak.

"According to the CIA, the analyst tracking the corvette was inexperienced. China and Venezuela have grown very close recently, after establishing some bi-lateral trade agreements. And Venezuela had announced some military exercises. The analyst thought the corvette was part of a cooperative training maneuver. But instead, the corvette continued on to Guyana before reporting mechanical problems and pulling in at Georgetown. At the time, the explanation was assumed to be authentic."

"And it just sat there for over four months?"

Langford nodded.

"Christ! Did they even bother to check on it?" Miller held up his hand before Langford could respond. "Forget I said that. We're talking about the CIA."

The other three men grinned even though it wasn't a joke.

Bartman leaned forward. "And a few weeks after this ship arrives, our mystery sub shows up. How did the Russians find out about it?"

"We don't know. But we do know there was equipment waiting when the Chinese showed up in Georgetown, likely from Venezuela."

"The trucks and earth moving equipment," Miller murmured. "So the big question is...what are they bringing back out of the jungle?"

They all looked back up at the large monitor. The frozen screen was displaying a close-up picture of the crate transfer aboard the corvette.

"And this has been going on for over five weeks?" Griffith inquired.

"Just about." Langford tapped his laptop and the video began to advance in slow motion.

"How about drugs?" Miller offered.

Griffith shook his head. "It wouldn't take five weeks to bring down a shipment of drugs."

"Unless it was a big shipment."

"No," Bartman agreed. "China has more than enough domestic production of drugs. They wouldn't need to come all the way over here for more."

"Well, I'm betting it ain't *sugar!*" Miller shot back, sarcastically.

"What else do they have?" asked Griffith.

Bartman was watching Langford and knew what his colleague's answer would be even before he said it.

"They do have *gold*."

Griffith raised his bushy eyebrows. "Gold?"

Bartman considered the idea. "Guyana is a small exporter of gold. It's a highly valuable commodity and it's portable. It might also explain the extreme security."

"Wait a minute," Griffith interrupted. "Guyana is a gold exporter. If they already sell it to other countries, why would they care about keeping shipments to China secret?"

Langford shrugged. "Maybe they've discovered a big deposit that they don't want anyone else to know about."

The room became silent as each of the men considered the possibility. China had been hoarding gold over the last several years, from all over the world. They had also been buying up mines in foreign countries. There was something they wanted gold for, and badly. No one knew why, but some suspected China was planning a major global economic event.

"Then why not bring something bigger?" asked Miller. "Like a freighter? And why not more trucks? Whatever it is, they could get it out a hell of a lot faster."

"And attract a lot more attention."

"Well, they evidently got the Russian's attention."

Langford sat, thinking. "On the other hand, maybe it's something immaterial."

"You mean something Guyana's government doesn't care about?"

"Right."

"Or," said Bartman, from the other side of the table, "they do care about it, but the Chinese has given them an offer they can't refuse." He paused and leaned back in his chair. "Well, at least sending the Bowditch was a good call." The Secretary of State didn't need to explain his statement. The relationship between the United States and China had become increasingly tenuous in recent years, to put it mildly. A more accurate word, which only a few dared to use, was *eroded*. The last thing the U.S. needed was to incite more military tension. That was why Langford had sent the Bowditch, a science vessel.

The conference phone on the table suddenly beeped. Langford glanced at the others as he reached for the phone. "I thought there was someone else we might want to have chime in on the subject." Langford pushed a button on the keyboard. "Langford."

"I have her on the line, Admiral," his secretary's voice came over the intercom.

"Put her through."

After a moment, the line clicked. Langford cleared his throat and spoke up. "Good morning, Doctor Lokke. Are you there?"

"Yes, Admiral. I am. I'm sorry for being tardy."

"That's quite all right. Have you had time to review the information I sent you?"

"I have indeed."

"Excellent. Standby while I add you." Langford leaned forward and studied the complicated phone's keypad for a moment, pushing one of the larger buttons. He looked up at the large monitor and saw Kathryn Lokke's video feed appear as a smaller window, overlaying the wide still frame from his own computer.

Kathryn Lokke stared into her camera. Her light complexion and short reddish-brown hair filled most of her window.

"Doctor Lokke, allow me to introduce Douglas Bartman, our Secretary of State. I believe you already know the rest of the group."

Lokke smiled curtly. "Yes, I do. Pleased to meet you, Mr. Bartman."

The Secretary nodded as Langford began. "Doctor, we were just discussing the video from Georgetown. More specifically, the crates being loaded onto the corvette ship and what they might contain. Drugs or agricultural commodities don't appear practical, but we're military men. You're the expert, and we'd like to hear your opinion."

Dr. Kathryn Lokke was the Director of the United States Geological Survey, the largest scientific and research department on the planet. She had taken over the department somewhat recently and had worked previously with Langford and others on his staff, under rather difficult circumstances. Langford thought very highly of her, as did the President. He also knew she was not someone to be trifled with.

Lokke took a deep breath, studying the footage on her own screen. "Well, it's not a liquid or gas, or else they would be using cylinders. I also agree it's not drugs. I doubt the Chinese would sit around for several months loading drugs on a ship. Drugs are moved quickly. As for other commodities, the quantity would have to be significant. But they're not, especially for someone like China."

"What about a commodity like gold?" Langford asked.

She frowned, thinking. "Gold is less a commodity than it is money. And there is a lot of mining going on in South America. But no, I doubt that's the answer, either."

Griffith squinted. "Are you sure?"

"No, I'm not sure," Lokke shrugged. "But gold is extremely dense and heavy, and those crates are relatively large. If they were filled with gold, there would be no way two men could carry it. Unless, of course, the quantities inside were much smaller than the crates, or if the men were twelve feet tall."

Langford's lip curled in his familiar way. "So either smaller amounts or it's something else."

"I think it's something else. Why put small amounts of gold in larger crates? It would be a waste of space, especially on a relatively small ship. Besides, there's a bigger problem. Mining gold, or even silver, for that matter, requires refining to get it into smaller blocks for shipping. But a refinery requires a lot of space and energy. Not something you would see in the jungle or on a mountain. It's not practical."

"So we rule out gold."

"Yes," she nodded. "Silver and platinum too."

"Well, we know they're doing something." Miller said. "They took up some earth movers, and they've been bringing something down ever since."

"Earth movers?" Lokke asked, with a raised brow. "I didn't catch that part."

Langford chimed in. "Yes, a few of them, as far we can determine."

"Hmm..." The men could see Kathryn Lokke lean back, thinking. She remained quiet for a long time before speaking up. "There is something that comes to mind. Something that might be far more strategic than gold. REEs."

"What's an REE?"

"Rare earth elements," Lokke explained, leaning forward again. She was surprised at their confused looks.

Langford looked at the others then back to the screen. "Fill us in."

"Rare earth elements, or REEs, are a group of seventeen specific elements on the periodic table which have become the equivalent of a modern day gold rush. These elements have very special properties that make them extremely valuable in a variety of modern technologies, especially technologies with military applications: things from lasers, to fiber optics, to missile guidance systems. These elements are also essential to many technological advances that make our modern way of life possible."

Griffith spoke up. "So they're rare."

"Actually, no," Lokke answered. "They're quite plentiful. In fact, cerium for example, is the twenty-fifth most abundant element on the planet. What's rare about them is not their existence: it's their *concentrations*. You see, REEs are common, but in deposits that are quite dispersed, which means uneconomical for mining. However, as modern technologies have advanced, rare earth mining has become more economically feasible; so much so that they've become a very important piece of political leverage, especially to China."

Langford suddenly remembered. "You're talking about China's export ban."

"Exactly. China has been absorbing rare earth mines for decades. So much that they ended up cornering the market by the early 2000s. No one cared because China, the world's largest exporter, sold them to the rest of the world as they did with many other commodities. But..." Lokke said. "That changed in 2009."

Bartman frowned. "What happened in 2009?"

"China stopped exporting them," Langford answered. "Or should we say, they restricted them."

"Right," said Lokke. "In a big way. Suddenly the

folly of allowing China to become the primary owner of rare earth metals became clear. Dozens of uneconomic rare earth projects, which had been abandoned around the world, were instantly in the spotlight again. Today, nearly all first world countries are desperately searching for rare earth deposits and trying to establish new mines."

Langford watched Lokke on the monitor. He could see the wheels in her head turning. "So you're saying the Chinese may have found a deposit in Guyana?"

Kathryn Lokke rubbed her finger gingerly back and forth across her lips. "Maybe. Or maybe they found '*The* Deposit.'"

"I thought you said they were all over the world?"

"They are. But there's something else. One of the early researchers of rare earths in the 1800s was a man named Delafontaine. I think Matt was his first name, or maybe Marc. Anyway, he studied them for over forty years and even developed a new form of spectroscopy. He also wrote a lot of papers on the subject. One of which was an idea on what he called "The Deposit." Remember, rare earths are common. In fact, many of them exist together, but always in varying densities. In other words, some deposits are denser than others. In several cases dating back to the early twentieth century, they found deposits that had surprisingly low concentrations. What Delafontaine posited was that based simply on arithmetic, or perhaps chance, there was probably another deposit somewhere out there of unusually *high* density. One that would be 'off the charts' compared to what's already been found. To him, it was mathematically inevitable."

"And was it ever found?"

Lokke shook her head. "No. But considering how dependent the world is on technology today, if the deposit did exist and was found, the strategic and economic value of it could be incalculable."

Everyone quietly stared back at the frozen video frame on the monitor, or more specifically, at the crates being transferred.

"Are you suggesting this is what the Chinese found in Guyana? 'The Deposit?'"

"I'm simply pointing out a possibility. One that is remote at best. Although I *will* say, rare earth searches are being conducted everywhere. In many respects, the geography of our continents is now pretty well mapped, all except one: South America. And most of South America is completely covered in dense jungle. So, if Delafontaine's deposit *did* exist, South America would be the one place that could still hide it."

# 24

"OKAY," LANGFORD PRESSED his fingers together in front of his face. "If this is true....if the Chinese found a special rare earth deposit, then what are in those crates of theirs?"

"Rocks."

"Rocks?"

Lokke nodded. "Most likely. Rocks that would look common to the average person, but to an expert they would be covered with signs of very dense and rare element content."

Griffith spoke up. "Would they need any special equipment or facilities? What about a refinery?"

"Possibly not. Rare earths do require an extraction process, but if the concentrations were *really* dense, you might only need basic equipment. Equipment like bulldozers or land movers. You could get them out quickly and worry about extraction and refinement later." Lokke noted the looks on the men's faces. "Remember, this is just a theory. The Chinese could very well be after something else, but a big rare earth find would fill a lot of the holes."

"Okay," said Miller. "Let's step back. Maybe the Chinese discovered a big deposit and maybe they didn't. If they didn't, what else could it be? We've already ruled out gold and other precious metals, plus agricultural possibilities. What else could be that valuable to them?"

"Maybe they found the Lost Ark," smiled Griffith. The others around the table chuckled.

Langford stopped and thought for a moment. "Is that possible?"

"What, finding the Ark?"

"No," frowned the Admiral. "Something else. Could it be some unknown archeological discovery?" He turned toward the screen. "Dr. Lokke?"

She shrugged. "It could certainly be a historical item. Although that's probably a stretch. If it was truly significant, I doubt the Guyana government would sit idly by while it was deconstructed and taken away piece by piece. Besides, what would the Chinese want with a piece of some Mayan type of history? I'm not an archeologist, but even a hidden temple or a tiny city couldn't be disassembled in a few months. Nor would it explain the need for earth moving equipment. Unless, of course, you were trying to destroy it, but that makes even less sense."

"What about some kind of ancient treasure?"

Bartman shook his head. "Aren't most ancient treasures made of gold or silver?"

"Right. Again, too heavy," conceded Langford. "I guess we're back to the rare earths theory."

Kathryn Lokke peered directly into her camera. "You know, the more I think of REEs, the more sense it makes. The Chinese have established a veritable stranglehold on the rest of the world with these elements. This has given them tremendous economic and technological leverage for a long time, even while other sources are found and brought online. So, if there was a super dense deposit out there, and I was the Chinese, I would grab it pretty darn quick."

Miller turned to Langford. "Okay, so either it is elements or it isn't. Either way, we need to get a look into those crates, and fast."

Langford nodded. "I'm working on that."

"What do you mean?"

Langford checked his watch. "I have two men who should be on the ground soon."

Miller stared at Langford for a moment before grinning wryly. "And which two men would that be?"

"John Clay and Steve Caesare."

"Why am I not surprised?"

* * *

The small city of Georgetown was clearly visible against

the bright green background of Guyana's rain-forested mountains. The Bowditch was still miles away, but by now was visible to anyone on shore, including the crew of the corvette.

Standing outside the bridge, Captain Krogstad lowered his binoculars and peered at the receding shape of the Oceanhawk helicopter, headed well south of the city. Next to him, Commander Lawton stared in the same direction.

Between that night's observations and further verification from Borger's footage, they had confirmed something sizable was indeed being loaded onto the Chinese ship. However, the crates were well sealed, leaving no visual clues as to what was inside. They had also verified that the ship had arrived just over four months prior, and while they could not achieve a positive confirmation, they suspected the Russian sub had arrived just a few weeks after the corvette. All the while, sitting quietly and watching.

Lawton was surprised to feel a tinge of worry for John Clay and Steve Caesare, who were both on the helicopter. She reluctantly admitted to herself that Caesare, while having a certain brashness to his personality, was also somewhat charming.

She straightened up taller next to the captain and quickly forced the thought out of her mind. They were grown men. They would be fine. Besides, she had a lot of work to do.

* * *

The chance of not being seen was almost zero, but it didn't mean they couldn't be subtle. As the chopper lifted off the ground and headed back out to sea for the Bowditch, Clay and Caesare hefted their packs up and over their shoulders. It would be a long hike into town, but the early morning coolness meant they would have a head start before the humidity and heat really set in.

They covered the first five miles in less than an hour, which was surprisingly good time considering they had to stay off the road and out of sight. They were also traveling in the most casual clothes they had, knowing they would need to blend in quickly when they reached Georgetown. Both were dressed in shorts, yet while Clay wore a comfortable, dark green polo shirt, Caesare wore a rather loud button up. It was the most casual clothing they could find and from Borger's suitcase no less.

Together they continued weaving in and out of the trees, picking up more moisture from the thick foliage than from the air. Both men stopped several times at the sound of a passing automobile, which was usually a truck headed north from New Amsterdam, carrying an early morning load of commercial goods.

When they neared the town, they crossed over the railroad and came in high up along Embankment Road.

Georgetown had a population of 750,000. However, it was the half million tourists it received annually which allowed Clay and Caesare to blend in. Originally settled as a Dutch colony, Georgetown was invaded and captured by the British in 1781, primarily due to its location at the base of the Demerara River. After decades of political friction between the local governing body and the policies of King George, the town finally received its city status in 1842. The wards and streets were named after the Dutch, French, and English, who administered the city through different periods of its history. As a result, and perhaps more notably, Guyana became the only country in South America with English as an official language.

It took them just under two hours to reach the city's downtown district and to find a small obscure hotel. Leaving their packs in the room, they promptly found a taxi and slid into the back seat.

The old driver peered at them both from the rearview mirror. "Good afternoon," he said, with a hint of a British accent.

"Hello, Mr.…Brennan," Caesare said, leaning forward and glancing at the driver's credentials overhead.

From under a thick mane of white hair, the driver turned and looked back over his shoulder while Clay slammed the back door shut. "Where can I take you lads?"

The two looked at each other in the back seat. "We're…new in town. Thought we'd take a tour of the city."

"Splendid." Those words were music to Brennan's ears. He grinned and set the meter before glancing over his shoulder and turning out into the lane. "Are you two with CARICOM?"

CARICOM was short for "Caribbean Community" and was an agreement to improve economic relations and foreign policies for fifteen Caribbean member nations. Guyana, and more specifically Georgetown, had the distinction of housing the CARICOM headquarters since its inception.

Clay shook his head at the question. "Afraid not.

We're here for a business meeting and taking a couple of personal days first."

The driver nodded and turned right onto Mandela Avenue, heading north. "Well, you couldn't find a better city for a holiday if you like the ocean and warm water. My family moved to Georgetown when I was six, 'course it looked a spot different back then. Been here ever since."

Clay and Caesare sat quietly for the next several minutes while the driver rattled off interesting tidbits about the city, including a drive-by of both the Georgetown Lighthouse and their National Museum. It was only when they'd reached the water and the renowned Georgetown "Sea Wall" that Clay spoke up and asked the older man to turn left.

He obliged and took them along the wall, which eventually curved onto Main Street and headed south along the Demerara River.

Brennan had been driving a taxi for over thirty years and couldn't remember the last time he had a couple of fares quite like these two in his cab. He couldn't put his finger on it, but there was something different about them. He watched his passengers from the mirror as he pointed out several of the city's most notable landmarks. Curiously, the two men in the back looked at very few of them.

After turning south, the two suddenly paid significantly more interest to the surrounding area. It was the area with the oldest and most rundown buildings in all of Georgetown. But it was when they made their way toward the tall bridge that the men really perked up.

Their eyes were locked on the gray Chinese warship as they passed.

After snapping a few pictures, they both turned forward again. "What kind of meeting are you chaps here for?" Brennan asked.

The edge of Caesare's lips curled as he glanced at Clay. The driver's question had a knowing tone. "It's more of a convention actually," Caesare answered.

"I see," replied Brennan, still watching them. "What kind of convention, if you don't mind my query?"

"Potato chips."

Brennan raised his eyebrows. "Potato chips?"

"Yes. I believe you call them 'crisps.'"

The driver sat upright and peered in the mirror at Caesare, who was now grinning widely.

Brennan suddenly laughed. "You're funning with me."

Clay reached forward and dropped a large bill onto the seat. "Mr. Brennan, perhaps you can find a quiet place to pull over."

The driver's expression changed from curiosity to nervousness. "Sure," he said, glancing down at the protruding microphone attached to his two-way radio. At the next block, he turned left and circled back onto the busy four-lane road of Mandela Avenue. "Any place in particular?" he asked, scanning the road.

"Here is fine," Clay answered, as he reached behind himself.

Brennan's apprehension grew as he quickly pulled to the side and stopped the car. He didn't know that the object Clay was reaching for was simply his wallet. Clay retrieved two bills and returned it to his back pocket.

"Mr. Brennan, you seem an intelligent man. It may not come as a big surprise that my friend and I would like to remain as 'unmemorable' to you as possible."

"Okay."

Clay smirked. "And please relax. We're not going to hurt you."

Brennan took a deep breath and calmly breathed out. "Well, I'm glad to hear that." He was more relieved than they knew. Despite their tourist apparel, it was clear to Brennan that these two men had an edge about them. They were polite, but he suspected his two passengers could be as physical as they needed to be.

"Well," Brennan said, with a humorous tone. "I presume you chaps aren't looking for a store to buy chips."

Both Clay and Caesare smiled. "Not exactly." Clay handed the two bills to the driver. "We're more interested in getting some information."

The old man noted the money in Clay's hand and took it calmly. It was his turn to smirk. "I suspect it has something to do with the Chinese ship then?"

"It does."

Brennan finally shook his head and chuckled. "Bloody hell," he said, running a hand through his white hair. "I thought for a minute you boys were going to off me."

Caesare laughed. "Your tour wasn't that bad."

The driver laughed as well. "Well, I'm happy to know *that's* settled." He put the car into park and shifted his body sideways to get a better look at the two in the back. "So what about that ship are you keen to find out? The bloody thing has been sitting here for a long time and the lot of us has been wondering why."

"So, you don't know?"

"No one does. No one can get near it. What you saw was as close as anyone is allowed to get." Brennan looked at them suspiciously. "And at night, no one is allowed on these streets at all."

"Why's that?" Caesare asked.

Brennan looked around outside the car and lowered his voice. "Because of the trucks."

"What trucks?"

The driver grinned at that. "Come now, boys. I reckon you wouldn't be here unless you knew a bit about the trucks yourself."

Clay acquiesced. "We know a bit, but not much. Do you know where the trucks are going?"

"No. That entire part of the jungle is now off-limits according to the government. It has been ever since that ship arrived." Brennan watched his two passengers exchange looks. "Do you know what they're carrying on those trucks?" asked the taller of the two.

"Nah, no one does. Except our government, of course."

"So, they're involved?"

"Oh yes," Brennan said, almost sarcastically. "Something changed when that Chinese boat arrived. Many of us have noticed that our dear, old government officials are driving a lot of spanking new automobiles around now. And their families are too. But that's not all. There's a lot of new money floating around lately, which is helping just about everyone. Hospitals, schools, the ferry, large stores, even small shop owners see it. The government has even been talking about paying down our debt and reducing taxes. And I can tell you lads this, that's something I haven't heard before in my lifetime."

# 25

"I THINK WE'RE READY." Juan stood up with the vest, unplugging both cables. He crossed the small cabin and stood next to DeeAnn, who looked up eagerly. From inside her cage, Dulce also gazed up from her half-eaten clump of celery.

"Really?"

"Yep."

DeeAnn was immediately up off her seat. Juan held out the vest while she slipped her arms through one at a time. He then clipped both sides together and cinched the large nylon strap.

"How does it feel?"

She wiggled back and forth. "Good. But heavy."

"It's only a few pounds heavier but probably feels like a lot more." Juan turned her around and reached under the vest's edges to make sure nothing was caught. With his fingertips, he felt for the wires under the thick material and made sure they traced cleanly back to the batteries. He turned her back around. "All right."

They both looked down at Dulce, who was still watching.

"Here's the on-off switch," he said, pointing to the front left side. "Pretty close to where the old one was. The microphone is here, as far from the speaker as we could get it. And the video camera is right here in the middle." He stepped back and pointed his arm straight at her torso. "Try to face Dulce straight on when you talk to her. Otherwise the camera may not pick it up."

"Okay." DeeAnn placed her finger lightly on the power switch. "Now?"

Juan nodded. "Now."

The switch clicked easily and a soft blue LED light illuminated the plastic switch. To minimize power consumption, it was the only indicator light on the vest.

Behind them, near the front, Alves rose from his seat and shuffled closer to watch.

With one more nod from Juan, DeeAnn cleared her throat and spoke loudly. "Hello, Dulce."

Her grin faded quickly when nothing came back out of the speaker. She started to say something else when Juan cut her off, motioning to her to stay quiet. Finally, almost thirty seconds later, the speaker broadcast the familiar pattern.

Dulce quickly rose to her feet with a giant grin. She gripped the steel bars and rocked back and forth while replying. The delay was as long as DeeAnn's.

*Me love Mommy.*

DeeAnn exhaled with obvious relief. "How are you?" she said, waiting.

*Me happy now.*

DeeAnn smiled and turned to Juan, who winked back at her. "Not bad for a couple of yahoos."

They both laughed. It was a favorite phrase of Lee's. Next to both of them, Alves was also grinning widely.

"Well done, Mr. Diaz. Well done."

"Thank you. I'm not done, but this will do until we get to your place. I'll see if I can tweak it a little more, but the slowness is mostly due to the system's limited processing power."

"Understandable," Alves nodded, as if he understood what Juan had just said. "But still impressive."

Both men watched as DeeAnn sat back down onto her seat somewhat awkwardly. She twisted her body to accommodate the stiff vest and leaned in close to the bars of the cage. She reached in and grabbed Dulce's hand. "Are you okay?"

*Yes.* She looked excited. *We fly like bird.*

"Yes, we are flying like the birds."

After a short silence, Dulce seemed to look around curiously. *Me need potty.*

DeeAnn nodded and stood back up. She twisted the small metal knob and swung the door outward. Dulce was gently led out by DeeAnn's hand before heading toward the restroom. "Gentlemen," she announced. "We'll be right back."

Juan watched them make their way forward to a large door, which DeeAnn held open for Dulce.

He was worried. One of the strange translation errors had already shown up on the new vest during testing.

He hoped their trip would be short. And that they could make a difference helping to find DeeAnn's friend Luke. Because the errors were increasing. And if he and Lee couldn't fix them soon, it had the potential to quickly undo *all* the translation progress DeeAnn and Dulce had made together. In other words, IMIS would have to be reprogrammed from scratch.

# 26

WHILE CLAY PEERED through a pair of 8x30mm military binoculars, Caesare silently unwrapped an energy bar and slipped the foil wrapper deep into his pack. After making it back to the hotel room and grabbing their gear, they headed west to the edge of town where they waited patiently out of sight.

After the sun went down, the two spotted a building set far enough back for them to be discreet. They watched a few patrols drive by before quickly passing through the shadows and climbing up the back ladder of the two-story structure. From the top of the roof, they had a clear, if perhaps distant, view of the Chinese ship, which remained motionless at the water's edge.

"Anything?" Caesare took another bite and looked around at the other rooftops, scanning for movement.

"Nope," Clay said, adjusting the binoculars. "There isn't the slightest movement on or inside that ship. Fascinating."

Caesare checked the faint red glow of his watch. "We still have a little while yet." After taking another bite of his bar, he looked behind them once more before settling down again below the rim of the roof. "You know, this reminds me of that time in Haiti."

Clay smiled from behind the glasses. "Without the gunfire."

Caesare lay down and propped a broad arm behind his head. He then examined the area around him. "This roof is cleaner too. It's like the Ritz."

Caesare looked up at a large patch of cloud passing overhead. As it passed by, the stars behind it blinked back into existence one by one. "I have to admit, John, there are a few things I still miss from the old days."

"Yeah, same here."

Neither of them had to say anything. They still remembered their first few years together very clearly. Although the mission in Haiti was the turning point for both of them, as well as a few fellow SEAL members.

The real "Operation Uphold Democracy" was very different from how it was explained to the media. Even though originally designed as a combat mission, it was billed as little more than a peacekeeping operation. The mission, as understood by the public, was to remove the regime that staged a coup in Haiti a few years earlier and overthrew the country's president. What was not known was that the new regime knew something the public didn't, and as the situation continued to erode, the United States decided it had to neutralize a risk, urgently.

The secret was that the bloody coup had been quietly instigated by the U.S., the very country who was now trying to get rid of a regime that was quickly losing support from its own citizens. Of course, both the media and the history books would report that the deployment of over twenty thousand peacekeeping troops eventually helped persuade the regime to step down. However, the truth was far less diplomatic. The primary driver, known only to a select few, was two Navy SEAL teams who silently found the head of the regime one night and eliminated him. Yet, while the public was none the wiser, it was the last straw for several of the SEAL team members. They'd had enough of cleaning up messes, particularly those created by idiotic politicians and an incompetent CIA.

* * *

Less than an hour later, Clay and Caesare heard what they were looking for, long before they saw them. And they were right on schedule. The rumbling of the trucks trudging down the hill in low gear was unmistakable. It took another several minutes to see the first flashes of headlights through the canopy of trees. Almost a mile out, the trucks emerged from the forest and reaching the bottom of the hill. Their engines roared louder as they picked up speed. Both Clay and Caesare watched intently, their eyes just over the lip of the roof.

There were six again, just as they'd seen on the satellite footage. All in a tight single file line. The lead truck veered toward the water, as did the others, and then followed along the river toward the ship. As they passed the old buildings, Clay and Caesare studied them carefully.

"Three axle and armor plated. Looks like Ural Typhoons."

"These guys don't mess around," Caesare responded.

"That means protected armor and glass. And bulletproof tires. Not what I was hoping for."

"Yeah, I was hoping for something more like…Chinese quality."

Clay followed each truck. "Unfortunately, I don't think any of these are going to fall apart on us anytime soon."

Both men fell silent and watched the short line of trucks continue along the river, just as the bright lights came on aboard the corvette ship. They both remained motionless, with their heads and binoculars barely above the roofline. They watched the first truck eventually slow, and then turn around. It backed up into place, stopping at the bottom of the wide gangway.

"No back-up beepers," mused Caesare. "Isn't that illegal?"

As the first truck shifted into park, the rest remained in their single file line, idling with headlights still on. Moments later, a small group of silhouettes emerged from the dark shroud around the ship to assist with the mysterious crates.

* * *

After each truck was unloaded, it was driven to a dark building not far from Clay and Caesare. A tall metal door opened and the rear end of a much larger tanker truck became visible. One by one, each Ural Typhoon stopped in front of the door for refueling. What neither Clay nor Caesare had spotted on Borger's monitor previously was that while each truck's tank was being refilled, more empty crates emerged from the darkened building and were quickly loaded into the back of each Typhoon.

"They're efficient, I'll give them that."

"Agreed." Clay turned his binoculars back to the ship where the last truck was being unloaded. They had noticed something earlier that Clay was trying to get a better look at now through the glare of the corvette's bright lights. The silhouettes of the sailors moved methodically back and forth, but standing on a higher part of the ship was a single individual who wasn't moving at all. Instead, he appeared to be watching the others, or maybe supervising them.

It was something else they had not noticed in the ARGUS footage. The person, who appeared slightly taller than the rest, was watching the transfer of crates very carefully. However, with one of the bright lights directly behind him, his face remained unseen.

Several minutes later, after the last Typhoon truck had reached the abandoned building for more fuel, the lights on and around the corvette instantly blinked out. The only light remaining was from the headlights of the trucks themselves, five of which had already headed back up the hill.

When the last truck had departed, the metal door was lowered, and the area plunged back into darkness and silence.

"Well, *that* was interesting."

Caesare watched the tail lights of the last truck finally disappear into the distance. "How far would you say those trucks can make it on a full tank of gas?"

Clay shrugged. "Uphill, with all that armor, maybe three hundred miles. They wouldn't use much gas coming down."

"That's what I was thinking."

A few hundred yards away, silence swept over the Chinese ship again as it rocked almost imperceptibly in the darkness. The mysterious man standing above the others watched his men disappear again below deck. He dropped his cigarette and mashed it out with the tip of his boot.

Lieutenant Wang Chao turned around and studied

the bright lights of Georgetown less than a mile away. He marveled at how well the government had kept the area clear given such a large nearby population. *Money spoke*, he thought.

Chao then turned and focused on the small group of lights further out at sea. It was a United States ship. A science vessel, he'd been told. Chao displayed a tight grin. He was surprised it had taken the U.S. so long. But it didn't matter. They had arrived too late. Soon Chao, his team, and their loaded ship would all be gone.

# 27

GENERAL ZHANG WEI stared absently at his desk as he laid the phone handset back into its cradle. In his late fifties, with cool eyes and close-cropped gray hair, he was not a man to get excited too soon. But he couldn't help but smile now. They had done it.

Lieutenant Chao had confirmed it. They were now days from completion, and the small science ship sent by the U.S. had only just arrived. They were far too late. Wei could not have hoped for a better result, especially since they expected, in all probability, to be discovered far earlier. It was a risk that had paid off handsomely. There was now nothing standing in their way. They had made the find of the century and with virtually no international contention at all. Yet when the world found out what the Chinese now possessed, it would leave them utterly shocked.

However, along with the good news from Chao came the unfortunate end to a problem that General Wei had known would have to be dealt with eventually. He reached forward and picked up the remote control to a large television screen on his wall. He powered it on and selected the special input feed he'd watched many times before.

The picture came to life displaying a dismal gray cell at an unidentified location, deep underground. In the corner was a small cot with a figure resting on top. His back was facing the camera.

The General stared silently at the screen. The truth was he felt a small amount of sympathy for the man. His name was Zang, and he had done his country the highest honor of anyone perhaps in China's entire three thousand year history. Even more difficult, Zang was a true patriot. He had returned to China with one of man's greatest discoveries, wanting only to enrich the country he loved so much.

In addition, it was clear from the hours of videotaped interrogation that he had absolutely no idea what he'd done wrong, or why he was being held captive. How could anyone who delivered a gift like his be treated so poorly? Zang could only imagine that there had been a terrible mistake. Perhaps the authorities thought he was trying to use this find to his own advantage: to leverage some kind of deal or payment. It was the only thing that made sense.

General Wei had watched for hours the barrage of questions put to Zang. The patriot never wavered from his explanation. More importantly, Zang showed himself to be wholly unable to think independently from the explanation his mind had created. At one point, Wei watched Zang try to ask if something was wrong with his explanation: whether the government had been unable to locate the find in Guyana.

Wei lit a cigarette at his desk and continued staring at Zang's cell. The problem wasn't that they could not find Zang's discovery. It was the opposite. They *had* found it, right where he said it was. And it was the very same reason that in a few days, Lieutenant Chao would have to kill every single one of his men in Guyana.

Wei picked up the phone and dialed. When the call was answered, he spoke softly and clearly, "End it."

When the door to Zang's cell swung quietly open, General Wei held up the remote and turned the television off. Less than sixty seconds later, Zang was dead.

# 28

ALISON GRIPPED THE stainless steel railing, unable to decide if she was nervous or scared... probably both. She looked to the port side of the boat at the sun peeking up over the line of the horizon, separating ocean from sky. The water was like glass this early in the morning, making it the perfect departure time.

It was the day they had all been preparing for. Alison looked down and watched Dirk and Sally leap excitedly through the calm water, just ahead of the boat's surging bow. They were as thrilled as she was and were leading their human friends out into the waters of the Caribbean.

It was a dream come true for any marine researcher but especially for Alison. Not just to observe, but to communicate and *participate* within the natural world of another species. To experience what they experienced, and to see the world from their eyes was more than she could ever have imagined. Now it was happening. At that moment, she realized it wasn't nervousness or fear. It was an unbridled excitement which she had never felt before: the point where dreams and miracles met.

Behind Alison, Kelly Carlson sat in the skipper's seat, looking out over the top of the cabin and scanning the ocean. She wore a tan baseball cap and a long, loose-fitting white T-shirt. Kelly leaned forward and reduced the throttle to match Dirk and Sally's pace.

Inside, down in the forward starboard hull, Chris stood behind Lee, who was running through yet more system checks on the servers. The sound on the graphs was spiking up and down along the top, much higher than normal. It was the underwater microphone picking up the noise from the boat's 267 horsepower John Deere diesel engine as they motored forward.

Lee glanced up and over his shoulder at Chris. "Here goes." He typed a command that activated a new algorithm designed to identify the signature of the engine and eliminate it. The large spike was immediately highlighted and disappeared from the graph, displaying a more normalized baseline.

"So this will allow us to hear the dolphins but not the other way around?"

"Right," Lee nodded. "We're receiving sound from the microphone, which is a lot easier to work with than what we'd be sending out through the speakers. This should allow us to hear them while running the engines in case they need to tell us something."

"Nice. Everything else look okay?"

"So far, so good." He glanced at the servers, now strapped to the floor near his feet. It was another benefit of the catamaran design. The amount of heeling or leaning was negligible, reducing the chance of the servers being tipped, even in rougher seas.

"Well, if you don't need me," said Chris, "I'm gonna head up top."

"Sure, go ahead. I'll be up in a little while after I've checked a few more things."

With a nod and a pat on Lee's shoulder, Chris stepped through the narrow oval doorway and climbed the half dozen steps into the salon. After stepping out in the warm breeze, he spotted Alison at the bow and trailed along the lifelines to join her. Looking past her, he could see Dirk and Sally swimming effortlessly out in front.

"Everything okay?"

Alison inhaled deeply and smiled. "Couldn't be better."

"Anything more from DeeAnn?"

She glanced at her watch. "Not yet. Not for a few more hours."

DeeAnn had phoned late the night before, letting Alison and the team know they landed safely. They had arrived at Alves' preserve just after nine o'clock. All told, it was a successful trip, and Dulce seemed to be doing well.

Alison couldn't hide her enthusiasm. Even though it was still early, everything was progressing according to plan. She crossed her fingers and hoped their good luck would continue.

* * *

DeeAnn awoke early and turned over, examining the room. The walls were a soft white, reflecting the early morning sun. The room was decorated in a stylish, natural theme. She spotted some beautiful orange flowers on her dresser and wondered what they were called. Finally, she rolled to the side of the bed and stood up. She dressed and picked up the new, thicker vest, before unplugging it from the wall.

She planned to give Dulce some time that day to acclimate before starting the search. DeeAnn was worried at the possibility of pushing Dulce too hard. Gorillas were introverted creatures, and the last thing she needed was Dulce becoming overly excited. Behaviorally speaking, it was a very small step from excited to frantic.

Alves had given DeeAnn the closest room to the fenced area downstairs, just seconds away. Descending the stairs quietly, she pushed the exterior door open gently to look for Dulce.

The fenced area was larger than it appeared the night before. It measured at least three hundred by another hundred and fifty yards. She spotted the black fur of Dulce's back hunched over in a nearby corner. DeeAnn watched as Dulce plucked a handful of flowers and sniffed at them, apparently unable to decide if they were edible.

Dulce turned when she heard the metal gate open behind her. She dropped the new handful of flowers and ran excitedly through the tall grass to DeeAnn.

*You here, you here.*

DeeAnn opened her arms just in time for Dulce to leap into them. At the last second, DeeAnn remembered the vest and cringed as Dulce's body landed with a thud against it. She promptly lowered Dulce to the ground. "Sensitive," she replied, tapping the vest. "We have to be careful."

Dulce gave her a toothy grin. *Okay. I careful.* She grabbed DeeAnn's hand and pulled her forward. *Come. New flowers. Pretty.*

Less than an hour later and after watching Dulce examine much of her new play area, the metal gate squeaked again and Juan Diaz stepped through into the fenced area. He tromped over the tall grass and met them with a smile.

"Morning, Dee."

"Good morning, Juan."

Juan watched as Dulce climbed up a small tree to its lowest branch. "How is she?"

DeeAnn began to speak but caught herself. She glanced down at the vest. "Where's the mute button?"

"We didn't have time to put one in."

DeeAnn nodded and instead placed her finger firmly over the small microphone. She also turned the vest away from Dulce just in case. "She's doing all right. She's showing some mild signs of anxiety." She motioned to the area around them. "But out here with us, she seems a little better."

"Yeah, I could see her starting to get a little upset on the plane."

"Right. Gorillas are introverted so what we see on the outside is only the tip of the iceberg. Unfortunately, when they hit their breaking point, we don't get much warning."

Juan noticed DeeAnn's attention shift and he turned to see where she was looking. Mateus Alves was approaching from the large building. Walking through the grass was difficult, even with his cane. A second man was with him, tall and broad, dressed in matching khaki shorts and shirt. DeeAnn and Juan left Dulce playing on the tree while they met the men at the fence.

"Mr. Alves."

"Greetings, Ms. Draper. Mr. Diaz. I hope you both slept well." He turned to the man standing just behind him. "I'd like to introduce our head of security, Miguel Blanco. He helps keep things running when I'm away."

DeeAnn smiled politely. "Pleased to meet you."

"Hi," Juan added.

"Good morning." Blanco gave them a slight nod. With dark, hawkish eyes and a deep tan, he looked like a seasoned soldier out of uniform.

Alves looked past DeeAnn. "And how is Dulce faring this morning?"

"So far, so good." She decided to keep the nuances about Dulce's behavior just between her and Juan.

"Wonderful. Shall we bring some food out?"

"Please. Otherwise, she's probably going to eat all of your flowers."

Alves laughed. "She's welcome to eat whatever she likes. Though I'm not sure everything would be to her liking. I must admit I'm not well educated on the differences in flora between our two continents. I'll have food brought out right away. As for the rest of the animals," he said, waving his arm, "we lost many during the vandalism." He motioned up the hill, past the nearby fences. "The rest of the preserve is wild and to where most of our remaining animals escaped. I'm afraid it will take some time to find them."

"I'm guessing that's where our capuchin monkey is?"

"Yes, we believe so."

DeeAnn nodded, still staring up the hill. She couldn't tell what was the preserve and what was...well, *Brazil.* It was all mountain and jungle as far as she could see. She felt her heart sink at the sheer expanse before them. She was finally faced with the thought she'd been avoiding this entire time. *How on earth were they supposed to find a monkey in all of this?*

DeeAnn took a deep breath. There was another topic she was dreading, one she couldn't put off any longer either. She turned to Juan and began unfastening the buckles on the vest. "Juan, would you mind looking after Dulce for a bit?"

"Sure, Dee."

DeeAnn looked at Alves. "Mr. Alves, can you show me Luke's room?"

* * *

Miguel Blanco unlocked the door and pushed it open. He then stepped out of the way to allow DeeAnn in.

When Blanco turned on the light behind her, DeeAnn gasped.

Alves stepped in from the hallway and put a gentle hand on her shoulder. "I'm sorry, Ms. Draper. We had to leave things as they were the night of the attack, for investigation purposes."

DeeAnn nodded absently and scanned the room.

Several things were turned over or broken and in some cases, both. Clothes were pulled from a small dresser, strewn across the floor. A large desk in the corner had been overturned.

"My God," she whispered, "what happened?" She turned to Alves and Blanco. "Were they looking for something?"

Alves shrugged. "It appears so. Though I'm afraid we don't know what. We weren't exactly working on anything secretive."

DeeAnn stepped over a broken lamp, suddenly afraid at the possibility of seeing blood. To her relief, there was none.

Alves spoke softly over her shoulder. "Footsteps outside suggest Luke made it out before disappearing. We believe he was picked up and carried from there. Everything we've learned seems to suggest it was a raid of vandalism, designed to ruin the preserve. Several systems, including the main air-conditioning system, were destroyed."

"Why would they want to ruin your preserve?"

Alves shook his head. "I don't know, Ms. Draper. As I said, I have many enemies who would love to see my businesses fail, but the preserve is different. It is the one thing I've done truly for the people of our country: for all the people of South America."

"Could Luke have seen something? Something he wasn't supposed to?"

"It's possible. If he recognized someone, it might explain why they would take him."

*Would it?* DeeAnn thought to herself. *Would it really explain anything?* She wanted desperately to believe Luke was still alive, but she was an analytical person. She couldn't help asking the obvious question in her head. If Luke had seen something he wasn't supposed to, why didn't they simply kill him? Her only explanation was that he didn't *see* something...instead, he probably *knew* something.

She stared at the items on the floor for a long time before turning back around to face her hosts. "And we're hoping to find this monkey Luke was working with...for what, exactly?"

"Anything," Blanco answered, in a deep voice. "Whoever did this covered their tracks well. We're hoping the capuchin can give us a clue as to who it was. A uniform, an insignia, anything. We have a number of pictures we can show him. We're hoping he can pick something out. At this point, it's the only option we have left."

DeeAnn shook her head. This was feeling more impossible by the minute. She stopped when she spotted a picture frame lying face down on the floor. She reached down to pick it up and turned it over. The photo hit her immediately. It was a picture of her and Luke, many years earlier, on the beach standing knee-high in the water. They were both laughing.

Tears began to well up in her eyes. She blinked hard, chasing them away. With a quick wipe from the back of her hand, DeeAnn looked back at Alves and Blanco. "So do you have any video or audio footage of this monkey Dexter?"

# 29

CHRIS FOUND ALISON, standing once again on the bow. She was eating a sandwich and watching the water as the boat drifted in place. The gentle swells of late afternoon sun reflected brightly off the water. Dirk and Sally had left to hunt for food, leaving them all with some down time.

"Ali!" Chris walked forward, keeping close to the stanchions.

She turned to see him approaching with the satellite phone in his hand. "Who is it?"

Chris smiled. "Guess."

She held it to her ear and answered. "Hello?"

"Hello, beautiful."

Alison grinned. "Well, hi there."

"How are things going? I presume you're at sea since your cell phone didn't pick up."

"We sure are. We're over seventy miles out already, almost within sight of St. Kitts. And you're very sweet for remembering. What are you up to?"

Clay looked at Caesare, who was downing a piece of pizza. "Just watching Steve eat," he joked. In reality they were less than a mile from the abandoned building they'd spent much of the night atop and were about to head back to it.

"You poor thing," Alison teased. She had seen Caesare's voracious appetite in action.

"Everything going all right?"

"Yes! Dirk and Sally are out finding dinner, and

Kelly is taking a nap, getting ready for the first watch. It sounds like we'll be there tomorrow."

"I bet you're busting with excitement."

"I am." She turned back out toward the water. "I really am. It's more than I could have ever hoped for, John." She paused. "I kinda wish you were here with me."

"So do I." His baritone voice said through the speaker. "It's just bad timing, I'm afraid."

"I know. I'm not mad. I just…" She struggled for a moment and decided to change the subject. "Wait, I haven't told you about DeeAnn!"

"Told me what?"

Alison spent the next ten minutes telling Clay about the visit from Alves and his assistant, the news about DeeAnn's friend, and her decision to take Dulce back with them. When she was finished, Clay remained quiet, thinking.

"What's the guy's name again?"

"Mateus Alves. Have you heard of him?"

"Can't say that I have, but that certainly doesn't mean anything."

"Lee and Juan both checked him out. And considering their snooping skills, he looks pretty trustworthy."

Clay was still thinking. "Can Dulce really communicate with another primate species?"

Alison shrugged. "We're not sure, but DeeAnn seemed to think it was possible. She said the way they communicate is very similar. Honestly though, I think she would have gone either way. I probably would have too."

"Have you heard from her since she left?" Clay was

again looking at Caesare who had picked up on the topic of their conversation and was now listening intently.

"Yes. She called last night. They arrived safe and sound. And the new vest seems to be working well. With any luck, they'll find something out about her friend quickly."

"You don't sound hopeful."

Alison sighed. She wanted to be hopeful, but all things considered, the odds were against them. Even if Dulce could find and talk to the smaller monkey, she couldn't imagine what he might tell them that would make a difference. She wanted to believe DeeAnn's friend was alive, but from the circumstances described by Alves, it sounded doubtful. "You know me," she told Clay. "Prepare for the worst but hope for the best."

Clay smiled on the other end. "You're very wise, Alison Shaw." He glanced at his watch. "I should probably go. Steve and I have some things to do before it gets too late. Stay safe. I'll try to call you again soon."

"Okay. Thanks for calling. You be safe too."

"I will."

Clay ended the call and powered off the phone, dropping it into a side pocket on his bag.

Caesare was still watching with raised eyebrows. "What's up with Dulce and DeeAnn?"

"It appears they've gone on a trip."

"Trip? To where?"

Clay zipped the side pocket closed and slung the bag over his shoulder. "Let's head out. I'll fill you in on the way."

Caesare nodded and picked up his own bag. They had a relatively short window in which to reach their target before dark. Once there, they would have to change back into their black fatigues and hightail it up the hill to get into position.

* * *

Just as they had the night before, the loud trucks angled slowly down the narrow road toward the bottom of the mountain. Even in first gear, the giant vehicles strained under their own weight, causing the transmissions to moan under protest. The bright headlights of the Typhoons eventually passed over a section of dense jungle where Clay and Caesare were lying quietly on their stomachs, waiting.

Talking to Langford earlier, he impressed upon them that the brass needed to know what was in those trucks as soon as possible, which meant they were going to have to improvise, and fast.

As the first truck passed, Caesare remained motionless, propped up onto his elbows in an overlook position with an M4 carbine tucked tightly into his shoulder. He pointed downhill into an open area, where he could give Clay emergency cover if needed.

A little further uphill from Caesare, Clay was squatting, waiting. The plan was simple, or at least as simple as they could come up with, given the time crunch. Caesare was also a better shot and Clay a faster runner, which was why Caesare was the one providing cover.

When the last truck rumbled past, Clay immediately leapt from his position and scampered up a small embankment. Within half a dozen steps, he was onto the road and in full sprint. Clay tore down the steep hill, chasing the truck's dark outline. He stumbled over the uneven ground, almost losing his balance. He recovered and quickened his pace, reaching out for the rear of the huge bouncing vehicle.

Clay's hand was just inches from one of the back handles when the grade changed and the truck abruptly sped up. He stumbled again and pushed harder. His boot dropped into a small hole, slightly twisting his ankle and causing him to fall onto a knee, just as he seized one of the large stainless steel handles. The ground raced beneath him, dragging Clay behind the truck as he managed to get another grip on the handle and lifted off both knees. He pulled himself up, hand over hand, until only his feet were dragging. Clay finally propped one, then both knees, up onto the bumper.

This new position was only slightly better than being drug, as the truck's heavy bouncing smashed Clay's knees against the hard metal. With another heave, he got a foot under himself and stood up straight, pulling himself in against the black metal door.

Less than twenty yards behind him, Caesare watched and rolled his one open eye before looking back into the scope. "What I wouldn't give for a camera."

Caesare kept the rifle trained on the truck as he watched Clay's dark figure twist the heavy handle then quickly pull the door open. With that, he disappeared inside and the door closed behind him.

In the darkness, Clay pulled a small light from a leg pocket and put it between his teeth. He bit down on the rubber tip and the tiny LED light came on, casting a faint glow around the dark gray interior. The mysterious crates were larger than he expected. All were stacked in front of him, secured to the sides and floor with thick nylon straps.

Clay quickly grasped a strap and loosened one of the ratchets, providing enough slack to pull one of the crates free. The truck's transmission groaned again and caused the vehicle to lurch, throwing Clay forward. He tumbled hard against the rest of the crates, then immediately stood back up and reached out for one. Clay was quite mindful that each second inside was carrying him further from Caesare's protection.

Inside the cab, the driver looked across the seat to the other soldier. "Did you hear something?"

"Sounded like something fell over."

The driver smashed his foot against the oversized pedal and the truck came to a grinding stop. He pressed the emergency brake down with his other foot and placed his hand on the ball of the gearshift. He motioned toward the back. "Check it out."

* * *

Further up the hill, Caesare let his second eye open briefly when he saw the brake lights come on, lighting up the area behind the truck in an eerie red glow.

"Get out, John," he quietly mumbled. A moment later, he heard the truck's emergency brake engage. "As in now!"

Next, he saw the passenger door open.

The soldier dropped to the ground and slung his rifle over his shoulder. Having a crate come loose and fall over wasn't that unusual. But they were given orders to investigate everything, no matter how small. Considering their cargo, they were to take absolutely no chances.

The soldier stood behind the truck, bathed in the red light. He pulled the rifle off his shoulder and tilted it toward the metal door. With a finger lightly against the trigger, he reached up high with his left hand and twisted the handle. In a burst of movement, he pulled the door open and leapt back, aiming his rifle inside.

## 30

IT WAS ON the floor.

The soldier kept his rifle pointed into the darkness of the truck while he examined the area around the crate. He then carefully climbed up through the door. Leaning his rifle against the metal wall and with a heave, the soldier grabbed and lifted the crate back up on top of the others. He calmly wrapped the end of the loose strap around his hand and pulled hard, ratcheting it back down firmly.

In the cab, the driver felt the door slam shut behind him. A moment later, the passenger door opened again. His comrade jumped back in next to him and pulled his door closed with a bang.

As the truck lurched forward and continued down the hill, Caesare dropped his trigger finger and exhaled. He pivoted his barrel and scope, searching. After a few minutes, he saw Clay's black outline rise from some nearby bushes and look around.

* * *

Neither of them moved for a long time, until well after the truck was out of sight. Clay listened carefully before stepping back out onto the road, still under the watchful eye of Caesare's scope.

It wasn't until Clay made it back up the hill and sat down next to him that Caesare relaxed. "That was exciting."

"And painful," replied Clay. He examined his pants at the knees, fingering some tears in the material.

"You're not going to go on about your bad knees again, are you?"

"Well, that sure as hell didn't help!"

Caesare chuckled and pushed himself up onto his own knees. He slung the M4 over his right shoulder. "So, any luck?"

Clay nodded and stood up. He ripped the Velcro top of his jacket open, then reached inside and pulled something out.

Caesare merely stared at him. When Clay failed to reach into his jacket for anything else, Caesare squinted disappointedly. "Wait, that's it? *That's* what was inside?"

Clay nodded silently.

Caesare shook his head. "You've got to be kidding me!"

* * *

Lieutenant Chao stormed down the corvette's gangway under the bright lights toward one of the Typhoon trucks. One of the men had found something on the last truck and called out to the others.

Several had gathered around the tailgate by the time Chao arrived, and he pushed his way through, yelling for them to get out of the way. He lifted himself up into the back where one of his men was examining a crate.

"What is it?"

"Sir, one of the crates is damaged." The man stepped back allowing Chao a closer look. "The driver said they had one fall off the top just a few kilometers back."

Chao could see the corner where some of the wood had been severely chipped.

"Sir," the man replied. He silently fingered the edge and raised the top of the hinged crate for Chao.

Chao looked inside. He instantly whipped around and jumped back down, out of the truck. "We have a breach!" he yelled to the others. "Three kilometers! GO!"

Chao's top men immediately scrambled for the truck, piled in around the crates, and unloaded them as fast as possible. Once empty, the rest climbed in and closed the metal door. The driver jammed the stick into first gear and watched Chao climb in next to him. He released the brake and the vehicle jerked forward.

The giant engine roared as it accelerated, forcing Chao to scream over the noise and into his radio.

Clay and Caesare stopped in their tracks. They were halfway down the mountain when they heard a sudden commotion. They ran to the top of a small hill and looked out over the clearing. The trucks were headed back uphill, and *fast*. They were coming for them.

Caesare turned to Clay. "What did you do, leave them a thank you note?"

Clay buckled his pack around his waist and cinched the straps down tight. "I guess that was a mistake."

Together the two men broke into a run, zigzagging eastward through the dark trees.

They found the spot not far from where the truck had stopped earlier. The vegetation was matted down, indicating where someone had been lying in wait. Chao's men quickly fanned out but couldn't find any tracks. Not surprising in the dark. It would take several hours before there was enough light to discover Clay and Caesare's tracks further down the road.

Chao examined the area with his flashlight. Nothing else was left behind. Just the matted flatness. He climbed back up the short embankment to the road and walked around the back of the truck. He shined his light over the door, then down lower and along the bumper.

Chao peered closer at something small stuck in the crevice between the bumper and the truck's back panel. He reached down and wiggled it forcefully until it came free. He examined it carefully, rubbing it between his fingers before looking back at the truck. He was familiar with the fabric.

* * *

General Zhang Wei awoke, peering sleepily at the small stand next to his bed and his cellular phone lying on top of it. The phone rang a third time before he reached out and picked it up. The screen was painfully bright in the dark room, causing him to squint as he tried to make out the incoming number. It was Chao.

The General accepted the call but continued watching the screen with one eye closed to make sure the encryption was established. Finally, he held the phone to his ear. "What is it?"

Chao's words were clear and unmistakable. "The Americans have found out."

The fog immediately cleared from General Wei's head, and he sat up on the edge of his bed, thinking. He wasn't surprised. It was inevitable once the science vessel had arrived. They were smart not to send a warship. Wei instinctively reached for his glasses and slid them on. "But do they know?"

On the other end, Chao held his own satellite phone to his ear and peered into the darkness beyond the glaringly bright glow from the truck's headlights. "They don't know yet, but they will. They took a sample."

"Dammit," Wei growled. It would take them some time to understand what they had, just as it had taken Wei's men in the beginning. But it wouldn't be long. Maybe days. "How much do we have now?"

"About sixty percent."

Wei nodded silently in the dark. He'd hoped for more, a lot more, but they would have to take what they had. He hesitated, wondering if there was any other way. Maybe the Americans wouldn't figure it out. Or maybe it would take them longer than he expected. Maybe the politicians would get wind of it and turn it into one of those bureaucratic fights for which the Americans were famous.

*Damn it!* He shook his head again. He couldn't take any chances. Those Americans had no idea just how *lucky* they were to have sent a science vessel. They would soon.

Wei gave a resigned sigh. "Three more days," he said. "We have at least that long. Then destroy what's left."

Chao acknowledged the instruction and hung up, leaving Wei solemn and thoughtful on the edge of his mattress, holding his phone. He finally lay back down on his bed. The other side was empty.

He couldn't take any chances. It was a once in a lifetime discovery. *No,* he thought to himself, *it was bigger than that, much bigger.*

# 31

CAPTAIN KROGSTAD STEPPED through the door and onto the bridge, still fastening the last button on his shirt. He gazed out over the shoulder of his Quartermaster of the Watch. An early morning fog surrounded the ship, giving a strange feeling of isolation.

"Where is it?" Krogstad asked.

The Quartermaster nodded straight ahead. "Just a few degrees to port, sir."

"How fast?"

"Just a poke, really. Maybe five knots."

Krogstad relaxed slightly, still staring out through the giant window. If someone was attacking the Bowditch, it was a ridiculously slow attack.

The communication's officer turned around. "Sir. I have a call coming in for you over satellite."

"Who is it?"

"It's John Clay, sir. He says it's them on the boat." The officer then smiled, "And not to shoot."

Krogstad rolled his eyes. *Yeah, like what was he going to shoot with?*

Ten minutes later, the strange boat slowly emerged from the fog. When Krogstad saw what it was, he almost laughed. A small fishing trawler.

The old half-rusted trawler slowed its engines and slid past the Bowditch's bow as the skipper expertly brought the two vessels almost within reach. The trawler's bumpers were down, but they wouldn't need them. Instead, they glided closer and closer until they approached one of the Bowditch's maintenance ladders running down the outside of its hull. With a rumble, the trawler's engines were thrown into reverse, which slowed the boat to a virtual standstill. The tip of its own bow crept closer. Clay and Caesare turned and acknowledged the skipper before jumping from the front of the trawler onto the Bowditch's exterior ladder.

When they reached the top, Captain Krogstad was standing over them with arms folded, along with his Officer of the Deck and the Quartermaster. "Nice ride," he commented, with a smirk.

Clay cleared the ladder and unbuckled his bag, giving the Captain a salute. "We had to leave rather quickly. I apologize for the dramatic entrance. I had some trouble getting routed to you through satellite."

Krogstad's lip curled. "What the hell. I don't get many wake-up calls like that anymore." He turned to Caesare as he joined them. "I presume your grand return means you found something."

"You could say that."

* * *

Thirty minutes later, Clay, Caesare, Captain Krogstad, and Will Borger sat around a small metal table in a semicircle. All four men sat facing the monitor. The conference capabilities onboard a ship while underway were much more limited, having to bounce the signal off a satellite first. But all technical limitations aside, the picture was still surprisingly clear. Aside from some occasional pixilation, they could see Admiral Langford and Secretary of Defense Miller quite well. In another window on the screen were National Security Advisor Griffith and Secretary of State Bartman. However, Clay and Caesare were both surprised to see Dr. Kathryn Lokke from the U.S.G.S. in a third window. They had met her the year before in what turned out to be one of the most memorable meetings they'd ever had.

After uploading a picture of what they found in the Chinese truck, Clay waited for the Admiral's response. The picture was now onscreen and Langford's reaction was exactly as Clay expected.

"You can't be serious?!" exclaimed Langford. *"A goddamn plant?!"*

"Yes, sir."

They could see Langford and Miller look at each other with disbelief.

"Are you saying," Miller spoke up, with a look of incredulity, "that all of this is over some PLANTS?!" The other three officials on the screen simply looked on, speechless.

Clay replied again, simply. "Yes, sir."

Langford shook his head and wrapped a hand over his mouth, while Griffith cut in. "All this time. All this secrecy. The black trucks, the midnight runs, everything…is over a bunch of plants." His tone was rhetorical.

Lokke's expression was the only one that had moved on from surprise to curiosity. "Commander," she said to Clay. "Are you sure the rest of the crates had the same things in them?"

"I am. There were a few gaps, allowing me to see inside. They were all carrying the same contents as the one I opened: giant plants wrapped in plastic."

Lokke raised her eyebrows. "How much of the plants were in plastic?"

"The whole plant, including the roots. It all appeared to be wrapped in some kind of special medium. As you can see from the one I retrieved, the plants are pretty large. I estimate they had about two dozen packed into each crate."

The picture Clay had uploaded to the screen was of a very thick and very green section of leaf, appearing to come from a much larger sample. In truth, it seemed to everyone to be a big and otherwise ordinary looking leaf. They had all seen larger leaves before, particularly palms.

"What in the hell would they want with a bunch of plants?" Langford asked. The others remained silent until Langford addressed Krogstad. "Rog, we need to get your people to look at this, ASAP."

"They already are. Clay gave the sample to our science team shortly after arriving back onboard."

"Good," replied Langford. "So far, I see two possibilities. One, there's something unique about these plants. Two is that the plants are somehow not the main objective of our Chinese friends."

"Or a ruse," added Miller.

Langford turned to him. "What do you mean?"

"Maybe these plants are part of the objective and maybe they're not." He paused, thinking. "The Chinese know we're here, and unless they're idiots, they know that we're here to find out what they're doing. And there's only one way to do that: get a look in those trucks."

Langford nodded. "So they're expecting us to show up, and instead of what they're really bringing out of the mountains, they pack the crates full of plants as a ploy."

"Exactly."

Langford considered it.

"Except," piped in Griffith, "they don't know *when* we would sneak in. A lot of these shipments would then have to become ploys, not just one." He spread his arms in a questioning manner. "And how long do they keep that up?"

"I agree," added Bartman. "Whatever it is they have, they're pretty serious about their extraction. I can't imagine they would suddenly start packing all their trucks with plants, hoping to throw us off. They would have to know a ploy is the first thing we would suspect. It's what we would do."

"Okay," replied Langford. "Scenario two then. The plants are only one of the things they're after." He noticed Clay shaking his head. "Clay?"

"It's possible, sir. But that whole truck was filled with them. Even if it were only part of the extraction, a whole truck full would mean it's a *big* part. It's possible, but more often than not, the simplest answer is usually the right one."

"That would mean these plants are, in fact, what they're after."

"Correct."

Next to Clay, Will Borger cleared his throat. "If I may, sir. I think Clay is right. I've been studying the satellite video, and it's clear to me, given how quickly they're unloading these crates, that they don't appear very heavy. It also supports the likelihood that all of the crates contain the same thing."

"Dr. Lokke? Any thoughts?"

Lokke slowly shook her head. "I'm not sure. I'd have to confer with some of my staff, but on the surface, it's certainly possible they found something of extreme interest. Taxonomy has arguably contributed more to modern society than anything else. Everything from glues to fabrics, to antibiotics, almost everything has roots back to...well, things with roots."

"So what kind of plant-based discovery would warrant this kind of secrecy?" asked Miller.

Lokke blinked, thinking. "God, it could be almost anything. My first guess would be something medicinal or biological."

"Or technological," interjected Caesare.

Langford turned to him. "Technological?"

"Maybe?" Caesare shrugged. "What is China most dependent on? Oil. Maybe there's a relationship."

"Synthetics!" exclaimed Borger, seeing where Caesare was headed. He looked back to the monitor. "That is a possibility, sir. And it might explain why the Chinese are trying to grab it."

"What are synthetics?"

"Synthetics are pretty much any compound that we've been able to duplicate from its original, organic source. Which, as Dr. Lokke pointed out, is usually some derivative of biology. "Synthetics" is mankind creating a superior product through more modern means, say through a chemical process. Oil is one of these products. In fact, synthetic oil goes all the way back to World War II. When the Nazis were running out of real oil, Hitler ordered an investigation into a synthetic alternative. And they found one. They were able to create huge amounts of oil and rubber synthetically to keep their armies moving. Even fuel. But the process wasn't all that sophisticated and required much more energy to create than they got from it. Which, of course, can only go on for so long. We've come a long way since then."

"Meaning?"

"Biofuels," Borger answered.

"Biofuels?"

Borger looked back and forth between Caesare and the screen. "Biofuels is a much more natural and cleaner process than synthetic fuels. There are all sorts of companies and governments working on it. The main problem is that even biofuels aren't as efficient as we need them to be. The plants just don't produce a high enough concentration of organic oil. What we really need is a plant source that produces at least twenty percent more to really achieve a self-sustaining biofuel."

"Are you suggesting this plant the Chinese have found in Guyana has more oil in it?"

"It's a possibility. If oil really is the focus here. But like Dr. Lokke said, it could be anything. Heck, maybe its photosynthesis."

"You mean as in light absorption?"

"Yes." Borger stopped to think and suddenly got an

excited expression. "Actually, if it's photosynthesis, that could be huge!"

"Will," the Admiral said. "Focus. You're losing us here."

"Sorry, sir," he replied sheepishly. "Photosynthesis, as you know, is a plant or tree's ability to absorb sunlight and turn it into energy. It's a biological process that is still far more efficient than we can achieve with things like solar panels."

"And?"

"China just happens to be the largest manufacturer and exporter of solar products, by a long shot."

Miller frowned. "So?"

"So," continued Borger. "What if the Chinese found a plant whose photosynthesis is ultra-efficient? Better yet, what if it allows them to better understand or *copy* the organic process?! There would be no other solar product in the world that could compete with that."

"Which might allow them to reduce their dependence on oil at the same time," offered Caesare.

"Oil is a finite commodity," agreed Lokke. "Some of the biggest oil wells in the world are beginning to run dry, like Cantarell in Mexico. The world is being forced to turn to shale. Eventually, the sources will either run dry or become so difficult to tap that only the richest countries will be able to afford it. And with a population of one and a half billion people, the Chinese are no doubt acutely aware of the importance of real, tangible resources."

Langford frowned. Wars were fought over resources like these. When resources become scarce, the only predictable human reaction is to fight for what is still left.

Energy is the lifeblood of modern society. Without it, any nation on the planet would perish. And whoever controlled it over the long term became the victors.

"So, oil or photosynthesis," Langford said.

"Well, those are just possibilities, sir. To be honest, if it is some kind of biological discovery, it could be almost anything."

Langford glanced at Miller before leaning back in his chair. "Okay," he said, turning to Krogstad. "Roger, keep your people on this. We need some answers. We need to understand exactly what we're talking about here. Mr. Borger, I want you to see if you can pinpoint where these trucks are going." He then looked at Lokke's image. "And Dr. Lokke, I'd like you to start getting a small team of experts together just in case we need a task force on the ground. Bring them in from wherever you need to but have them ready within a few days."

Lokke nodded. "Absolutely."

Langford and Miller looked at each other again. This time they shared the same weary expression. If this "discovery" were as important to anyone else as it apparently was to China, things could get very ugly. They hoped it wouldn't, but their expressions were telling. If the simplest explanation was the right one, then the message was clear. The Chinese had gone to a lot of trouble and expense over these plants, which meant they were probably ready to fight for them too.

# 32

DEEANN COULD FEEL a sense of worry growing within herself. Dulce wasn't as talkative as usual, and she wasn't sure if it was due to stress or nervousness, or whether a result of the increasing errors from the vest's computer system. Juan had looked at it the night before and confirmed the frequency of errors was still increasing.

On top of it all, DeeAnn's heart was sinking at the realization that the chance of finding the capuchin monkey was remote at best. Alves' preserve was simply too big.

They had spent almost four hours in the field yesterday. Alves and his head of security Blanco had escorted them into areas of the preserve not yet searched. But the place was just too *huge*. They would never be able to cover the area, even in Alves' giant four-wheel drive vehicle. But getting out and hiking through the jungle was the only way Dulce could listen for the monkey. Without at least some idea of where Dexter might be, it was quickly feeling hopeless.

DeeAnn watched as Dulce examined more trees. There were thousands of trees in the preserve, maybe tens of thousands.

DeeAnn had been quietly, yet reluctantly, thinking of an exit plan. What she was worried about the most was the vest. If she lost the ability to communicate with a frightened gorilla in the wild, things could get much worse for them.

She realized her mind had drifted off and looked back to find Dulce now watching her.

*No monkey,* Dulce said, matter-of-factly.

DeeAnn smiled and shook her head. "Not yet. Should we go look again today?"

*Yes,* Dulce replied, looking up at DeeAnn. *Look more.*

"Okay, we look more," DeeAnn smiled, placing her chin gently on Dulce's furry head and rubbing her back. "We look more."

Upstairs on the top floor of the state-of-art facility, Alves and Blanco observed DeeAnn and Dulce from the inside, through a tall window.

"How long are we going to search?" asked Blanco. It was a difficult question but one that needed to be asked.

Alves answered without looking away from the window. "As long as necessary."

Carolina, Alves' assistant, approached and joined them. "Everything is ready."

Alves nodded.

Carolina waited for a reply, but getting none, she continued. "And everyone is looking for you."

*Who cares?* Alves thought. Business could wait. It *would* wait. The businesses could run themselves for a long time.

He continued watching DeeAnn and Dulce out in the grass. This was far more important. It was *the* most important thing he had ever done, and in the end, nothing else mattered. Nothing.

Blanco wasn't convinced. He was sure there were

other ways, but it wasn't up to him. He would do as he was told. At least for now.

Standing behind Alves, Carolina looked at the hardened Blanco, who then glanced briefly at her. They would both do what they were told. For now.

* * *

Brazil's unrelenting humidity made wearing the thick vest almost unbearable, especially through the peak heat of the afternoon. The only relief was the wind flowing over the open top of the vehicle. DeeAnn couldn't tell what model it was, but it reminded her of the old military Jeeps she had seen as a girl. These, however, were much nicer.

She turned and looked at Dulce, who was sitting on the bench seat between her and Juan. Dulce was smiling the entire way. Bouncing up and down while they drove over the rough ground, Dulce loved every minute of the ride. It was a nice change. The young gorilla looked up to the open sky at a group of birds darting away from a nearby tree.

DeeAnn still held Dulce's leash firmly in her hand, worried that a sudden movement or shift could result in her falling out. A motherly instinct that was never fostered through a child of her own, she clearly still had it.

Blanco slowed the vehicle and brought it to a stop in another open field. A vast sea of trees began a few hundred yards away and continued on, high into the mountains.

Juan promptly jumped out and helped Dulce down. DeeAnn followed closely behind, careful to keep extra slack in the leash. It took only seconds for her to feel the sweat return under her vest.

Alves hobbled around the back from the passenger's seat. "This is another area Luke had taken Dexter to. They'd spent a few days out here last month."

DeeAnn turned and scanned the area. Luke probably brought Dexter out periodically to keep him calm. Wild primates often became agitated with too much time in a captive environment, even one as nice as Alves' facility. However, with Dulce, DeeAnn had the opposite challenge. She was born in captivity and now being *outside* her normal environment was causing her stress.

Together, they crossed the small field and passed into the edge of dark green forest. The group continued following Dulce as she knuckle-walked from place to place, looking and listening.

DeeAnn watched the others who were idly scanning the area. All except Alves, of course. He was intently watching Dulce as he had been all day. She had to admit it was beginning to feel a little odd. His interest was beginning to go beyond mere curiosity.

Juan checked his watch and gave DeeAnn a concerned look. He was forever thinking about the system and was no doubt estimating how much battery life they had left for the day. That and, of course, the errors. The vest still seemed to be working well, but he didn't know for how much longer that would continue.

DeeAnn noticed Dulce examining something on the ground and walked up behind her to have a look. She frowned when she discovered that Dulce was looking at the remains of a bird nest. Four tiny pink bodies were lying next to it on a wide rock. DeeAnn looked up at the tall tree above them. The nest must have fallen, causing the hatchlings to tumble out. They were much too small to move about on their own, which meant they likely died on the rock.

Dulce used her rough brown finger and reached out to touch one of them. She poked the featherless pink body gently and waited. Nothing happened. She then poked the others one by one. Finally, she turned to DeeAnn with her lower lip drooping sadly. *Babies die.*

DeeAnn frowned and knelt next to her. "Yes, the babies died. It's very sad." She was surprised when Dulce turned back, gently picked up the four little bodies from the rock, and placed them into her palm. Using her free hand, Dulce then turned and dug her fingers into the soft earth, creating a small hole. She placed them all carefully into the cavity and laid a leaf on top. Finally, she began covering them with the dirt.

DeeAnn was awestruck. She couldn't believe what she had just witnessed, on so many levels.

*Me no like die.*

DeeAnn shifted her eyes to look at the amazing little gorilla in front of her. "Me either."

# 33

W*E HERE ALISON.*

Alison smiled and quickly stepped out of the salon, into the boat's spacious cockpit. She trotted to the side and peeked over the starboard hull. Sally was waiting with her head poking out, gently batting the water with her fins to stay up. "Are we here?"

Dirk abruptly popped his head out of the water next to Sally. *We here.*

Kelly immediately killed the engine and allowed the boat to drift to a stop. "Thank goodness."

*Thank goodness, indeed,* Alison thought. It was much further than they were expecting, repeatedly promised by Dirk and Sally to be just a little further. That "little" further had taken them well south of their expected location, almost within sight of the small island of Grenada. She knew that dolphins had a sharp understanding of distance, but they seemed almost purposefully vague this time. It was something they had never witnessed before with Dirk or Sally. Their conclusion was that the dolphins' *home* wasn't stationary. It moved.

*Come Alison come.*

"I'm coming," she said, with a touch of sarcasm. "Just give us some time."

* * *

In the time it took them to get set up, more dolphins began to arrive. Many more. Alison pulled the second fin onto her foot and wiggled it while she looked out over the water. There were *hundreds* of dolphins now.

"Chris, look at this," she said, standing up.

"Wow!"

The number of dolphins swimming in and around each other seemed to be growing bigger right before their eyes.

Lee turned back from the water to look at Alison. He was excited too, wanting to see how his new "aqua vest" worked in the real world. "How's that?" he looked over the straps on the vest.

"It feels fine."

"Okay, good. Let's get the rebreather on now." Chris, standing behind her, lifted the tank and BCD up high enough for her to slide the unit on. Next, Chris lifted the thick oxygen hose over Alison's head and handed it to Lee, who aligned the hose with the facemask and attached it to the bottom.

"Test, please," he said, handing the full mask to Alison.

She held it to her face and breathed in. "Yep. Got air."

Next, Chris snaked the weight belt around her waist and Lee buckled it in front.

Alison pulled the mask strap over her head, while Lee examined the three lights on the vest's shoulder. All three were lit and steady.

"We have power, link, and camera." Lee then turned to his laptop on the white fiberglass table to verify connectivity with the onboard servers. "Looking good." He turned back to Alison. "Ready to test?"

"Sure."

He activated the translation software and made a motion with his hand for her to speak.

"Hello," Alison said, inside the mask.

The familiar whistle and clicks were heard almost immediately through the speaker.

"Good. Now remember," he reminded her, "you have to be *looking* at them for IMIS to pick it up."

"I remember."

Lee looked past Alison's shoulder to Chris. "Are we good?"

"Yep, we're good."

"Okay, Ali. Let's turn around."

She nodded and slowly turned around to face the wide, built-in steps at the end of the boat's starboard hull. She gave them a thumbs-up and grasped the top of the rail on each side. With careful movements, she descended each step until she reached the last one at the water line. She could feel the lapping of the water over her fins and feet.

She looked out over the water at the peaceful blue horizon. With a deep breath, Alison jumped.

* * *

Compared to the stifling warm air above, the ocean felt cool and instantly refreshing. It took a few seconds to get her bearings, but Alison adjusted herself and tilted her head back and forth, looking for water leaks in the mask. After verifying that all was still secure, she popped her head up above the waves and twisted around to find the boat.

Alison smiled and gave them the "A-OK" sign before dipping her face back into the water. Less than twenty feet below, hundreds of dolphins were swirling beneath her in every direction.

Alison was searching for them when Sally swam by and playfully bumped her from behind. *Alison, you here.*

"I am here," she replied. "Thanks to you." A moment later, she heard the familiar buzz indicating a translation error. It didn't matter.

"Where is Dirk?"

*I here,* he answered, swimming to her excitedly. *We home Alison, we home. We show you.*

Alison pivoted forward and kicked after them. "Yes, show me."

Together, Dirk and Sally descended into the darkening blue water and turned for a moment, waiting for Alison. When she caught up, they dove further, before stopping to wait again. *Come Alison.*

She laughed and rolled her eyes inside her mask. "I'm coming!"

She let more air out of her BCD and sank further, into the heart of the immense pod. The dolphins she had seen from above now swarmed from every direction, darting past her with amazing precision. Alison reached out and grazed one with her fingertip as it glided up and around her. She turned and watched in awe. Dolphins were everywhere.

She noticed several dolphins bump one another and jet away as if playing a game.

*Incredible,* she thought, listening to the translations.

*Come we*

*Metal*

*Get food*

*Find them leave*

*Where*

Alison blinked and twisted back around. Dirk and Sally had disappeared, and she realized she was becoming surrounded. The chatter in her earphone was now coming from everywhere. "Sally, Dirk? Where are you?" She looked below, then up above. All she could see was the giant shadow of the boat floating overhead.

*Going*

*People here*
*She talk*
*I hear talk too*
*People talk*

Alison turned again and found several dolphins had stopped a few feet in front of her, watching her curiously.

*You talk,* one of them said.

*She talk*
*Who she*
*She talking*

Alison tried to identify which dolphin was speaking, but there were too many. She turned back to those closest to her, still unable to find Dirk and Sally.

"Hello," Alison simply said.

The dolphins moved their tails excitedly. *You talk us. How you talk.*

The pod was still surrounding her, but now more dolphins were slowing and staring at her.

Alison thought for a moment and spoke slowly. "My name is Alison. I talk with this metal." She heard the translation come through the speaker, noting the different combination of whistles and clicks that identified her name. It was a crude, but unique compilation they had created in the lab to designate her name. It probably sounded like gibberish, but at least it was a pattern the dolphins could repeat.

*Alison*
*Alison*
*Name Alison*
*Alison Dirk Sally friend*
*Talk again*

"Wait," Alison said. She was trying to follow who

was speaking but turning her head to hear one would cut off the sentence from another. She was suddenly bumped by a dolphin from behind, who appeared to be examining her rebreather tanks. As she tried to steady herself, she was gently bumped again from the side.

*Metal here down come talk*

Alison whipped around again. "Wait, easy!" She put out a hand that got bumped as well, spinning her around. "I can't-

*From metal come trip talk metal here down come with us trip metal talk talk Dirk here down Sally*

"Wait! Wait!" Alison shook her head and pushed away, clamping a hand over the side of her mask. "Lee, Chris! Can you hear me?!"

Thirty feet above them, Lee leaned forward and grabbed the microphone off the small desk. "Alison, can you hear me?! Alison!"

She couldn't hear him. The translations were inundating her system so that she couldn't hear anything over the constant flood of words. There were now dozens of dolphins closely surrounding and trying to speak to her. She was getting bumped from all directions by those curious to find out where her voice was coming from.

"Chris, Lee!" she yelled. "Are you there?!"

*Come us metal many friends talk trip come-*

Suddenly everything went silent.

"Alison. Alison, can you hear me?" It was Lee's voice, clear and alone.

"Lee, yes!" She was still getting jostled around and looked at the dolphins who were still talking. "What's happening?"

"I had to disable the translation. I've turned off your microphone and speaker. Can you get to the surface?"

"I think so." Alison pushed away hard and pumped her legs, sending her to the surface. When she reached the top, she looked around through the fogged mask and spotted Chris. He was already on the bottom step waiting for her. She reached up and he clasped her hands before pulling her up forcefully, which caused her to stumble and fall into his arms. In one quick motion, Chris reached over her head and pulled the mask from her face.

"Are you okay?"

She had to catch her breath. "Y-e-s." She looked back to see that many of the dolphins had followed her to the surface and were bobbing above the water. They were still talking excitedly.

Lee came running out of the salon and helped her up the rest of the steps. They quickly removed her mask along with the tanks from her back, freeing her from most of the weight.

"What happened?" she asked, still out of breath.

Lee frowned. "I think IMIS got confused."

"Confused?"

"Yeah. It was trying to process too many translations from different directions. It got overwhelmed until it couldn't sync the words correctly. I'm sorry."

Alison took a deep breath to calm her nerves. "It wasn't your fault. I guess we should have expected something like that."

Chris nodded in agreement. "That's definitely a response we weren't ready for."

"Agreed." Lee knelt down and helped Alison off with her fins. "You sure you're okay?"

Alison smirked with amusement and glanced back at the dolphins crowding around the stern of the boat, all still trying to talk. "I didn't expect them to be more excited than I was."

* * *

Lee was studying his screen when Alison approached from behind with a mug of tea. His monitor was filled with graphs and computer logs from the portable IMIS servers below. The window in the middle of the screen displayed a jumble of crisscrossing lines, presenting all of the different conversations that IMIS had been trying to translate through Alison's vest unit.

"Wow. That's what it looks like?"

Lee pursed his lips but kept his eyes on the graph. "Most of it. The problem is the vest."

"What do you mean?"

"Well, not the vest per se. It's because it's mobile. The camera is too limited. Back at the lab, we have multiple cameras all synched with each other. It provides a complete picture of the tank from almost any angle, which means nothing gets lost. But the vest has only one camera and it's small, which means a relatively narrow viewing angle. It's one thing to view a three-dimensional area like the tank, but it's another to be right in the middle of it."

"Meaning it's easier to lose track of moving objects?"

"Exactly." Lee leaned back in his hard plastic chair and crossed his arms. "The other problem is that with so many dolphins present, IMIS can't keep track of who is saying what. The camera limitation just compounds the issue. I should have anticipated that."

Alison took a sip and laid a hand on Lee's shoulder. "We can't think of everything."

He shook his head. "I should have thought of *this*."

"So what do we do?"

"Unfortunately, there's nothing I can do about the camera, at least not here. That's going to take some design work and a whole lot of testing." He sighed, still staring at the scrambled lines on the screen. "But I might be able to figure out a workaround. The one thing we haven't told IMIS to do is to listen for individual tones or pitches. We never had to. We only had two dolphins to worry about. But now it simply can't differentiate between so many different conversations."

"Are these servers strong enough to do that?"

Lee nodded. "I think so. I just need to figure out how, and then try to code it."

"Well, I know this is a long shot, but is there anything I can do to help?"

Lee looked up and smiled. "Nah. Thanks, Ali. It's just something I need to figure out."

"I figured as much. What if I at least bring you some dinner?"

"That's a deal."

Alison patted him again on the shoulder and stepped through the narrow doorway, heading for the stairs.

Back in the salon, she passed behind Chris at the compact stove. He stood stirring a pot of pasta.

Alison leaned in and sniffed. "Smells good."

Chris winked. "It's kind of hard to screw up spaghetti. How's Lee coming along?"

"He's trying to find a way to separate the strings of conversation."

Chris shook his head. "I don't know how he figures all that stuff out. I pretty much give up when my email doesn't work."

"Or when they come from me," Alison teased.

They both looked at the open sliding glass door as Kelly stepped in from outside. The fading light had turned the sky behind her a dark crimson red. "Okay, the drogue is down, so we shouldn't drift too far tonight. And we should have pretty good weather for the next couple days."

"Any sign of Dirk and Sally?"

"Yeah, they've come by a couple times to check on us. I think they know we're having trouble with the translations right now." She cocked her head for a moment. "At least I *think* it's Dirk and Sally."

Alison laughed. "Oh well, I'm sure they could use the rest." She reached behind Chris and grabbed some plates. "I'm just hoping Lee can work one of his computer miracles."

* * *

A noise woke Alison up and she rolled over, forcing one eye open in the darkness. It took her a moment to remember where she was and finally recognize the boat's smooth, white fiberglass walls and ceiling. They were only visible thanks to the soft glow coming through her door.

She cleared her mind and squinted toward the light. She swung her legs over the edge of the bed and stood up in her shorts and tank top. Suspiciously, she walked softly down the tiny hallway, following the light.

She knew what she was going to find, but it didn't make her any less irritated. She pushed the oval door open and stepped out into the small converted cabin. "What on earth are you still doing up?"

The sarcasm was lost on Lee, who looked at her excitedly. "Good, you're up!" he said, almost jumping out of his chair. "I need to talk to you."

Alison glared at him. "You know the sun is going to be up in a couple hours, right?"

He couldn't hide the brief look of guilt. "Uh...yeah. Sorry, I couldn't sleep."

A drowsy Chris came downstairs, nearing the end of his watch. "What's going on?"

"Someone's been up all night."

Chris turned to Lee, who was grinning.

"Okay, that's true," Lee confessed. "But I have good news!"

Alison's eyes opened in anticipation. "Did you fix it?"

"I did."

"Really?'

He shrugged innocently. "It wasn't that hard. I identified several segments of Dirk and Sally's speech and overlaid them onto the speech patterns from the other dolphins. Then I removed the differences, which gave me a tonal signature. I've now added it to the translation process, so it should filter Dirk and Sally's speech from the others. It will help keep IMIS from getting confused. Unfortunately, it also means the other dolphins can't talk directly to you. They'll have to talk through Dirk and Sally. It's the best I can do for now."

Alison and Chris looked at each other. "Lee, you're amazing!"

"Tell that to my wife."

Alison started looking away but stopped when she noticed that Lee was still smiling. "What?"

"That's not what I was working on all night."

She eyed him suspiciously. "What *were* you working on then?"

"I have something else to show you guys." He grabbed the chair and promptly sat back down. He pulled up a new window on his screen that Alison had seen before in Puerto Rico. On one side was video footage. The other side displayed a long list of text, some of which was highlighted in red. The video held a still frame of DeeAnn and Dulce in it. "Recognize this?"

"Aren't those the translation errors you've been trying to figure out?"

"Yes, they are."

Chris lifted his eyebrows. "Did you find something out?"

Lee smiled. "I think so." He turned back to the screen. "I was working on the tonality problem when something suddenly occurred to me. When you were underwater today, Alison, and were having problems, I was afraid we were going to find the same synchronizing errors we've been having with Dulce: the ones where some of the translated speech is time-stamped incorrectly. Luckily for us, there weren't any errors. Instead, it was a limitation of how IMIS was instructed to process the data." He turned back around to them. "But that got me thinking…what if the errors we've been having with Dulce weren't really errors either?"

Now both Chris and Alison were listening intently.

"Think about this. The one thing that was confusing the hell out of me was that I could see the errors occurring on the screen, but I couldn't *detect* any speech related errors in the video. And neither did DeeAnn or Dulce. Therefore, I had to assume they were subtle and still infrequent enough that they would eventually begin to appear as translation drops. But they never did."

"So, are you saying the errors are not real?"

"Yes! That's exactly what I'm saying!" The excitement in Lee's voice was growing. "At least in a sense. After all, how can you have a problem with a cause, but no effect?" He looked back and forth between them. "The answer is...you don't! It's because the effect *is* the problem! In other words, if you can't observe the effect, there is no problem."

Chris furrowed his brow. "I think you just lost me."

"What I'm saying, is that I was trying to find a cause to something that wasn't really a problem."

"But," Alison cut in, looking back at Lee's monitor. "I thought the computer errors were the problem?"

"That's what I thought," Lee nodded. "But then I asked myself, what if the computer was wrong? What if it was confused, like it was today with the vest?"

"So you're saying there's no problem?"

Lee was smiling widely now. "Right."

"And the log entries in the computer are wrong." Chris continued.

Lee suddenly held up his finger at what Chris said. "Actually, no!"

"No?" Chris looked back to Alison, confused. "I'm lost again."

"This is the exciting part," Lee replied. "My point is that there is no translation problem, and the entries in the log *are* valid!"

Chris squinted at Lee. "How can that be?"

"Because," Alison said, thinking through it. "Those log entries mean something else."

"Exactly!" cried Lee.

"So what do they mean?"

Lee's grin grew even wider. "For this, you two might want to sit down."

## 34

ALISON AND CHRIS both turned around, then shot Lee a sarcastic look.

"Sit down where?"

Lee looked past them at the small empty hallway. "Oh, sorry. Never mind." After a chuckle, he whirled around in his chair and restarted his video of DeeAnn and Dulce. "Like I said, I couldn't find any noticeable discrepancies in the translations. Of course, that doesn't mean they're not present, but if these were true errors, the frequency alone means we should have seen several hiccups. Words being wrong or maybe a little out of context. But so far, nada. If anything, IMIS is getting faster, which is exactly how it worked with Dirk and Sally on the old system."

Alison watched the video while she listened. "Okay, so they aren't errors, but we still don't know what they are?"

Lee smiled slyly. "Or maybe we do." He slowed the video down dramatically then zoomed in on DeeAnn and Dulce in the middle of the frame. Their slow motion images became clear enough to see their facial expressions. They watched DeeAnn ask Dulce a question.

"They look like they're trapped in molasses," Chris joked.

After an unusually long wait due to the slow motion, Alison and Chris could see the translated text appear up on Lee's screen.

"Would...you...like...to...play...another....game?" she asked.

The three watched while the sound emanated from DeeAnn's old vest. They could barely see Dulce's expression start to change or her mouth move when the red letters abruptly appeared in the computer logs.

"There!" cried Lee, stopping the video. "Right there! There's one!" He pointed at the red lettering on the screen. "From here, you see that it takes almost three seconds for Dulce to speak. Yet as far as IMIS is concerned, the translation already happened. We've never seen this with Dirk and Sally before."

Alison and Chris remained fixed on his screen.

"And Dulce's translations have never been wrong?" Alison asked.

"Not as far as I can tell."

"Maybe the camera's audio and video are out of sync."

"Good guess," Lee offered to Chris. "But they're not, I checked. Remember, we have multiple cameras surrounding her habitat."

"Well, if the translations are happening early, and

they're correct, then IMIS must be *anticipating* the words to be translated."

Lee pointed to her. "I thought the same thing. But our algorithms can't actively predict behavior. At least not yet. Which leaves only one more possibility. IMIS is picking up on something *else*."

"Something else? Like what?"

"Okay, remember what DeeAnn told us…that gorillas are quiet communicators. That they're calm and thoughtful. I remember that because she told me about a thousand times while I was helping code the new software to study primates. Calm and thoughtful. Which means nonverbal, something else DeeAnn says all the time, 'most of their communications are *non*-verbal.'"

"Oh, my gosh," mumbled Alison, as Lee's words began to dawn on her.

"You see," Lee continued, "the system was never broken. It was just the opposite. If anything, IMIS was working *too* well. So well in fact, that I think IMIS has begun translating a language with Dulce on a level that *humans can't even detect!*"

* * *

Alison and Chris stared at Lee before finally turning to each other. They wore the same look on their faces.

"Did you say an undetectable language?"

"Yes!" Lee was so excited that he had to force himself to keep his voice down for Kelly, who miraculously was still sleeping. "It's the only thing that fits. Dulce is able to communicate on a level, a primate level, which only IMIS is able to pick up on. And it's fast!"

Alison took a deep breath. "Wow."

Lee eagerly looked back and forth between them. "And *that* is why I haven't slept all night."

Chris smirked, with the look of shock still on his face. "Well, that's about the best excuse I've ever heard."

Alison stood silently, thinking, with the back of her hand covering her mouth. "So, what kind of language is it?" she asked out loud.

Lee shook his head. "I have no idea."

Alison blinked out of her trance and looked down at Lee, who was still seated. "Well, I guess we can be happy the software isn't broken."

"Uh, yeah," he chuckled in agreement. Just moments later, he became serious again. "This is huge guys. I mean really HUGE."

"I agree. And it means we need to get a hold of Dee-Ann for a couple of reasons," Alison said, reading her watch.

Chris eyed her curiously. "What's the second?"

She turned to both of them. "Well, we're going to need her help trying to validate what Lee just found. And secondly, I'm guessing she'll want to know that there may not be anything wrong with that new vest of hers after all."

# 35

THE SUN'S FIRST rays of the new morning broke over the distant blue horizon and raced across the surface of the earth, illuminating the coast of South America. The trees lit up in a bright green hue, reflecting the lushness of the mysterious jungle laden continent.

The early twilight splashed over everything close to the water, including Alves' preserve and Dulce, who was huddled into the corner of her fenced area. She was hiding with her small black head tucked down, from a fear that was now causing her fingers to shake. She was beginning to feel nervous and more than a little irritable. She wanted to help and make DeeAnn happy but deep down, more than anything, she wanted to go home.

She'd been awake most of the night and a growing wisp of exhaustion was beginning to take its toll on her. She was waiting quietly for her mother.

The sound from a nearby group of black-goggled tanagers filled the air as the jungle awakened to the cool, humid morning. Other birds began to join in, adding their own morning calls. But it was a different noise that caught Dulce's attention. It was a very peculiar sound.

Dulce silently raised her head and looked around behind her, scanning the nearby building less than thirty yards away. She kept watching and listening until she heard it again, this time louder.

She turned her attention to a small area of the building where the lower wall overlapped with the next structure, providing a darkly shaded corner section of the roof. It was there that Dulce continued to stare until she saw it. A small gray head appeared from the shadow and glanced around. When the small capuchin monkey spotted Dulce observing from the ground, he quickly ducked back into the shadows.

Dulce's eyes opened wide and she wrapped her fingers eagerly through the chain link fence. She continued watching the hidden area for several minutes before the gray head appeared again. This time, it was staring curiously at Dulce. After a moment, he tipped his head as if trying to figure her out.

Thirty minutes later, DeeAnn was surprised when she opened the outside door and found Dulce standing attentively at the fence. She followed Dulce's gaze up to the roof but couldn't see what she was looking at. Her curiosity grew when she approached the caged area to find that Dulce was still ignoring her.

DeeAnn gingerly unlocked the gate and stepped inside, still observing the young gorilla. She began to close the gate when she suddenly froze. Up along the first roofline, she could see something protruding out from the shadows. She eased her breath out slowly. It was the small gray head of Dexter, the capuchin monkey they had spent the last two days searching for. The monkey had never left!

DeeAnn rolled her eyes. *Of course! Why didn't she realize?* With as much time as Luke spent with him, Dexter could just as easily have become comfortable at Luke's home, especially since his own was so far away. In fact, Dexter probably wouldn't have left a familiar environment for the unknown unless he was being chased. Instead, frightened from the attack, he found what he considered the safest and closest place to hide. *How could she not have thought of that?*

DeeAnn turned as the exterior door to the building opened again, and Juan stepped out. She immediately put her finger over her lips and signaled him to come quickly.

* * *

It took Juan just a few minutes to locate a ladder near a nearby utility shed. It wasn't quite tall enough to reach the lower roof, but it was enough to allow Dulce to get within eight feet of the monkey. DeeAnn kept her distance and remained further down the ladder, just within reach of Dulce's dangling leash. Juan stood immediately behind her, securing the bottom of the aluminum ladder.

Unfortunately, they couldn't understand what Dulce was saying to Dexter at the top of the ladder. DeeAnn could not point the vest upward at the correct angle, and Dulce was facing away from her, making a translation impossible. But speak, she did. Dulce stood poised at the top, carefully studying Dexter and exchanging an unending series of sounds and gestures.

Dexter's sounds were higher pitched, sounding less like an exchange and more like a screaming match; but step by step, his head and body gradually emerged into the morning sunlight. When he reached the edge of the roof, DeeAnn slowly shook her head in wonder. The full significance of the event would have been lost on anyone else, but to DeeAnn, what she had just witnessed was nothing short of earth shattering.

# 36

THE METAL DOOR burst open, and Alves charged down the hall with Carolina hurrying behind him. Miguel Blanco was waiting near the end of the hallway with arms folded, gazing through another smaller window. He calmly turned when Alves reached him.

"Tell me!"

"He was here all along," Blanco smirked, "hiding upstairs." He motioned back outside. "We have him contained."

"Is he talking?!" Alves blurted, excitedly.

"Don't know. The woman asked us to stay inside. She said they needed to establish a level of trust with the monkey first."

Alves peered eagerly through the exterior window and across a small open area to where several cages sat at the base of the group of trees. They were too far away to hear. "We need a feed on them!"

"Enrique's working on that," Blanco replied smoothly. He glanced at his watch. "He said he'd have video and audio in ten minutes."

Alves nodded anxiously. "Good." From their angle, they could only see part of Dexter's tiny frame outside, but it was him. He was sure. After a long pause studying him, Alves turned back to Blanco. "He doesn't get out of that containment cage! Understand? No matter what!"

The roof was just the beginning. Coaxing Dexter down

was one thing, but once on the ground, watching Dulce ask Dexter a question and then relay the answer *back to them* left DeeAnn in awe. She was sure she had just witnessed IMIS do something of which Lee Kenwood had never dreamed.

DeeAnn continued watching, still dumbfounded, as Dulce handed Dexter a small chunk of celery and asked, *Hungry*?

The tiny gray monkey studied the vegetable for a moment, but then seized it in a flash. He finished it within seconds. Dulce tilted her head and grinned, then reached for another.

The two were now in a different caged area. It was smaller and located under the canopy and shade of several dark green, mid-sized mango trees. DeeAnn and Juan were both inside but leaning against the chain link, a distance which Dexter appeared to deem safe.

They watched intently, and DeeAnn kept her vest pointed carefully, as to allow her to capture both primates within the tiny camera's field of view.

What was interesting though was that over the last couple days, the IMIS vest had grown increasingly efficient at translating for DeeAnn, and yet it was unable to translate the exchange between Dulce and Dexter. DeeAnn pondered what that meant. Was there something else happening with the communicatio between the primates?

As was the case in human communication, words, gestures, context, and tone were also very commonly used by primates. In fact, many primates knew what humor was and enjoyed playing tricks on their researchers. Even more fascinating was their practice at varying levels of deception. They also demonstrated human characteristics like greed, jealousy, and ire. *So why couldn't IMIS translate their speech?* A thought suddenly occurred to DeeAnn, and she dropped her head, contemplating. *Unless it was something humans couldn't do. Or something humans had evolved out of.*

Dulce spoke with Dexter again, who seemed to say something back. Dulce rolled her head sideways with a curious expression and looked at DeeAnn. When she spoke, the words emanated a moment later from the vest's speaker. *He hiding.*

DeeAnn replied softly. "Ask him why he is hiding."

They watched Dulce turn back to Dexter, who was barely half as tall as she. His near white fur had a peppering of black, which from a distance gave him a gray hue. After another blurted exchange with yelps and motions, Dulce turned to them again. *He hide from bad people.*

DeeAnn looked at Juan with widening eyes. "Do you think that means he *saw* them?

"Maybe," Juan whispered back.

DeeAnn cleared her voice. "Who are bad people, Dulce?"

Dulce spoke to Dexter again and waited. *He want out cage.*

"Soon. But first, who are bad people?"

After another exchange, Dulce replied again. *Bad people hurt friend.*

DeeAnn gasped. *Luke! Was Luke the friend?* She took a deep breath, struggling to remain calm. "Who was his friend?"

Dulce stared at her a moment, trying to understand

the question. When she turned and spoke to Dexter, his reply was brief. *Teacher.*

"Yes, Dulce! Teacher!" DeeAnn said, gripping one of Juan's sleeves. "Who hurt the teacher?"

*Teacher friend.*

"Yes, yes. Teacher is friend. Who hurt teacher? Where is teacher?!"

Dulce asked again. IMIS didn't translate, but DeeAnn could tell Dexter's answer was different this time. She stared apprehensively at Dulce, waiting.

Dulce looked at DeeAnn but didn't speak immediately. She waited, staring, as her small face slowly changed expressions to one of sadness. Her answer struck DeeAnn like a freight train. *Teacher die.*

Juan's eyes widened and he turned to DeeAnn. Her face went instantly white. Her knees wobbled and she looked as though she were going to collapse when Juan quickly reached out and grabbed her.

Dulce watched DeeAnn with sorrow and finished the translation. *Friend die teacher.*

# 37

DEEANN'S EYELIDS FLUTTERED open, and she looked around with blurry eyes. After taking some time for them to adjust, she finally recognized her room on Alves' estate.

She turned her head and saw Juan's face hovering above her. Alves and Blanco stood behind him, looking questioningly.

"Dee, can you hear me?"

"Yes." She blinked and focused on Juan's young, tan face. "What happened?"

"You fainted."

"Fainted?" she said, confused. "I did?"

"Yeah." Juan looked to the other two men, then back down at her. "How do you feel?"

DeeAnn blinked again. "Fine." Her mind was fully aware now and trying to rewind. All at once, she remembered and was instantly overcome with heartbreak. *Luke!*

She remembered what Dulce had repeated. Even worse, she knew what it meant. She had been hoping against hope that Luke was still alive, but she always knew the chances were remote. Deep down she knew that Luke was dead, but she wouldn't let herself come to believe it. Until now. They were just words. From a monkey, no less, but she knew it was true. She finally had to admit it. Luke was gone.

Her eyes began to well up until streams fell from the corners, running down each of her cheeks. DeeAnn closed her eyes and gently rolled her head back and forth. What on earth was she doing here? She just wanted to go home.

She opened her eyes again and reached for Juan's hand. "Help me up."

"Hold on." He loosened his grip and gently placed his other hand on her shoulder. Leaning forward, he brushed her hair off her forehead. "I think there's more here than just fainting. You look like you might have a case of heatstroke. You're sweating quite a bit. Are you thirsty?"

"Yes."

"You've been pushing yourself pretty hard, Dee. I think you need take it easy for a while."

She took a deep breath and forced her limbs to relax. "What about Dulce and Dexter?"

Alves peered over Juan's shoulder with a concerned look. "Don't you worry about them. They're safe and they're not going anywhere. You need some rest. In fact," he said, with a sigh, "I think we all do."

DeeAnn nodded. "They need to be separated without me in there with them. And fed too."

"Already done," smiled Juan. "Let's just take the afternoon to get some rest." He turned to Alves and Blanco. "If you gentlemen don't mind."

A flash of surprise passed over both of them, but they nodded and headed for the door. With a quick glance back, they stepped out and Blanco closed the door softly behind them.

DeeAnn looked up at Juan and shook her head. "I'm sorry, Juan. I brought us on a wild goose chase, and I shouldn't have." She reached up and laid a hand over her eye. "I thought I could do something to help Luke before it was too late. But in my heart, I already knew it was too late. And now I'm worried about Dulce. I know you can't tell, but she's not coping well. And here I am, with a case of heatstroke." She took a deep breath and let it out quickly. "I know this sounds harsh, Juan, but if Luke really is gone, I don't think we're going to find out who did it. At least not soon. I think it would take a while. Longer than Dulce could handle." She frowned at him. "We need to go home. Before things get worse."

"I understand." Juan nodded and gingerly patted her hand. "Are you sure you're okay?"

DeeAnn nodded. "I'm fine."

"Good," said Juan, lowering his voice. This time it was his turn to take a deep breath. "Because I think we have a problem."

DeeAnn wrinkled her brow. "What?"

Juan leaned in and almost whispered. "I said I think we have a problem."

"What are you talking about?"

He looked up and scanned the room, wondering if he would be able to spot a bug, even if there was one. "Listen. Did you notice anything while Dulce was talking to Dexter outside?"

"Like what?"

"When you were talking to Dulce, I heard something. When I looked up, one of Alves' men had opened a window and aimed a video camera right at us."

"They were recording us?" she asked.

"I think they only caught the last bit, but yes, they were recording."

"That's a little weird. We could just give them a copy of the translations."

Juan nodded, still using a low voice. "That's what I was thinking. And there's something else. I know you may still be a little groggy, but do you remember the last thing Dulce translated before you fainted?"

DeeAnn thought a moment. "Teacher die?"

"No," Juan shook his head. "She said something else right after that. She said, *Friend die teacher.*"

DeeAnn's eyes narrowed as she thought about it. "Friend die teacher?"

Juan nodded but said nothing.

After thinking, DeeAnn looked at him curiously. "Redundant translation?"

"Maybe. Maybe it was a redundant reference or maybe it was one of those system errors beginning to cause problems. But if it was, the timing would be extremely coincidental."

DeeAnn propped herself up on her elbows. "Well, you know the system better than I do. What are you saying?"

Juan turned and looked cautiously at the door. "The IMIS software catches most redundant translations. It's not perfect, but it's pretty effective."

DeeAnn's eyes narrowed further. "Spill it, Juan. What are you getting at?"

He bit his lip, thinking. Finally, he leaned forward again. "I don't think it was redundant. I think the word 'friend' may have been a reference to a third person."

DeeAnn gave him a contemplative stare. Suddenly she bolted up. "Oh my god, *friend die teacher*. You think it was a reference to who killed Luke!"

"Shh!" Juan held up both hands. "Look, I don't know. I don't know what exactly was happening between Dulce and Dexter, but considering how accurate our other translations from Dulce have been, I think it's very possible."

"Oh, my god!" DeeAnn repeated, with both hands over her mouth. "Do you think 'die' means *kill*?"

"It's a possibility. But Dee, we don't know this for sure."

DeeAnn dropped her hands. "With what you know of IMIS, how much of a possibility are we talking about?"

"Well," Juan replied, glancing at the door again. "A few minutes ago, I would have said something like forty percent. But..."

"But what?"

With one hand, Juan reached down past the side of her bed and came back up holding his cell phone. He unlocked the screen and turned it toward her. "Remember when Alves told us he had a cellular repeater on site here? The one we've been using for calls? Well, after you fainted, my cellular signal *disappeared*."

# 38

A MILD SOUTHWESTERLY PRODUCED a morning chop over the deep blue waters of the Caribbean; though for the open ocean, it was still considered relatively calm. The swaying of the boat over the small rolling waves had increased, making it slightly more difficult for Alison to keep her balance. Chris and Lee loaded her up with the diving equipment again. Behind her, a soft sunrise shone through a veil of light clouds on the horizon.

It was already nearly eighty degrees when Chris opened the valve and Alison tested the airflow once more, giving another thumbs-up.

Lee stood in front of her. "Okay, so remember, you're only going to hear Dirk and Sally this time. It's the only way not to overwhelm the system."

Alison pulled the mask from her face. "Got it."

After a few test translations, followed by the addition of her weight belt, Chris helped Alison back to the stern. Dozens of dolphins were waiting for her again with their heads up out of the water. One by one, they bobbed higher as the small waves brushed past them. Alison smiled when she spotted Dirk and Sally in the middle of the group.

Her jump this time was more controlled and her splash smaller. She immediately spun around to signal Chris. After a short pause, she reached down to let some air out of her BCD and slipped below the surface, descending in slow motion through the emerald water.

The dolphins wasted no time circling her, all still trying to speak, but this time she felt a sense of calm as Dirk and Sally approached.

"Dirk, Sally, the metal is broken. I can only talk to you."

She wasn't sure what she was expecting. Dolphins didn't exactly nod. Instead, they just watched her and replied. *You talk us only.*

"Yes."

*Okay.*

Dozens of dolphins continued to swarm around her excitedly.

*We all happy you here. We like talk.*

Alison smiled from inside the glass facemask. "So am I, Dirk. So am I." She watched as he shot past and stopped behind her. He came in closer to examine her tanks.

*Metal no broken.*

She rolled her eyes. "Trust me, it's broken." The familiar buzz sounded in her ear, signaling a bad translation.

Alison watched Sally turn slightly and speak, most of

which generated only more buzzing, courtesy of IMIS. Out of the string, there were only two words translated correctly: *she here.*

She waited in anticipation as Dirk came out from behind her. The field of swirling dolphins began to quickly thin until only a few were left, yet even they distanced themselves. From a distance, Alison could see three faint shapes approaching. All three swam in a tight group. They moved steadily until they slowed next to Dirk and Sally.

The three looked noticeably larger than the others but not by much. Instead, with their size and slow movements, they struck Alison as older.

Sally turned and drifted closer to Alison. *Here our heads.*

Alison stared at her with a puzzled expression. "Your head?" *What does that mean…what heads?* She pondered Sally's comment for a moment and shrugged beneath her vest. "I don't understand."

Sally blinked, continuing to drift in. *Our heads. Old.*

"Your heads are old? I don't…" Alison stopped in midsentence. "Wait," her eyes lit up, "you mean your elders?!"

*Yes. Old heads.*

"Old heads," Alison repeated, inside her mask. She looked back at the three older dolphins who seemed to be studying her. One of them appeared to speak, but Alison couldn't hear it. She could only hear what Sally repeated to her.

*How you speak.*

"I speak with a metal,"

After Sally had repeated Alison's reply, the elder spoke again. *How many humans talk.*

Alison smiled, feeling a surge of excitement. "Just me now. But soon, many will talk!" She considered explaining what "soon" meant but left it alone. She knew the IMIS system was wildly complex, not to mention expensive. It would take time. Years maybe. But one day it would come. One day everyone would be able to do it.

Another elder spoke to Sally, who repeated again to Alison. *How old you.*

She chuckled, creating a small patch of fog inside her mask. Clearly dolphins didn't have the same hang ups with age that humans did. She briefly wondered if they had any hang-ups at all.

"I'm thirty-four."

Finally, the third dolphin spoke through Sally. *We happy talk again.* Before Alison could reply the elder added, *You come journey.*

Alison gave a brief shake of her head. "What?"

*We journey. You come.*

"Journey? You're going on a journey?"

*Yes. You come. We go to beautiful.*

Alison stared at them, surprised. "Isn't this your home?"

*We go — home now. — Beautiful — —.*

Alison's earpiece buzzed again with more unrecognized words. She reached down and found the glowing button on her vest that muted the speaker. "Lee, are you getting this?"

Lee's voice was clear and crisp. "We sure are."

"Who's there with you?"

Lee glanced up at Chris and Kelly. "We're all here, Ali."

"They're leaving," Alison said, looking at the dolphins.

"It sure seems that way," he replied.

Alison was afraid to ask the obvious question. They were, after all, out in the middle of the ocean and farther from land than any of them thought they ought to be. She swallowed silently. "What do you guys think we should do?"

Lee looked at Chris, who then looked at Kelly. With a smile, Lee leaned in close to the microphone. "Didn't we hear an invitation in there?"

Alison was relieved to find the rest of the team was as excited as she was. After some assurance from the elders that their journey destination was close, Kelly was confident the boat would be fine. They had more than enough fuel and food.

Several hours of motoring later, Alison was woken by Chris shaking her vigorously. She had managed to catch up on some sleep, but when she blinked up at him, he had an urgent look on his face.

"Ali! Ali! You've got to get up!"

Her eyes darted around the small cabin in a panic. "What's wrong?! Is something wrong with the boat?!"

Chris simply grabbed her hand and pulled her toward him. "Just get up! You need to see something!"

Alison shook the cobwebs from her mind and slid out of the bed, onto the cool wooden floorboards. Still being pulled by Chris, she stumbled up the stairs behind him and into the salon. Lee's laptop sat abandoned on the round table.

Chris yanked on her hand again, pulling her outside into the wide cockpit, where both Lee and Kelly were staring out across the water.

Alison blinked again and this time when her eyes cleared, she gasped. "Oh my god!" She turned and looked past the stern, then over to port. "OH MY GOD!"

She finished a three hundred and sixty degree scan before turning back to Chris and the others. She was speechless.

Together, they all stared incredulously. That morning, during Alison's second dive, they had seen more dolphins than ever before. Hundreds of them.

But that paled in comparison to what they were seeing now. They were now surrounded by *thousands* of dolphins. No, *tens of thousands!* As far as they could see in any direction were the familiar gray shapes and dorsal fins rising rhythmically up and out of the water, everywhere!

Alison stepped forward, completely bewildered. "My god," she whispered to the others. "This isn't a journey. This is a *pilgrimage!*"

## 39

DEEANN PEERED OVER Juan's shoulder at his laptop screen, watching as he typed. He tried again and waited. Finally, he shook his head and leaned back in the chair.

"Still nothing. It's dead."

DeeAnn remained bent over. "Maybe it's a fluke," she whispered. "I mean internet lines go down, right?"

"Not like this," he said. "I can't even ping the router. Which means either a failure inside the building itself..."

"Or?"

Juan shrugged. "Or we've been cut off." He checked his phone again. "And we still have no cell signal."

"Couldn't they both be down at the same time?"

He nodded. "Yes, but these are two different signal types. They could certainly both be plugged into the same bad power circuit but that would be the worst example of putting everything in one basket." He spun around, still keeping his voice low. "And Alves doesn't strike me as a person who cuts a lot of corners."

"Maybe the power's just out," DeeAnn offered. She turned to the small lamp on the table, then reached under the shade and rolled the switch. It lit up immediately. "Okay, maybe not."

In another room, Alves and Blanco watched them from the high-definition feed of a hidden camera. Both DeeAnn and Juan could be seen near the top of the picture, hunched over the desk in Juan's small room. It was difficult to see his computer screen, but their whispering was easily picked up by the camera's microphone.

* * *

"Why don't we just ask them?"

Juan could be seen looking at her sarcastically. "Because then they would know that we know."

"Then what do you suggest we do?"

"I think the sooner we get out of here, the better. I have a feeling that this is all related to that monkey. They sure wanted to find him awfully bad."

DeeAnn nodded, almost reluctantly, before adding, "To find Luke."

"At least that's what they said." Juan leaned in closer to her, pressing his hands together thoughtfully. "Let me ask you a question," he whispered. "First, let me say that I'm really sorry about your friend, Dee. I really am. But…do you really think he's already…you know?"

"Gone?"

"Right." Juan watched DeeAnn's composure deflate.

"I think so."

He waited a moment before continuing. "Well, if it's true, what if Alves already *knew* that?"

DeeAnn's eyes immediately grew wider. "What do you mean?"

"I've been thinking more about Dulce's last translation from Dexter."

She paused, trying to recall it. "Friend die teacher?"

Juan nodded silently then leveled his gaze. "If that little monkey is right, who do you think the 'friend' is?"

The two sat silently, staring at each other.

There was a loud knock at the door. They both jumped and spun around. DeeAnn and Juan nervously watched the door but said nothing. A few moments later, there was a second knock.

"What do we do?" she whispered.

"I don't know!"

They remained frozen, making no sound. Finally, they could hear the back and forth movement of the doorknob as it was turned from side to side. Juan had locked it. He shot to his feet and cleared his voice.

"Yes. Who is it?"

The reply was muffled through the thick door. "It's Mateus. Is Ms. Draper still with you?"

There was no point in lying. "Yes. Yes, she is."

"May I come in? I'd like to talk to you."

He frowned worriedly at DeeAnn but moved hesitantly toward the door. He reached out and unlocked the knob, then turned it and pulled the door open. On the other side stood Alves in the doorway. Behind him was Blanco, towering above his boss and wearing his usual stone-cold expression.

"May I come in?" Alves asked.

"Uh, yeah, sure." Juan stepped to the side, feigning a welcoming gesture.

Both men immediately entered the room. Alves smiled at DeeAnn, who stood near the window. She grinned and nervously tucked a strand of hair behind one ear.

"Ah, hello, Ms. Draper. How are you feeling?"

"Good. Fine."

"I'm very relieved. We were quite worried about you."

As Alves crossed the room, something about him seemed different. She wasn't sure whether something had changed or if it was her own nervousness.

"I'm fine, really. Thank you. I just needed some rest. It's been a hectic few days."

"It has indeed," agreed Alves. "I'm sorry we've been so pressed." His smile was still on his face as he scanned the room. He gazed at Juan's open laptop and frowned.

"Still working hard, I see." He turned back to Juan. "But not too hard, I hope."

Juan shrugged. "Oh, you know, just going through the logs again."

Alves nodded. "Of course. Have you found anything interesting?"

"Not really," Juan lied. "Just standard system stuff."

Alves grinned and stepped closer to the laptop. He bent forward slightly, squinting to see the screen. "Just finishing up, I guess." He turned back around. "It's been quite a day, yes? I must say, it never occurred to me that Dexter was still here."

DeeAnn shrugged. "They are unpredictable."

"Indeed. I've been eager to hear what you found out this morning. Was the communication with Dulce successful?"

DeeAnn looked at Juan before turning back to Alves, trying not to appear nervous. It felt like she was failing, miserably. "Not much yet, I'm afraid. Mostly trying to establish some common words and trust. I'm afraid it's going to take a while, but it looks promising." DeeAnn felt a streak of panic rush through her. She suddenly remembered what Juan told her: that they had set up a video camera to record them. If true, it meant they undoubtedly would have heard Dulce's words through the speaker on DeeAnn's vest. But if Alves knew she was lying, he didn't let it show.

"Well, at least it's a big step," he said. "I hope we can make progress quickly. For Luke's sake."

DeeAnn, who had found herself nodding while Alves spoke, abruptly stopped. His last line about Luke had an unmistakable tone. It sounded like an insinuation. Dee-

Ann's nervousness came flooding back. *Did Alves know about Luke after all?* If he did, it meant he had been playing them all along. She looked Alves over again and realized what it was that had changed.

"Where is your cane?" she asked.

There was a flash of genuine surprise as Alves looked down out of reflex. He stopped and, with a smile, raised his head again. "Very perceptive of you, Ms. Draper."

If DeeAnn's face showed a moment of faint smugness, it instantly disappeared when something in Alves' voice changed. His Portuguese accent was heavier.

Juan looked up at Blanco who, with arms folded, remained steadfast in front of the door.

Alves stood, thinking, and absently scratched above his eyebrow. Finally, he grinned. There was no more point to the facade.

"So, here we are," he finally conceded. "Planning an escape are we?"

DeeAnn checked Juan's reaction, then put her hands on her hips and glared at Alves. "Where is Luke?"

He breathed in and let it out slowly. "Well, I'm afraid Luke Greenwood...was just a tad too difficult."

DeeAnn felt a jolt to her heart. Her eyes began to well up at the emotional confirmation that Luke was dead. She knew now it was true. Yet she could still feel part of herself struggling to find another possibility. She felt a tear roll down her check but maintained her stance. "You killed him?"

Alves grabbed the desk chair and sat down smoothly. "I suppose there comes a time when we all must take a stand on what we believe in, no?" He waved his hand casually as he spoke. "I suppose you could say we found out what Luke's stance was."

DeeAnn shook her head defiantly. Her eyes filling quickly with tears. "You killed him, you bastard!"

Alves smirked, dismissing her without a hint of remorse. "It was unavoidable. I did try to reason with him. But he remained an obstacle."

"An obstacle?" she cried. "An obstacle to what? More power? More money? What happened…did he find out about some fraud you were involved in?!"

Alves surprised her with a burst of laughter. He leaned back in his chair, recovering slowly. "Oh, Ms. Draper, you are naïve. You believe this is over a business deal? Over money? What a simple world you must live in." He reached up and wiped a tear of laughter from the corner of his wrinkled eye. "No, Mr. Greenwood didn't have much business sense. He was lucky to figure out his email." Alves shook his head, traces of laughter still on his face. "You really have no idea what's happening here, do you?"

"I know you've cut off our cellular and internet access, so we must know something we're not supposed to."

Alves laughed again but not as hard this time. "And what is it that you *know*?" he challenged.

DeeAnn looked back to Juan. The truth was that they hadn't the slightest idea. The only thing they really knew was that Alves killed Luke. They had nothing else.

Alves watched her fumble. "You haven't even asked the question of *why* yet." He looked past her to Blanco, who remained as still as a rock, listening. Alves' laugh fell to a mild chuckle. "Why would I go out of my way to bring you here?"

He watched with amusement as the question sank in and marveled at their naivety. "I didn't bring you here to find Luke, *DeeAnn*."

She glared at his sarcasm.

"I brought you to find his monkey. Dexter."

"Why?"

"Dexter was Luke Greenwood's *stand*. His line. It was Luke who let Dexter escape in the first place. He was a smart man; I'll give him that. But as you know, his sense of ethics bordered on obsessive. In the end, that was his liability, blinding himself to rational thought. And more importantly, his own mortality."

"Yeah," DeeAnn was seething. "Well, I'm sure it's hard for someone like you to believe, but sometimes even innocent animals are worth dying for."

Alves rolled his eyes. "Please. It wasn't the monkey he gave his life for. Dexter was merely a symbol. No, Luke Greenwood gave his life for something much bigger. I suppose he should be commended for that. Even though he failed, thanks to you."

DeeAnn was still confused. "Failed?"

"Yes. After all, you found the monkey he tried to free. After Dexter's accidental capture, Luke realized there was something very special about him. They are exceedingly smart for monkeys. *Organ grinders,* I believe you call them. But this one had unusually high levels of intelligence and dexterity. Luke said it was 'off the charts.' He became obsessive in studying the monkey and, in the end, even more rabid in his moral convictions to protect him." Alves' eyes almost seemed to grow darker. "It turned out that while Dexter may have been a symbol for Luke's convictions, what Luke ultimately discovered about him proved to be a *much* bigger surprise. A secret no one was expecting."

"A secret worth killing for," DeeAnn snarled.

Alves' lips curled into a sordid grin. "Very much so. And thanks to you, one we have now recaptured."

"So," Juan spoke up, "bringing us here to find Dexter was just so you could figure out how to make yourself smarter?"

Alves suddenly laughed again, harder. He pushed himself up and out of the chair. "My, you Americans are dim. No, Mr. Diaz, that's not why you're here." He motioned past them to Blanco, who smoothly removed a .40 caliber Glock from behind his back. "Not even close."

# 40

IT WAS TRULY a pilgrimage and bigger than anything Alison could ever have imagined. They had been surrounded by a veritable sea of dolphins for hours before IMIS picked up Dirk and Sally's words again, calling to her.

The sun was steadily falling down toward the horizon when Alison finally slipped beneath the cool waves once again. "Can you guys hear me?"

"We're here, Ali." Lee reassured her through his microphone. "Are you okay?"

"So far." Alison was surrounded by a wall of dolphins, all swirling around her, endlessly. They all adjusted their path to keep just out of reach as if she were in her own bubble. As she descended in her small space, she could see glimpses of bright colors below.

It was once she passed thirty feet that the dolphins began to thin and disperse. At forty feet, she broke out below them. Dolphins were mammals, which meant lungs to breathe air. Most activity was spent closer to the surface. They could venture much deeper. However, at the moment, Alison still felt as though she were swimming beneath a living, moving ceiling.

Yet, it was what she saw on the ocean floor that nearly drained the blood from her face. The entire floor was a section of raised seabed spreading as far as her visibility could see. But more than that, it was what covered the entire bottom: seagrass.

Different from seaweed, the seagrass was bright green in color and comprised of many forms of underwater vegetation, including flowers, roots and leaves. The growth here was as dense as Alison had ever seen it, so green and lush that it almost glowed against a background of blue water. Both in and above the seagrass were countless starfish, urchins, and crustaceans of dizzying numbers. There were life forms of all kinds, including *billions* of smaller fish with bright colors that resembled a giant underwater kaleidoscope.

Alison was stunned. She simply floated in place, without a sound, taking in a landscape that was beyond green with sea life of every imaginable color. It was not until she heard Lee and the others gasp over her headset that she managed to speak.

"Are you guys *seeing* this?!"

"Amazing!" whispered Lee. Kelly and Chris were both staring over his shoulder at the monitor, transfixed.

Kelly slowly shook her head. "It's the most beautiful thing I've ever seen."

Beneath the boat, Dirk and Sally finally appeared next to Alison. She glanced at them and tried to form words. "It's…incredible."

*See Alison*, replied Sally. *World is good. Beautiful.*

Alison nodded. "It is…beautiful." She simply could not believe how full and vibrant everything was. "How long has this been here?" she whispered.

Dirk wiggled his tail. *Forever.*

The entire crew sat on the back of the boat in the darkness, staring out over the water and the endless sea of frolicking dolphins. With no moon out, only the stars were left to shine faintly across the choppy waves.

Chris held his empty plate while the others continued eating under the bright glow of the overhead deck lights. "It looks so normal from up here. No one would ever imagine what was below us."

They all stopped and considered his words. With a smile, Alison lowered her dish. "Tomorrow you all have to go down. You have to see it up close."

Chris gripped an overhead stainless steel bar as he stood up and agreed, "Amen to that."

* * *

Josias stood on the bow as they quietly motored through the mass of dolphins around them. Something they had seen many times before during the same time of year.

But tonight Josias' eyes were focused dead ahead. The lights from the distant boat could be seen easily from several kilometers out. He couldn't tell what kind it was, but judging from the number of lights, it was most likely a small private craft. He turned to look at the other two men behind him. One stood at the wheel and the other was busily checking the AK-47s. All three men were dressed in black. The same color as their boat.

Josias didn't meet the standard image of a pirate. He was short and slight with fairly well-groomed dark hair. No one would ever take him for a murderer. But why should they? The handful of people he had killed were all unintentional. They were victims of circumstance, usually a skipper or crewmember who tried to resist. During a hijacking, even on a small yacht, things could get out of hand quickly. But he wasn't a monster. He had remorse. He regretted those people being dead, but he had rationalized long ago that it was their own stupid fault. He was never looking to kill anyone. Josias was simply looking to feed his family.

Many countries throughout the South Caribbean were heavily populated with poor, starving citizens. Subjected to bad political regimes and devastating storms, life throughout the islands was hard. Much harder than for the yacht owners. If they could afford such an expensive boat, they sure as hell could afford the insurance to go with it. And some were still dumb enough to resist.

Of course, Carlo was probably largely to blame. Josias looked back to Carlo at the stern and watched as he lowered one rifle then picked up another, making sure each was fully loaded. Josias and their skipper, Junior, were both men just trying to keep their families alive, but Carlo was very different. Carlo had no family. He was young, big, and grew up sleeping on the streets of Haiti. He learned at a young age that the only way to get ahead was to find what you needed and take it; by using more force than the person you were taking from.

Carlo glanced up and caught Josias' eye, still watching him. He smiled and made a crazed, hungry motion with the AK still in his hands. He then laughed and set it down, picking up a third rifle. For Carlo, it wasn't just about surviving. He liked to hurt the people. Something his large size made all too easy.

Junior, their skipper, standing next to Carlo, kept his head down. Like Josias, he hoped it was a quick raid. And that Carlo was in a good mood.

With less than two kilometers left, Josias grabbed the old rusted lifeline and made his way back to the cockpit. It looked like it was going to be a good score.

* * *

Alison sat on the bench seat at the main table, casually observing Lee's work on his laptop. She leaned back against the thin cushion and watched Kelly help Chris with the dishes. He made a joke, and Kelly feigned a look of shock before pushing him playfully.

Alison shook her head. She couldn't tell whether there was something more than friendship there. Chris had a few years on her, but Kelly had a great mature, yet playful, way about her. Not to mention a tall, curvy figure.

Lee continued typing but curled his lip, knowing what Alison was thinking. When she leaned forward to speak to him, he stopped typing.

"Lee, when we go down again tomorrow, can you record the video?"

"I should be able to. The signal was a little weak with all the dolphins in the way, but it may still be strong enough to get a good picture."

"Good. If anything is worth recording, this is."

"You can say that again."

Alison let herself fall gently back against the cushion again. She was in a great mood. Everything was going well. They still had more than enough food and fuel, the weather was holding, and IMIS was working well... with a few exceptions, of course. Although, it was peculiar that she hadn't heard from DeeAnn recently. She no doubt had her own hands full.

"Any more ideas on how long it might take to give IMIS the ability to differentiate between more than two dolphins?"

Lee let a burst of air out of his mouth as he considered the question. "That's a good question. A couple months maybe, including testing. I'm presuming you want that as a priority."

Alison gave him an exaggerated smile. "Please."

"You do realize I have about a dozen things for you, all sharing the number one spot."

"It's because you're just so amazing!" she teased.

"Yeah, tell that to my wife."

Alison tilted her head and wrapped her arms around her bare knees. "Speaking of whom, aren't you supposed to call her?"

"I will. I didn't want to run down the battery on the sat-phone before you called John."

"Very funny," she squinted.

"Hey," Chris called out to the pair from his position at the sink. "Anyone mind if I put on some tunes?"

"Please do." Alison jumped from the seat and walked toward the steps. "I'm going to take a shower." With that, she grabbed Chris' music player and handed it to him as she headed downstairs.

It was less than twenty minutes before they heard it or, rather, felt it. With the music playing loudly, no one had the slightest idea that a vessel was approaching. It wasn't until Kelly felt the slight bump on the side of their boat that anyone looked outside. By then it was too late.

The three darkly clad men silently coasted their aging speedboat in, next to the side of the Prowler catamaran. Junior, with line in hand, was already tying the boats together by the time Carlo and Josias jumped aboard. When they reached the sliding cabin door, Kelly was just stepping out to investigate.

Without the slightest hesitation, Carlo grabbed her with his giant fist, pulled her forcefully out into the cockpit, and threw Kelly to the deck.

"Kelly?" Chris' voice called from inside upon hearing something hit the cockpit's thick fiberglass floor.

Instantly, Chris was pulled out next into the darkness, but much harder this time. He stumbled forward and tripped over Kelly, smashing headfirst into one of the hard bench seats and careening sideways.

"What the-" was all he got out before Carlo stepped in and hit him hard in the face with the buttstock of his AK-47.

"Shut up!" Carlo growled. He turned back and forced the sliding door completely open.

Lee's shocked expression kept him still just long enough for Carlo to step inside and level the barrel of his gun at Lee's chest. Outside, at the same time, Josias stepped smoothly over Chris and jammed his muzzle into his back.

Carlo stepped closer to Lee and held a finger over his lips. "How many aboard?" he whispered, in a thick Haitian accent.

Lee stared at him and decided lying was a bad idea. They would probably search the boat anyway. Something told Lee that the beast standing in front of him didn't like surprises. Without a word, Lee held up four fingers.

## 41

ALL FOUR WERE sprawled on the floor of the cockpit. With hands bound behind their backs, they lay as Carlo and Josias searched the boat for valuables. The two quickly rounded up the jerry cans of fuel and most of the food.

Josias was downstairs, staring at the IMIS servers, when Carlo came in behind him.

"What are those, computers?"

Josias nodded. "Expensive ones."

"Can we sell them?"

"Yes. My cousin would buy them."

"Fine." Carlo quickly scanned the rest of the confined cabin and ducked back out.

Fifteen minutes later, they were back up top and *furious*. They were expecting much more than a few phones and computer tablets. The diving equipment and computers were the only things of considerable value. For a boat that nice, it was beginning to look like a major bust.

Carlo stood over Alison and the others, fuming. There had to be more. They were hiding something.

He looked at Lee and kicked him hard in the stomach. "Where is it?!" he yelled.

Lee shuddered violently from the pain. He coughed up some spittle and struggled to speak. "Where's… what?"

"Money! You have some, I know it!"

"We don't!" cried Alison. "I swear."

Josias stood off to the side and sneered. "Bullsheet." His accent was even stronger.

"I swear we don't. We're researchers."

Carlo turned and stared at Josias. There was a brief moment of silence when the satellite phone suddenly rang behind them.

Carlo leaned through the door and spotted the ringing phone on the counter. Its buttons were lit in a bright orange hue while it continued ringing.

He turned and peered back down at Alison. "Who is calling?"

Alison, still partially on her side, twisted around but wasn't even close to the phone. "I have no idea."

"Yeah?" Carlo cried. He reached in and grabbed the phone, then stepped back outside. "You don't know?"

"No," Alison sighed. "Maybe you should answer it."

Carlo examined the phone, still ringing. He scoffed and, in an instant, flung it overboard into the ocean.

* * *

Steve Caesare finished dinner and returned down the narrow hallway toward their rooms. When he reached the end, he spotted Clay's open door and peered inside. Clay was sitting on the small bunk with one knee propped up and an arm resting across the top. On the bed next to Clay was the small, flat silver cube.

"Any ideas yet?"

Clay raised an eyebrow at him and looked down at the cube. "Not yet."

"You'll get it," Caesare winked. "You always do."

Clay reacted as though he might chuckle. "You know this isn't like a word puzzle."

"Really? I thought it was a deck of cards."

Clay smiled. "If it is, then it's a pain to shuffle."

"I bet," Caesare said, with a brief laugh. He motioned to Clay's dangling hand, which was holding a phone. "Talk to Alison?"

Clay turned back. "No. She's not answering."

"Did you tell her to keep it on?"

"I did," Clay replied, with a slow and deliberate nod.

Caesare looked curiously at the phone again. "How many times did you try?"

"Four." Clay shook his head. "It's not like her."

"Where was their last position?"

"Just a little east of Trinidad."

"Really?! What are they doing so far south?

Clay stared at the wall in front of him before turning back to Caesare. "Where's Borger?"

* * *

Josias finally dropped the last of the servers onto the cockpit floor with a "clunk." The pile was nearly waist high with all three servers, the diving gear, the boat's marine radio that had been ripped out, all navigational instruments, fuel, some food, and several electronic devices. Not a huge bounty, but it turned out not to be a complete loss either. Josias twisted his wrist and glanced at the watch he'd taken off Chris. They had less than four hours before first light, and they were going to need all of it to put as much distance possible between them and the Prowler. He just needed to get Carlo off before things got any worse.

Just then, Carlo stepped back outside behind them. He dropped the boat's water maker onto the pile in disgust. Four people had to have more than this, but he couldn't find anything else. He'd beaten the two men, but they revealed nothing more than what they'd already found. But there was still one more thing.

He glanced at Josias standing next to him with his rifle slung loosely over one shoulder. Junior was now on their boat, leaning over the edge with a hand on the side on the Prowler waiting to bring things aboard.

"It's getting late," Josias said. "We have to go."

Carlo checked his own watch. "Not yet." With a snarl, he looked at the four people still bound and gagged on the floor. The men's faces were beginning to turn black and blue. One of them looked to be unconscious. He turned to the two women, lying still at his feet.

Josias watched with grim acceptance as Carlo's face took on a seething, sickening appearance. The women on the floor were both exceptionally attractive, and he was hoping Carlo's reluctance to harm them was intentional. But now, watching him stare at them on the floor, Josias knew he was wrong.

Carlo's upper lip seemed to curl up strangely, revealing his mangled teeth. He abruptly reached down, pulled Kelly up off the floor, and flung her over his back. Without a word, he marched back inside and down the stairs to one of the bedrooms. Less than a minute later, he came back for Alison.

He dropped Alison onto the mattress next to Kelly. Both lay on their backs, neither able to move their hands beneath them.

They both watched in horror as Carlo turned and slammed the cabin door shut. When he stepped toward them, he realized why both had remained so calm outside.

Both women were saving their energy, and almost at once, they released it in a torrent. They began kicking Carlo with every ounce of strength they had, beating him in the chest and face, sending him stumbling backward.

* * *

Outside, Josias shook his head and set his rifle down. He picked up two of the heavy jerry cans and scurried to the port side.

Junior straightened up and pulled harder on the line to retie the two boats together. A warm wind was picking up and the two vessels were trying to drift away from each other.

It was the wind that helped. That and the struggling women below deck, of course. Together, along with the sound of the waves around them, both Josias and Junior were prevented from hearing the sound until it was almost on top of them.

The sound of helicopter rotor blades.

## 42

"CARLO!" JOSIAS BURST in through the cabin door. "We have trouble!"

Carlo jumped and whirled around. Behind him, Josias could see the shorter woman's blouse was torn, exposing her bikini top underneath. Carlo didn't bother replying. He followed Josias back out and up the short set of steps. From there, they ran back out into the darkness to find a giant Oceanhawk helicopter circling the boat.

"Shit!" cried Carlo. He turned and followed the helicopter as it circled less than a hundred yards away around the port side of the boat, then the stern. "Is it the Coast Guard?"

Junior shook his head. "I think it's their Navy."

"Throw me a light," Carlo barked.

Junior rushed to a nearby storage compartment and lifted the old lid. He withdrew a giant flashlight and swung his arm out, throwing it across.

Carlo snatched the light out of the air and turned it on, still watching the chopper as it began another slow circle around the boat. The light was bright enough to partially illuminate the aircraft and revealed the giant side door that was open. Sitting on the inside, someone was leaning out with half of his face behind the night vision scope of an M40A5 sniper rifle.

They remained frozen, continuing to follow the helicopter as it slowly circled a third time, then a fourth. When it completed the fifth circle, the Oceanhawk slowed and stopped near the stern, hovering in place. Steve Caesare, holding the M40A5 rifle tight against his shoulder, never wavered.

The three men gripped their AK-47s tightly. Carlo glanced around the Prowler's cockpit. It was a mess. There was no chance of lying their way out of this. He let his finger find the trigger guard on the gun, then snake its way around the trigger. "Don't do anything!" Carlo yelled over the thundering blades. "Wait and see what they do."

No one moved for a long time. They waited, continuing to watch the helicopter that was still hovering.

Finally, Josias twisted his mouth toward Carlo. "What are they doing?"

"I don't know." Carlo continued staring. The U.S. military was ruthless. They would not be fooled no matter how fast he talked. To them, attacking an American boat was basically an act of war. There was no chance of getting off the boat easily with a Navy helicopter and sniper overhead. They would have to make their own exit. "How many do you see?" he asked loudly.

"Just one," Josias replied.

"Junior?"

Junior looked carefully into the flashlight's beam, still shining against the helicopter. "I see only one."

Carlo's eye narrowed. He was no scholar, but he could count. The sniper might be a good shot, but if the three of them opened fire at the same time, two of them might get away. Especially if they could make it to the launcher on their boat. "Junior," he said, looking sideways. "Start the engine."

Junior began to move but quickly froze again. Carlo growled at him for not following orders but suddenly saw the look on Junior's face. With eyes wide, he was staring across the boat and over Carlo's right shoulder.

Josias turned and gasped as well, forcing Carlo to slowly turn around. A man was standing on the white fiberglass roof of the Prowler's salon. He was dressed in black fatigues, which were soaked and dripping with water. Carlo stared briefly at the man's bare feet and quickly followed them up his legs to the barrel of an M4 assault rifle. There was no doubt where it was pointed. It was aimed directly at Carlo's head.

John Clay spoke from behind the sights. "Don't… move."

They didn't. They remained very still, moving only with the gentle rocking of the boat. Carlo could clearly see Clay's finger on the M4's trigger.

From the roof, Clay glanced down into the cockpit. "Where are the women?"

"Down below."

"Alive?"

"Yes."

Clay looked directly at Carlo. "Tell your men to throw their guns in the water."

Carlo repeated the command, and both Josias and Junior threw their AKs over the stern into the dark rolling waves.

"Now you do the same."

Carlo complied, reluctantly.

Clay kept his right finger on the trigger and reached up to his ear with his left hand. He pressed the small ear bud in firmly. "You there, Steve?"

"Affirmative."

"Light 'em up."

A moment later, a bright red dot from Caesare's scope appeared on Carlo's back.

Clay turned to Carlo and his men. "Face down on the deck. Hands flat on the back of your head. Right now."

All three simultaneously dropped onto their stomachs and reached back behind their heads, as instructed.

The red dot from Caesare's rifle followed Carlo down, where it continued dancing within a small circle on his back.

Clay stepped back and raised his weapon. He spoke to Caesare, loudly enough for the others to hear. "They're yours. If one of them so much as raises his head, take it off."

"Nothing would make me happier."

With that, Clay instantly turned and ducked inside.

He quickly scanned the salon and ran down the starboard stairs, searching both cabins. Nothing. He ran back up, across the salon, and down into the port hull. There he saw both women bound on the bed, struggling to get the gags out of their mouths.

Clay rushed into the cabin and grabbed Alison, checking her for injuries. Seeing none, he eased the gag out and turned to Kelly. She had a small laceration on her cheek, but otherwise looked unharmed.

"John!" Alison sputtered, clearing her mouth.

"You okay, honey?"

"What are you doing here?"

"We weren't that far away." Removing the gag from Kelly's jaws, he then gently rolled her over and withdrew a large knife from behind his back. It sliced through the duct tape effortlessly. "Are you hurt, Kelly?"

She felt her cut. "It could be a lot worse."

Clay turned to free Alison. After returning the knife to its sleeve, he grabbed her and pulled her in close. She wrapped her arms tightly around him.

"Boy, are you a sight for sore eyes."

Clay smiled and pushed Alison back just enough to kiss her.

After a long moment, Alison leaned back with warm, watery eyes. "I think you forgot your shining armor."

Clay smiled at her attempt at humor, before standing back up. "Too heavy. I left it on the chopper." He pulled both women to their feet. "I need to check on Chris and Lee."

As he reached out and pushed the door back, Caesare's voice broke in over his headset. "Clay, we've got an urgent call from Langford."

"Take a message."

Back up top, Clay found Chris just regaining consciousness. Clay double-checked his pulse and removed the tape from his hands. He then gently bent one of Chris' knees and rolled him onto his side. He retrieved a cushion from a nearby seat, sliding it under his head.

Lee's face, like Chris', was covered in cuts that were beginning to bruise. Clay freed his hands and helped him up into a sitting position. He lightly patted down his legs, looking for anything else. "Anything hurt?"

Lee shook his head. "Not below my head." He forced

a smile through his cut lips. "I'm very glad to see you, Mr. Clay."

Clay smiled and rose up. He clapped Lee gently on the shoulder. "So am I, Lee."

He found the tape inside the cabin and knelt back down, jamming the ball of his knee painfully into Carlo's back. Pulling the man's arms down behind him, Clay wrapped them together tightly at the wrist. He then moved to the other two.

When Clay finally stood back up, Caesare's red dot disappeared. A few minutes later, the helicopter drifted over the boat, allowing Caesare to rappel down. He unclipped and stepped over Chris with Kelly kneeling at his side.

Caesare crossed the cockpit and stopped next to Carlo. With one of his boots, he dug into Carlo's gut and forced him over onto his back. Caesare squatted down next to the Haitian and looked into his dark eyes. There was no trace of remorse.

He raised his voice over the thundering helicopter above. "You sure picked the wrong boat, eh?"

Carlo jerked his head up and spat, but Caesare's reaction was instant. He drove a powerful fist straight into Carlo's face, slamming his head against the cockpit floor.

Caesare stood up, watching Carlo's eyes roll upward. He came in close to Alison so she could hear him and nodded out toward the swirling water. "Any chance dolphins would eat a human?"

"I wish."

He frowned and then addressed Clay. "Langford says you need to get back to the Bowditch, pronto."

"You've got to be kidding."

"He said it was urgent. He asked me to apologize to Alison." He looked at her. "Which is rare for the Admiral. Don't worry, John, I'll stay and bring them in."

Alison gripped Clay's arm. "Do you have to go right this second?"

He peered at the Oceanhawk with its blades still beating the air above them. One of the pilots had his helmet against his side window, looking down and waiting.

"I'm afraid so," he sighed. "They're burning fuel." Clay sized up the jerry cans in front of him. "You should have more than enough to reach the Bowditch."

He surprised Alison when he wrapped his arms around her and gave her a long kiss. "You'll be fine with Steve. He should have you to the ship by noon at the latest. Just get some rest and take care of Lee and Chris."

"Okay, we will."

He nodded at Caesare. "The bag is on the bow."

Clay smiled at Kelly before grabbing the harness, still lying on the deck. He clipped himself in, grabbed the rope, and gave the signal to raise him.

From the deck, Alison watched Clay quickly ascend towards the helicopter. From there, the copilot reached out and pulled him in, not letting go until Clay got his footing.

The front of the helicopter immediately dipped forward and accelerated. Within moments, it was gone, and the thundering blades faded into the night.

* * *

Carlo fell hard, striking his face against the filthy deck of his speedboat. The craft was larger than one would have expected, which meant it was likely stolen from a previous victim.

"Whoops. Sorry about that," Caesare said, then dropped Josias next to Carlo with the same force and bounced him off Junior, who was already face down.

Caesare turned and stepped back over the side. With a short hop, he landed on the edge of the Prowler and stepped down next to one of the seats. He opened Clay's large waterproof bag and withdrew a Springfield .40 caliber semi-automatic. Before he returned to the speedboat, he glanced over his shoulder to Alison and Kelly, who were both watching. "Cover your ears."

They watched him hop back into the other boat. The women suddenly froze when he pointed the gun down and, without hesitation, rapidly unloaded the entire magazine.

*Oh, my god!* Alison stood horrified. They were both speechless…until Caesare reached down and turned something. He then pulled up on a large panel, which looked to have over a dozen neatly placed holes in it.

It was one of the panels to the engine compartment. Even without direct light, Caesare could make out the dark fluids squirting out of the thick damaged hoses and pooling at the bottom of the compartment. With a satisfied nod, he dropped the panel and let it clang shut. "That'll do."

The men were still watching wide-eyed from the floor of their boat when Caesare crossed back over, untied the line, and pushed off.

As they floated away, he called out a heartfelt, "Bon voyage!"

# 43

IT WAS STILL dark when deckhands guided the Oceanhawk down onto the Bowditch's pad. Clay slid the heavy door open and jumped down beneath the slowing rotor blades. He trotted to the base of the metal stairs where Neely Lawton was waiting for him.

"They're waiting for us," she said, waving him up the stairs as she started climbing. Clay followed her up and checked his watch. It was four thirty-five a.m.

When they reached the small conference room, Captain Krogstad and Will Borger were already seated at the table. On-screen were a tired looking Admiral Langford and Merl Miller. Kathryn Lokke appeared surprisingly alert.

Clay and Lawton sat down on opposite sides, keeping all of them just within frame of the small camera above the monitor.

"Everyone," Krogstad said, "I'd like to introduce Commander Neely Lawton, our resident biology expert and head of the research team aboard this ship. She is the one who requested this meeting. I can also assure you she is as sharp as they come."

If the introduction bothered Lawton, she didn't show it. Only Langford knew that she was also Krogstad's daughter.

Lawton cleared her voice. "I'm sorry to bother all of you at this early hour, but I have some information that I think you will all agree warranted an immediate call. As you know, my team has been studying the sample which Commander Clay brought aboard from one of the Chinese trucks." She pressed a button on her laptop and a picture of the sample appeared on the monitor for all to see.

"Now, please be aware that we have had less than forty-eight hours to study it, so for all intents and purposes this should be considered a preliminary finding." She paused for any questions. Receiving none, she continued. "We began with tests on all of the plant cells' organelles: nucleus, ribosomes, mitochondria, everything. Finding nothing unusual, we then examined the plant's chloroplast and thylakoid spaces and measured its photosynthesis properties."

"And?" asked Langford.

"Its photosynthesis capacity appears to be above average, but not by much."

"So, you're saying there is nothing special about its photosynthesis?" Langford asked.

"Correct. Nor is there any significant oil composition or production that we can detect. Again, this is a preliminary examination. There are still more tests to carry out, but I can say with some degree of confidence that these initial measurements are accurate."

Miller rubbed his eyes. "Commander Lawton, I presume there is at least something noteworthy for us to discuss on this call."

"Yes, sir. After finding nothing in the preliminary tests, we decided to dig deeper. As you may know, DNA has already been mapped for many modern plants, but to do a complete mapping here would take months, even in a larger laboratory. But we did study its chromosomes. In particular: their lengths, the position of centromeres, and branding patterns. The name of this kind of study is called karyology, and we found something interesting."

"The somatic cells of humans, as we all know, have forty-six chromosomes. Orangutans and gorillas have forty-eight. Animals like bears and wolves range through the sixties and seventies. Plants, on the other hand, generally have a lot less. So these somatic numbers vary from species to species."

Miller nodded. "I presume you are going to tell us how many our mystery plant has?"

"Eighteen, sir," was Lawton's reply. "But the number is not all that important. What is important is the behavior of those chromosomes. My intention is not to turn this call into a biology lesson, but I thought it worthwhile to refresh everyone's memory on a few subjects. Chromosomes are organized structures of existing DNA and proteins. They essentially package portions of DNA and control its various functions."

"The reason for my primer is that we found something interesting regarding the chromosomal behavior of Commander Clay's plant. As a matter of fact, 'interesting' wouldn't be the right word. What we found is rather staggering, and it has to do with a very specific part of the chromosome."

"And what part is that?"

Lawton glanced at the screen with a hint of apprehension. "Telomeres, sir."

Langford watched Clay and Borger look at each other. "What's a telomere?" he asked.

"Telomeres are nucleotide sequences that reside at the end of each of our cell's chromosomes. They act as a sort of 'cap' to prevent problems when DNA is replicated. For example, during cell division, when chromosomes are replicated, it's the telomere caps that protect against accidental mutation or fusion with each other. Every chromosome has them, and the telomeres grow slightly shorter with each new replication."

Lawson continued. "About fifteen years before their discovery, a man named Hayflick discovered that there was a finite limit to these cellular divisions, after which the cells would simply stop replicating and die. It's called the 'Hayflick Limit.' Telomeres were discovered to literally be the switch behind the Hayflick Limit. Telomeres grow shorter and shorter with each replication until they reach a critical point. That point or limit is the *switch,* which disables the ability for cells and chromosomes to replicate any further. It's the point that we humans refer to as 'old age.' "

"Over the last few decades, researchers have been trying to find ways to turn that switch off. To allow the cells to continue replicating. As it currently stands, all cell types, except for one, have these limits which force them to die and subsequently brings on the terminal decline of old age."

The room became quiet while everyone digested Lawton's explanation. Kathryn Lokke was the first to lean forward and speak. "You said there was one type of cell that didn't have these limits?"

"That's right," Lawton nodded. "But it's not that the cell doesn't have a limit. It's that its switch has been turned off. In other words, their telomeres don't grow shorter as they are supposed to. This allows the cells to continue dividing indefinitely to a point of immortalization." She paused and took a short breath. "I'm talking about *cancer* cells."

Everyone looked at Lawton with a startled expression as she continued.

"Cancer cells have DNA that has been damaged through a process of mutation, a process that we still don't understand. But it allows the cells to live for an extremely long time. In fact, there is one infamous line of cancer cells that *never* die."

"You're talking about the HeLa cells," Borger said.

"That's right," Lawton nodded. "The HeLa cells are named after a woman named Henrietta Lacks. She died of cancer but not before her doctor took a biopsy from her cancerous tumor. It turned out to be one of the most surprising discoveries in the field of cytology. The cells from her tumor simply won't die. In virtually any environment, they continued to replicate indefinitely. They are still alive today and are the most widely distributed cell culture in history. There was an interesting book written on the subject not too long ago."

"Okay," Miller said, peering into his camera. "So what does this have to do with Clay's plant?"

"Well, not surprisingly, the behavior in cancer cells has captured the imaginations of many researchers around the world. If telomeres can somehow be intentionally deactivated to allow cell replication to continue, perhaps they can achieve what cancer cells have already managed to do: perpetual cell replication, but this time in healthy cells."

Miller frowned, thoughtfully. "You mean, as in stopping diseases?"

"No, sir," Lawton replied simply. "I mean as in stopping the aging process itself."

Everyone on-screen and in the room stared at Lawton, frozen. Everyone except Borger.

Neely Lawton waited for questions but receiving none, continued again. "For some time, scientists have been trying to find a way to turn off the automatic shortening of telomeres when they replicate. Or, perhaps as in the process of telomerase, to *re-lengthen* them. Researchers are getting closer, but ultimately telomerase is an interventionist approach. The holy grail would be something much more holistic." She turned and looked at Clay. "Enter Commander Clay's plant."

Lawton reached out to her laptop. "The plant sample Mr. Clay delivered may provide the answer. On the screen is a picture of the plant we received." She typed a command on the keyboard and a second picture appeared on the screen. "And this is the same plant now. Less than forty-eight hours later."

"Oh, my god," mumbled Langford.

Lokke was equally stunned. "That's the same plant?"

"Yes, ma'am," Lawton replied. Forcing herself to stay calm, she clicked a button and enhanced both images. "As you can see, the second picture of the plant is noticeably larger than the first."

"Unbelievable."

Lawton couldn't help but grin. "This plant is the first one I've ever seen with the same telomere disabling properties that cancer cells have. But unlike cancer cells, it doesn't kill the host."

"And that's why it's growing?" asked Lokke.

"Actually, no." The excitement in Lawton's voice

was now obvious. "There is something even more exciting about this plant. Not only are the telomeres disabled but, somewhere in the gene sequence, the replication schedule is wildly accelerated. This means that not only does it *not* have a Hayflick Limit…its genetic code is programmed to replicate much faster than that of a normal plant cell. You can see this in the picture. Not only is the torn leaf regenerating itself, but it's actually in the process of re-growing a new *stem and root system!*"

This time even Borger was surprised. "Whoa!"

"I take it this never happens either," Miller asked, rhetorically.

"Actually it does, sir. Just not this fast. Many known plant types can propagate into a new plant. But not this fast and they don't regenerate their missing parts. In fact, if I had to guess, I would estimate that Commander Clay's plant here will regrow itself entirely in a couple weeks, maybe less."

Langford stared at the pictures on his screen for a long time. "So that's what the Chinese have found."

"And why they've been so secretive," added Miller.

Lawton nodded. "You can all see now why I deemed this call urgent."

"Commander Lawton," Clay spoke up. "What would you say are the scientific ramifications of this?"

She took a deep breath and shook her head, considering the question. "Generally speaking, I'd say pretty darn big. As far as I know, the characteristics of this plant are something no one else has seen anywhere else on the planet. I mean just the speed at which its cells are replicating make cancer cells look slow. Theoretically, if this process can be harnessed or replicated, or even somehow distilled, I cannot even begin to imagine its possibilities. Reversing disease is one thing, but the ability to completely arrest the aging process at the cellular level is… well," she shrugged, "into the realm of fantasy."

"Jesus," Langford muttered, leaning forward into his hand.

Kathryn Lokke cleared her throat. "Ms. Lawton, I know you said you haven't had time yet to fully examine or test this sample. Is there any chance at all that we're wrong here? I mean the picture obviously speaks for itself, but is there any chance that we've misdiagnosed what's causing this?"

"Yes, there could be other factors," Lawton nodded. "But given the tests we've already run, I would be very surprised to find another explanation. What is far more important, however, is the possibility of whether these chromosomal attributes can be crossbred with other plants. Which I bet is exactly what the Chinese are thinking. If so, that is one enormous game changer!"

"What do you mean?"

"What I mean is we could be talking about something that virtually any country on earth would be willing to go to war to obtain. An entire agricultural system comprised of plants that never die. Imagine what that would be worth. But what's really frightening is the question of whether these DNA attributes can be transferred beyond just *plants.*"

"Is that even possible?!"

Lawton stared at the screen. "I'm not sure if it is or isn't, but considering what we've already accomplished with genetic engineering, it may very well be in the realm of possibility."

On the screen, Lokke took a deep breath before turning her attention back to Langford. "Well, Admiral, I guess the only question now is what we do about it?"

Langford thought it over. "Secretary Miller and I need to make some calls. This is going to require a full cabinet briefing, and quickly. Mr. Borger, have you been able to pinpoint a location yet?"

"I believe so. It's hard to see through the thick canopy, but I believe the source is approximately one hundred and twenty miles into the Guyana rainforest. Due south and about fifteen hundred feet in elevation. At least that's where their trucks stop."

Langford nodded. "Okay, I want you and Clay to continue gathering whatever intelligence you can on the location. Doctor Lokke, please continue to gather and prepare your team but remain on standby for now." He leaned forward with a grave expression. "And Captain Krogstad, do NOT under any circumstances, allow that corvette out of dock!"

## 44

THE DAMP MORNING chill hung in the air as Alves' goon, Blanco, escorted DeeAnn up the grassy slope toward the helicopter. His grip around her upper arm was like a vice and felt as though it was beginning to cut off her circulation.

Still, she tried to remain calm for Dulce's sake. DeeAnn's hand was wrapped tenderly around the small gorilla's, which was squeezing her hand firmly. She could sense the nervousness in Dulce's hold.

Alves was standing near the giant helicopter, an AgustaWestland AW101. It was one of the most expensive private helicopters on the market. One look inside would explain why. It looked more like the interior of a private jet than a helicopter.

DeeAnn paid no attention to the aircraft. Instead, she glared angrily at Alves, who appeared to have changed dramatically from the man she first met. He no longer made an effort to hide his real accent, nor was there even the slightest hint of compassion in his eyes. His face now looked dark and stone-like. The transformation was truly sickening.

They reached the short set of metal stairs and were pushed forward by Blanco without pause, sending both DeeAnn and Dulce stumbling up and into the cabin. Behind them, they heard a screaming Dexter approaching. He was being toted up the hill in a cage, by one of Blanco's henchmen.

Inside, DeeAnn hated having to put Dulce back into a cage, but she had no choice. It was for her own good, and frankly Alves and his men were no longer here to help. They were simply giving orders.

DeeAnn closed the metal door behind Dulce until it clicked shut. She then turned and sat down in the next seat, looking at Blanco and noting the large gun in his holster. DeeAnn turned away and peered out the window, back towards the large building. There was no sign of Juan. Why would there be? She didn't expect to see him, yet it made her feel even sicker to her stomach.

As it turned out, Alves' men *did* record some of the

communication between Dulce and Dexter. And they knew exactly what Dexter had revealed. There was no hiding it now. That, along with Alves' devastating admission the evening before, exposed just how little freedom she and Juan ever really had.

From the very beginning, they were there for a purpose. Any appearance of a collaborative effort was strictly intended to get them on the plane and away from Puerto Rico. Alves was after Dexter all along, for very different reasons. And DeeAnn and Dulce were little more than Alves' bait.

Now the game had become deadly. Juan was being held until DeeAnn and Dulce fulfilled their orders. Of that, Alves was imminently clear. And he promised them that if they refused, Juan would be dead within minutes.

DeeAnn closed her eyes and tried desperately to keep it together. Dulce was on the verge of an anxiety attack, Juan was being held at gunpoint, and yet DeeAnn somehow had to get Dexter to lead them to some place that no one but the monkey had ever been before: his home in the jungle.

Dexter's cage was lifted inside and slid in next to Dulce. The small capuchin quickly scrambled back to the far corner of his cage and fearfully wrapped his tail over his mouth.

After several more minutes, Blanco and two of his men, including the handler of Dexter's cage, climbed in and sat in seats at the front. They watched DeeAnn and the two primates with an expression of dark ambivalence.

Alves had a word with the pilots before sitting down in a rear facing seat directly across from DeeAnn.

"Are you at least going to tell me why?" she sneered.

Alves barely reacted. "What exactly do you feel you need to know?"

"Why are you trying to find out where Dexter came from? What is so damn special about him that made you kill Luke over it?"

Shadows appeared through the cabin windows as the extra-long blades of the chopper overhead began to turn. They flashed eerily over Alves' face as the motion accelerated.

"And I suppose you think this knowledge will somehow help you in your effort with the monkey?" Alves asked sarcastically.

"It might."

Alves shook his head, irritated, but he relented. "Your ignorance knows no bounds. Luke knew the monkey was special. That was very obvious from his intelligence alone. But other things indicated there was something more. Things like his hair and teeth. They suggested that Dexter was much older than expected, given the normal lifespan of capuchins." Alves paused and glanced out the window as they felt the helicopter lift off the ground. "So Luke did a DNA test. He wanted to match it against the current gene mapping for capuchins. But he found something none of us were expecting. Something that made everything else pale in comparison."

"That he was smarter than you?"

The old Alves would have at least grinned at the insult. This Alves simply looked at her with increased irritation. "He found that the monkey's gene sequencing was different. It wasn't just older than normal, it was a *lot* older!"

The nasty look on DeeAnn's face fell away as an innate curiosity overtook her. "How old?"

"Most capuchins live a maximum age of twenty-five years in the wild. But your Luke Greenwood was convinced that Dexter was well over a *hundred*."

# 45

ADMIRAL LANGFORD KEPT his head against the headrest, trying to relax in the back seat of the town car. He rolled it sideways and peered out of one of the darkened windows. Even at six a.m., the traffic heading into downtown Washington, D.C., was beginning to slow with congestion. The only consolation was knowing that several others from the President's security cabinet were having to endure the same conditions.

The folder on the seat next to him was filled with copies of pictures, diagrams, and the hasty write-up sent over by Commander Lawton after their call. Given how rapidly the cabinet meeting was put together, only the President and Vice President had an inkling of what it was about. The rest would find out soon enough.

Langford's cell phone rang. He reached into his inside coat pocket to retrieve it. It was a number he didn't recognize.

"Langford here."

"Admiral, this is Caesare."

"Caesare? Aren't you supposed to be on a boat headed for the Bowditch?"

"Yes, sir. I am. But something urgent has just come to my attention that I need to speak to you about."

Langford looked outside again at the ever slowing traffic. "I appear to have plenty of time."

President Carr looked up from his copy of Lawton's write-up and back to Admiral Langford with raised eyebrows. "Is this *real*?"

"We believe it to be authentic, Mr. President."

"Jesus Christ!" He put the paper down in front of him and looked at the high-resolution pictures again. "How the hell did the Chinese find out about this?"

Vice President Bailey put down his own copy. "And how did they convince Guyana to just roll over for it?"

Miller answered. "We don't know who or how they found it. But it appears they convinced the government of Guyana the old fashioned way."

"They bought them off," Baily acknowledged.

Carr smirked. "You say that as if we wouldn't have done the same thing." He rubbed his forehead absently. "How can we be sure about the implications this Commander Lawton is laying out here? I mean, how many scientific discoveries do we hear about every day that end up meaning nothing? Not everything pans out."

"That's true," agreed Secretary of State Bartman, from across the table. "If I had a nickel for every medical or technological advancement that promised to be a breakthrough, I'd be a rich man."

Next to Miller, Langford shrugged. "The fact is, sir, we don't know."

"How long have we been testing this thing, forty-eight hours?" Bartman asked, with a hint of sarcasm. "Look, I'm not saying this isn't what she claims, but how on earth can we be sure after just forty-eight hours? Other advancements have turned out to be nonviable after months, even years."

The Admiral sat motionless, listening. Finally, he frowned and scratched his cheek. "Well, the Chinese have had months to study it, maybe longer. And they sent a *warship* to go get it."

The others became silent.

Langford shrugged. "We can sit here and debate how viable this is, and we can decide to wait until we've tested more. But all the while, there's a fully armed Chinese ship scooping up this plant by the truckload, and it's doing it as quietly as possible. Maybe we should consider the logistics of what it would take for us to do something like that, while trying to keep it secret at the same time. That's a lot of moving pieces, and the Chinese appear to have moved on it awfully fast. If you ask me, I don't think we should be spending our time discussing the odds of this being real. I think we need to be considering the ramifications if it is." Langford looked at Carr. "How wrong are we willing to be, Mr. President?"

"And what if we're wrong, Admiral?" the Vice President asked. "What do you recommend, a blockade? Our relationship with China is already on delicate footing. What if we rush in and manage to elicit a situation that escalates into something even bigger? How would we feel starting up a military conflict with them, come to find out this big 'secret' discovery turns out to be a fascinating new toothpaste?!"

President Carr nodded his head solemnly. "Ramifications can go both ways, gentlemen. The Chinese and the Russians continue to strengthen their alliance. Considering our problems with Russia, this certainly doesn't help matters. The last thing we need to do is to inflame the relationship even more."

The room was silent again, allowing Secretary of State Bartman the opportunity to interject. "Let's assume for a moment that this discovery is as important as you say. And we don't try to stop them. Why not send our own team in to retrieve specimens? Hell, even if we don't, we can steal whatever secrets the Chinese derive from this plant. If they document anything, we can eventually get it."

"We're starting to add a lot of 'ifs' to our thinking," Miller noted.

"That may be, but I think it's less risky than inadvertently creating a geopolitical conflict."

The President turned to National Security Advisor Griffith, sitting quietly in his seat. "Stan? Thoughts?"

Griffith was leaning forward with his chin perched on his palm. He blinked and looked up. "Espionage is never a sure thing. And it often causes more long-term damage than one would expect. Look at the NSA and their surveillance snooping. We lost a lot of credibility after that, not to mention some important allies. I do agree that risk is less about the odds of something happening and more about the ultimate ramifications." He picked up and examined his own set of pictures again. "How much do we know about Commander Neely Lawton?"

"She graduated cum laude and one year early from Harvard before getting her Masters," Langford replied.

"After joining the Navy, she was part of a team, who two years ago, discovered an algae capable of cleansing toxic metals from polluted water five times faster than any other known method. An algae that several corporations are now working to commercialize. She's as sharp as anyone I've met in the field." He looked around the table before concluding, "And she thinks this plant the Chinese have found is a pretty damn big deal."

Sam Johnston, the Commandant of Marines, leaned forward onto the table with hands interlocked. "It seems to me the one thing we don't want to do is to try second guessing how important this discovery may ultimately be. We should be focused on getting someone in there to find out exactly what the Chinese team is doing. There's a lot of speculation on what's actually happening at the top of that mountain. I suggest observation be our first priority."

"We can still get ships in the area if we need them, without making anyone nervous," added the Chief of Naval Operations, sitting next to Johnston.

"If it's that important," Griffith added, turning toward the President, "we can put a non-military team on the ground and stake a claim without screwing around with that corvette."

The President thought it over. Everyone knew the Chinese had been stockpiling virtually every essential commodity for years: gold, silver, copper, iron ore, and a dozen more. They were preparing for something. Yet even with all the other commodities, they had never moved as quickly as they had in Guyana. They knew something, something that no one else did.

"Mr. President, Commander Lawton believes this

may just be the tip of the iceberg on what the Chinese have actually found. If that's true, to what lengths do you think they will go to keep it?" After a pause, Langford added with a grave tone, "What lengths would any of us go to?"

## 46

THE STREETS WERE virtually empty. The pollution in Beijing was worse than normal and most people remained indoors. The few who did venture outside covered their faces with white masks and walked briskly from building to building.

The growth of China over the last four decades had been tremendous, raising the country from a veritable third world status to the second largest superpower in the world. It was a level of growth like nothing the modern world had seen. Hundreds of new cities with gleaming skyscrapers and endless shopping malls now littered China's eastern seaboard. The country was now home to a faster growing number of millionaires and billionaires than any other country in the world, including the United States. And they had just overtaken Russia's ranking for the second largest military on the planet.

Yet the explosive growth of China's modern industrial gold rush came at a price. Production remained in overdrive as their factories worked to keep up with both a global and now domestic demand for goods. It also meant a lack of standards and every incentive to cut corners. Regulations were nowhere close to keeping up with production. Not to mention they came without any semblance of safety, particularly with incentives for fraud and corruption oozing from every public office. It was unsustainable. Their red-hot economy was going to have to slow eventually. When it did, the impact would be harsh.

Wei's Mercedes crossed over the Landmark River on Xindong Road, the thick veil of smog leaving him unable to see past the edge of the structure's steel railing. The pollution was getting worse. More and more days were deemed unfit for breathing and each of those meant a significant loss in productivity. Change was no longer avoidable. It was only a matter of time.

The general looked at his watch. Of all his meetings, this was one he could not be late for. In reality, it was less a meeting than it was a summons.

The seven people that waited for Wei were beyond authority. They were beyond any real definition of accountability, yet everything that happened in China fell under their ultimate control. They were the government elite, the Politburo Standing Committee of the Communist Party of China, and the seven men who determined the path of China's future. It was the same group who secretly appointed nearly all heads of state and the military. And they were the same group who had appointed Wei.

Regardless of their ultimate disconnect from the average citizen, the Politburo Standing Committee steered the political, economic, and military courses of China's future with a deft hand. A hand that also had the ability to instantly clench into the most ruthless of fists. While justice in other modern countries was bound by at least a facade of judicial fairness, the masters of China had no such requirements. Punishment was occasionally handed down from them with a stunning lack of mercy, usually in the form of executions. Swift and strategic, the executions of high-ranking public officials were performed just as often to make a point rather than to actually deliver 'justice.' In fact, out of a number of officials executed for their role in deeply rooted corruption, Wei suspected several were never involved at all.

It was what made the recognition by the group of seven as much of a curse as a blessing. Power and wealth could be granted with the wave of a hand, yet it could be withdrawn even faster with the swing of a sword.

Wei's mood grew even more somber as his driver turned onto the byway and the image of a giant complex emerged through the suffocating brown smog. The Mercedes made its final turn into the half-circle entrance under an enormous glass overhang. After the car stopped, Wei barely had time to unfasten his seatbelt before the door was promptly opened from the other side.

He was escorted to the eightieth floor where the elevator dinged and opened its silver doors. Wei walked forward into the expansive room, which was the top floor. Glass walls, on all sides, looked out over a heavily obscured cityscape.

They motioned him to a chair on the far end of the oval table. He sat and looked up at the serious faces of each of the seven members.

On the other side of the table, Xinzhen began immediately. So much for etiquette.

"So the Americans have arrived."

"Yes," Wei answered.

"Are you prepared?"

Wei nodded. "Yes. We will protect it at all costs."

"Even if it leads to conflict?"

Wei tried to appear relaxed. "We always knew that was a possibility."

The man nodded slowly. Another of the Committee members spoke up, the brashest of the group.

"And what about the extraction?"

"It is nearly complete," Wei reassured. "You will have it soon."

The man's eyes narrowed. "I hope so. Time runs short, General."

"Careful steps must be taken, Mr. Secretary." Wei had explained it all to them many times before. Each meeting was almost like the first, yet Wei revealed none of his irritation.

After all…he knew something that the Committee didn't.

* * *

Lieutenant Chao stood on the deck of the corvette class ship, this time in direct sunlight. Secrecy no longer mattered. The Americans knew. They had gotten a sample and by now, no doubt, had discovered the secret of the plant. But ironically, they wouldn't realize its full potential for at least another week. Nevertheless, they knew enough now to understand what Chao and his men were up to.

The boat sat surreally silent, rocking gently with the help of the mild incoming ocean surge. There were no more shipments, no more transfers in the dark, and no more running the crates back to the hangar for the next load of trucks.

In fact, General Wei was probably sitting in front of the Committee now, being questioned for the hundredth time. They wanted to make sure their prize was safe. It was their future. And it would ensure survivability for China's supreme ruling class and their political structure, regardless of the coming devastation their economic rot would bring. At least that's what they were expecting.

Chao looked up at the distant mountains of Guyana. Who would have thought that crazy explorer Zang had been telling the truth? And that it would turn out to be a discovery that would change the path of human history, a history of which Chao was an astute student. He wondered how many explorers had dreamt of this find. How many had spent their entire lives searching for one of the world's greatest legends? Only to have someone else stumble upon it by accident. What fools.

He raised his binoculars and looked out across the ocean. The American ship was still there. They were no doubt running around desperately trying to figure out what to do. A grin crawled across his tight lips.

Soon they would come in with guns blazing like the Americans always did. But this time, their only discovery would be that they were too late, that their mighty empire missed out on the most epic of revelations. He only wished he could be there to see it.

But he couldn't. What was going to happen that evening remained far more important. It was their last trip back into the mountains. Yet this time, the trucks were loaded with more than just crates.

And most of his men would never come back out.

Several miles across the water, Clay stood on a metal grating just outside the Bowditch's bridge. He remained still, with his binoculars up, studying the corvette ship. For a moment, he thought he saw a glimmer of reflection from something.

Standing next to him, Captain Krogstad looked through his own pair. He scanned the waterfront from side to side and muttered to himself. "'Don't let them out of the dock,' he says. How the hell am I supposed to do that with an unarmed science vessel?"

Clay mused and turned to scan the rest of the southern shoreline. He panned, looking out over the northwest horizon. He froze and, after a brief pause, dropped the binoculars. He couldn't help but smile. "Vessel sighted."

Krogstad spun with his glasses still up. The small white object was clearly visible against the dark blue water, even with the unaided eye. The azure sky stretching overhead lacked even a wisp of cloud.

The object was the Prowler catamaran steaming ahead at twelve knots.

Krogstad noted the time on his watch. "They're even early. Well done, son."

It took almost an hour for the boat to reach them, eventually rounding the stern and coming under the same maintenance ladder Clay and Caesare had used. Peering over the edge, Clay smiled at the sight of Caesare at the helm. He was wearing a T-shirt and someone's baseball cap to block the sun.

Lee and Chris were the first to climb the ladder.

With some difficulty, they reached the top and were immediately escorted off to sickbay by Krogstad's crew. Next came Kelly, followed by Alison. Considering recent events, the women seemed no worse for the wear. When Alison spotted Clay standing off to the side, she quickly covered the distance to him, smiling all the way. She wasn't sure what would be deemed appropriate on an official ship with an official crew and was pleasantly surprised when Clay put an arm around her.

"How are you?" he asked warmly.

Alison beamed. "Good now, thanks to you and Steve. How did you know where we were?"

"Borger found you."

"Ah, the mysterious Mr. Borger I hear so much about. Does that mean I finally get to meet him?"

Clay smiled. "In the flesh. Though you might want to keep your sunglasses on. His shirts can be a little hard on the eyes." He let the smile fade from his face. "How are Chris and Lee?"

"Pretty good. Steve couldn't find any signs of critical injuries, but their wounds will take some time to heal."

"Well, they're in good hands now." Clay looked at the ladder just as Caesare appeared. He climbed over the edge effortlessly and nodded to the Captain before approaching Clay.

"Nice job, sailor," said Clay, pausing when he noticed that Caesare was not smiling.

Instead, he looked at Clay with a serious face. "I'm not staying long."

"What?"

"We have a problem." Caesare gave a slight nod to

Alison. "It seems DeeAnn Draper and Juan Diaz have gone missing. Along with Dulce."

"For how long?"

Alison peered up at him. "We haven't heard from either one of them in a few days."

"I called a friend at the CIA," Caesare said. "There's been no activity on their cell phones from the tower they were connecting to outside of São Luis. I also had him dig deeper into our billionaire, Mr. Alves. It seems he's not quite the Boy Scout philanthropist he seemed. He's involved with some bad elements in Brazil."

Captain Krogstad walked up behind them. "Trouble?" he asked.

"You could say that," Clay answered, then turned back to Caesare. "So, do you have a plan?"

'Yeah, my plan is to find them," Caesare stated flatly. His face became even more serious. "I talked to Langford and got clearance. As long as you stay here working with Borger and Commander Lawton."

Even though it wasn't a surprise, Clay still didn't like hearing it. He wasn't one for staying behind. "Do you need anything?"

"Nope. I've got what I need on the boat. I'll need to hold onto your bag. Langford diverted a transport plane on its way down. It should be waiting at Georgetown's airport by the time I get there. Which means I should be in São Luis by sundown." Caesare turned to Krogstad. "Captain, can I borrow one of your crew? I can take the Prowler to shore, but I need someone to bring it back."

"Of course. Whenever you're ready."

Caesare opened his mouth to speak but was interrupted by someone shouting from across the deck. It was

Borger. He was waving frantically and running toward them. When he reached them, he spit out the words and bent over as though someone had just given him the Heimlich maneuver. "You guys gotta get in here!" He pointed back the way he came and rested his other hand on his knee, nearly hyperventilating.

"What's wrong?"

Borger couldn't reply. He was desperately trying to catch his breath. After several more inhalations, he finally got it out. "Hurry! The lab!"

The other five immediately bolted for the stairs less than a hundred feet away. Rapid pounding on the gray metal steps could be heard as they made their way up.

Clay reached the lab first. He grabbed the door and pushed it open forcefully, stepping inside along with it. Behind him, Caesare entered, followed by the two women, Krogstad, and finally Borger in a distant last.

Startled, Commander Lawton jerked her head away from the large monitor in front of her. There was an instant before she spoke when her eyes flashed on Caesare, a gesture which only Alison and Kelly caught.

"We have a problem," she stated as she stood up. "A big one!"

"What?"

Lawton smiled politely at the women and turned back to the screen. "Look at this."

Instinctively, everyone stepped in closer behind her.

Lawton enlarged a window on the screen and it zoomed in, displaying the twisted shape of a simple life form.

"What's that?" asked Clay.

"Bacteria. A human intestinal bacteria to be exact."

She turned back around, facing them. "I wanted to try something. Any of you guys familiar with 'horizontal' gene transfer, or HGT?"

Borger looked down the line and then meekly raised his hand in the affirmative.

Lawton rolled her eyes. "I don't mean you, Mr. Borger." Seeing five blank stares, she continued. "Horizontal gene transfer refers to the passing of genes to other organisms, not including traditional reproduction. It's most commonly used to refer to gene transfers between two *dissimilar* organisms. And 'artificial' HGT is essentially what we refer to today as genetic engineering. For example, transferring a glowing gene to a fish so it glows in the dark. That one makes a neat pet."

"But even without artificial assistance, some genes in genetically modified foods, such as soy and wheat, have been documented to actually 'jump' to another organism such as bacteria. One study observed it happening in human digestive bacteria, which is why I chose that one."

*They still appeared to be with her.* Lawton went on.

"I wanted to see if Clay's plant had a similar ability, to 'jump.' Therefore, I extracted the chromosomal DNA I told you about and injected it directly into one of the bacterial cells." She motioned with her hand to the onscreen picture behind her. "See Exhibit A."

"And?"

"And it worked."

"Impressive," Clay said.

She shrugged. "Not so much. There are much more efficient ways to do it than my brute force technique. But bacteria are a single cell organism, so it's not horribly difficult to do. Besides, I don't know if 'impressive' is the word you'll want to use when I tell you the next part." She turned and retrieved a small petri dish from the table behind her. "This," she said, presenting it in her palm, "is what it looked like two hours ago."

They all peered into the clear dish which didn't appear much different than water.

"Okay," Lawton nodded briefly. She turned and set the dish down, while picking up another. "And this is what it looks like now."

The others behind her let out a collective gasp. The dish no longer resembled water. Now it looked like a thick pink soup.

"What happened?" asked Krogstad.

"It grew, sir. A lot. These are all new bacteria, all from the one I transferred the plant's genes into." She reached into the dish and gently lifted an edge of the pink material with a fingertip. She let it drop back down into the dish for effect, complete with a squishing sound.

"All that in two hours?"

"Yep. Of course, given the right growing medium, bacteria can grow quickly. But not like this."

Clay was still watching the dish. "I take it this is a result of the telomere not allowing them to die?"

"Actually, no," Lawton replied. "It's because of the other attribute, the rapid regeneration. I don't know what piece of DNA code is responsible for that, but it's in there somewhere."

"Okay. So, you're saying we have an HGT transfer from the plant to a bacteria."

"A human bacteria," Lawton corrected. "And now for the next part, and our problem." She folded her arms and turned back to the screen. "Fortunately, human bacteria don't transfer their genes into regular human cells. At least they didn't until a couple years ago. That's when a team of scientists at the University of Maryland School of Medicine published a report showing evidence that it *does* happen. They demonstrated that their bacteria can, on occasion, transfer its genes into healthy human cells."

"On occasion," Clay repeated curiously.

"Yes, in a small percentage of cases."

"I sense a surprise coming."

Lawton nodded. "You're right." She reached down and picked up the same pink colored petri dish again. "This is the surprise!"

"Oh, wow," Borger mumbled.

Clay wasn't following. "Will?"

Borger looked at Lawton then back to Clay. "It's a numbers game, John."

"A numbers game?"

"I think what Commander Lawton is saying is that given the *normal* speed at which bacteria replicates, their numbers still aren't enough to matter against our trillions of other cells." Borger motioned at the pink petri dish still in her hand. "But with a much faster replication rate, it could be a problem."

"Exactly," Lawton said. "Over time, with a faster replication *and* the bacteria cells no longer dying a timely death, they could theoretically go on to grow indefinitely. Which means, given enough time, even a DNA jump that only occasionally happens could still eventually infect every single cell in our bodies. In fact, it wouldn't even need to get to every cell. It would only need to change a large enough number for the body to physiologically react to it. Or to *absorb* it."

Clay eyed her curiously. "And how long would that take?"

"I'm not sure," she shrugged. "Without the cells dying and given the compounding effect of accelerated replication, probably less than a year. But the point is that getting that plant's DNA into human cells may be a lot easier to do than we thought. Especially if you were to use a friendlier strain of bacteria, like Bacillus Coagulans."

"Given enough time," said Clay.

"Exactly."

"Damn," Caesare folded his arms. "A guy can miss a lot in twenty-four hours."

Lawton winked at him and shrugged. "Just the biggest biological find in history."

Clay looked at Krogstad. "This is huge." He then remembered something and asked Lawton, "So this is the problem you were talking about?"

"Not entirely," she said.

"Meaning what?"

"Meaning that if we know what these 'plants' of theirs can *really* do, then the Chinese must know it too."

Alison shook her head. "I'm confused. Are the Chinese the only ones who have this organism?"

"Yes."

Krogstad looked grimly at Clay. "And I have a feeling they're not in a sharing mood."

# 47

DEEANN STROKED DULCE'S trembling hand through the cage bars. The small gorilla was beginning to whimper. Dexter was still cornered in his own cage, shaking. With fingers gripped around the thin metal bars, he was frantically looking back and forth between the helicopter's windows out to the blue sky beyond.

Alves watched the primates with interest but little concern. Behind him, Blanco was watching them all.

"I hope this is worth it," DeeAnn said, in a snide tone.

It took a moment for Alves to respond, as if deciding whether he felt like it. "I hope so too."

"I knew you couldn't be trusted."

Alves grinned wryly. "And yet you did."

"Because I was stupid."

"Agreed." Alves tilted his head. "By the way, I know about your romantic relationship with Luke Greenwood." His tone was mocking. "A woman, still in love, coming to save her man. Very romantic."

"Go to hell."

He was still grinning but took a deep breath. "Hopefully not for a very long time."

"So, I guess your plan is to just fly up into the jungle to find out what makes Dexter so old. Just like that."

He stared at her. "Ms. Draper, do you know what the ultimate irony is?"

She didn't respond.

"It's being rich."

She displayed a puzzled look but still didn't reply.

"The greatest desire, as it turns out, is also the greatest irony of all: to be rich. To have more money than you will ever need. The irony is that shortly after becoming rich, you realize that what you *really* need, what everyone needs, is time. You see, a rich person doesn't want to die, but plenty of poor people do. Sure, there are exceptions, but there is much more suffering on the bottom than on the top. After all, when you have the means to be king, who would ever want it to end? The answer is no one."

"So you want to live forever."

Alves laughed. "Oh, please! Don't be trite. It doesn't become you. You are still a woman of considerable intelligence, mostly." He glanced out one of the side windows. "Even pragmatists can dream, no? We just dream, *realistically*. No, Ms. Draper. I don't harbor any silly fantasies about living forever, but I most certainly do pursue those things that may extend my health. And health *is* time. Would you believe me if I told you I was eighty-three years old?"

The surprise on her face was obvious.

"I didn't think so. You see, there are many things we can do to extend our health. Some easy, some hard. And some more than a little strange. I've done them all, and still do many of them today. Do you know why?"

He leaned forward when she didn't answer. "Because one must be ready. Ready for even the briefest of opportunities. A *real* opportunity."

"You mean like Dexter."

"Yes. Like Dexter." He looked down at the frightened monkey. "Just as in business, you must be prepared for any opportunity that presents itself, no matter how short or unorthodox. Because death can come at any moment, from a thousand different directions. A sudden heart attack, a fall," he said, spreading his hands, "even a helicopter accident. Life is unpredictable, but opportunity favors the prepared."

"And the rich."

Alves smiled. "Being prepared with means, no doubt improves one's odds."

"Maybe you should just think about living a life that's worth living?"

"Ah, the ethical choice," he mused. "The golden rule, live as you want to be remembered, leave the world a better place." He laughed again. "All sage advice, from the belly of mediocrity. No doubt you have many friends living by such a noble ethos, yes?"

She glared at him. "Luke was one."

The humor dropped from Alves' face. "Yes, I suppose he was. Then again, maybe he wasn't."

DeeAnn's eyes narrowed, questioningly.

"Did it ever occur to you, Ms. Draper, that your precious Luke was driven by motivations that were more… human?"

"No."

Alves sighed. "I marvel at how one-dimensional your mind is. Luke Greenwood spent his life rescuing poor, abused animals from nasty people. People like me, perhaps. He was a hero. A man of the earth!" Alves shook his head. "Tell me. What do you think he enjoyed more, rescuing those poor animals or *hurting* the evil abusers?"

"What's the difference?"

"Ah, there's the single dimension again. What is the

difference, indeed? Revenge, regardless of whom you deliver it upon, is still a human trait, is it not?"

DeeAnn answered reluctantly. "I suppose."

"Of course it is. So then I ask you; if your dear Luke were getting more pleasure from hurting those who are evil, how virtuous would his fundamental motivation truly be?"

DeeAnn quietly brushed a dangling strand of hair back over her ear.

"I have news for you, Ms. Draper. Human beings are motivated by their own interests and nothing more. Of course, we can all paint a different agenda or insist we act under a more noble value system, but in the end, all of our actions are self-motivated. No matter how small or how slight." He gestured to Dulce. "And it's the same with your animals."

"So then you're saying, why fight it?'"

Alves smiled broadly. "Why indeed."

"And your self-interest now is to find out how Dexter has lived so long and to find a way to copy it."

"We can only hope."

"So, all of this, all of this deception and deceit, was just so you could eventually go live like a monkey?" She scoffed. "Knock yourself out. I'm only doing this for Juan."

This time Alves didn't answer. He merely shrugged. It didn't matter. It didn't matter to him why she was doing it or how she had to rationalize it to herself. The simple truth was that when it was over, neither Juan Diaz or DeeAnn Draper would ever be seen again.

When Caesare reached the Georgetown airport, the Grumman C-2 Greyhound transport plane was waiting for him on the tarmac. First built in 1966, the silver-colored, twin-engine C-2s were used by the Navy for various cargo missions and had flown millions of miles. And of the thousands of missions flown, the aircraft's primary and most respected missions were delivering pieces of paper to aircraft carriers. Papers in the form of letters. Yet now with the digital age, the old C-2s flew far less often.

Caesare sprinted across the hot tarmac toward the plane. His large bag bobbed up and down as he ran, strapped tightly across his back. The various gear inside, particularly the rifle and ammunition, weighed him down considerably.

He reached the C-2 and, with a short leap, jumped through the lower positioned door. A crew member nodded then looked outside before pulling the heavy metal door shut. He gave the okay to the pilots. As the engines roared to life, he yelled over the noise to Caesare.

"Make yourself comfortable, sir!"

In his black fatigues, Caesare nodded and looked around. With no place to sit, he simply removed his bag and fell backward onto the dozens of oversized, stuffed mailbags.

## 48

LESS THAN TEN miles away, aboard the corvette, Lieutenant Wang Chao watched over the shoulder of Hoa Ling, his lead biologist. Like Chao, Ling had been handpicked by General Wei, as were the other four members of Ling's team. They were the best in China, and probably in all of Asia. And if any of them were bothered by their extreme working conditions below deck, none showed it.

What the Americans didn't know was that their ship wasn't much of a corvette class at all, at least not anymore. Below deck, it had been completely gutted. Virtually all armaments and weaponry systems had been replaced with a science lab and even larger storage area. The only parts that had been kept were those that ensured the ship would float. Even the living quarters were reduced to the point of sheer necessity. With a minimal crew and science team, the gutting was the only thing that made it possible to store five weeks of extraction efforts in the cool, dark recesses of the boat's bow. Chao's ship was a corvette in appearance only.

Standing before both of them was a giant machine called a nanoscale magnetic torque transducer. Or as Ling's team called it, the 'nano-mag.' It was required for the painstaking process in molecular biology referred to as *transduction*. In 1951, researchers in Wisconsin demonstrated the process of using a common virus to elicit an enzyme reaction, which then allowed for the DNA in one cell to be replicated or 'cloned' to another. And while the process had been honed over the years for better efficiency, the fundamental steps were surprisingly similar to those first steps documented over fifty years before.

Ling removed a small vial of clear liquid from the machine and screwed on the top. He then placed it into a thin, rectangular box next to him, which held two more vials. The inside lining of the box was ice cold, constructed specifically to house the vials at a near zero temperature during transit. Ling closed the lid and secured the clasp before presenting the box to Chao.

"They're ready."

Chao took the box and examined it, impressed. The exterior did not feel any noticeably cooler to the touch. What he held in his hands was the first complete extraction of the plant's genome and biological material. The vials were filled with thousands of bacteria cells, all painstakingly injected with the plant's chromosomal DNA through transduction. The cells were held dormant by the ice cold medium inside. Only above temperatures of thirty degrees Fahrenheit would they thaw and become active.

Chao went to a nearby station and wrapped a thick metal band around the box. Next to it, he wrapped another band of thick paper, with an intricate wax seal. If the box were opened, the recipient would know it. Of course, it was overkill in Chao's opinion. After all, there would only be four people who touched the box, including Ling and Chao.

Chao immediately left the lab and carried the package up the metal ladder. He emerged from the ship and onto the deck. He then crossed the gangway where a soldier was waiting at attention. Another lieutenant, and one of impeccable reputation.

The man saluted to Chao, who returned it before handing the box to him. There were no misunderstandings. Either the man delivered the box personally, or he and his entire family had better already be dead.

Chao watched the man walk briskly to the truck and climb in. *Would he make it?* Chao wondered. Then another thought occurred to him. *Did he even care?*

Chao was also selected personally by General Wei but for a very different reason. Chao was ruthless. And ruthless in ways that literally redefined the word.

He'd served under the General before, and his reputation became well-known after one of their incursions. After a particularly nasty battle, Chao's team had won the fight. But what he had done to enemy survivors left his entire platoon in disbelief.

But he was here now. Chao had been tapped again by Wei to get a job done, and to get it done without any emotional interference. What it really meant was to do it without any emotional baggage.

Oddly, Chao had always found the whole thing puzzling, if not entertaining. Being able to completely distance yourself from human emotion was an asset, not a liability. After all, how many commanding officers were willing to kill their own men?

Chao watched the small truck disappear to the east and turned to watch three of his Typhoons pull up. He climbed a small weeded slope to reach a dirt plateau where the trucks had stopped. He walked around to the back of the first truck while the driver eagerly got out and ran back to meet him. The driver inserted a key and opened the heavy door.

Inside, he could see them. Their dull green tanks

were still barely visible within the truck's darkened interior. Chao stepped inside and examined one. The harness was old and the straps frayed. Not surprising, given they hadn't been used since the Vietnam War. Most countries had discontinued their use or even banned them outright. Of course, they were always a contingency, but Chao never expected to have to use them, and certainly not this soon. Yet, in the end, a plan that remained flexible was a plan that won.

Chao browsed the dozens of additional tanks stacked neatly behind each backpack. Each was filled with liquid propane. They were called 'mechanical incendiary devices' but they were known the world over by a more distinct name: flamethrowers.

The best and most ironic part was the original manufacturer: the United States military.

* * *

Twenty minutes later, Chao tossed a large bag onto the seat then climbed into the cab of the first truck. He gave the order to move out.

The tires on each of the Ural Typhoons dug into the ground and surged forward. Chao looked out his window and into the truck's side view mirror, watching the ship slowly shrink behind them.

It would be his last trip up.

# 49

SÃO LUIS WAS the capital of the Brazilian state of Maranhão, and the only one of Brazil's state capitals originally founded by France. With two major sea ports and almost a million residents, São Luis was a burgeoning South American metropolis.

Jose Vierra had lived in São Luis his entire life and paid no attention to the overhead noise from the nearby airport. Frankly, in his stupor, he was simply too drunk to notice. Instead he was cursing at his girlfriend, telling her for the last time to get onto his damn motorcycle!

His girlfriend stood at the top of the steps with her arms folded defiantly. Even as buzzed as she was, she wasn't getting on with him.

Finally, Jose screamed at her and grew more incensed when she proceeded to flip him off. She then turned around and stormed back inside the bar.

Seething, he fumbled to get the kickstand down and turn the motorcycle off again. He was just about to dismount when he noticed a figure appear out of the darkness, carrying a large bag.

Steve Caesare smiled at him, having observed the exchange. "Honeymoon must not be going well, eh?"

Vierra made a puzzled face from under his thick, sweaty brow.

Caesare shrugged. The man didn't speak English. It didn't matter. He needed transportation, and this fellow looked like just the type of generous person he was hoping for.

* * *

DeeAnn could see the outlines of the small shacks just within range of the campfire light. The roaring flames leapt high off the tall pile of wood, illuminating everything around them, including the trucks and even the faint glow of Alves' white helicopter in the distance.

Several yards behind DeeAnn was a large area with rows of wood and wire mesh cages. They were old and rusted, some of the framing barely holding together. It was a disgusting sight, reminding her of that terrible compound in Mexico. She refused to look and instead kept her eyes on Dulce and Dexter, both caged next to her.

"Can we please let them out? Just for a few minutes?" she pleaded.

Alves seemed to be growing even more indifferent. On the other side of the fire, he sat in a wooden chair and lifted a large bottle to his lips, drinking what resembled a green sludge. He lowered the bottle and looked at her, wiping his lips with a cloth napkin. "No."

"What is wrong with you?!" she cried. "You're torturing them!" Dulce was visibly trembling now, and Dexter was still gripping his cage tightly. She could smell Dexter's fear as he repeatedly urinated.

Alves made no attempt to answer.

"Listen," DeeAnn continued, "you don't understand what you're doing! You still need them, don't you? How are you going to learn where he's from if they're both too frightened to speak?!"

Alves took a breath, and finally turned to her. "And how would I find out if we took them out and they escaped?" He paused, waiting rhetorically. "I'll take my chances." He calmly raised his bottle and took another gulp of sludge.

The man had no idea. Dulce hadn't spoken since they'd landed and she was now sweating profusely. It was so much that DeeAnn could see the sheen on her fur in the firelight.

Even worse was where they were. It was the poacher camp where Dexter was first captured while trying to free the other monkeys. Just the mental trauma alone from being here was probably enough to keep Dexter from ever talking again.

DeeAnn was now very frightened. If Alves had no concern for them now, then he would have even less after he found what he was looking for. The sickening feeling in DeeAnn's chest was growing stronger. She knew that she was never coming back. She felt even sicker when she thought about Juan and how she'd brought him into this mess.

Across the fire, Alves stared off into the darkness, his white hair glistening in the light. His body slumped forward, tired. Even though the others couldn't tell, his old lungs could feel the change in elevation and were having to work harder to compensate. In the last several years, his efforts had become more of an obsession than a quest. Each year, he was growing more desperate with the knowledge that his time was nearing an end. How much longer could he keep going?

Alves peered into the black expanse all around them, no longer hearing the sounds of the jungle or those around him. Why was he so desperate to live when all of the people who really mattered to him were already gone? His brothers and sisters, his wife, the friends he played with as a boy. Everyone who was a part of any pleasant memory he had was gone. He remembered playing games with his brothers and sisters, constantly laughing and running. Those were some of the purest memories of life that he could recall, and yet his loved ones had all gone, one after another.

But still, he remained. He remained and persevered, finding ways to hold onto every last minute he could grasp. *Why? Why did he cling so desperately*? He knew the answer before he even asked it. It was because everyone close to him, those who had left, did so with the same reluctance. The same look on their face that said no matter how old, no matter how much pain they had, they didn't want to leave the game. Alves felt it too. He didn't want to leave. Not because he was afraid of what waited for him on the other side. But because when you were out, you were out forever, never to return. And forever was a very long time.

Behind Alves sat Blanco, along with his two men. The two were smoking cigarettes and conversing about how well their famed soccer team had been doing. Yet Blanco paid no attention.

Out of earshot, DeeAnn wondered what the men were talking about. But even more than that, she wondered what Blanco was thinking behind his cold dark eyes.

Juan Diaz sat in complete darkness, unable to see anything. His eyes had long since adjusted to the windowless room he was in. There was no light, not even the slightest glimmer, to offer him.

From where he was, it sounded like the entire preserve had been abandoned. No sound from the outside reached him at all. The only thing he ever heard was an occasional noise from just a few rooms over, from the man who had put him here.

Diaz had no idea what time it was. However, he did remember two voices clearly talking about Alves' assistant Carolina. According to the few words he was able to pick out, she had fled not long after Alves and the others had left. But he didn't know whether that was four hours ago, or twelve. He didn't know how many times he had fallen asleep or for how long. The only things that had woken him up were the pain in his shoulders from his hands being bound behind him and the rumbling in his stomach.

He had called out several times for food, loud enough that Blanco's man must have heard him, but there was no reply. Letting him use the bathroom before throwing him in the closet was the last outside contact he'd had. But why? They were supposed to be holding him as insurance, to force DeeAnn into helping them. If they were going to keep him alive, they *had* to feed him. But they hadn't. Over the course of many hours, the reality slowly dawned on Juan as he lay in the blackness with his face against the cold, smelly concrete. They weren't feeding him for a reason.

The terrible feeling of despair was nearly overwhelming. Juan rolled his forehead helplessly against the hard floor, feeling the small pebbles press painfully into his skin. A tear escaped and rolled sideways off his cheek. *He wasn't going to make it out of here. He wasn't going to see anyone ever again.*

He thought of his parents. They were so proud of him being the first to go to college, a real college. And then he saw his younger sister. She looked up to Juan, and she was everything to him. He pictured how her small face would look when she was told that Juan had died. Then the tears let loose, and he wept.

# 50

JUAN AWOKE WITH a start. He still couldn't see anything, but a noise had woken him. He was frantically trying to recall what it might have been, when he heard it again. Something in the other room. Something loud. An argument, maybe. The next sound was even louder, but he couldn't figure out what it was.

*No! They were getting ready. They were coming for him.* They were going to do to him what they did to Luke Greenwood.

Juan desperately pulled at his bindings again. He strained, trying to break what was holding him. It felt like tape, but it didn't budge. He tried again, feeling the veins in his temples bulge. Nothing.

He kicked his feet and tried to pull one up away from the other, but the tape held. *Jesus! What kind of tape was it?!*

*Wait!* He paused when he heard something else. *Was that the other door opening?* He continued kicking, now in a panic, trying desperately to break the tape. It wouldn't give. He scooted himself backwards on the concrete floor, searching for anything behind him. His fingers touched something. It was metal, a tool maybe.

But it was too late. Juan froze when the door to his room was violently kicked open. The light was turned on, blinding him and causing him to clamp his eyes shut. When he felt hands grab him, he shrieked and bucked wildly on the floor. He used the moment to roll onto his back, kicking at the bastards as hard as he could. "No! No!" he screamed. "Get away from me!"

With a victorious thud, Juan's right heel made contact with something. He tried again kicking in the same area but couldn't find the target again. It had moved away. He couldn't find anything. He opened his eyes into the bright glare and spotted the silhouette. He lunged with both legs together, using everything he had, and struck the shadow dead center, sending it reeling back against the wall. Juan blinked hard, looking around for anyone else. What he heard next caused his heart to sink. It was the sound of laughter.

They were actually chuckling. The shadow stepped forward, this time grabbing Juan's legs when he kicked hard toward his captor again. When the man spoke, his words were clear and unmistakable.

"Well, you're definitely alive."

The words were in English. Juan felt his legs drop to the floor with a thud. His vision finished adjusting until finally a familiar face materialized before him.

The man standing over him smiled and dabbed his own lip with one of his fingers. He pulled it back to reveal a small streak of blood. It was Steve Caesare.

"Mr. Caesare!" Juan croaked. His eyes wide with shock, Juan's brow furrowed and the sudden elation triggered an emotional release. Juan stared up at a grinning Caesare as his survival instinct gave way and he began sobbing.

Caesare knelt down next to him and put a thick paw on his shoulder. "It's okay, Juan. I got ya, buddy."

Juan pursed his lips, barely able to see Caesare through his blurry eyes. He tried to speak but couldn't.

"Don't try to talk." Caesare gently patted him. "Just relax a minute." In a smooth motion, Caesare drew a giant knife from somewhere behind him. As he reached down to cut the tape away, Juan could have sworn the blade had blood on it.

It took a few minutes for him to recover. All the while, Caesare stayed next to him, talking in a calm voice. Finally, Juan blinked the remaining tears out of his eyes and took a deep breath. He eased himself up onto his rear and wrapped his arms around his knees.

"You okay?"

He sniffed and nodded. "I…I'm sorry."

Caesare smiled. "Don't ever be sorry. Not about this. I've had my share of moments just being thrilled to be alive."

Juan forced a smile of his own. "I guess you really are a Navy SEAL, huh?"

Caesare laughed and stood up. "Unfortunately for them." He lowered his hand and waited for Juan to take it. When he did, Caesare pulled him up onto his feet. "So where are DeeAnn and Dulce?"

"Alves took them. In a helicopter."

"How long ago?"

"I don't know. What time is it now?"

Caesare peered at his watch. "A little after midnight."

"It was early this morning. Six or so, I guess. At least I think it was this morning."

"Where'd they go?"

"I don't know," Juan shook his head. "We came here to help them find a monkey. To try to find out what happened to DeeAnn's friend. But it was Alves. He killed her friend and lied to get us to come. And it was all to find that monkey."

"Why would he go to all that trouble over a monkey?"

"I don't know exactly. There's something about him that Alves is after. He's trying to find out where Dexter came from, but I don't know where that is, or which direction they went."

Caesare nodded, thinking. "How many were here guarding you?"

"I only saw two."

"Well, at least that's good news. Let's get out of here." He motioned toward the door and stepped out into the hallway, checking both directions. Juan noticed the gun in Caesare's hand. He hadn't even seen him pull it out.

They headed up the hallway and stopped at the door. Juan gave a start when he realized it was the room from which they were monitoring him. And also because Blanco's man, who was watching him, was now lying face down on the floor.

He looked back at Caesare, who was already heading further up the hall. "You did that?"

There was no answer.

When they reached the door to the outside, Caesare opened it slowly and quietly, listening. Hearing nothing, he opened it wider and slipped out, holding it for

Juan. He laid a finger over his lips and made a motion to be quiet.

They passed beyond the glow of the building's overhead lights and into a section of dense trees. After a hundred feet or so, Caesare abruptly stopped, causing Juan to almost run into him.

On the ground was another of Blanco's men. This one was lying on his back, clutching his side where his clothing was covered by a large dark stain. The man was gasping for breath and held a knife in his right hand.

"I see we found a knife." Without the slightest hint of sympathy, Caesare stepped forward, placing his heavy boot on the man's upper arm and pinning his right side. "Speak English?'

Blanco's henchman stared at him defiantly but reluctantly nodded.

"Then listen carefully. You tell me what I want to know and I'll leave you here, with a chance to live." Caesare raised the gun and pointed it at the man's forehead. "If not, I won't. Understand?"

The man nodded and relaxed his hand, letting his knife tumble to the moist dirt next to his head.

"Where did they go?"

Blanco's man coughed. "The mountains."

"Where in the mountains?"

"Northwest."

Caesare's jaw flexed. "How far?"

"South to Sipaliwini. Is a poacher's camp."

He motioned toward Juan. "How long were you keeping him here?"

The reply was broken. "Until Blanco call."

"And then what?"

The mercenary hesitated and looked nervously at Juan.

Caesare pressed hard on his arm. "I said, *then what*?!"

"To kill him," he blurted out.

Caesare's eyes grew dark. "How? How was he going to call you?"

The man grimaced. "The phone. In the office."

Caesare peered around through the trees. "Anyone else here?" There were two Humvees parked near the building on the south side.

The mercenary shook his head. His breathing was growing steadily worse.

"Keys."

The man tried to move the arm that Caesare was standing on but couldn't. Instead, he twisted his wrist and tried to point downward.

Caesare reached down and felt through the man's pockets. When he found what he was looking for, he reached inside and pulled out a set of several keys. He took his boot off of him and stepped back. He then turned to Juan. "Anything else?"

"Yeah," Juan said. He stepped forward and kicked the man as hard as he could in the groin, causing him to double over and howl in pain. Then Juan cursed in Spanish and spit on him.

Caesare nodded. "Well said."

They left him lying in the darkness and quietly reentered the building. Together, they moved slowly down the hallway in case Caesare had missed someone. Juan's former capturer was still lying face down in the room, lifeless. Caesare found the small phone and dropped it into his own pocket.

"Juan, if we can find the server room, can you shut everything down?"

"Hell, yes, I can!"

It took two and a half hours to reach Belem and find the hotel. When the two walked into the well-lit lobby, Mariana was startled to see Caesare again. She recognized him immediately. But this time, his face did not appear nearly as jovial.

"You're back, senhor." She glanced curiously at Juan, who was standing weakly next to Caesare. "Would you like a room?"

"No." Caesare shook his head and approached the old, run-down counter. "Actually, I'd like to see your brother again."

Mariana's lip curled with a hint of humor. "Another late night swim?"

Caesare turned toward Juan, who was looking at him with raised eyebrows. "Don't ask."

* * *

Lucas arrived within minutes, as the men stood waiting in the lobby. He stuck his head in the doorway and motioned for Caesare and Juan to come outside. They followed him out and Caesare smiled when he saw the same old Chevy Malibu. He and Clay had returned it to the hotel after borrowing it the week before, just prior to hightailing it out of Belem.

Lucas and his friend, who was standing on the other side of the car, looked Juan up and down. "Is he okay?"

"Someone tried to rough him up."

Lucas nodded. He was unfamiliar with the phrase, but he got the idea. "No swimming tonight?" Lucas asked with a grin.

*What is it with the swimming jokes?* "No," Caesare replied, dryly. "I need a helicopter."

Lucas' face became serious. With a concerned look, he peered at his friend over the roof of the car.

"Not the whole thing," Caesare clarified. "Just a ride."

"Senhor...that is expensive."

"It's urgent."

"Do you have money?" Lucas asked.

"No, I don't," Caesare replied. He reached into his pants pocket and withdrew a key ring. "But how would you like a new Humvee?"

Lucas remained silent for a few long seconds. "I may know someone."

"I thought you might."

* * *

It took them less than thirty minutes to reach the old airfield. Completely dark, it looked like a skeleton of its former self. Unfortunately, even broad daylight wouldn't have helped its appearance much.

Lucas drove his new Humvee up an open embankment to an old building. All four doors opened and they climbed out, hearing the sound immediately.

Soon after, they saw two bright flashing lights appear over the treetops, followed by the faint outline of a large helicopter. It approached and began to descend, finally bouncing down on the open grass in front of them.

Caesare was not the slightest bit surprised to see that

it was a Brazilian Army chopper. Given the poor economy, someone was obviously moonlighting.

The side door on the gray helicopter slid open and a man dressed in the same color fatigues waved them forward.

Caesare hefted the heavy bag up on to his shoulder and turned to Juan. "You're staying here." He yelled over the noise of the rotors.

"Huh?!"

Caesare pulled Lucas in close so he could be heard. "Get him to the airport!" He pointed at Juan. "And put him on the first plane to Puerto Rico!"

Lucas nodded. "I will. Right away."

Caesare gave Lucas a stern gaze. "If anything happens to him, I'm coming after you!"

"Yes, yes. No problem. You can trust me."

He nodded at Lucas before turning to clap Juan on the shoulder. "Everything will be fine. Just get yourself home, alright?"

Juan nodded and hugged Caesare's larger frame. "You're going to find them, right?"

Caesare nodded with a cold stare. "Damn right, I am!"

# 51

AT THE FIRST ray of light, the entire camp instantly awoke to Dexter screaming at the top of his tiny lungs. He rocked the cage frantically, throwing his small furry body against the inner metal bars over and over, nearly tipping it over.

DeeAnn was the first on her feet. For a moment, it almost looked as if the cage were being shaken angrily with Dexter simply trapped inside. But it was only Dexter, and he was completely unglued. Next to him, Dulce watched with wide eyes from within her own cage.

"Dulce, what's wrong with him?" she asked. There was no response. She began to repeat her words when she caught herself. She wasn't wearing the vest. "Damn it!" DeeAnn turned and ran back to her bag where the vest was carefully laid out on a large rock.

"What is it?" Alves cried. He was wobbling, trying to quickly get to his feet.

"I don't know!" DeeAnn pulled the vest down onto her shoulders and clasped the side buckles together. She flipped the power button and looked to see if the blue light was on.

And then she noticed it. Following her frozen gaze, they all did. High above them, on the distant horizon beyond the mountain's peak, they could see it billowing up into the sky like a dark blanket.

Smoke.

# 52

THEY WERE OUT of time. The sun was up and the smoke would now be visible from every direction. He had to get out.

Chao surveyed the damage. Everything was either burning or smoldering, for almost twenty acres in every direction. He and his men had used the rest of their extra gasoline supply to douse all the giant plants they hadn't excavated and then torched them with the flamethrowers. Most of the fire was still raging and quickly spreading out to the other trees and plants. Before long, it would cover the entire area, all the way to the cliff's face.

What they had found would never be shared. Their discovery would give China abilities far surpassing any other nation or people. They would not just be the next super power; they would be a super power like the world had never seen.

Of course, the Americans would figure it out soon. And they would no doubt arrive here too. But they would find nothing left to harvest. Only decimation. What the fire didn't destroy, the 2,4,5-T that laced the gasoline would finish. It would soak into the root systems and kill every last strand. Something they had already tested.

Chao watched one of his men work with his flamethrower, still spreading the bright orange streams of death onto everything he touched. With any luck, the fire would continue far enough that the Americans wouldn't be able to determine where it even began.

He turned to the truck. It had more than enough

fuel to make it back down, especially now that the cargo hold was empty. None of his men noticed when Chao walked over and opened the driver's side door, withdrawing the .45 caliber pistol from his bag. He pulled out a short black cylinder and screwed it onto the tip of the barrel. No one had ever gotten a close look at his gun and its threaded barrel. He double-checked his magazine and pulled the slide back, chambering the first round.

The flames were high enough that few of his men could see each other. And the smoke created a thick brown curtain all around them. The time had come.

This was where Chao's gift really shined. Most executioners would at least suffer from a nervous trembling in their hands, but Chao felt nothing at all as he approached the nearest of his men. A sergeant who had served him well. A man of intense loyalty, both to Chao and to the Motherland. Young, idealistic, and the father of two young children.

He never saw Chao, who quietly walked up behind him, raised his gun, and pulled the trigger.

Seventeen more.

# 53

DEEANN GRIPPED THE cages tight with her fingers, trying to keep them steady as the truck threw her from side to side. The road was little more than a worn path through the grass, with mounds and dips large enough even for her to see from the back.

"Hurry!" screamed Alves. He was sitting behind the driver, clutching the back of the seat. In the front passenger seat, Blanco sat gripping the overhead handle, trying to withstand the wild motion of the vehicle.

The driver had the pedal mashed to the floor, hitting every obstacle in the road at almost full speed. He was wrestling the steering wheel at the same time, trying to keep them from sliding down the embankment on Blanco's side.

DeeAnn tried unsuccessfully to keep the cages from thrashing against the interior sides of the truck. The shaking was too hard. She, along with Dulce and Dexter, were all thrown back and forth together. Dexter's shrieking had been replaced with a deep, guttural moaning, even as he crashed back and forth against the sides of his cage. Dulce was eerily silent. She was sopping wet and her eyes filled with fear.

DeeAnn couldn't help but think that if the fire site really was their destination, then Alves may not need any of them at all anymore.

Suddenly the driver slammed on his brakes, causing everyone to tumble forward. The road had disappeared. He peered intently through the dirty windshield, searching.

"There, there!" yelled Blanco, pointing to the right. It was overgrown with wild grass but remained barely visible.

The driver drove forward slowly, cranking the wheel hard to the right. He inched the front tires up and over a group of small boulders before getting the truck back onto the path. From there, he slowed and climbed carefully.

As they passed a clearing, DeeAnn caught a glimpse up the mountain from the side window.

*Dear god,* she thought. *We're not even close!*

* * *

On the other side of the same mountain, Chao was descending as rapidly as he could. With an empty truck and much better road, he was well past the halfway mark before DeeAnn's group even laid eyes on the summit.

He turned through a tight corner then pressed hard on the gas pedal, opening it up before having to brake hard again for the next turn.

Eventually, Chao broke out from beneath the canopy of trees and could see the glimmering ocean far in the distance. He quickly followed the river and glanced the dull gray ship waiting patiently at the dock.

Chao couldn't stop the smile from spreading across his face. He'd made it and without any serious problems. A few of his men had turned around in time to see the gun, but it was too late. It was over. Everything had gone his way, and now they were shipping out. And in three short months, he would be wealthy beyond his wildest imagination.

The last hour was the easiest. The road was smoother and the hills at the base of the mountain provided a gentler decline. Chao gripped the wheel and pushed the accelerator down further.

Finally, he was close enough to see the crewmembers from his ship moving on the dock, waiting to cast off the gigantic lines holding the corvette in place.

Chao instinctively looked down and noticed the condition of his light gray jacket. He cursed and slowed the Typhoon. With one hand on the wheel, he snaked an arm out of the jacket, then switched and pulled the other arm free. He grabbed the garment and held it up before throwing it out the window. He returned both hands to the steering wheel and sped up again.

Better to arrive out of dress than in a jacket with blood spatter all over it.

## 54

A MORNING FOG HAD settled further down the canyon, far beneath the camp. The extra moisture helped blanket some of the sound, but it also gave the large Brazilian helicopter an ominous image as it rose up, out of the mist.

As they breached the top into a clear blue morning sky, both helicopter pilots looked up through their windshield with wonder. There appeared to be an enormous fire at the top of the mountain, which was very rare given how green the area was.

They cleared the next plateau and spotted the small poachers' camp. It appeared to be little more than a few shanty structures with old vehicles and no one visible on the ground. The one thing out of place was an enormous, multi-million dollar, white AgustaWestland helicopter resting idly in a nearby clearing. The copilot beckoned Caesare forward to the cockpit and pointed to the craft.

Caesare nodded and clapped him on the shoulder.

He made a "down" signal with his fingers and rushed back to the fuselage to prepare the drop line.

The pilots came in low, circling the camp to look for an ideal spot. Behind them, the left side door slid open and Caesare stepped forward, wearing the thick nylon harness with the rope snaked through the rappel ring. Over one shoulder hung his M4 assault rifle.

He clung to the large steel handles on either side of the door as the chopper came around the south side and began to slow.

The aircraft finally stopped circling and fell another ten feet into a hover. The powerful force from the overhead blades flattened a giant circle of tall grass beneath them. Seeing no one below, Caesare dropped his black bag out and gave Lucas and his friend a friendly salute.

But just as he turned back toward the door, it happened. Alves' two pilots burst from one of the structures carrying rifles. In a flash, they aimed at the chopper and opened fire.

Caesare jumped as bullets ricocheted off the thick armor around the door and the left side landing gear on which he was standing. He immediately fell back inside the protection of the fuselage when the pilots instinctively pitched hard away from the shooters.

"Get down! Get down!" Caesare yelled over the beating rotors. He lunged and grabbed the handle on the nearest seat while the airman next to him hit the floor. Lucas and his friend followed.

The chopper leaned hard and sped toward the edge of the plateau, where it disappeared.

In the cockpit, the pilots were yelling backward over their shoulders in Portuguese. Caesare didn't know what the words meant, but he understood the general meaning: *get the hell out!* He quickly pulled himself back up into a sitting position by the door and searched himself for injuries. Nothing. Just a rip in the side of his pants. He was lucky.

The pilots continued downhill, dropping below a nearby tree line before leveling out again. The airman slapped Caesare on the back just before the Navy SEAL gripped the line and pushed out into the open.

The rope unraveled quickly, causing Caesare to drop faster than normal. Too fast. He hit the ground hard with his boots at an angle, pitching out and slamming sideways into the dried dirt.

Caesare groaned and immediately dropped his gun. Wasting no time, he rolled onto his back and began unclasping the harness. Within seconds, he was out. He threw it away from him and waved up at the helicopter. The line instantly rose back into the air as the helicopter pitched once more, heading further downhill and disappearing again into the fog.

He was on his own. Caesare sat up, probed his rib cage, and winced when he pressed on his bottom rib. It was cracked. Lucky again.

He twisted around, looking through the trees and back up the hill. He got down low and waited for a few minutes, but didn't see anyone coming down. He quietly re-slung the M4. If those two were any good, they would be expecting him to round the base of the hill and come up from behind. And if they were ready for that, then they might be ready for him to come straight up instead. Or better yet, from one of their flanks, where the terrain was easier.

As it turned out, neither lackey was very good. When Caesare came up and over the top of the hill behind them, neither of the men were watching. Instead, they were both turned and looking down the front of the slope where they had last seen the helicopter. One was trying to dial someone on a phone while the other glanced nervously back and forth between the slope and his partner. The first man began cursing at the large phone in his hand. They were the pilots all right.

Caesare came up behind them smoothly, with the carbine pressed tight against his cheek. By the time they heard him, he was right on top of them. The pair froze at the sound of Caesare's boots.

"How many?!" Caesare growled, in a low voice.

Both men peered at him without moving.

Caesare circled wide and stopped next to an old International pickup truck. Its fenders and doors had more rust than paint. He kept the barrel on the pilots and glanced around the camp. "How many others?"

Still no response. *Christ.* "Speak ENGLISH?"

The two men, both dressed in light colored khakis, looked at each other. When they turned back, one of them raised a hand and held his index finger and thumb just an inch apart.

"A little. *Great,*" Caesare mumbled sarcastically. "How many?" he asked again, sweeping his arm across the camp.

The pilot Caesare was talking to was shorter than the other, with hair barely an inch long. "No," he said. He pointed back and forth between him and his partner as if to say *just us*.

Caesare motioned for them to get onto the ground,

and they complied without hesitation. Both lay face down while Caesare checked inside the three rundown structures. They were so poorly constructed that Caesare wondered if someone had run out of nails. They probably would have been better off with tents.

He examined the second vehicle, an old style U.S. Jeep which clearly had seen better days. It looked to have been out of commission for years.

With his ears listening for anything behind him, he approached the pilots again as they lay still on the ground. He stood to the side where they could clearly see the carbine pointed at their heads. "Where?!" he yelled.

The shorter pilot looked up with a questioning look.

"I said *where*?! Where did they go?!"

The pilot pivoted his head. He then tilted it and pointed up at the mountain.

Caesare followed his finger toward the smoke. He studied the situation while his gun remained on the pilots.

"Alves?" he asked and pointed the same way.

The man on the ground nodded.

"How long ago?" After more silence, Caesare yelled again and pointed at his watch. "HOW LONG?!"

The pilot displayed four fingers.

Caesare stepped forward and picked up the phone that was dropped when the pilots both lowered themselves to the ground.

*Four hours.*

One by one, he tied the men to the old Jeep with one at each end, using a nylon line from his bag. When he finally stood up, neither man said a word. Almost half

Caesare's age, they simply glared at him from their positions in the dirt.

"You know I should have killed you both."

Neither replied.

"Not even a thank you." Caesare shook his head. "I weep for the future."

He scanned the camp once more before running through the tall grass over to the AgustaWestland. He approached, pausing for a moment outside to admire the aircraft, and then reached up high and pulled the door open.

If he thought it was nice from the outside, he was stunned at the inside. "Good God," he thought to himself and examined the ornate interior. The walls were decorated in a combination of soft white and lightly colored maple wood. The white leather seats gave it a noticeably elegant touch. But his eyes quickly fell to the open area on the left side where the carpet was matted down, leaving square-shaped impressions. *Cages.*

Caesare immediately turned and entered the cockpit. The instrument panel was as modern as he had ever seen. He dropped his bag on the copilot seat and slid into the other. After a short pause, he was startled when the leather seat began to slide forward for him.

"You've got to be kidding." He held his hands up until the seat finished its positioning, then dropped one hand onto the stick and felt it out. After scanning the rest of the panel, he reached out and powered up the electrical system. Lights all around the cockpit instantly illuminated and two large screens in front of him flickered to life. He leaned forward and inspected the fuel gauges.

"Just enough fuel to make it back," he said aloud. A devilish grin began to spread across Caesare's face.

General Wei sat quietly in his darkened office. It was very early in the morning and he was the only one in the building. Still in his uniform, he sat waiting with hands resting on the expansive black, polished desktop.

In hindsight, he supposed it had been inevitable. There were a thousand variables that could have easily yielded a different outcome, but deep down he knew it would eventually come to this. He had seen his share of battle, often skirmishes obscured by the veil of political posturing, but warfare was the same no matter where it was and no matter which uniform you wore.

Wei was one of a few soldiers who had ever made it so high up the military ladder without any strong political or blood relationships. In truth, he was an anomaly more than anything else. Born and raised by humble means, he'd entered the Chinese Army when he was only sixteen and the country was in the throes of the greatest political shift in modern Chinese history. It was an overthrow of the old regime by a new one that, in the end, would be different in words only.

His skills as a leader were recognized early in his career by one of the new government's ideologists and guided him down a path of advancement that few would ever experience. But ironically, it was his skill of remaining politically neutral that helped Wei eventually become one of China's most powerful military leaders.

But he had no illusions as to where his fate now lay. Wei was one of China's only honest generals, perhaps *the* only one, which is why "the seven" selected him for this job. But when it was over, he would be too.

Wei jumped when his phone suddenly vibrated against the hard wood of the desk, illuminating the area around him in an eerie glow. Wei picked it up and looked at the screen. It was the message he had been waiting for: a message from Chao.

Wei read the text and put the phone down again. He sat for several minutes in the darkness. Deep inside, he had somehow hoped it wouldn't come to this. That there was still some way out. There wasn't.

There was a fleeting attempt at consolation, remembering an old proverb about the hardest decisions having to be made by the strongest men. It didn't help.

He picked up his desk phone and dialed a number. The other end was picked up immediately. Wei gave the order and gently returned the receiver to his cradle.

As he usually did, Wei thought of his late wife: the most beautiful of souls whom he had ever known. *What would she think of her husband now?*

# 55

ALISON DUNKED HER tea bag several times before laying it to the side and taking a tentative taste from her mug. Satisfied, she removed the pouch and set it gently on the edge of her saucer. She raised the cup with both hands and took a longer sip.

"So what's on your agenda today?" she asked.

Sitting across from her, Clay lowered his glass of

orange juice. "I've got to find Will and go over the new satellite data. See what else we can find out."

"In the lab?"

"Yes."

"I guess I'll see you there," Alison winked. "I've got an appointment with Commander Lawton."

Clay raised his eyebrows curiously. "Yeah?"

"Mmm hmm." She returned her mug and grabbed a fork, picking through her bowl of fruit. "She's interested in the work we're doing with IMIS. I told her I would give her a full briefing on it. She also has some interesting things to share on the marine biology front with some of the work they've been doing."

"That would be interesting. I'll do my best to eavesdrop."

Alison laughed. After a moment, her face became serious. "So, listen. This thing that you're working on with Commander Lawton and Mr. Borger, it's obviously classified. But we're not going to get thrown off the ship again, are we?"

Clay smiled. She was referring to what happened last year on Captain Emerson's Pathfinder, which required all of the civilian personnel to be unloaded in a hurry. "Well, hopefully not quite that fevered. But I believe we will need to get you ashore as soon as Chris and Lee are well enough."

"How long is that?"

"A few days probably."

Alison frowned. She began to speak but hesitated. "I wish...that we didn't have to leave. I kind of like being here with you."

Clay smiled again. "Kind of?"

She dropped her chin sarcastically. "You know what I mean."

He chuckled and then looked deeply into her eyes. "Well, I like you being here *a lot*."

Alison smiled nervously and reached up, fingering part of her long dark braid. She remembered how much John liked her hair braided. "This is the most time we've spent together. Of course, it's far from an ideal date."

Clay was about to speak when he noticed the ship's First Officer enter the small mess hall and look around. Upon spotting Clay, he swiftly crossed the room.

"Commander Clay, you're needed on the bridge." He glanced apologetically at Alison. "Immediately, sir."

Clay squeezed Alison's hand. "Sorry. I'll see you in the lab later." As he stood up, he heard a loud and unmistakable sound. It was the ship's giant anchor chain.

Once outside, both men ran toward the middle of the ship and up the nearest ladder. Another level up, they raced to the end of the catwalk where they yanked open the door and entered the bridge.

Clay approached Krogstad, who was standing at the helm and staring out the giant window through his binoculars.

"I've been looking for you," he said to Clay, dryly.

Clay followed his glare toward the shore. "What's happening? Are we raising anchor?"

"Affirmative." He handed the binoculars to Clay. "It appears our Chinese friends are preparing to leave."

Clay could see the tip of the Chinese corvette slowly appear beyond the far end of the Georgetown seawall. At the same time, he could hear the tempo of the pounding anchor chain speed up outside.

"Sir," the ship's Communication Officer looked at Krogstad, "I have Admiral Langford on the line."

"Good." Krogstad nodded at his pilot as he picked up the receiver. "Bring us around." He returned his gaze to the corvette as it continued sliding out into view. "Admiral Langford."

Langford had just returned to his office and was leaning over his desk phone with palms on either side. "Captain Krogstad, go ahead."

"Sir, the corvette is leaving port."

"Are you sure?"

Krogstad could now see the faint image of the ship gradually emerging. "Pretty sure."

"Damn it!" Langford turned his head in irritation. The White House was still ignoring his request to send reinforcements at the risk of inciting something with the Chinese. And now it was too late! He had only been authorized to send non-combat vessels, which may as well have been nothing at all. "How fast?" he asked.

"Slow. Maybe eight to ten knots."

*God damn it!* "Okay, then block them in."

Krogstad raised his eyebrows. "Block them in?"

"You heard me, Captain. I said block them in!"

"Admiral, we're not close enough."

Langford gritted his teeth, frustrated. Christ, was he the only one who understood what was at stake?! "Listen to me, Krogstad. I don't care how you do it, but you are NOT to allow that ship to leave!"

"Admiral, may I remind you that this is a science vessel? We have no weapons."

"I don't care if you're in a rowboat, Captain!" Langford bellowed. "Do whatever you have to do! *Ram them if you have to!*"

Langford hung up and immediately selected another line. When it was picked up, his voice had reached an angry pitch. "Get me the White House!"

Standing on the bridge, Krogstad peered silently at Clay and his First Officer, who were both still next to him. With a simple "aye," he heard the line disconnect and returned the receiver to its cradle. He blinked, thinking, and finally looked at his pilot. "Full speed."

Krogstad turned to his first officer. "Get everyone on this boat to the stern of the ship, immediately."

The First Officer and Clay looked at each other. "Sir?"

* * *

Two decks below, Kelly caught up just as Alison had left the mess hall and was headed for the science lab. Kelly had just come from sick bay. It was determined that Chris had sustained a concussion, so the doctor wanted to keep them both resting for another twenty-four hours. Kelly left, promising to inquire about a cabin for them to use.

She walked next to Alison, watching her. "So, I take it you're not in a big hurry to leave."

"What do you mean?"

"You're kidding, right? I can see it all over your face, Alison."

"Fine…I admit, it would be nice to spend a little more time with John."

"I don't blame you. He's so dreamy," she teased. "So, have you talked to him? About the…*exclusivity*?"

Alison eyed her as she stepped aside to let a female officer pass. "Someone is sure full of questions." She continued walking but suddenly noticed she was alone. She turned around to find Kelly standing still, looking at her with folded arms. Alison rolled her eyes. "Okay, no. I haven't. It's not exactly the best time and place."

"Ali, there's no time like the present."

Alison really wished she would stop saying that.

"Besides," Kelly joined her again, "for all you know, he may just be about to ask you the same thing."

They continued down the catwalk in silence, which was interrupted when they reached the door of the science lab. Alison yanked her hand back when Borger suddenly burst out through its door.

His eyes grew wide at seeing Alison. He searched past them with a look of urgency and instinctively grabbed her arm. "Alison, do you know where Clay is?!"

"Um, yeah. He just went up to the bridge."

"Thanks." Borger pushed his large frame past them and ran as fast as he could to the stairs, following the same path Clay had taken. However, unlike Clay, Borger was well out of breath by the time he stepped into the wheelhouse, just as Captain Krogstad's first officer was coming out.

"Clay!" he blurted. "We got a problem!"

Clay raised the binoculars again. "We can see that, Will."

"What?"

Krogstad gave Borger a hard stare. "Son, you need to get off my bridge."

Borger wasn't listening. "Oh geez," he said, looking out the window with Clay. "Is it leaving?!"

"Mr. Borger!" Krogstad raised his voice.

Clay suddenly turned to Borger. "Wait a minute, what problem were *you* talking about?"

He looked nervously between Clay and Krogstad. "The mountain is on fire."

"What mountain?"

"THE mountain. The Chinese camp. The source of the plants! The whole area is on fire!"

"Since when?"

"Since this morning. And it's big!"

Clay and Krogstad looked at each other then spun back to the window. The corvette was still moving. And the Bowditch was accelerating quickly towards it.

"My God," Clay said, "they destroyed what they couldn't take!"

"That's not the worst part," Borger said. He lowered his voice so no one else on the bridge could hear him.

"What's the worst part?"

"The Forel is gone. The Russian sub…it's gone!"

"What do you mean gone?"

"Gone, as in not there anymore. The dock outside of Belem…it's empty."

Krogstad looked at Borger with a trace of worry. "When?"

"According to the satellite feed, it left last night."

"Do you have a bearing?"

Borger took a deep breath. "I can't be sure. It left in the middle of the night, when the ARGUS couldn't see it. But I think my servers picked up a glimmer of it this morning. I'm not positive though."

"And where did it *look* like it was headed?" asked Clay slowly.

Borger was almost afraid to say it. "Towards us."

"Jesus Christ!" Krogstad cursed under his breath. The Bowditch was now surging through the calm water at sixteen knots. The distant Chinese ship was growing larger.

"SIR!" called the sonar operator in front of them. He whipped around with his young eyes suddenly as big as saucers. "Sonar is picking up something in the water! I think it's a torpedo!"

"WHAT?!"

Everyone on the bridge turned and stared at the operator, who looked back at his screen. "Five thousand yards, sir, and closing! It's definitely a *fish*, Captain!"

"The Forel!" whispered Borger.

"That's not possible," said Clay. "The Forel was never combat capable!"

"Well, someone sure as hell forgot to tell them!" Krogstad barked. His gaze was trained on his sonar operator. "Speed?!"

"Eighty knots! Impact in approximately seven minutes!"

It was the worst possible thing Krogstad could face and he knew it. The Bowditch was not a combat boat, which meant they had no decoys. They had virtually nothing in the way of countermeasures.

Krogstad turned to his communications officer. "Try to jam it!" To the pilot, his next message could not have been clearer. "Now move this bucket of bolts!"

Their only chance lay in the ship's massive diesel engines; more specifically, how much they could extend the amount of time before impact. They couldn't outrun it, but every second they could add back to that clock was a second they could use. They might be able to jam the acoustical contact with the torpedo, but if it was "wire guided," Krogstad knew it wouldn't help.

Clay stared out the front window with a look of urgency. "Captain, the Oceanhawk!"

Krogstad looked below to the helicopter and the maintenance crew working on it. "Find the pilots!" he barked at Clay and then bolted through the outside door. From the catwalk, Krogstad leaned over the railing and yelled to the helicopter crew at the top of his lungs. "GET THAT CHOPPER IN THE AIR, RIGHT NOW!"

* * *

Richard Hines had served as Chief Engineer aboard the Bowditch for over nine years. Short, with a powerful chest and arms, he was no-nonsense. And he ran his crew with the same dogged efficiency as the oldest veterans.

Hines was standing below on the Quarterdeck when the phone blared behind him. A level below Hines, on the engine platform, the four enormous diesel engines were howling. They were now running at one hundred and five percent, a pace that could not be maintained for long. But what Hines heard when he pressed the receiver to his ear nearly straightened every strand of his short, dark curly hair.

Immediately, and without a word, he slammed the phone back down and grabbed the microphone for the engine room's loudspeakers. "TORPEDO IN THE WATER!"

* * *

The startled crew of the Oceanhawk helicopter looked up at the bridge to see the Captain screaming at them. But it wasn't until he repeated the command that they jumped into action.

If it weren't for Clay, Krogstad would have overlooked the Oceanhawk until it was too late. It was a version of the Sikorsky S-70 family, and a multi-mission helicopter. Each variant was designated a special and unique military function. The UH-60 Blackhawk was designed for land based warfare. The "Rescue Hawk" was a naval search and rescue chopper. But the Oceanhawk was a SeaHawk variant, and SeaHawks were *anti-submarine* aircraft!

The problem was the new design. With a folding tail section, it allowed the helicopters to be stored in a much tighter space, but it also meant it took longer to ready the aircraft for flight.

They had less than seven minutes. How much less Krogstad didn't know, especially with what he was about to do.

Even cutting out most of the pre-flight checklist, readying the tail section and firing up the twin engines would likely take more than seven minutes. But they had to try.

*Clay had better find those pilots.*

* * *

Clay was flying down the ladder to the main deck when the piercing siren sounded overhead. Loud enough to be heard throughout the entire ship, everyone instantly froze in their tracks when they heard it. The siren stopped almost as quickly as it started and was replaced by Krogstad's voice.

"All hands, move immediately to the stern of the ship! I repeat, move to the stern of the ship!" The next three words instantly struck fear into the hearts of the ship's officers and crew. "BRACE FOR IMPACT!"

The crew flew into action, ducking in and out of every room, pulling along their fellow sailors and anyone else they could find.

Clay pushed past the dozens of people who began filling the narrow catwalks, rushing toward the back of the ship. He spotted a senior officer and stopped him. "Where's the flight crew?!"

In the science lab, Commander Lawton was urging everyone out quickly through the doors. She pushed her hands against both Alison and Kelly's backs, following them out just behind Borger and two of her researchers. The catwalk outside was already filled with people, but Lawton kept pushing through the bottleneck.

* * *

Below deck, the ship's engineering team was the only group who remained where they were. Chief Hines had one hand holding the phone to his ear, talking to the Control Room. With the other, he grasped the microphone tightly, shouting orders loud enough to be heard even over his crew's double-layered ear protection.

This was no "buttercup" drill. This was the real thing. The giant SHT pumps were primed and ready, manned by two men on each side. Everyone else held their positions, with their infrared scopes dangling upon their chests.

* * *

"Four minutes, Captain!"

Krogstad's communications officer kept shaking his head. "We can't jam it, sir! It must be wire guided."

*Damn it!* He knew the chances of jamming were low, given the age of the technology. It left Krogstad with only one option. He gazed through the bridge's window again. He could clearly see the corvette now, much larger and beginning to turn out of Georgetown's port. It was turning toward them. *God damn it! Of all the ships to be on!*

He didn't have a choice now. The corvette was no longer a priority. The Bowditch and everyone aboard were all that mattered. And the Bowditch was no match for either a corvette or sub.

He had to give the order now, or there wouldn't be enough time. It meant they were going to *lose* most of the time left on their clock. But there was nothing else he could do.

"Full reverse men! Come about to port…HARD!"

* * *

Chief Hines got the message and yelled it out immediately. "ALL STATIONS, STAND FAST! FULL REVERSE! COME ABOUT LEFT TO PORT!"

It only took thirty seconds for the bus-sized engines to fully reverse. But it would take longer for a ship that size to come about. It began with the thunderous shuddering that vibrated through the entire hull, as the thick steel was put through tremendous strain. But begin to turn, it did.

The mighty engines began pulling the ship backward through the water towards the torpedo, which was still charging straight at their stern at almost eighty knots.

From the bridge, Captain Krogstad watched the horizon begin to spin in an agonizing crawl. The full city of Georgetown came into view. Second by second, he could gradually see the cliffs at the south end of town.

"Two minutes!"

Krogstad brought the microphone up to his mouth. "All hands, to the stern! NOW!"

He could hear the echo of his own voice through the outside speaker system. What he couldn't see, however, were the rotor blades of the Oceanhawk below, gathering speed. Nor did he see the two helicopter pilots sprinting across the deck toward the chopper.

Behind them, Clay turned and ran for the stern, his boots pounding the metal grating hard with every step. When he reached the back, he found the rear of the ship littered with crew and passengers. Everyone frantically searched for a secure place to squirm into or something solid to wrap their arms around.

He spotted Alison near the side and ran to her. Behind her stood Kelly, Chris, and Lee. All huddled together and held on tightly to a thick railing. Borger was nearby, holding onto the base of a mechanical crane. His eyes held a fearful look, but one that knew what was coming.

Clay wrapped his arms protectively around Alison, and she pressed herself into his chest. "Hold on," he hollered to everyone. "This is going to hurt!"

The ship continued its agonizing turn, with the bow finally beginning to swing into the path of the torpedo.

The best Krogstad could do was to keep everyone near the stern, where lifeboats would be easier to deploy, and to allow the front of the ship to take the full force of the impact.

At twenty seconds, Krogstad's voice came over the speakers one last time.

"BRACE..."

"FOR..."

"IMPACT!"

## 56

THE EXPLOSION WAS immense. The Bowditch's bow had not quite swung all the way around, resulting in a detonation along the front port side.

The force was so great that it pushed the front of the ship up almost five feet before the ascent stopped. The hull came crashing back down onto the surface, sending a wall of water out in both directions. And the concussion hit the Bowditch like a hammer, causing nearly everyone to lose their grip and fall forward against the hard metal deck. Arms flailed and hands searched desperately for a new anchor.

But it was the Oceanhawk that Krogstad watched from the wheelhouse; at least in the seconds before his own body hit the floor. Unfortunately, the rotors never reached their full speed to create enough lift.

Instead, the helicopter, along with its pilots and crew, was thrown into the air. They then smashed violently back down onto the steel deck. The entire aircraft pitched and rolled over, causing the whirling blades to strike the deck and break into long pieces of flying shrapnel. In an instant, orange flames appeared below the fuselage. An explosion completely engulfed the area in a black fireball. As the fireball curled inward under itself and rose into the air, the warped shape of the helicopter began to roll backward. In near slow motion, it continued rolling off, and over, the end of what was left of the bow. The remaining pieces of rotor were still turning, resembling a set of fumbling fingers reaching for help, as both the craft and its pilots disappeared over the edge and tumbled into the sea.

What no one could see yet was the port side bow, ripped open as though the Bowditch had been gutted. An enormous gaping hole, within a ring of twisted, tortured metal, provided a cavernous entry for the water to rush in. And rush in, it did. The hole extended down through the bottom of the Bowditch's hull, which caused the water to surge in from the underneath as well as the side.

With the loss of much of its underside support, the bow slumped hard, pitching the entire ship at a forward angle.

* * *

Chief Hines was screaming below deck. The overhead system had been knocked out, leaving only the direct radio to radio within their masks to communicate. And even that was barely loud enough to hear over the incoming flood of water.

Their forward port pump was gone, and the one against the starboard bow was damaged beyond repair.

It left them with only the two aft pumps. And that wasn't enough.

The forward section of the quarterdeck was also gone, crumpled below onto the engine platform as if it were tinfoil. But the fire was Hines' biggest problem.

Using his infrared scope, he was unable to locate anyone forward of him. Seeing through smoke was one thing, but the sheer heat radiating from the flames rendered the scope useless. Hines had no option but to search through the smoke and flame with his naked eyes.

He could hear the fire suppression system trying to suck the oxygen out as quickly as possible. Someone grabbed him from behind and Hines whirled around to see Daniel Harden, one of his second engineers.

"Pumps one and two are out!"

Hines nodded. He already knew that. The rush of water was simply too much. It was now just a matter of time.

"The hole's too big! Get everyone out!" yelled Hines. "I'm going to search forward!"

Harden nodded and disappeared into a shroud of smoke.

Hines called out over the radio. "Adams! Vierra! Velasquez! Who's there?!" He listened, hearing only Harden shouting to the remaining crew behind him. "Forward crew," Hines yelled again. "Who's there?!"

After a long silence, he heard something. It sounded like a cough. A moment later, a weak voice called back. "It's Velasquez. I'm down."

* * *

On the bridge, Krogstad and the other men climbed back into their seats and tried to assess the damage.

"Is there another fish in the water?!"

His sonar operator shook his head. "No, sir."

*Thank god.* "Get me a damage report!"

His communication's officer turned with the receiver still against his ear. "Forward pumps are out, sir. Fire forward of the quarterdeck. One engine is gone and two more offline. Two men missing." He paused then turned to the Captain with a grave expression. "The breach is too big, sir. The pumps can't handle it."

"How fast?"

"Too fast. Hines says the breach is even bigger than he thought. He estimates ten minutes before the lower decks are flooded."

Krogstad felt the plane of the ship begin to pitch further forward. He raised the back of his hand and absently wiped a trickle of blood from his forehead. "All right, head for Georgetown."

"Sir, even with only one engine, we will increase the flow of the water below deck by reversing course.

Krogstad rolled his eyes. "Then keep going backwards."

"Aye, aye."

Georgetown wasn't that far away, but with one engine and the ship filling rapidly, the boat was also getting heavier. And getting heavier fast. The more water they took on, the less the engine would be able to move them. And the more the engine moved them, the faster the water would fill.

"Can we make it six miles?"

The officer spoke into the mouthpiece and waited. He shook his head. "Hines says not a chance."

*Dammit.* Most ships took time to sink, sometimes even hours, but some took only minutes. And his was going to be one of them.

Krogstad stood thinking, desperately searching his brain for a way out. There wasn't one. His face took on a look of painful resignation. "Tell the Chief to get out."

* * *

Below deck, Hines was searching for Velasquez. The fire was almost out, thanks to the CO2, but the water was rising rapidly.

He grabbed what was left of the railing from the quarterdeck and leaned over, trying to see forward through the eerie red hue of the emergency lights.

He saw something.

The object was floating on top of the water among the debris but wasn't moving. The water's powerful surge caused the dark mass to swirl in a wide circle, bumping against the starboard hull and slowly circling back toward Hines.

It was just out of reach. Hines gripped the railing tighter, leaned out, and stretched as far as he could. The object bobbed closer, almost within range. It was Velasquez. And thankfully, he was on his back, but it was unclear whether he was still breathing. Hines reached out further, straining the length of his arms. Velasquez was closer now. Closer. Closer.

The surge suddenly shifted and Velasquez began to move away. Hines pawed at the water trying to draw him in. The further Velasquez moved, the more forcefully

Hines splashed at the water in front of him. For a split second, it seemed as though Hines was winning, but a wave of dread spread across his face when he realized he was wrong. The abrupt change wasn't because Velasquez was coming closer again; it was because the remaining deck that Hines was standing on was *moving*. In that moment, the deck bent outward just before the steel grating broke and Hines plunged into the black water.

* * *

"I lost contact with Hines, sir!"

"Are we still moving?"

"Yes, sir! But we're getting heavy and slowing. I don't know how much further we'll get."

Just minutes after the explosion, Krogstad reached the sickening realization that he was out of options. The world seemed to slow for a moment as Krogstad considered his next and last command. It was a command that no captain ever wanted to give. He headed for the door and yelled to his men.

"Kill the engine and sound the horn! Then get out!'

* * *

Below, on the rear of the main deck, Clay helped pull people to their feet and looked them over for serious injuries. The explosion had flattened everyone, but none was too bad. Some broken bones and a little blood but most could at least stand on their own. The medical staff was moving from person to person, examining them.

Krogstad had done it. He had managed to absorb as much of the torpedo's explosion as possible with minimal loss of life.

Clay abruptly felt his balance change as the ship began to roll to port. He grasped a nearby vertical support and wrapped an arm around Alison, while the others stumbled and bumped into each other. The ship was beginning to list.

Then he heard it. They all heard it. In fact, everyone within a twenty-mile radius heard it: the ship's deafening horn. The powerful sound resonated outward so deeply that it caused everyone's chest bones to vibrate. And it was so overwhelming that not a single sound could be heard over it.

The four long blasts were a signal that no one could miss, nor its message.

ABANDON SHIP.

## 57

AN EMERGENCY SITUATION aboard a ship filled with a trained military crew was far different than one filled with civilian tourists. The first instinct of the tourists was usually fear, followed by screaming. On a Navy boat, the first instinct was remembering the drill.

In less than fifteen seconds, the nearby crew had reached the tubular storage containers on each side of the stern. The seals were immediately broken and lids lifted up to reveal the inflatable life rafts packed inside. From the center of the stern deck, the Chief Mate was barking commands, watching each side remove and prepare to lower the rafts. The drill required the rafts be out in two minutes. The Bowditch crew would do it in a minute and a half.

Clay motioned to Commander Lawton and together they ushered Alison and her team to the front of the line. After the rafts were lowered over the side, the civilians were corralled toward the ladder and instructed to descend over the outside of the ship. Alison went last, but when she cleared the edge, she stopped and looked at Clay curiously. He hadn't moved.

"John?"

Clay moved to the ladder and lowered his voice. "Get in the raft, Alison. I'll be right behind you."

Her face grew anxious, and she stared at him for what seemed like a long moment. But the others climbing onto the ladder forced Alison's progress.

Clay smiled. "Don't worry."

Alison was nearly shoved down the ladder by the others scrambling past and Clay disappeared from view. It was only when she was out of sight that he turned and ran. He had to get to the science lab.

* * *

Clay had barely reached the ladder in the center of the first deck when he saw Captain Krogstad descending from above. The rest of his crew from the bridge followed closely behind him. Krogstad spotted Clay and promptly stepped aside when reaching the bottom, allowing the rest of his men to pass.

"Get those life rafts in the water!" Krogstad called after them. He looked at Clay. "Clay, come with me."

"Where to?"

"We've got men below deck."

Clay nodded in acknowledgement, immediately running after Krogstad. The plant would have to wait.

Together the two rushed down a nearby ladder to the second deck. The entire length of the walk was solid metal. The oversized doors they passed along the starboard side housed various maintenance equipment and tools. The largest was the ship's condenser, which created fresh water from vapor, and could still be heard running when Krogstad and Clay passed it. Much of the power was still on.

The next ladder led down to the quarterdeck and was already submerged in water. They slid down and splashed up to their waists.

The dark surging water was ominous. Debris from the destruction floated everywhere they looked. Much of it were chunks of plastic and other materials, but some were larger pieces of metal, twirling on end, with only the tip exposed above the water. The sheer power of the surge kept the objects eerily suspended far above the bottom.

"HINES!" called Krogstad. "HINES, WHERE ARE YOU?!"

Clay turned around and repeated the call back toward the stern. After a brief pause for listening, they both called out again, louder.

There was no sign of anyone. The only sound was the merciless seawater surging around them and rising quickly.

They continued calling, eyes straining through the dim light. Both men could feel the limits of the thin oxygen, supplied only by the openings from the decks above. They called again, searching more frantically as the cold water reached their chests.

Hines was gone.

The rising water and its increasing weight on the port side caused the ship to suddenly list again. Both men instantly steadied themselves with the ladder, but the listing did not stop. The ship continued to roll, passing thirty-five, then forty degrees.

Clay and Krogstad scrambled awkwardly back up the ladder to the second deck, trying to make their way up the catwalk. As they reached the next ladder, the momentum of the roll reached the critical forty-five degrees, and all hell broke loose.

Outside, water no longer constricted by the tall sides of the ship's hull rushed in over the edge of the top deck, down into the ports and stairwells. The incredible deluge swept with it everything from the deck that was not nailed down and, in some cases, even those that were.

# 58

CHAO WATCHED CALMLY from the deck of his ship as it passed within a kilometer of the Bowditch. He'd never seen a ship destroyed up close before. It was fascinating.

His dark eyes watched the devastation unfold as the Bowditch suddenly began to roll, tipping its port side down below the water line and allowing a massive curtain of water to cascade over the top. The destruction was fantastic.

He turned his eyes to the half dozen life rafts floating away from the stern. Several figures could be seen still trying to get off the ship in time but were instead swept away by the deluge. The rest were desperately trying to paddle away from the enormous stern that was turning upside down right in front of them.

There was no sympathy in Chao's gaze, just observational curiosity. He didn't care whether any of them lived or died. Death was a fact of life. Some just met their end sooner than others. Although deep down, Chao did feel a spark of gratification as the largest empire in the world was caught completely off guard again.

The front of the Bowditch was sinking faster now as the flow of seawater into its damaged bow continued to outpace the rest of the ship. The forward section of the main deck was already underwater, and it continued its slide beneath the heavy waves that would soon entomb it, forever.

* * *

The sudden roll of the Bowditch took everyone by surprise. Alison jumped to her feet and screamed, watching the sea wash over the side of the ship and envelope the last of the crewmembers still on its stern. "NO!"

Alison had been clinging to hopes that Clay and the Captain would still appear on deck and make it out in time, but any hope she had left was instantly washed away with the last of the crewmembers.

She stood in the raft, motionless, watching the last of the giant waves pour over the end of the stern. No. It wasn't possible. *It wasn't possible! Clay was still aboard!*

Alison's bottom lip began to tremble as Kelly stood

up behind her and wrapped her arms around Ali's shoulders. Tears began to well up. She felt the hands of Chris and Lee each slip into hers and squeeze gently.

Behind her, Borger watched, completely stunned. The moaning of the ship's steel hull and the roar of the receding water was all that could be heard. No sirens. No horns. No calls for help. Nothing.

An overwhelming sense of dread silenced everyone, as the reality of what had just happened settled over the survivors. It was a sickening feeling of death.

* * *

It took less than ten minutes for the last of the Bowditch's gray hull to slip silently beneath the waves. All that was left behind by the last bit of the stern was a gentle turbulence in the water.

In the distance, Borger watched Chao's corvette disappear to the south. The moment was punctuated by the sound of Alison weeping openly on Kelly's shoulder.

The survivors watched solemnly as dozens of small craft could be seen leaving Georgetown, heading for them. It was comforting but did nothing to ease the misery.

What did help came just a moment later: a loud sound behind them. Almost in unison, more than one hundred and twenty heads turned around and spotted the distant object. Alison had to wipe the tears from her eyes to see clearly. When she saw it, she knew exactly what it was.

On the horizon was the unmistakable white hull of a ship she had been on before.

It was the Bowditch's sister ship, *Pathfinder*, commanded by Captain Rudolph Emerson. The sound the survivors had heard was a long steady blast from the Pathfinder's horn. With engines roaring, Emerson and his crew were charging south as fast as they possibly could.

# 59

CAPTAIN EMERSON STOOD stoically inside the Pathfinder's bridge. They had been running hard all through the night and had received the Bowditch's final distress call just minutes earlier. Still, Emerson was stunned at what he saw: six life rafts, bobbing helplessly on the distant swells, surrounded by an ocean of debris. Nothing else.

The Bowditch was *gone*.

"All hands," he barked into his microphone. "I repeat: all hands, report to the main deck and prepare to receive passengers!"

He dropped the microphone to his side and with steely blue eyes took in the scene through the giant window as they slowly approached.

"Get me Admiral Langford."

* * *

Langford's head hung low with both hands on his desk. After a long pause, he collapsed into his chair. He hung up with Emerson and switched back to the other line. When he spoke again, his voice was very different than it had been just two minutes ago.

"Mr. President," Langford's tone was as heavy as his heart. "The Bowditch has been destroyed."

The call fell silent for several long seconds. When the President's voice spoke again, it was only one word.

"Survivors?"

Langford nodded. "Yes. But I don't know how many yet."

The White House had been wrong. They'd underestimated the lengths the Chinese would go to protect their discovery. Commander Lawton had said it was something countries would fight over, and she was right. Which meant the potential of this new plant was every bit as accurate as she claimed, maybe more. It wasn't a fluke, or a mistake, or anything else the President's cabinet had suggested. It was something so powerful that the Chinese had just started a *war*. And given how quickly they did it, he wondered to what lengths the second most powerful nation on earth was really willing to take it?

President Carr and everyone involved had prevented Langford from doing anything until it was too late, all in an effort to avoid conflict. And by doing so, they had incited something far worse.

The point was not lost on anyone on Langford's call. They had been wrong and those on the Bowditch had paid the ultimate price.

"Are you still there, Admiral?"

"I am."

"Good." The President's voice was clear and sharp. "I want you to listen carefully. As of this moment, I authorize you to send whatever forces you need."

Langford did not answer. He remained staring at the wall. He had ordered Krogstad to stop the Chinese corvette, even if it meant ramming it. *Christ, all of this was his fault.*

"Did you hear me, Admiral?"

Langford blinked out of his daze. "Yes."

"All right," said Carr. The President then addressed his Chief of Staff. "I want my entire security team on a call in fifteen minutes."

* * *

The rescue was swift and smooth. The Pathfinder's rear platform had a lower height due to the remote control rovers with which they frequently experimented. After relocating two large cranes on the platform, it served as the boarding point for the Bowditch's survivors.

As one person after another was pulled up to safety, the expressions of thanks were everywhere. Yet, when Alison finally climbed off the last raft, she displayed no such expression. Her look was one of complete devastation.

Emerson spotted her and pressed through the crowd that was growing quickly. "Where's Clay?"

The Captain's expression melted when Alison burst into tears. Behind her, a black and blue Chris Ramirez frowned at the Captain and shook his head slowly from side to side.

Emerson couldn't hide his disbelief. *Dear lord, we lost Clay!* He barely noticed when the rest of Alison's team approached and surrounded her. Emerson blinked several times, still stunned. Finally, he asked the second question. "And Captain Krogstad?" He was met with nothing but silence.

The muscles in Emerson's jaw clenched angrily. *If he still had a warship, he would have gone after that damn sub.* But he didn't. Both gradually and reluctantly, he accepted his primary objective: the safety of the survivors. And for better or worse, the submarine appeared to be gone.

Even though the Pathfinder was a little smaller than the Bowditch, its crew managed to accommodate everyone by clearing space in the infirmary and mess hall. It was tight, but within an hour, everyone had been checked out. Emerson's medical staff reported only a few more injuries.

However, the bodies of the Bowditch's crewmembers that drowned in the deluge were still being recovered, hefted aboard, and bagged. It was a painfully somber picture.

* * *

Alison and her team were sitting in a corner of the crowded mess hall as Will Borger came through the gray steel door, scanning the room. When he spotted them, he hurried through the crowd. His bright Hawaiian shirt stuck out like a beacon.

"Ms. Shaw."

Alison peered up at him through puffy red eyes but said nothing.

Borger stopped and abruptly considered what he was about to say. He chose his words carefully. "Someone wants to talk to you outside."

She lowered her head almost as if she hadn't heard him speak. "I'm not in the mood," she whispered.

Borger was hurting as much as they were. He'd worked with Clay for years and had the highest regard for him. He was an incredible officer. Clay was smart, resourceful, and always treated people with respect. Even more than that, he was an amazing friend.

Borger could see that Alison was devastated but he persisted. "Ms. Shaw. It's important."

Alison looked up again with irritation. But before she could reply, Borger cut her off.

"Trust me."

She rolled her eyes and looked at the others, then rose slowly. Frankly, she didn't care if it was the *President* outside. With a silent huff, she followed Borger back through the throngs of people. Kelly, Chris, and Lee followed in single file behind her.

Brushing past people as she pushed her way through felt surreal. Everyone Alison passed was talking in low voices about the Bowditch or Captain Krogstad. But she didn't hear anyone talking about Clay. Most of them probably hadn't even noticed him onboard.

Where the crowd became too thick, Borger reached back and gently guided her at the elbow. He leaned forward and forced their way through, seemingly in a hurry.

Once outside, Alison stopped and looked around. "What?"

"This way." He led them all up along the port side of the ship until they were within twenty feet of the bow, where he turned back and addressed them. "Captain Emerson was just about to give the order to head for Georgetown when we saw them."

"Saw who?"

Borger grinned and nodded over the side of the ship. When the group of four spread out and peered over, they were all shocked to see Dirk and Sally in the waves below, staring up.

Alison's eyes widened and she gasped. "Sally! Dirk!"

Both dolphins kept their heads above water and spoke back with a series of whistles and clicks.

As excited as Alison was to see them, a look of disappointment instantly replaced her momentary joy. She hadn't thought about their Prowler boat until now. She scanned the horizon but found nothing. It must have sunk as well. After all, it was still tied to the Bowditch at the time of the attack.

"The servers," she said.

Lee knew what she was thinking the minute she looked out at the water. "The servers were on the Prowler. So was the vest. There's no way to talk to them."

Defeated, Alison watched silently as the dolphins continued speaking.

Chris, who hadn't said anything, watched them too, curiously. After about fifteen seconds of listening, he turned to her. "Ali, are you noticing anything with Dirk and Sally?"

She turned to him listlessly. "I don't know. What?"

Chris went back to watching them. "Don't they seem a little excited to you?"

"I guess so."

"No, I mean *unusually* excited."

"Maybe they're hungry."

Chris' eyes narrowed on her and he bumped her in the shoulder intently. "I'm serious. Look at them."

Trying to concentrate, Alison watched both dolphins. She couldn't understand them without the IMIS system, but she had grown familiar with some of their sounds. Her brow furrowed as she listened closely.

Dirk suddenly disappeared underwater, but Sally continued talking just as quickly. Something wasn't right.

Lee noticed the exchanges between Ali and Chris. "What is it?"

"They're trying to talk to us."

"No kidding."

Chris was still looking down at the water. "I think they're trying to tell Alison something."

"But we don't have the servers."

Borger cocked his balding head and ponytail. "What kind of servers do you need?"

"It's not just the hardware," Lee replied. "It's the data. Without that, we can't do any local translations."

Borger thought a minute. "Do you have copies of the data?"

"Of course, but it is back at the lab, on IMIS. The production system."

"Do you ever connect remotely?" asked Borger. "Like with a tunnel?'

"All the time. But the amount of data we're talking about would take forever to copy remotely. Especially out here on a boat. If we tried to copy it over satellite, we'd be retired long before it finished, and by then we wouldn't remember why we needed it."

Borger grinned at the joke. "Well, that may be true over commercial satellite networks. But the military satellites are lower in orbit, and consequently, much faster."

"How much faster?"

"*A lot* faster."

"Well, I don't think it can do a hundred megabits. And that's pretty much what we'd need for a live feed from the main system." Lee almost turned away but noticed that Borger was still thinking.

After a moment, Borger leaned closer and lowered his voice. "I think I might be able to do it." He winked at Lee. "But you can't tell anyone."

* * *

It took less than thirty minutes for Borger to bundle the satellite channels into a single connection with enough throughput capacity. The easy part was then passing the signal through his laptop to an underwater speaker and microphone they'd borrowed from the Pathfinder's engineering crew. By establishing an encrypted tunnel into the lab back in Puerto Rico and with the higher speed of his satellite connection, no processing of data had to happen on Borger's laptop. Instead, the processing would all happen directly on the giant IMIS system itself.

The tradeoff was that Borger had secretly commandeered most of the satellite network's capacity, which meant a lot of other military users would be scratching their heads for a while, wondering why the system had slowed to a standstill. Borger was hoping they would be done by then.

Outside, Alison and Chris had managed to get Sally and Dirk to come around to the Pathfinder's stern with its lower deck. Sally was still speaking rapidly, and Dirk had returned after disappearing several times. He seemed…agitated.

Lee and Borger approached with Borger carrying his laptop. "Okay," Lee announced. "We're ready. This may be a little kludgy, but it should work. We'll need to talk through Mr. Borger's laptop. The translations are going to be slower too because of the satellite connection. So, we may need to be patient."

Alison watched Dirk suddenly disappear again. Each time it was for a longer duration. "Anything else?"

"Yes," replied Lee. "Speak slowly. And assume there's no voice recognition on our side. There's too much background noise out here."

Alison and Chris nodded at each other. Behind them, Captain Emerson quietly approached to observe.

Borger placed his laptop down carefully on one of the ship's large storage compartments. The faded metal stood nearly waist high and approximately eight feet from the edge. Lee stepped in next to him and looked up at Alison. "Ready to turn it on?"

Alison turned back to Sally, who was still talking excitedly less than ten feet further out. "Hit it."

Behind her, Lee activated the software and the familiar translation screen came up. The colored, dancing lines that represented IMIS' translation process with intersecting data points came up on the display. The computer's system log data appeared in a second pane. As soon as the application started running, the "Translating" button began flashing on the screen. IMIS was instantly taking in the sounds from Sally.

In their lab, most of the translations to and from the dolphins happened very fast, especially since much of their language had now been identified. But the new delay over the satellites meant it would take longer for IMIS to spit Sally's words back out into English.

Nevertheless, when the first translation of Sally's frantic words came back through the laptop's speakers, none of them was prepared for what they heard.

# 60

SOUNDS UNDER WATER. *Help need. Hurry.*

It took only seconds for Alison to understand what Sally was saying. "Oh my god!" she cried and whirled around to Lee and Borger, who were both staring intently at the screen.

"Does that mean what I think it does?" asked Borger.

Alison urgently pushed past both men and typed a response on the keyboard. "What do you hear, Sally?"

After a long pause, the translation came back from IMIS and was piped out over the underwater speakers. It took even longer to wait for Sally's response. *Hear sound below. Short short short long long long short short short. Many time.*

Borger's face became very serious. "That's SOS in Morse code!"

* * *

It was called a "Gumby" suit and the earliest version successfully used was in 1930, deep in the Atlantic. They were conceived and designed from a single need for sailors trapped in dangerous situations below deck: *survival.*

Colored bright orange and made from thick, closed cell-foam neoprene, Gumby suits sported a wide opening allowing them to be donned and zipped up in mere seconds. Their high collars sealed quickly over the mouth and nose, and an internal oxygen tank provided up to two hours of breathable air. And Gumby suits had long since become standard equipment for every Navy ship.

The rigid design was inflexible. And without a mask,

only a familiar blurriness was visible underwater. But the suits worked. Had they not been stored on the ship's second deck, neither Clay nor Krogstad would have survived the crushing wave of water that filled the ship when it came plunging down from above.

It was pure luck, as was the large underwater reef off the coast of Georgetown on which the wreckage of the Bowditch had landed, preventing it from descending into a much deeper abyss. But in spite of their initial good fortune, both Clay and Krogstad were now almost out of oxygen.

Movement was extremely limited within the suits, and they could barely see each other's blurry shapes under the water, against the ship's dimming emergency lights.

Clay couldn't communicate with Krogstad, so instead he concentrated on forcing himself past the body's natural panic reaction. He knew how quickly hyperventilating would use up his precious air and tried to remain calm as possible. But the raw emotion of fear was relentless. He repeatedly felt his body's survival instincts attempt to seize control, and each time he forced himself through it. He had to think. It was the only way to fight, so Clay floated motionless, going through the logistics. *How much air did he have? How fast was he breathing?*

He remembered equalizing the pressure in his ears three times on the way down, which meant his depth was probably between eighty and a hundred feet. And that meant his compressed air would not last long. Thankfully, he was in excellent shape, which gave his respiratory system a higher level of efficiency.

He had gingerly reached around in an effort to

find something, anything. His thick, gloved hand had brushed several small items before he found a pipe on the floor beneath him. It had been thrown free from one of the maintenance closets after being ripped open by the torpedo blast. With it, he proceeded to tap out the letters S…O…S on what he believed to be a wall close to the outside hull.

After almost an hour of tapping, Clay took another break and cracked open one of his eyes. The red lights appeared to be fading overhead. How long would they stay on? Without them, he wouldn't be able to see anything at all.

But it wasn't the lights that were fading. It was his brain. The air in the suit was nearing depletion. Clay's brain was suffering from the inability of his lungs to draw in and supply him with enough oxygen. His thoughts were slowing and becoming more difficult to follow.

He opened his eyes wider and looked again for Krogstad, whose gray silhouette was no longer moving. He was older than Clay, which meant he most likely was drawing his breaths faster. Clay reached out with his foot and bumped the captain. There was no reaction from Krogstad. He simply floated silently a few feet away.

Clay's body shuddered for a second time. He could feel the beads of sweat forming on his skin. His renewed banging of the pipe against the inside hull was now beginning to slow, until it finally stopped altogether. His eyelids began to close on him and the pipe fell from his grasp.

It was then that Clay could see. He could see Alison's beautiful face looking at him, saddened. A wave of remorse washed over him. Remorse of what his death would do to her. She didn't need any more grieving in her life. Alison's image was replaced by his parents. They were standing together, young, before the divorce, and beaming at him with proud smiles. The feeling of remorse faded and was replaced by something warmer, something *comforting*. They were waiting for him and ready to welcome him into their eternal arms.

As his remaining air faded, Clay's last lucid thought was a pleasant one: the image of a dolphin. He would always remember how happy they looked with their curved mouth and perpetual smile.

* * *

It took Dirk four tries to navigate through the labyrinth of mangled ship and find where the sound was coming from. Then just as he did, the banging abruptly ended.

There were two of them, surrounded in strange shapes that resembled large crabs. And neither was moving. Dirk knew that when humans became still in the water, it was very bad. He quickly latched his teeth onto the nearest of the two figures and pulled him backward. He then circled around, pressed his nose against the limp body inside, and pushed it forward. Together they moved through the maze, over giant shards of twisted metal and missing decks, and through the fields of floating debris.

* * *

Jim Lightfoot was Captain Emerson's go-to guy for water dives. Lightfoot was part of the research team, and at six foot three he was young and strong. More importantly, he had been a championship swimmer in a former life.

Dressed in nothing but a pair of blue swim trunks, Lightfoot hurtled onto the bench seat on the ship's stern while several crewmen frantically added his gear. Two men slipped fins on his feet while two more lifted the heavy tanks onto his back. He quickly tested his regulator and nodded, then pulled the mask down over his tan face.

As he stood, Alison turned away from Borger's laptop and peered up at Lightfoot.

"Hold on to Sally. She'll take you!"

"Okay." Lightfoot nodded and returned the regulator back between his lips. Without hesitation, he took three exaggerated steps with his fins and plunged into the blue water.

After performing a short self-check, Lightfoot swam forward to where Sally was waiting. He wrapped his right hand around her large dorsal fin and held on tight as she kicked her powerful tail and dove. Together, they descended through the shimmering blue water into the darkness below.

Lightfoot kept his left hand on his nose and continually cleared his ears as Sally raced straight down. The stern of the sunken Bowditch quickly came into view, propped eerily on its side in the watery tomb. Sally continued along the underside of the hull and leveled them out near the mid-section. The light from above had now stopped reflecting any color but deep blue, creating strange shadows along the side of the ship as they passed.

When they neared the bow of the ship, Lightfoot saw the enormous hole extending far beneath and out of sight. No wonder it sank so fast.

As they neared the hole, Lightfoot saw what they

were looking for. A second dolphin emerged, dwarfed by the giant hole and pushing a human shape into the open. Lightfoot nearly lost his grip as Sally accelerated. With his right hand, he equalized his ears one last time and reached behind him. He found the second line and followed it to the end where he gripped the second regulator. He then brought it around in front of him and tested the button on top, producing a small explosion of bubbles. It was ready.

When Sally neared, Lightfoot let go of her fin and kicked forward with the momentum. He reached out and grabbed the thick Gumby suit to pull the figure closer to him. There was no movement at all.

Lightfoot immediately fingered the seal across the figure's face and glanced at the second regulator in this right hand. The switch would have to be very fast.

* * *

Everyone on the stern of the Pathfinder waited impatiently, barely breathing. Alison stood on the edge, gripping the rail with both hands and staring intently down into the water. She couldn't see anything. *"Please,"* she pleaded under her breath. *"Pleeease!"*

After a torturous silence, Lee broke the tension from his spot behind them. "I think they're coming up!"

Alison ran to the screen and stared at Sally's last message. *We come back.* She could barely stand it. She stepped back to the rail and tried to anticipate the steps. Lightfoot had to come up very slowly due to decompression. And if things were going well, he'd probably stop again about twenty feet down for the nitrogen to gas off. She glanced at her watch. They'd been down several minutes already, which meant the delay could either be good news, or very, very bad.

But if it were good, how on earth could anyone survive for that long underwater? A sudden, devastating thought occurred to her. What if the sound the dolphins heard was just some metal banging together? What if what Dirk was trying to bring up was simply someone's *remains*?

Kelly stepped in next to her and wrapped an arm around Ali's shoulders just as her knees began to weaken. "Easy, Ali," she whispered.

But Alison never heard her. The fear of what Dirk might *really* be bringing back to them had just taken her breath away.

* * *

When Lightfoot appeared, he came without warning. Most of his ascent had been directly beneath the Pathfinder, so when he reached the surface, the crew jumped. They eagerly pulled him aboard, along with the orange figure floating next to him.

They lifted the figure up and onto the metal deck of the stern just as the ship's doctor barged through.

"Move!" The doctor yelled and knelt down over the unconscious man.

Behind him, Alison pushed forward, trying to catch a glimpse of the man's face. It was obscured by both the crew crowding before her as well as the Gumby suit's oversized cap and face cover.

Doctor Khanna made several compressions against the person's chest and then leaned back. "Get him onto his side!"

The crewmembers complied and rolled the figure onto his left side, allowing a small stream of seawater to drain from his mouth and lungs. When it had stopped, they quickly rolled him back onto his back, where Khanna performed CPR. After a full minute, he heard something and leaned back onto his knees, expectantly.

Finally, with a violent convulsion, John Clay coughed.

# 61

CLAY'S EYES FLUTTERED open painfully under the bright sun, and he quickly rolled his head away. Several silhouettes loomed over him, seemingly all speaking at once. Inside, his mind was racing, trying to piece together the last clear memories he had.

He had been below deck…with Krogstad. They were searching for someone, a crewmember, when the ship moved. It moved quickly. They could hear the flood of water coming. The suits were nearby. Thank god.

His mind skipped forward. He was under the water then surfaced again. Sounds of the surging water were all around him, and he was breathing through the suit. But he had to slow down. He was going to hyperventilate.

Clay suddenly convulsed and clasped the arm of one of the silhouettes above his head. *The suit was out of air! He couldn't breathe!*

But he was breathing now. Clay drew in deeply. And that blinding glare was the sun. *He was alive.*

Clay was now fully aware and rolled his head back to

center. He bent his arm over his eyes to block the bright light. Finally, the silhouettes became faces. He recognized one of them as Khanna. Clay's memory scanned its data bank. Khanna was a doctor. But what was he doing here? He served on Emerson's ship. The Pathfinder. He blinked repeatedly and looked at the other faces.

There was only one other face that he recognized. And it was the only one he cared about at that moment: Alison.

She was peering over the shoulder of one of the crewmen with a desperate look on her face. When she saw Clay notice *her*, she tried to smile but lost it. Instead, she broke down and pushed through the others, falling onto her knees next to him.

Clay reached out and pulled her down onto his chest. He could hear her crying and wrapped his arms tightly around her. After a long moment, he pushed Alison up by the shoulders to look at her. Her eyes were filled.

A reassuring smile formed on Clay's handsome face. "Well, that was close."

Alison shook her head and covered her face with her hands. "For God's sake, stop doing that!"

Dr. Khanna breathed a little easier and leaned back further to give them some room.

Clay watched Khanna stand up. "Where's Krogstad?"

The doctor frowned. "They've gone back down for him."

Breathing deep, Clay covered one eye with the heel of his hand. *He was still down there.* Then the memory flashed back. *Krogstad had stopped moving long before Clay's air ran out.* He shook his head in sorrow.

"Where's Borger?" He searched the faces of the people still kneeling around him. None of them knew of whom Clay was referring. Finally, Alison wiped her tears away and rose up, scanning the area. She spotted him at the back of the crowd and waved him in closer.

Borger came around in front of Clay then twisted his head to match Clay's orientation. "Howdy, Clay."

"Will, what happened?"

Borger took a deep breath. "Uh, well, the Bowditch sunk. And it almost took you with it."

Clay nodded. "Thanks for finding me."

"Yeah, well, I wish I could say 'you're welcome.' But it wasn't us." Borger grinned at Alison.

"Dirk found you," she said, with a sniff.

"Dirk?"

"He heard you banging on the wall."

Clay furrowed his brow. He'd forgotten that part. "I'll be damned."

"I think you're going to owe him a boatload of fish for this one," Borger joked.

"Indeed." His expression became serious. "Who hit us, Will?"

"The torpedo? I don't know. But I agree with what you said earlier. The Forel was never designed for weapons. Unless it was done after the fact."

"That's what the brass is going to think."

"They probably already are."

Clay reached out to both Alison and Borger. "Help me up." Once on his feet, he kept his hands on their shoulders, steadying himself. He spotted Captain Emerson, who stepped in towards him.

Emerson shook his head, smiling. "You have nine

lives my friend." He put his hand out. "Now I'm wondering how many you have left."

Clay shook his outstretched hand. "Thanks for coming to the rescue."

"Any time." Emerson's face turned somber as he glanced over at his crew. They were still standing in anticipation at the edge of the ship, waiting for Krogstad. Or more likely, Krogstad's body. "I was supposed to call Langford," Emerson commented. "But maybe you should instead."

***

Langford picked up the call on the first ring. He was relieved to hear Clay's voice and immediately asked about Krogstad. His voice became quiet when he heard they were still waiting. He was a Navy man, and he knew what that meant.

Clay changed the subject. "Sir, what's our response?"

Langford knew he meant the U.S. *military* response. "We don't know yet. We're trying to figure that out. There are a lot of factors in play here."

"I'm not so sure it was the Russians, sir. It would have taken a massive design change on the Forel."

"Well, we know they've already modified some things on that sub. Now we need to find out how much. The CIA is on it. In the meantime, we're considering our options."

"Yes, sir. However, we appear to have another problem." Clay looked at Borger as he spoke. "Borger says there's a fire on top of our mountain, where the Chinese were sourcing whatever they took. A big fire."

"Damn it." Langford turned around, thinking. He

was standing quietly in the corner of the President's Situation Room. "How do you feel, Clay?"

"I feel fine," he lied.

"What do you need?"

Clay peered at Alison and Borger as he spoke. "Some transportation."

"Let me make some phone calls."

## 62

IT TOOK THEM hours to finally reach the top of the mountain. With the vehicle's powerful engine constantly roaring up the steep inclines, DeeAnn couldn't even hear herself think. Next to her, both Dulce and Dexter were still trapped in their cages and fearfully peered through the steel bars. DeeAnn was trying to comfort them, but the noise was too loud for her vest to translate anything. It was without a doubt the longest ride of her life.

The smoke from the fire was extremely heavy due to the jungle's damp air. Rather than rising, some of the brown layers descended outward and down the mountainside. And the thick smoke made their climb over the final hill even more shocking, when they finally saw the fire in curtains of wild dancing flames all around them. In some areas, it caused the dark smoke to glow a crimson red.

Once he had a full view, Alves' driver stopped and everyone's mouth fell open. The breadth of the destruction was immense.

Alves' hope of a miracle promptly evaporated, and at the same moment, Dexter went completely ballistic. He screamed at the top of his tiny lungs and pulled even harder against the bars of his cage. His desperate hands searched the outside lock and frantically tried to finger it open.

Dulce was visibly shaking while watching Dexter. A helpless feeling washed over DeeAnn as she realized that she couldn't help either primate. Both had devolved into full panic attacks, and no amount of training could help now.

A desperate Alves pushed open his door and jumped out onto the smoldering earth. He stood there in shock, watching the flames stretching up into the brown sky. *No! NO!*

From a distance, the black earth looked utterly lifeless. He could not even ascertain what had originally been on the ground before it was burned beyond all recognition. Alves abruptly pulled a white handkerchief from his pocket and placed it over his mouth to reduce his coughing.

Dexter was still screaming when Blanco's man pulled the cages out of the back of the vehicle and dropped them onto the ground. DeeAnn spotted the fur around the capuchin's miniature hands, soaked red with blood as he tried fiercely to move the bars. His dark pupils were wide with fear.

"Let them out!" DeeAnn screamed.

But Alves didn't hear her. He and the other men were taking in the sheer destruction before them with a sense of awe. For Alves, the scene caused a gut wrenching sense of mortality. His mind tried to understand how something like this was even possible, here in the mountains of the Amazon.

Then both Alves and Blanco spotted it at the same time. Less than fifty yards away, lying on top of the burnt ground were *boots*. They were protruding out from behind a large group of rocks. One of the dark boots was pointing up with the other twisted sideways against the ground. Both men hurried across the scorched ground with Alves moving surprisingly fast without his cane.

When they rounded the enormous rock, the entire body became visible on the ground. Dressed in a gray, partially burnt uniform, the man was twisted onto his side and wearing a giant, mechanical pack. On it, they could see two metal tanks with a long hose dangling to the ground. The dead man remained motionless with his right cheek against the ground, goggles pulled down over his face. Both Alves and Blanco stared at the lifeless body with confusion.

The soldier's face was frozen in a look of agony and part of the skin was blackened as well. Yet his characteristics were still clearly Chinese, with dark eyes gazing upward at the sky. The corpse's left arm was still under one of the straps, appearing as though the figure had been trying to get the pack off when he entered the eternal realm. Blanco circled around the body and pushed it over further with his boot. On the back of his uniform was a large patch of blood.

"He was shot from behind."

Alves recognized the flamethrower and shook his head, dumbfounded. He was still holding the handkerchief over his mouth. "Why? Why would they do this? If they got here first, why would they destroy it?"

Blanco coughed and covered his mouth with his sleeve. He scanned the area and spotted another body further away, also on the ground. "Maybe they didn't know what they were doing."

Alves followed Blanco's eyes to the second body. "Or they were used."

"Or both."

Alves stepped away before reaching down to pick up a scorched piece of vegetation off the ground. He wiggled his fingers and watched it break apart into pieces of ash and drift away.

Further down the slope, he could see a much larger section completely untouched by the fire. The soil looked lumpy, like it had been turned up. His eyes grew wide when he realized what it meant. Excavation!

Behind them, the sound of Dexter's screaming abruptly ceased. They both whirled around and Alves' face drained in a panic. "NOOO!" he screamed.

DeeAnn had managed to open the cage. Alves watched helplessly from a distance as Dexter bolted away from them and disappeared into a wisp of swirling brown smoke.

Alves was *livid!* With the area destroyed, the monkey's genome was his last and only hope. "Get him!" he yelled to one of Blanco's men who stood peering after the monkey, uncertain of what to do.

"GET HIM!"

The man gave a brief nod and ran after the monkey, disappearing into the smoke.

Alves stormed back up the small incline. DeeAnn, who had also let Dulce out of the second cage, stood defiantly, firmly grasping Dulce's hand

"You'll pay for that!" Alves growled. "You will PAY!" Out of breath, he stopped less than ten feet from her. The second of Blanco's men promptly stepped in from behind and seized DeeAnn by the back of the neck. She stumbled forward from the impact but managed to hold onto Dulce.

Alves' mouth curled into pure hatred and his face turned dark red. "Tell the gorilla to go find him!"

DeeAnn did not answer.

"I SAID, TELL THE GORILLA TO FIND HIM!"

DeeAnn continued staring. When she spoke, it was a single, unmistakable word. "No."

Alves' eyes looked as though they would pop from their sockets. He turned to Blanco. "Kill him! Kill Diaz! Now!"

"You were going to kill us anyway."

Standing next to Alves, Blanco's dark eyes jumped to DeeAnn and studied her. At the same time, a sinister smile crept across his rugged face, sending shivers down DeeAnn's spine. He was enjoying this.

Without a word, Blanco approached DeeAnn's side and replaced the other man's hand with his own iron grip on her neck. Dulce whimpered and darted behind DeeAnn's leg.

"Go get the phone," motioned Blanco. Without a word, his man nodded and headed back toward the vehicle behind them. It was slowly being enveloped by a small curtain of smoke.

"Jesus, what a stupid woman!" growled Alves. He glanced at Blanco and nodded his head. "Take it off."

Blanco immediately reached his thick arm over Dee-Ann's shoulder and down across her chest. With two quick motions, he tore it loose, allowing the vest to fall to the ground.

Alves stepped forward and picked it up. He then slid his arms through and tightened the Velcro straps.

"Then I'll tell her. I'm sure she'll want to save *your* life." He turned the vest toward Dulce, who was peering out from behind DeeAnn. "Dulce," Alves commanded in a stern voice. "Go find Dexter."

Dulce didn't move.

Alves looked down at the unit. Nothing came out of the speaker. He flipped the power button up and down and repeated.

Still nothing.

He glared at DeeAnn. "What did you do to it?!"

DeeAnn merely shook her head, silently.

"Tell me!" Alves yelled.

Her response was smart. "Your idiot driver should have slowed down. The vest is broken."

Alves' eyes narrowed. He checked the vest again and spoke one more time. Nothing.

"It's over," DeeAnn said. "Your crazy obsession for immortality is *over*."

To her surprise, Alves laughed. "Over? You think this is over? Nothing's over. The monkey's still out there, probably along with many more like him. And even if I can't find them, whatever *was* here hasn't just been destroyed. Some of it has been removed and taken somewhere." He displayed a delirious grin. "Which means I can find it. I have more resources than you can imagine. Billions of dollars and an army of people. And I'll spend every last dime finding what was taken from here. No, it's not over. It's just beginning!"

DeeAnn was staring in disbelief at Alves, when she felt Blanco's body weight subtly shift behind her. She gasped when his gun appeared over her shoulder.

Alves was still watching DeeAnn when he suddenly noticed the same thing. He looked at Blanco with a puzzled expression. The gun was pointed at *him*.

"What are you doing?"

Blanco was still squeezing DeeAnn's neck, yet leveled the barrel of his gun directly at Alves' chest. "Enough of your insanity."

Alves was thoroughly confused. His mind was having trouble processing what his eyes were seeing.

"You would," Blanco said accusingly. "You have more money than most people could ever imagine, and I believe that you *would* spend every last dime trying to escape your own fate. It's not bad enough that you've raped our country for your fortune, now you want to use your blood money to cheat death too, a fate many of your victims have already faced."

Alves' expression changed from confusion to concern.

"How many families could live a good life from your money?" Blanco continued. "Families like *mine*. Instead, you would spend every last bit trying to extend one life already lived like a king."

"What are you talking about?" Alves cried. "I pay you well. You know that!"

Blanco smiled. "Yes, and now you're about to pay me even better. It's time for someone else to assume the throne."

"You can't," Alves challenged. "It's all in my name. Killing me gets you nothing."

"It's not all in your name. Carolina has access to more than enough."

"Carolina?" Alves' eyes escalated to a look of panic. He was right. Carolina had enough signing authority. It wouldn't get Blanco all of it, but it would still make him rich. "She would never do it."

Blanco's smile was mocking. "You underestimate the loyalty of a woman in love. She already *has*."

"You can't do this."

Blanco shifted his head, unmercifully. "You said death could come from anywhere, no?"

It was the last sentence Alves ever heard. Before he could respond, Blanco pulled the trigger and fired a round straight into his chest, ripping a gaping hole through the right ventricle of Alves' heart. The old man was dead before he hit the ground.

DeeAnn screamed, then became frozen, stunned from both the explosion of the gun and the instantaneous death of Mateus Alves. She stared helplessly when Dulce screamed and abruptly bounded away down the mountainous slope.

Blanco marched forward with DeeAnn stumbling beside him. He stood over Alves and fired a second round into his chest. Then he turned and looked back toward the smoke. *Where were his men?* "Luis! Marco! Get out here!"

He yanked DeeAnn down. He slapped her hard across the face, causing her to collapse onto the ground in a daze. He used her shirt to wipe the gun clean then grabbed her right hand, wrapping it around the butt. Finally, he forced her fingers through the guard and over the trigger.

"Get out here, damn it!" Blanco yelled louder over his shoulder. DeeAnn blinked repeatedly, still trying to process what had happened and to think of what to do next.

Blanco looked up as a figure finally appeared out of the smoke. He opened his mouth to yell something else but stopped. The figure didn't look like either of his men. This one was muscular and wide and dressed entirely in black. Blanco paused, wondering whether his eyes and the smoke were simply deceiving him. As the figure approached, he strained to see who it was.

DeeAnn recognized him immediately, if not from his face then from his profile. The black hair and mustache were unmistakable. The instant relief she felt was overwhelming and DeeAnn began to cry.

Steve Caesare stopped and looked down, assessing. In his right hand was the outline of a large gun. He smiled at Blanco. "Luis and Marco aren't doing too well."

"Who are you?!" Blanco spat.

"I'm the Cavalry."

Blanco quickly grabbed the gun back out of DeeAnn's weak hand. He moved his left hand around to the front of her neck and pressed the gun into her cheek. "Take another step forward and she's dead."

Caesare calmly raised his gun and motioned over his shoulder. "You're going to have to go through me to get to that Jeep."

Blanco snarled and pressed his gun harder into DeeAnn's face. "I'll take her with me."

Caesare smiled again, condescendingly. "You're not taking her anywhere."

"No?" He got to his feet, pulling her up along with him. "Drop your gun, or I'll kill her now."

"What is this, a movie?" Caesare mocked. "I'm sensing you don't think very far ahead. If you kill her, I'll kill you. And believe me, you won't like the way I do it."

Blanco was growing nervous. He pulled the barrel away from DeeAnn and pointed it at Caesare. "Then you die."

"I'll take you with me." Caesare's eyes grew cold and hard. "That I promise you."

Blanco didn't answer. Instead, he glanced around feverously.

"If you kill her, you die. If you kill me, you die. So, the only way you make it out of here alive is to let her go."

"I…" Blanco heard a noise and cut himself off. Something was coming toward them. "What is that?"

Caesare listened then smiled. He recognized the faint pitch easily. "That's the sound of *prison*."

* * *

Less than a hundred feet away, Dulce remained hidden behind a boulder. She peered carefully around the side of the rock, keeping her eyes on the embankment above. Were the bad men coming? She didn't know what to do.

She watched the wisps of smoke glide through the air, as she listened and waited. The crying had stopped, but the bad men had her mommy. Then something else. Another voice. A deeper voice. Dulce's eyes opened excitedly. It was a voice she recognized.

When she heard it again, Dulce jumped out from behind the rock and scurried back up the grassy embankment. When she reached the top, she continued straight through the smoke at Caesare. *He here! He here!*

* * *

Caesare was staring intently at Blanco, waiting for an opportunity, when he noticed something come bounding up the hill. He kept his gun pointed at Blanco and glanced to the side. *It was Dulce!* His heart softened momentarily until he realized that she was headed for him at full speed. He put out his palm, "DULCE, NO!"

She didn't stop. Scared out of her wits, she ran for one of the few people she knew could keep her safe.

"NO!" was all Caesare got out before Dulce closed the distance and leapt for him, diving into his arms and knocking him backward.

Caesare had been waiting for an opportunity, but so had Blanco. As soon as the gorilla hit Caesare, Blanco fired.

# 63

CAESARE STUMBLED BACK again as the bullet tore through his right side and exited his lower back. Blanco aimed again but didn't fire. Rather, he froze as the faint sound he had heard moments ago quickly became a roar, and a helicopter suddenly thundered over their heads.

Caesare collapsed onto one knee but still managed to get a shot off, striking Blanco in his exposed shoulder.

Blanco yelled and threw DeeAnn to the ground. He

sprinted away at an angle and fired twice more for cover. Neither bullet found their mark, but it was all he needed to make it to the protection of another patch of smoke floating idly past. In an instant, Blanco was gone.

The moment he was hit, Caesare felt Dulce go limp in his arms. She tried to scream but couldn't. The bullet had gone through her small body before hitting him. He kept her in his arms and rolled her gently onto her back. Her eyes softly staring at him, Dulce tried to talk but nothing came out. The bullet had gone right through her lungs. Her hands tried to grip Caesare but couldn't. Instead, she fell backward in his arms and cried her final tears.

* * *

John Clay made a tight circle and landed the small helicopter as quickly as he could. With a hard thump onto the ground, he powered it down and kicked his door open before jumping out. From the second seat, Alison opened her own door and climbed down followed by Will Borger. Even with the air obscured, they knew exactly where the others were…by following the sound of DeeAnn's screaming.

When they came into view, Caesare was sitting on the ground, propped up against a large rock, trying to press his hands against both sides of his wound. DeeAnn stood next to him, frantically hugging Dulce and sobbing. Unaware of the others running toward them across the charred field, DeeAnn knelt down and laid Dulce on the dirt. She quickly lifted her tiny chin and blew into her mouth. She then locked her fingers together and began pumping Dulce's chest.

Caesare's red eyes looked up at Clay as he approached, then fell back down to Dulce. "Help her, John!" he said, with gritted teeth.

Clay started to kneel but suddenly stopped. "Where's my bag?!"

Caesare blinked, thinking. "Back there, about thirty yards."

Bolting past Caesare, Clay ran up the short incline. He spotted the bag on the ground, close to where a vehicle had been parked, judging by the tread marks. He sprinted over and ripped the bag open. When he found the small pocket inside, he pulled out what he was looking for and came back running.

When he returned, Alison was on the ground, next to DeeAnn, blowing air through Dulce's wide lips while DeeAnn kept pumping. It wasn't working.

Clay stopped before them and locked eyes with Caesare, who was staring curiously back at him. He opened his hand and studied the square, silver cube in his palm. A year ago, the device had changed history in the blink of an eye.

Clay knelt to the ground at Caesare's feet, watching his labored breathing. He looked at him one more time before turning to Dulce. Then Clay pressed the cube against her soft, furry chest.

Nothing happened.

He pressed it firmly against Dulce's body. "Come on. Come on!"

DeeAnn and Alison paused and looked at the object. Beneath Clay's hand, Dulce's body merely sagged under the pressure. She was as still as a rag doll. After several attempts, Clay removed his hand and stood up, taking a step backwards.

Both women were looking at Clay, wondering what he was doing. Then it happened. A bright blue flash emanated from the silver cube and rippled outward over Dulce's small figure.

The elements inside the cube activated. With a bright flash, the cube's mysterious element created a powerful magnetic circle, which instantaneously began to fuse the deuterium core. The inside of the circle glowed bright blue at first. Then suddenly it turned black as all light was sucked out, and the portal reached out to connect through time and space.

Alison and DeeAnn, along with Borger standing behind them, all gaped in stunned silence as the gateway opened. Clay and Caesare had seen it before.

It took only seconds before a human figure appeared within the glowing portal, which had now stretched itself into the shape of an oval. The figure was shorter than average and peered out at the black ground in front of him with a puzzled expression.

He had a smooth bald head and deep blue eyes. He stepped out of the portal, looking surprisingly calm as his gaze found the women. He then followed their arms down to Dulce.

Palin looked up from the gorilla's small body and over to Clay, just as two more men came out of the portal behind him. "You're learning."

# 64

WHILE THE TWO other men examined Dulce, Palin turned to Caesare on the ground and examined him curiously. "You appear to get shot frequently."

Caesare tried to laugh but couldn't. Instead, he coughed up a small drop of bloody spittle.

A minute later, after quickly bandaging Dulce, one of Palin's men rose with the small gorilla in his arms and headed for the portal. The second man moved to Caesare and began examining his wound.

Palin remained still, observing, before his blue eyes turned to Clay. "Hello, John Clay."

Clay grinned. "Hello, Palin."

"We are pleased to see you again."

"So are we."

They both glanced back when Caesare groaned painfully. Palin's medic was pressing a thin silver patch against his lower abdomen with another to his back. Clay quickly stepped forward to help as the medic began to pull Caesare up onto his feet.

Once up, the medic tucked his head under Caesare's arm for support. Without a word, he walked Caesare forward to the portal and stepped through, just as the first man carrying Dulce had done.

Palin clasped his hands behind his back and, with a hint of humor, raised an eyebrow at Alison, DeeAnn, and Borger. None of them had moved an inch. "Have you not informed your friends about our first meeting?"

"Oh, I have," Clay mused. "But there is nothing like seeing this first hand."

Palin nodded and kept his smirk. He stepped back to the portal before turning around to face Clay and the others again. He looked curiously at them. "Are you coming?"

# 65

THE TEMPERATURE CHANGE stepping into the portal was a shock. The hot, humid, and smoky air was instantly replaced by a cool and crisp atmosphere. In his mind, it triggered an old memory for Clay: like jumping from a hot tub into a cold swimming pool.

The place they followed Palin into was wide and clean. The lighting was also slightly dimmer, telling Clay that they were indoors. He judged the room to be roughly a hundred feet by another sixty wide. It appeared to be a perfectly cut rectangular area within lightly colored stone that resembled granite. While he scanned the walls, Clay instinctively turned back for Alison as she stepped timidly through. Behind her came a very startled DeeAnn and a fascinated Will Borger.

Grasping Alison's hand, Clay turned back around to Palin and the strange room. It was filled with people running back and forth. Few seemed to even notice them. They were speaking a different language. Caesare and Dulce were nowhere to be seen.

Not far away, another bright flash of light burst from

the air and a second portal opened. Two people, a man and a woman, dressed in identical light blue clothing, rushed past Clay and disappeared into its black center.

"Where are we?" Clay asked.

"This is our planet."

Clay's gaze followed several others who rushed past. "What is this place?"

Palin smiled, watching a mesmerized Borger study the entire room behind them. The stone walls towered over their heads, each with wide hallways at floor level. "It's a hospital."

"A hospital?"

Clay watched as the two who had run into the other portal came back out carrying a lifeless figure. A third worker instantly arrived, pushing a floating gurney onto which they lowered the figure carefully. They all then disappeared together down one of the hallways.

DeeAnn stepped forward. "Where's Dulce?"

Palin studied her for a moment. "Dulce is your gorilla?"

"Yes."

"The gorilla is being attended to. As is Mr. Caesare."

"Attended to? What does that mean?"

"I mean, being cared for."

DeeAnn's eyes became huge and she had to keep herself from leaping forward to grab him. "Wait, she's alive?!"

"Probably."

"But…she…"

Palin answered DeeAnn before she could finish. "Died? She may have. We'll know soon. Mr. Clay did activate the portal quickly which means your gorilla has a much better chance now." He turned back to Clay. "I'm quite certain Mr. Caesare will survive his wounds."

"So it *is* a life saving device."

"That is correct. A combination energy source and computer, designed to fuse in the event of a critically incapacitated host. You may remember having seen one before."

"Uh, yeah," Clay nearly chuckled. *How could he forget? It was Palin's device that had been activated.* Clay thought of something. "What did you mean back there when you said, 'you're learning?'"

"You used the device I gave you to save the gorilla, did you not?"

"Yes."

"And you knew it could be used only once."

"I suspected."

Palin's face softened. "Then I meant exactly what I spoke. You are learning, John Clay. You're learning that there is more to life than simply being at the top of the food chain."

On the far side of the room, Borger witnessed the appearance of a third portal, and more people hurrying toward it. "Does everyone have a cube?"

"Not everyone," Palin replied.

"How do they work? How much energy do they require?"

"The energy required is very large. Two-way tunnels can be activated from great distances with the help of these devices. However, a one-way tunnel is much more limited, both in distance and energy."

Alison gasped. "That's how you did it? That's how you saved him!"

Palin cocked his head. "Saved who?"

"Dirk. Our dolphin! When you were on Earth!"

"Correct," he nodded. "It was at great cost, but your facility was just within range for a one-way tunnel."

"What great cost?"

"These portals are very complex. They require large amounts of energy to establish a tunnel. A two-way tunnel, initiated from one of our portable energy sources, is more efficient and requires less energy. A one-way tunnel doesn't have an initiating endpoint. Instead, the process is far more difficult. Without a source, the one side must bore a hole, which requires an enormous amount of energy. Energy of which we have little left."

"But you still did it."

"We did it twice, Ms. Shaw," Palin corrected. "The first was pulling your dolphin out from under an explosive device. The second time was delivering him back to you. In hindsight, given how much energy we lost, it was not a wise decision."

"Then why did you do it?"

"Because we were grateful. Your dolphin saved us, and as I said, there is much more to life than being at the top of the food chain."

DeeAnn interrupted. "I'm sorry, but I need to see Dulce. I need to know if she is all right!"

Palin nodded. "Very well."

He led them into another hallway, cut from the same stone as the rest of the room. As they walked, Borger studied the low ceiling, which appeared lit, but he couldn't find any lights. It was almost as if the air itself was illuminated. They passed several doors and felt the refreshing wisps of dry, cool air against the perspiration on their skin. Palin slowed at the fifth door and pushed it quietly open. Inside was the medic that had carried Dulce from the smoke strewn jungle.

Dulce's still body lay on a smooth examination table with several strange devices hanging over her from above. The medic was moving a flat surface from one of the devices back and forth across her small furry body.

"What is that?"

"The cells in our body, just as in yours, are energy driven. And energy travels in frequencies. The device he is using radiates special frequencies that stimulate cellular activity and, in this case, repair."

"Is she alive?"

"The definition of life, or death, extends beyond what your world currently understands. Life within a body is comprised according to our cellular structure. And cells remain usable longer than you know." Palin turned from Dulce's body back to DeeAnn. "Death does not always come quite as swiftly as you may think."

"How much longer are cells usable?" Borger asked.

"Not long, but long enough that your world might see it as bringing someone back from death. In reality, the body had not fully died yet."

Palin turned to the medic who looked back and nodded. "It seems your gorilla will live."

DeeAnn inhaled, placing her hands over her open mouth. "Oh, thank God. Will she…remember?"

"Her cells will remember." Palin nodded. "Perhaps you would like to stay here while we check on Mr. Caesare."

"Yes, I would."

Moments later, Palin led the other three to another

nearby room where they found Caesare reclining on a similar table. His shirt was off with each of his wounds covered in clean patches. A different, smallish device was pulled in close to his abdomen, shining a bright light on one of the patches.

He smiled with only a trace of pain when they entered. "What took you so long?"

"We were filling out medical forms."

Caesare grimaced. "How's Dulce?"

"Palin says she's going to make it."

"Good." He grinned at Clay. "I guess you figured out that silver block after all."

"Actually, you did."

"What do you mean?"

"You were right, Steve. I wasn't supposed to figure it out. I realized it might simply be a life saving device. Which means it's not *supposed* to be activated manually. After all, once paired with a person, that person probably wouldn't be conscious when it was really needed."

"So, it would know what to do. All by itself."

Palin looked at them curiously. "So tell me, Mr. Clay, what were you doing in a burning jungle?"

Clay explained the story, describing the remarkable biological discovery in Guyana and the Chinese warship that absconded with it. He also explained the attack on the Bowditch that allowed the warship to flee, even at the risk of creating a major geopolitical event. If Palin was surprised at Clay's story, he didn't show it. Instead, he listened thoughtfully as Clay spoke. When he was finished, Palin shook his head.

"There is great danger in your discovery."

There was a brief silence as Clay and Caesare looked

at each other. An anxious Borger interrupted by extending his hand. "Mr. Palin, my name is Will Borger."

Palin smiled and took his hand. "We know who you are, Mr. Borger. We are grateful for the help you provided to Mr. Clay and Mr. Caesare. The pleasure is mine."

Caught a little off guard, Borger took a deep breath. "I...uh, have a lot of questions. Like how your portal works? What's the unknown element inside the silver cubes? And what are these cellular frequencies that you're using for healing? There's just so much-"

Palin raised his hand and stopped Borger. "Mr. Borger, we come from the same carbon based origins. Given the common patterns of carbon evolution, we are more similar than you know. We both have humanoid brains, and we both are creatures of tools and knowledge. And our thirst for knowledge is constant." He nodded to Clay. "Mr. Clay also had many questions the last time we spoke."

Clay frowned at Borger. "You're not going to like his answer, Will."

"And what was my answer, John Clay?"

"You said it was unwise for a race to gain knowledge too quickly."

"You remember well," Palin replied. "But do you *understand*?"

"I understand. But I'm not sure I agree."

Palin sighed. "My answer was not an attempt to be evasive or trite. It was not to keep you from achievement. It's a truth of being human. We long to know answers, even when we lack the capability to bear those answers. Knowledge is only as safe as our wisdom. My people are no different. Further along, perhaps, but not so different fundamentally. Consider advancements in your own history and within your own skills of ingenuity. Things like gunpowder, or fission, or chemical weapons. These discoveries were borne from advancement, yet they radically changed the course of your planet's history. They eventually became tools of unimaginable power."

"But they also brought about good things."

"That is true," Palin wore a knowing frown. "But which outweighs the other, the good or the bad? Our histories have many similarities. The circumstances are different, but the lessons are the same. It took a cataclysmic event and the near extinction of our people to finally rise above our differences. To understand that true wisdom is not about being right, it's about the unintended consequences of our decisions." He paused, watching Borger. "You know that portals are possible now, even practical. And you will one day discover the element we use to create them. But with them comes the ability to harness unimaginable levels of energy. How well do you believe your people would handle a true *leap* in knowledge, given their current use of fission and fusion devices? How well would they manage frequencies that can harm as well as heal? Mr. Borger, ingenuity is the ultimate gift of humankind. And conquest is the ultimate curse. They cannot be separated. Not yet. Not until you face the gravest threat to your planet's existence. Until you face mortality as a species, not as individual groups. Only then can you glimpse true wisdom."

The room fell silent, and Palin watched Will Borger lower his gaze to the floor before he continued. "We came to your planet to save ourselves. It was a journey fraught with problems and danger. We came for the only resource that could save us: water, a resource that you have in abundance beyond your own comprehension. Water is not rare in the universe, but a planet covered in so *much* water is exceptionally rare. And you don't have the wisdom yet to even appreciate what you have. But it will come. It will come because your water is highly visible. If we can see it, so can others. Your water makes your planet Earth a *beacon* to all who can see you."

Clay's eyes narrowed. "How many others?"

"More than you have dreamed. I pray that your race matures faster than ours did."

"Wait," Alison spoke up. "Isn't that even more reason to share your knowledge with us?"

"You are wiser than most, Alison Shaw. But wisdom on a global level takes a very long time. You and your team have achieved a giant step forward for your people. You have broken the barrier of communication that has kept you isolated for so very long. You have regained an ability you once had natively, but have since lost. Your breakthrough may prove to be the most important turning point for your race in understanding the world around you. An understanding that will reveal your world as more than just a planet of resources. Life is not simply a matter of breathing or thinking. Life is *connectedness* on a planetary scale."

Alison stared at Palin, shocked and suddenly dumbfounded. "Oh my gosh!"

Clay and the others turned to her. "What?"

"That's what it is," she murmured, almost to herself. "That's what it is! It was staring me right in the face this whole time."

"What are you talking about?"

"Don't you see?" She looked back and forth at them, excitedly. "That's what Sally was telling me! She said they were 'happy to talk' again! I never understood what she meant. I thought it was just a translation issue, but it wasn't. She knew! Sally and Dirk *knew* that we used to be able to communicate before! And now, with the IMIS system, we aren't communicating with dolphins for the first time, we're communicating with them AGAIN!"

From the table, Caesare's eyes opened wide. "Whoa!"

"It's true!" Alison cried. "And Dulce proved it." She grabbed Clay's arm. "I haven't told you about what we discovered about the errors in IMIS! Lee found out that they weren't errors at all. They were real translations happening beyond human speech. On a level that we don't understand, but Dulce does! And IMIS has picked up on it!" Alison whipped back to Palin. "That's what you're talking about!"

Palin smiled. "Because of you, Alison Shaw, your world will someday become one again. A lesson that my people wished we had learned much sooner."

## 66

THE FRONT WALL was floor-to-ceiling glass, looking out from within the orange-red stone. The room was larger, cut from the face of towering cliffs that traveled as far as they could see.

Clay stared outward through what he had assumed were giant, clear panes of glass, but after closer inspection, he realized there was no *glass*. The clear wall between them and the outside world was simply air. And beyond it, a small blue ocean stretched out before them.

"Is this all of it?" Clay asked.

"Yes. For now. The impact that devastated our planet was almost inconceivable. It killed most of our people and the majority of our planet's other inhabitants. Our two largest oceans were vaporized from a force great enough to send most of it out into space."

"You mean you'll never get it back?"

"We will in time. Most of our oceans are now in the form of ice crystals floating outside our atmosphere. With each year, as we pass through the clouds, the gravity of our planet attracts a little at a time, causing it to thaw and fall back to the surface. It's how water originally arrived on our planet, but it will take a great many years to regain it all. In the meantime, the water we now have, thanks to you, is enough to begin the reconstruction of our complex ecosystems. We have a long road ahead of us."

Clay started to reply but stopped when a woman walked into the room behind them. She was tall with blonde hair flowing far past her shoulders. He had met her once before.

Laana moved with a grace that made her appear to be gliding across the floor with her long blue dress trailing behind. She smiled kindly at the four of them as Palin nodded and stepped back.

"Welcome," she said, in a smooth voice. "And hello again, Mr. Clay."

"Laana," Clay nodded respectfully, still unsure what her title or position was.

Alison watched the beautiful woman look over them and was sure she noticed a twinkle in Laana's eyes upon studying her and Clay.

Laana examined Caesare's side which was now covered with bandages and clothing. "How are we feeling, Mr. Caesare?"

Caesare's looked surprised. "I'm well, thank you."

"We're surprised to see you again," she said, returning her eyes to Clay. "However, we are pleased with your decision."

"It didn't feel like much of a decision at the time."

"Which means it was the right one." She turned and looked out over the glistening water. A deep red from their large sun reflected off the surface. "I see Palin has been giving you a tour." She waved one of her arms outward. "This is our planet's last city. Protected deep within the rock of these great cliffs." Laana gazed out over the picturesque horizon. "Great battles were once fought here, many years ago. It has an important place in our history, though not as important as now. It will forever be sacred and known as the city that saved the last of our race. And the place where your water saved more than just a race, it saved an entire planet."

Laana turned back. "Thanks to you, we are growing again. Slowly, but growing."

"Palin told us you would get your water back eventually," Alison said.

"Yes, in time. Until then, we are learning patience on a scale we would never have imagined before." Laana's voice promptly took an upbeat tone as she studied one of the cliffs in the distance. "Not far from that spot is where we launched our ship to travel to your planet.

It took several years. Of course, Palin and I were much younger then. It was a very frightening time." She took a deep breath and exhaled. "We owe you so much."

"Eh..." Caesare grinned broadly. "We know you're good for it."

Laana looked at him curiously then laughed. "We are thankful for your courage and hope that someday we can repay it."

Alison was still smiling from Caesare's joke. "Well, let's hope that won't be necessary."

Laana nodded and peered past them. DeeAnn entered the room, escorted by a medic. Dulce lay unconscious in her arms, heavily bandaged.

"How is she?" Caesare asked, as DeeAnn approached.

"Good. She'll sleep for a few days, but she'll be okay."

More footsteps were heard as Will Borger entered the room. Next to him walked one of Palin's men, an engineer whom Palin had summoned. He had been working with Borger for the last hour to analyze a sample of soil Borger had collected immediately upon landing in the helicopter.

Borger was beaming. "She was right. Commander Lawton was right about the soil."

"What did you find out?" asked Clay.

"Actually, she was more right than she knew. The Commander suspected there could be something in the soil, which is why she asked me to get a sample from near the fire."

"What is it about the soil?"

Borger nodded. "It's not the soil itself. It's what is *in* the soil." He stared at the others, as if waiting for them to guess. When they didn't, he blurted out, "It's the water!"

"Water?"

"Yep. There's an enzyme in the water that neither of us has ever seen before. And it looks like that may be what is creating the special DNA mutations in the plants!"

Clay raised an eyebrow. "What kind of enzyme?"

"I'm not sure, but it looks synthetic. And it's glowing."

"Any idea where it's coming from?"

"Nope. But thanks to our friends," Borger said, reaching into his pocket and withdrawing a small instrument, "we now have something to use to find the source."

Clay looked at Palin. "I suppose that's our cue."

"It appears so," he replied. "Your portal won't remain open much longer anyway."

Laana and Palin escorted them back through several rooms to the main area where the portal was still shimmering. One by one, they thanked Laana and Palin and stepped back through the black oval.

Clay turned to leave last when Palin stopped him. "John Clay."

Clay stared back, awash in the bright blue outline of the portal. "Yes?"

Palin stepped forward. "I don't know what your search will reveal or what knowledge you may glean. But remember, great knowledge requires great wisdom. *Beware of the leap.*"

# 67

THE HUMIDITY AND smoke overwhelmed them immediately. Coupled with the heat, it felt as though they had walked back into a damp furnace. Some smoke had dissipated, allowing them to breathe a little easier. However, much of the mountainside was still obscured.

Clay coughed and looked at Borger. "Okay, Will, where to?"

Borger looked around. If it was the water they were after, there was only one logical direction: *uphill.* He peered over a slow moving bank of smoke to the top of the mountain. There was a small cliff where part of the peak had long since eroded and fallen away. Under the afternoon sun, it resembled a half dome with its one side sheared off.

Clay stopped them before they started up the embankment. "We need to get Dulce someplace where she can rest."

"Agreed," replied Caesare. "You three go ahead. I'll take them."

"Where are you going?"

Caesare coughed then smiled devilishly. "I have an expensive and rather comfortable helicopter they can stay in."

Clay nodded and began trudging up the rocky hill with Alison and Borger.

They stopped periodically for Borger to sink the instrument

into the soil and wait for a readout. As he suspected, the frequency of enzymes in the water decreased as they moved to either side of the incline but increased as they climbed higher. The source was above them.

The enzyme concentrations increased rapidly as they neared the top and the half dome-shaped wall. And once they reached the base of the cliff, the measurements went through the roof.

"Wow!" Borger shouted. He looked up at the sheer rock before him, rising almost eighty feet over his head. There was a thin streak of water running down the face. Clay and Alison watched as Borger stood up and placed the instrument against the trickling stream of water.

The display on the instrument went to zero. Borger tried again in another spot. Still nothing.

"That's weird. The enzyme count just disappeared."

Alison peeked over his shoulder. "How could it disappear? It's the same water."

Borger traced the stream down to the ground with his finger. "It *is* the same water." He raised the sensor up again and placed its metal spike against the water one more time. "What happened to it?"

"Maybe there's another stream."

They spread out and looked for more running water.

"Here's one."

Borger ran over to Alison and measured it in multiple spots. Nothing. They found two more streams but no enzymes.

"I don't understand." Borger stepped back and looked to the top of the rock wall.

Clay moved behind them, studying the rock face. It seemed unusually smooth, as did the rock on which they were standing. He followed the original streak of water all the way down, from the top of the wall to the bottom of the hard, gray speckled stone beneath their feet.

Then it hit him.

Clay moved in closer again and examined the bottom of the cliff. "It's not coming from the top," he said, looking at both of them. "It's coming from *inside* the rock."

The two ran over to the base of the rock, where Clay was watching the water trickle down over the tip of his black boot. Borger measured to the right and left, finding strong signals on both sides.

"You're right. There's gotta be something inside."

Clay took a small step back and studied the face again. He repeatedly looked to the right then back to the left. There was something very different about the face directly above them.

"I'm no expert, but does this section look different to you two?"

Alison and Borger stepped back with him and stared at it. "It looks flatter."

"Yeah, it does."

"Look at that." Clay pointed to a tiny indentation in the stone that ran straight up the face. There was another on the other side of the water. He stepped back further and examined the stone beneath their feet. "And does this rock look unusually *level* to you?"

"It does."

Clay walked forward again and touched the cliff face with his hand. "There's something on the other side of this."

# 68

THE STRIPS OF interior lights came on automatically, and everyone in the cabin instinctively looked up. The sun was nearly past the horizon and evening was setting in. With all the windows and vents closed, very little of the smoke got inside the immaculate cabin. The helicopter's auxiliary system powered everything except the air conditioning, making the inside more than comfortable if only a bit warm.

With his pack on the floor and leaning against the table, Borger focused intently on his laptop screen. From behind him, Clay looked on over his shoulder. In the back of the cabin, Alison and DeeAnn foraged through the small kitchen and found enough food for several meals. Or at least several salads.

"Man, this guy wasn't a health nut…he was a health freak."

"You have no idea." DeeAnn glanced out at Dulce, still lying comfortably on one of the soft leather seats next to a dozing Steve Caesare. The thought that Alves' body was laying somewhere outside gave her the creeps.

A few minutes later, the two women brought the food out and set it down, just on the other side of Borger's computer. On the screen, both men studied a still frame satellite image of the mountain. They were zoomed in on the cliff.

Borger tapped one of his keys and the image slowly rotated. "Not much to see from the air."

"No, there isn't." Clay tilted his head at the picture. "We can't see the cliff face."

"And there's nothing noticeable on the back side either."

Clay straightened back up and folded his arms. It had taken them the remainder of the afternoon to hike around the back slope of the mountain, and they had found nothing. Nor did using Borger's instrument help them find any trace of the synthetic enzyme. Whatever was coming out of that rock was coming out from within the cliff face.

He sighed and took a break, thanking Alison when she handed him a bowl of salad with a few pieces of salmon on top. He took a bite and leaned back onto the arm of one of the seats behind him, thinking. If this mysterious enzyme *was* the true source behind the giant plants and their special replicating abilities, then the Chinese had jumped the gun. They had something truly amazing, but it may not be the source they believed it to be. And if the plants were that valuable, he wondered what the enzyme itself was capable of.

* * *

Clay's eyes opened in the darkness to find Borger shaking him by the arm. The lights in the cabin were out, leaving only the glow of Borger's laptop to illuminate the white seats nearest the table.

"Clay!" Borger whispered. "You awake?"

He blinked his eyes and forced them open. "Yes. What is it?"

"Come here!"

Clay pushed himself quietly out of the chair, careful not to wake Alison who was reclining next to him. He followed Borger back to the computer and squinted at the bright screen. He was still displaying the aerial view of the mountain.

Borger sat down in front of him. "I think I found something. This is the picture we were looking at earlier, right?"

"Right."

Borger nodded. "Okay, do you see anything different?"

Clay squinted closer at the screen. "No."

"That's correct." Borger looked back over his shoulder amusedly and whispered. "Sorry, that was a trick question. Look at the picture again and tell me if you see any trees or plants around the cliff base."

"Nope."

"Exactly. Strange don't you think?"

"Yes. It is."

"See, I got to thinking…if whatever is in this water can make those plants grow like that, then why isn't anything growing closer to the rock face? You'd think everything would be a hundred feet tall, right?"

Clay looked curiously down at Borger. "Right. Maybe the terrain is too rocky."

"I thought about that." Borger's whispering was getting louder. "But how rocky would it need to be for something not to grow with *this* water?! I mean, geez, it would probably have to be molten lava or something." Borger turned back around to Clay. "But what if…nothing was *supposed* to grow there?!"

Clay eyed Borger and looked back to the screen. "You mean, as in, by design."

"Right. Remember how flat the base is, and those lines you saw going straight up the rock. On top of that, we have something coming out of the rock that we've never seen before. Now we have an area in front of it where nothing grows. Not even with this super water. Don't you think those are a lot of coincidences?"

"It's artificial." Clay finished Borger's thought.

"Exactly! And here's the biggest clue of all. I kept thinking, 'why isn't anything growing there? Why are there only rocks?'"

Clay suddenly grabbed Borger's shoulder. "The rocks!"

"The rocks!" Borger nodded. He zoomed the picture in and leaned back out of Clay's way. "Now look at the picture and ignore the top of the mountain and the cliff. Look just at the rocks, and bear in mind they look like rocks on the screen, but they're actually boulders."

Clay studied the screen for several seconds. "Are those…shapes?"

"It sure looks like it, doesn't it?" Borger began typing. "Now look what happens when I invert the color in the picture."

The picture color instantly switched. The areas that were dark now appeared in shades of white. And the light areas, including the rocks, appeared black.

Clay immediately shot a look at Borger. "Those are definitely shapes!"

"I think those giant boulders on the ground were 'arranged.'"

Clay remained quiet, studying the black shapes. They were hard to identify, but the curves and angles were unmistakable. The boulder groupings also appeared to be laid out in three separate places, together forming a perfect triangle near the base of the cliff.

"I think they might be hieroglyphs," Borger whispered.

"I've never seen hieroglyphs like that," commented a female voice.

Borger jumped in his seat, and both men spun around to see Alison standing behind them in the dark.

"Geez, Alison! You scared the crap out of me!"

He hadn't jumped, but Clay was grinning at her. "That was impressive."

Alison shrugged, playfully.

They turned back to Borger's glowing screen. "Do you know a lot about hieroglyphs?" Clay asked.

"Not really. I took some courses in college," she said quietly. "But I've never seen anything quite like those." She leaned in between the two men. "Hmm."

"What?"

"There may be some similarities to the Mayan stuff. But I can't be sure. It's been a long time."

"What about Egyptian hieroglyphs?"

Alison shook her head. "No. Those look very different. Egyptian's wrote in long lines of script. These are more like the picture blocks used in the Central Americas."

"Do you think they can be translated?"

Alison thought about the question and shook her head again. "I have no idea. Maybe if other drawings have been documented somewhere else, but that's a long shot. Even the Rosetta Stone, which contained detailed one-to-one translations, took years. Here, we only have three pictograms to go on. And that's not enough."

Borger slouched back in the chair, folding his arms in frustration.

"Or..."

Alison and Borger looked at Clay. "Or what?"

"Or we try something else." Clay turned and grinned at them. "It just so happens, I know a beautiful woman who has a hell of a computer system, designed specifically for translating languages."

## 69

THE GIANT PATHFINDER ship rocked gently over the ripples rolling across the western Caribbean. The white hulled ship was anchored less than a mile from Georgetown. Overhead, the dark sky was filled with bright stars from both the northern and southern hemispheres, complimented by a faint sliver of moon. Aside from the watch crew, there was virtually no movement or sound to be heard. It made the hand that shook Lee Kenwood awake even more startling.

Lee jumped in his bed and peered up into the darkness at the outline of Captain Emerson.

"Mr. Kenwood," he whispered, careful not to wake Chris Ramirez in a nearby bunk.

Lee rubbed his eyes and squinted. "Captain Emerson?"

"Come with me."

"Huh?"

"I need you to come with me, son. You have a phone call."

"For me?"

"Yes." His silhouette stood up straight. "Please hurry."

Lee scrambled out of his bunk and followed him outside in nothing but a pair of swim trunks. They passed through three different metal doors before emerging into the warm Caribbean air. Emerson stopped and turned to face Lee, handing him a phone.

He fumbled for a moment but managed to get it to his ear. "Hello?"

"Lee, it's Alison."

"Ali? Where are you? What time is it?"

"Never mind. Listen, I need to ask you something important about IMIS."

"What is it?"

"How hard would it be to translate one written language to another?"

Lee looked confused. "For IMIS? It would be a piece of cake."

"What about an old language? And I mean really old, as in ancient?"

"Uh, I don't know. I guess it would depend on what it was. You mean like Latin or something?"

"I mean hieroglyphs."

Lee raised his head, surprised. Captain Emerson stood next to him, still watching. "Hieroglyphs? You mean as in Egyptian?"

"More like Mayan."

Lee scratched the back of his scalp, thinking. "Yeah, I think we could. We'd have to feed in a lot of data and do some programming, but yeah, we could do it."

"How long would that take?"

"For the data? Not long. It would take me some time to program though. Then there's testing and debugging. Probably a few weeks."

"How about a few hours?"

"What?!"

"We need to do it in a few hours."

"Are you kidding?!"

On the other end of the phone, Alison glanced at Clay. They knew it was only a matter of time before one or more of the nearby countries responded to the fire. And according to Clay, Admiral Langford was trying to delay that, but his misdirection would only last so long. "No, Lee, I'm not kidding."

Lee exhaled and ran a hand through his messy hair. "I don't think we can make it, Ali. Even if I can do some quick and dirty programming, with no testing or debugging, we have no way to manually feed any existing data into IMIS. I wouldn't be able to do it fast enough from this ship."

"Okay," she replied grimly. "Hold on."

Alison covered the microphone and looked at Clay. "Lee thinks it's possible, but not without someone on the ground. Which, we don't have."

Clay and Borger frowned in unison.

"Oh, I believe we do." Caesare was awake and delicately eased his seat up from a reclining position. With a grin, he stood up and came into the light.

"You believe we do *what*?"

"I believe we have someone on the ground."

* * *

The single bed was small, even for him. But he didn't mind. Truth be told, he actually relished it, especially right now. He hadn't slept all night and he was beginning to lose feeling in his left arm, but Juan Diaz didn't care. Instead, he stared down lovingly at the sleeping face of his six-year-old sister.

Her little face, with olive skin and dark eyelashes, looked almost angelic as she breathed quietly beside him. It wasn't his idea, but she begged him to stay with her. Diaz had arrived home less than twelve hours ago and headed directly to his parents' house. Angelina was thrilled to see her big brother and immediately ran into his arms. If he didn't know better, he would have suspected she somehow knew just how close he had come to death in Brazil. After that, all he wanted to do was to see his family.

Diaz suddenly raised his head when he heard his cell phone ring in the living room. In one controlled fluid movement, he quickly slid off the side of Angelina's bed and loped lightly down the hall.

He held the phone up in the darkness and peered at the number. He didn't recognize it. With a low voice, he accepted the call. "Hello?"

"Juan! It's Alison!"

"Ali?"

"Juan, where are you?"

"I'm home. At my parents' house. Where are you?"

"You wouldn't believe me if I told you. But we have an emergency and we need your help!"

"Sure, Ali. Anything."

"Good. Listen carefully."

* * *

The 1970s style gray building was three stories high with an unusually long overhang above the main entrance. The double automatic doors were locked, and the only visible light was glowing from a few small fixtures left on throughout the night for maintenance purposes.

The University of Puerto Rico was founded in 1900 as the first higher education center on the island. It had since grown to become the best University system throughout the Caribbean. But at four in the morning, most of those University buildings were closed. The three-story Mayagüez Campus Library was no exception.

What was an exception was that for the first time in twenty-three years, Superintendent Jose Mignucci had been awoken in the middle of the night and by the governor of Puerto Rico himself. Fifteen minutes later, Mignucci stood in front of the library building, waiting patiently and wondering what the hell it was all about.

In the distance, a single pair of headlights turned onto the main street, which wound around the vast lawn and eventually passed the library on its way to the campus admissions building. The revving of the car's engine could be easily heard as it sped around the gradual curve and braked hard upon approach to the intersection. With a hard right turn, the small Toyota squealed around and up the driveway toward the library where it finally skidded to a stop.

Mignucci watched with curiosity as a man jumped from the driver's seat and sprinted up the long walkway toward him.

"Good morning." Mignucci greeted the man with a dose of sarcasm.

Juan Diaz waved briefly and bent over to catch his breath. "Morning!"

Mignucci calmly spun around and inserted his key into the lock. With a quick turn, the bolt within the steel frame dropped, allowing him to manually pull one side open. He held it open and waved Diaz in.

Juan spotted the library's directory computer and ran to it while Mignucci turned on all of the interior lights. Juan barely noticed when the entire floor lit up behind him. Instead, he scanned the screen, found the search option and typed in "archeology and hieroglyphs." The result listed dozens of books. He printed the list and took off again, this time up the wide carpeted stairs heading for the second floor.

Thirty-five minutes later, Diaz burst through the administration office of their team's research lab across town, struggling under an armful of heavy books. He crossed the room and dropped them onto the long wooden table next to their digital scanner. He quickly picked up the nearest book and flipped through the pages as if pretending to speed-read. He immediately stopped when he spotted the first page of pictograms, along with their translations.

Diaz turned it over and pressed the book down flat against the scanner's clear glass, then hit the large green "scan" button. After the machine saved the image into memory. Diaz picked the book up again and continued flipping through.

* * *

There were several open-source computer code algorithms commonly used for telling a computer how to distinguish between pictures and text on the same piece of paper. But none of them were working. Lee Kenwood growled in frustration, looking for the error in his code. After changing some syntax, he clicked the "compile" button on his screen and waited for the result. Another error.

*Damn it, what am I missing?* He pounded on the table and opened up his coding window again. Finding the line causing the problem, he made another change. Still no dice.

"Come on!" He slapped the metal desk next to him with his palm and the pain instantly reminded him why that was a bad idea. Lee rubbed it and leaned closer to his screen, examining the list of variables he had added. He made another change and saved it, then clicked "compile" again.

This time there were no errors.

Lee thrust a fist in the air. "Yes!" He quickly scanned the local data repository and found the hundreds of graphic files Juan had uploaded. Now done with the books, Juan had already begun adding website links to the list. All were resources that IMIS would use to find patterns and cross reference against one another and lastly against the satellite image that Will Borger had sent them.

Taking a deep breath and with fingers crossed, Lee uploaded his computer code into IMIS' server cluster and launched it.

* * *

Alison was still sitting in front of Borger's laptop three hours later, studying the rock shapes in the image. She glanced up when she heard rain begin to fall onto the roof of the helicopter's cabin. It started slow, quickly increasing until it became a veritable downpour. She moved to the window but couldn't see the men outside.

Clay, Caesare, and Borger were over a half mile away, surveying the ongoing fire as dawn broke over the distant mountains. Fortunately, the dampness of the jungle had finally won out over the raging flames. Now, rather than expanding, the ring of fire was quickly fizzling out. The rain was the final straw.

They were soaked by the time the three made it back to Alves' giant helicopter, and the sun had already risen whole into the morning sky. DeeAnn was still asleep with one hand wrapped tenderly around Dulce's curved back. The men passed by them quietly and surrounded the nearby table where Alison sat.

"How's the brushing up going?" Clay whispered.

"Okay." She leaned back and briefly rubbed her eyes. "I wish I could talk to one of my professors."

"Find anything out?"

"The shapes definitely share some characteristics with Mayan pictograms, maybe even Olmec. But there are only three symbols, which isn't much to go on. It would be nice if we knew how old they were." She pointed to one of the three. "This one is most similar to a Mayan bird. And this other one is clearly a circle with inward facing arrows, but I have no idea what it means. I haven't found anything even remotely similar. And the third shape is anyone's guess."

"So we don't know if it's Mayan or not."

Alison didn't answer.

"Ali?"

She looked up at them reluctantly and then exhaled. "It's hard to say. Without knowing their age..." She paused. "The Mayan's were amazing. They knew some things that are beyond current explanation. For example, they calculated the length of a day down to two one-thousandths of what our modern atomic clocks calculate it to be. And that was two thousand years ago. Their understanding of astronomy and mathematics were… well, inexplicable. The problem is…they didn't come this far south." She crossed her arms. With a look of frustration, she began to say something but stopped.

"What is it?"

"This is going to sound crazy, but if these shapes are old enough, they may not have been influenced by the Mayan or the Olmec languages at all. Instead, those languages may have been influenced by *this*."

"Whoa," said Caesare. "That's heavy."

The buzzing of Clay's phone interrupted them. He quickly fished it out of his pocket. He examined the number and handed it down at Alison. "It's Lee."

She accepted the call and held it to her ear. "Hi, Lee."

"Hey, Ali," he replied. "I think I have something for you. IMIS thinks it has translations for two of the symbols."

"Two?"

He shrugged. "It seems to think so. Are you ready?"

Alison glanced at the three men surrounding her. "Go ahead."

"IMIS believes the middle shape, the one that looks like a bird, means 'large' or 'strong.' The one below it, and more to the right, means 'weak.'"

Alison jotted it down. "Large and strong…and weak. Is that it? Nothing on the third one?"

"No, nothing on the circle."

"Any idea as to accuracy?"

"Fifty-four and fifty-eight percent. So not great."

Alison nodded. "Okay. Thanks, Lee. Keep us posted."

"Will do."

"Oh, and Lee," Alison stopped him before he hung up.

"Yeah?"

"Great work!"

He chuckled. "Thanks, Ali. We'll see."

She hung up and handed the phone back to Clay.

"So strong and weak?" said Borger.

"Yeah. But Lee said the accuracy is barely above fifty percent. I'm not sure how much better off we are."

"It's better than nothing."

She nodded in agreement and continued staring at the screen.

"Maybe there's some meaning in the triangle itself. Maybe it points to something." Borger reached over Alison's shoulder and zoomed out. "Then again, maybe not. Looks like three directions that just point away from the cliff."

Clay stood behind Alison, transfixed on the screen. "If we assume IMIS is wrong about the shapes, then we have nothing. So let's assume it's right. Which gives us what?"

"A triangle, three symbols, three possible points of direction, and two words; strong and weak."

"And," Alison thought out loud, "if the shapes have single word definitions, then we're not looking for a sentence. We're looking for some kind of relationship between all three."

"Maybe there's a mathematical significance to the number three."

"Prime number?"

"There are a lot of prime numbers. Why not two or five?"

Clay kept staring at the third shape on the screen. The circle with inward pointing arrows. *Strong and weak. Strong and weak. And a circle. Circle with something traveling inward. Traveling inward. Traveling inward. Coming inward in all directions. But what? And from where?*

Caesare thought about it tactically. "You said those were boulders, right?"

"Right."

"Big boulders?"

"Yes."

"That means if you were standing next to them and looking horizontally, you probably couldn't tell what they were."

"That's right," Borger said.

"So you could only see the shapes if you were at the top of the cliff, looking down. From high ground."

"That is true!"

"Or from the air," reminded Alison.

Suddenly Clay turned. "That's it!"

"What?"

"From the air! You can see these from the air, or the sky." He turned to Borger. "Or from space!"

"Right. But then what does the triangle mean?"

Clay's eyes lit up. He began searching for something then spotted a piece of paper sticking out of Borger's pack. He grabbed the paper and unfolded it, laying it on the table. "I need a pen."

"Here." Borger dug deeper into his bag and pulled one out.

Clay grabbed the pen and brushed the wrinkled paper out straight. He then scribbled the three symbols in the same formation: one to the left and the others to the right, with one above the other. He leaned on the table and looked at the others. "What if there is no triangle?" He paused. "What if it's not even three?!"

"I'm not following."

"Think about it. What are we missing?"

They looked at his paper. Alison saw it first. "The cliff. We're missing the cliff."

"Exactly." Clay reached down and scrawled the cliff to the right of the three symbols. "It's not a triangle," he said, connecting them all with straight lines. "It's a *square!*"

Borger nodded. "It's four points, not three."

"And four meanings." Clay wrote the words 'strong' and 'weak' under two of the symbols. The other two, the circle and the cliff, remained blank. "Two out of four. Strong and weak!"

Borger shook his head. "Okay. So what do the other two mean?"

"Four meanings, Will. Only viewable from space!" He waited. Finally, he laughed and slapped Borger on the back. "Remember your astrophysics, Will!"

It took three seconds before the light went on. "The Four Forces!"

Alison looked back and forth between them. "What? What?!"

Borger jumped back in front of his computer. "The Four Forces of Nature! In astrophysics, four primary forces control everything. A strong force, a weak force, gravity…and electromagnetism." He pointed to the third shape. It was the circle with four arrows pointing inward. "Gravity!"

"Which means the last one is electromagnetism," added Caesare.

"So what does that mean?" asked Alison. "The cliff is electromagnetism?"

"I'll tell you what it means," Clay said, leveling his gaze at Caesare. "It means that cliff face is not a wall. *It's a door!*"

## 70

DEEANN AWOKE TO the sound of something breaking. She checked Dulce, who was still out, and looked around frantically. The noise was coming from the rear of the cabin. Both Caesare and Clay were tearing a large cupboard apart.

Caesare cut the power to several power plugs and proceeded to kick holes along the bottom of an interior wall. He checked to make sure there was no charge before reaching in and yanking out the electrical wiring. When it got to the end, he gripped the wire tight and gave a giant pull, snapping the other end off inside the wall.

Behind him, Clay removed part of Alves' specially modified interior power system. He disconnected a set of thick cables from one of the cabin's many twelve-volt batteries. Clay then lifted it out from the bottom of the storage area.

Caesare stepped past him, his eyes fixated on the

long-necked sink faucet. He instantly wrapped his big hand around the top and jerked, snapping it off at the base.

Alison and Borger stood quietly, waiting at the door.

"What's going on?" DeeAnn asked.

"We're going back out," Caesare answered, brushing past her. "Take care of Dulce. We'll be right back."

She blinked, watching them file out of the door, one by one, into the pouring rain. "Be careful!"

* * *

Together, they hiked back uphill to the cliff. Its entire face was now covered in a sheen of water, cascading down from the heavy rainfall. They approached the area in the rock where the two subtle grooves, almost ten feet apart, traveled together straight up.

Clay dropped the battery and held out the metal faucet pipe from Caesare. In one hand, Caesare gripped the pipe and one end of the wire together. With straining muscles, he then wrapped the thick wire around the pipe one pass at a time. In a few minutes, he had coiled most of the wire around the pipe. He grabbed the dangling ends, shaping them into hooks. With that, Caesare reached down and picked up the large battery, hooking the wire ends to the positive and negative battery terminals.

Alison brushed several soaked strands of hair from her eyes. "What's that?"

Clay winked. "An electromagnet." He looked at Caesare who nodded, then held the coiled rod up and pressed it against the rock.

Nothing happened.

Clay moved the rod to another place against the rock. Still nothing. Section by section, he moved the magnet across the cliff face and touched it to the hard surface.

Clay and Caesare suddenly looked at each other when they heard a heavy "clunk." A moment later, the rock began to shake and loose pieces fell away from the vertical grooves above. With a low, deep rumble, the face began to push outward from between the grooves.

It continued sliding forward until a large black entrance appeared. All four stood together in the rain... speechless.

Alison shook her head. "This is definitely *not* Mayan."

Clay dropped the magnet and glanced over his shoulder. He carefully approached the dark entrance. When he was close enough, he took a single step inside and looked around.

"Whoa!"

## 71

THE OTHER THREE followed Clay in as a rush of stale air blew past, forced outside by the light breeze behind them. Inside, the room was large, reaching well above their heads. Its depth and width quickly disappeared into the darkness. But they barely noticed the room's size. It was the contents that stunned them, leaving their mouths agape.

The room was radiating a bright green glow. The color looked almost fluorescent. Yet the most startling of all…were the tubes: rows and rows of thick clear tubes, standing nearly ten feet high. Hundreds of tubes. And each was filled with what appeared to be a bright glowing green liquid.

Side by side, all four of them stood in awe, slowly scanning the room.

"Okay," Caesare murmured. "This is pretty much the most amazing thing I've ever seen."

"What in the world is this?" whispered Borger.

They stepped further inside, approaching the closest tube. Inside, they could see the glowing liquid, swirling around ever so gently.

Clay looked at the smooth stone floor, appearing green from the hue of the tubes. He brought his right boot forward and gently placed it onto the floor in front of him. He then raised it up again revealing a deep footprint beneath.

Alison peered down and did the same thing, creating a smaller print in the thick layer of dust. "This place," whispered Alison, "is really old."

"What are these things?"

Clay shook his head at Borger's question, dumbfounded.

The green ambient glow revealed a stone ceiling several feet above the top of the tubes. Their clear casing appeared to be thick glass. When Borger reached out to touch one, a ripple of light burst from the glass, and he drew his hand back quickly. "Ouch!"

"Is it hot?"

"No, it's ice cold."

Clay moved forward and closed in, just a few inches away. The green glowing fluid was clearly moving. But there was something inside that the fluid was swirling around.

"There's something in the middle of this tube."

The others joined him and peered inside. "They look like bubbles," Alison said. Her voice echoed softly against the thick walls.

"Or tiny spheres." Caesare raised his head, following the spiraling strands of spheres to the top of the tube. "There's thousands of them."

Borger stepped away and examined the next closest tube. "They all have them." He looked closer. "Wait a minute, there's something inside of the spheres. It looks like little dots."

"And different sizes." Clay slowly circled around the first column and peered at the strands from the other side. "Very different sizes."

Borger looked more closely, staring intently through his eyeglasses. "You're right. Some of these are bigger."

"What do you think they are?"

Borger looked back at Clay. "I think they're *seeds*."

* * *

The four moved deeper toward the back of the room. Every tube appeared to have strings of spheres wrapped inside, twisting in a way that reminded Clay of a double helix shape. Although these contained ten or more strands each. "There are no machines in here," he remarked to the others.

"I don't see any either. Unless they're behind the walls."

"I don't hear anything. You'd think there would be some kind of sound, even if it were behind a wall."

Caesare considered it. "If there are no machines, then where's the power source? What's keeping all of this cold? And what's causing the glow? A chemical reaction?"

"That would last *this* long? You'd have to add more chemicals, but these tubes look like they're sealed on both ends."

The four fanned out quietly, examining more of the columns. A few minutes later, Borger called out from the other side of the room. They ran to find him back near the door in the cliff.

"Look at this!"

They peered down at the floor near his feet and could see a faint jagged etching through the dust, making its way to the door.

"What is it?"

Borger touched his finger to it then raised his hand and sniffed. "I think it's water."

They turned around and traced the tiny stream back to one of the nearby tubes."

"Is it leaking?!"

Clay crouched down and checked the glass. "I don't think so. In fact," he stood up, looking all the way to the top, "I don't think it's the fluid at all." He spotted a tiny flash near the ceiling. "I think the water found a way inside this cavern, and it's dripping down this tube and onto the floor; then it trails to the door."

"I think you're right." Borger careened his neck to the ceiling until he saw the same reflection from a drop of falling water. "That's how it's seeping back outside and changing the soil."

Both Clay and Borger observed a tiny flash emitted

near the top of the tube each time a drop of water hit the glass.

Alison stared through the tube nearest to her. "So, maybe this glowing liquid is some kind of power source. Or maybe some kind of nutrient."

"Or maybe it's both."

"Hey," Caesare called from behind them, "come take a look at this."

They found him a few aisles over, examining some of the spheres. "Take a look at these bubbles right here, closest to the edge. Tell me what they look like to you."

As soon as they saw what Caesare was pointing at, the others froze.

"Oh my gosh," Alison whispered. "Those look like some kind of embryos!"

"That's what I was thinking."

Instinctively, they all took a step back and scanned the glowing room with a very different expression. One by one, they backed up, retreating toward the door. When they reached it, they made sure it was still open and remained near the exit.

"Alison," Clay spoke softly. "How old do you think this place is?"

"I have no idea."

"Just a ballpark."

She shrugged. "Well, judging from how worn the boulders are outside and the amount of undisturbed dust inside, I'd say pretty old. I don't think this thing has been opened for hundreds of years, maybe thousands."

"Will and Steve, in your opinion, is there any possibility that something like this could have been made by us?"

Caesare looked at Borger then shook his head. "Are you kidding?"

Clay nodded pensively. "So, does anyone believe this place is *not* storing an extraordinary amount of DNA material?"

"DNA that doesn't belong to us," added Caesare.

Borger gasped. "Holy cow! It's another vault!"

"What do you mean 'another' vault?"

"I mean the seed vault. In Norway. On the island!" Borger gave them a sarcastic stare when he saw their questioning faces. "You don't know about the seed vault? The *Global* Seed Vault! It's a large complex on a Norwegian island that has been stockpiling copies of seeds for years, from all over the world."

"Why?"

"To protect them in the event of a major catastrophe. It's got something like a hundred thousand different seeds, all from different continents. The complex was supposedly built to last hundreds of years." Borger waved his arms emphatically in front of himself. "That's what this is! It's another vault!"

"Whose vault?"

Borger turned to Clay. "Well, clearly not ours. Someone else. An alien race."

"*Another* alien race?"

"Why not?" Borger asked. "Remember what Palin said. The amount of water that Earth has is not common, which makes us stand out to anyone who can see us. Like a beacon."

Alison frowned. "But why would some alien race put copies of their seeds on Earth?"

"The same reason as us," Borger replied. "In case of

a catastrophe. But right now, we can't go very far. They can. And if you're going to locate a seed vault anywhere, I'm guessing you'd want to do it on a planet that you *knew* could sustain you."

Everyone turned back to the columns in front of them.

Alison broke the silence with a whisper. "So what do we do now?" She looked back and forth between the three men, none of whom answered. "Guys?"

To her right both Caesare and Borger finally shrugged. She looked to her left. "John?

Clay blinked but continued staring, transfixed.

"John?"

Quietly, he inhaled then spoke under his breath without taking his eyes away. "Beware of the leap."

"Huh?"

"Beware of the leap," he repeated, louder.

"What leap?"

"It's what Palin said to me before we came back through."

Caesare looked at him curiously. "What does it mean?"

"We've seen what those plants can do. Which was probably nothing compared to the water itself." He turned to the others. "And that water is only touching the glass in here. What do you think the solution inside those tubes is capable of?"

No one answered.

"We could be talking about something so far beyond our current abilities and understanding that it would seem like *magic*." Clay scanned the entire room again. "Commander Lawton was so amazed by the DNA in those plants that she was sure countries would go to war over it. How far would they go over something like this?"

Caesare squinted at Clay. "All the way."

Clay stood thinking. "You're right. So, the question is how many lives is it worth? A thousand? A million?"

"There could be a lot of good," Borger offered.

"Would it be worth it, Will?"

Borger shrugged.

"Would those who died still think it was worth it?" Clay sighed. "A lot of advancements are vindicated as the cost of progress. But it's an easy question when you're only asking the survivors, isn't it?"

They continued to watch Clay, each of them silently thinking.

"Who knows what would be unleashed from these things. Or from the DNA they're protecting."

"It's a sleeping giant," said Caesare.

Clay looked at them, gravely. "Who thinks we should find out?"

When no one raised their hand, he looked back up at the nearest tube. The glowing green mixture struck him as having an odd beauty about it. In the end, Palin had tried to warn them about what they might find. About wisdom. *How often did humans really learn? What about governments?*

"So what do we do?" asked Alison. "It won't be long before people start showing up."

Clay's voice dropped almost to a whisper. "I say we leave it alone."

"Someone else will find it, John."

"Not if we bury it."

Caesare raised an eyebrow. "Bury it? Bury it with what?"

Clay turned and peered outside. The rain was still pouring. "Didn't our Chinese friends leave some bulldozers behind?"

Caesare stared at him. "John, we can't bury the whole damn cliff."

"We don't have to," he replied with eyes still fixed outside. "We only need to bury the sign posts. Or better yet, remove the boulders."

"Then how will whoever put it here find it, assuming they ever come back for it?"

Clay frowned. "If we don't hide it, there might not be anything for them to come back for."

## 72

IT DIDN'T TAKE long. Two of the earth movers were still operational. Moving only a few pieces from each of the three boulder groups, their shapes appeared as random as any of the others.

After redirecting the water leak, and with another press of their makeshift magnet against the wall, the heavy door clicked and slid smoothly back into place. The vertical seams appeared to change very little, with only small jagged pieces missing from the separation. Ironically, it made the cliff face look more natural than it had before.

When the four returned to the helicopter, they were soaking wet. They smiled when they stepped inside to find Dulce awake, lying against DeeAnn. Even as tired as the small gorilla was, her warm eyes managed to open wider when she spotted Caesare.

No one said anything. From the chair, DeeAnn observed the faces of the others and decided she didn't want to know what they'd been doing outside. She just wanted to leave.

She had been through hell. But she still had Dulce. And she and Juan were both alive. It was more than enough for her. Now she just wanted to go home.

She watched Borger sit down in front of his laptop. Clay followed and stood behind him. After a few minutes, Borger leaned back, sharing the screen with him.

"I'd say it's pretty unrecognizable."

"Let's hope so."

Alison and Caesare came over to take a look and nodded in agreement.

Caesare looked at his watch. "Who wants to get out of here? We should still have enough fuel to make it down the other side of the mountain to Georgetown."

Clay motioned outside. "Good, I'll follow you down. I need to return the other one."

"I'll go with you."

Clay smiled at Alison. "How could I give up my favorite copilot?"

Borger was fast at work on the last piece. He was getting into the system and removing the video data recorded from the ARGUS satellite. He wouldn't remove everything, just the data covering the top of the mountain back to the satellite's launch date. In fact, he wouldn't even delete it. The NSA, not surprisingly, kept copious backups of their data. Instead of deleting the files, he would corrupt them and leave them in place. With a little extra help from Borger, the corrupted versions of those files would soon replace all of those in the backups, leaving only unusable files in the NSA's repository. Hopefully, by the time they realized the problem, it would be too late. And Borger would remove all traces as to who did it.

With any luck, the distraction over the sinking of the Bowditch would give him enough time to finish.

Less than fifteen minutes later, both helicopters lifted off the ground and banked left in tandem. Together, they smoothly descended the north side of the mountain and headed for the thin blue line of ocean on the horizon.

# 73

GENERAL WEI STOOD in front of his large office window with his hands crossed behind his back. Outside, the smog had lightened enough to allow most of the citizens to go back outside again. Long gone were the clear blue skies he remembered from his youth. It had all changed. It seemed the poisonous smog was now simply a cost of progress for Beijing, and many other cities. The industrial progress of the country had been too much and too fast for nature to keep up. And they were now paying for it.

There was a knock on the door behind him. He replied and turned to see his secretary enter, escorting in the young lieutenant. Wei knew him only by reputation and examined the man's strong, youthful face. A face that many still had, one of unswerving love for his country and army. Wei wished he still had it.

Wei's secretary ducked back out, closing the door. He continued studying the man and his wrinkled uniform. "Has anyone else seen this?"

The lieutenant's dark eyes were like stone. "No, sir! I brought it straight from Lieutenant Chao." He held out his arms and offered the small box to Wei.

The seal was unbroken. "You've done well, Lieutenant. You will receive a personal commendation for this."

Wei kept his bemused expression from showing. In a few hours, a commendation with General Wei's name on it was more likely to harm the man's career than help it. Nevertheless, he saluted and dismissed him.

When the door closed again, Wei placed the box on his desk. He momentarily admired the box's ornate exterior before breaking the wax seal and unlocking it. Inside were three large vials of clear, frozen liquid. The DNA was from some of the first plants captured in Guyana. He held one up and examined it.

Was it possible it had been tampered with or switched? Of course. There was always a way. However, ultimately, Wei had little left to rely on but practicality.

He placed the vial back in its place and closed the lid. He then reached out and picked up his phone. Wei was about to give his last order as one of China's most decorated generals.

He had long known he would be the sacrificial lamb of his political masters. Yet what he was about to do would cause his family name to end up as one of the most publicly hated in China's history.

Their sacrificial lamb was about to leave its masters utterly stunned.

## 74

LIEUTENANT CHAO STOOD on the deck of his corvette, too far away to see even the faintest hint of land. Behind him, the fading sun was beginning to set against the watery horizon. A sunset he hardly noticed.

He had very little time now. The U.S. and Brazil were undoubtedly pursuing them which meant his stop in the middle of the ocean had to be swift.

The corvette and the Russian submarine Forel were side-by-side with a makeshift gangplank running between the vessels. The two Chinese submarines escorting them south would know they'd stopped and were undoubtedly waiting for them, just ahead out of sight.

The transfer of the packaged plants off the corvette and onto the Forel was quick. They weren't taking many: just enough to grow and then sell the DNA on the black market. It was Chao's ticket to ultimate wealth.

With the help of his Russian partners, he was about to completely disappear. It was the only way. Until, of course, one day when *everyone* finally had the formula, and he would be able to buy his way back into China, into their aristocracy. It was one of the constants in history; money always forgave.

Twenty crates. That's all he needed. Hell, it took longer to tie up the boats than to transfer the precious cargo.

When the last crate was tossed aboard the Forel, Chao stepped aboard. His life of hiding was about to begin.

Chao pushed the thick board away and watched it clamor down between the metal hulls, splashing into the ocean. It was so loud that he didn't hear the yelling at first. However, as the gangplank sank below the water, he caught the sound of someone yelling below deck and frantically clambering up the ladder. Chao turned to find himself looking into the ashen face of the Russian captain. He screamed a single word at the top of his lungs, which took Chao a split second to register through the heavy accent.

"Torpedoes!"

Chao's eyes bolted open and he whipped around. Not far away, he could clearly see four separate drafts speeding toward them in the water. His last thought was one of confusion. *The only submarines close enough to fire on them were their own.*

All four torpedoes found their mark just seconds apart. Together, the corvette and the Forel erupted in dual explosions. Each of their hulls was ripped apart in the blink of an eye, along with their contents and crew. Multiple fireballs billowed into the air and large pieces of burning metal shot outward over the water. The explosions momentarily lifted both vessels before they promptly crashed back down together, plunging through the surface.

The ocean wasted no time, immediately surging over and inside the gaping wounds. Once fully underwater, the hulls gradually twisted away from one another and descended rapidly toward their watery grave.

The explosions were tremendous, but they were still too far away to be seen from the white sandy beaches of Rio de Janeiro, where the trim figure of Carolina tiptoed over the sand and back to their chairs.

Blanco sat reclining, facing the sparkling blue ocean in front of him. The soothing sound of the cascading waves tried to hypnotize him over the cool breeze.

Carolina set his bottle down on the arm of the wide wooden chair and sat down in the adjoining recliner. Without a word, Blanco reached for the beer and took a long drink.

Even with the limited authority she had, Carolina had been able to take control of enough of Alves' assets to last them a lifetime. The vast majority of the billionaire's wealth still belonged to the corporations, which didn't bother him. It was best not to be greedy and draw too much attention. Blanco was also pleasantly surprised at how easy it was to modify someone's living will. Especially when the parties involved stood to benefit handsomely.

As expected, the investigation would go on for some time. Blanco's explanation of their fight with the Chinese on the mountain and the resulting deaths of Alves and his men met little resistance. And now they had enough money to keep it that way. He did regret having to kill the two pilots when he found them at the poacher's camp, but it was the only way. There would have been too many inconvenient facts left to explain.

As for Alves, Blanco held little remorse. The man had made a great many enemies and yet still lived a long, wealthy life of which most others could only dream. Given South America's long tumultuous history, Alves enjoyed a better ride than almost anyone. He should have been more appreciative.

Blanco adjusted his position and felt the searing pain in his shoulder. He wondered about the man in black whom he had shot before fleeing the mountain. The man was most likely dead. Thankfully, Blanco had gotten a better shot off, but he was still damn lucky the stranger only got him in the shoulder.

Blanco made an imperceptible shrug. *Better him than me.*

## 75

GENERAL WEI WATCHED the tall trees pass by with a surreal sense of loss as he drove deeper into the mountains of Northern China. *Why had he never fully appreciated the detail of the world around him until the end? Why didn't anyone?*

Hours later, his car turned off the old road and into the gravel parking lot of a tiny hospital. He was several hundred kilometers outside of Beijing, in a small rural town that the country's reckless industrial expansion seemed to have forgotten. He brought the car to a stop and slid the gearshift into park, then opened his door and immediately stepped out.

Retrieving a large satchel from the back seat, Wei marched briskly toward the old, faded double doors. He pulled one open and walked down a narrow hallway. When he reached the last door, he paused and gently pushed it open.

She was just as he had left her. Lying in bed, with eyes closed. She was so beautiful. Her smooth face and delicate hands still looked as tender as he could ever remember. It was only her accelerated breathing that gave away her illness. He lowered himself onto her bed and placed his old hand over hers.

She wasn't diagnosed with degenerative heart disease until after her mother had died. A small part of him was thankful for that. Watching his daughter slip away was torture enough, but the thought of having to hold his wife while she watched would have been unbearable.

Wei stood up and turned around in the same motion, setting his satchel down on the old table. He unlocked it and promptly pulled out a small brown paper bag. He tilted the bag down, causing the first vial to slide out into his palm. He then held the cylinder up and shook it. The fluid was now completely thawed. Inserting the needle of a syringe into the top, he pulled the small plunger back, withdrawing the clear liquid.

He stared at his angel for only a moment before finally inserting the needle into her IV tube and discharging the bacterial solution. Next, he calmly, but quickly, began withdrawing the solution from the second vial.

* * *

When he was done, Wei slipped the bag and the empty vials into his coat pocket. He left the rest of the contents in the satchel.

He sat back down on his daughter's bed and held

her hand for the last time. God, she was so beautiful. So perfect. Just like her mother. She had been his sunshine in a world of darkness, with her eyes always so bright and pure.

Now, her heart was in the last stages, and a final gift was all he had left to offer. When he'd learned of the discovery in Guyana, he knew it was his last hope. His only hope. And he had moved heaven and earth to make it happen.

Now his precious seventeen-year-old daughter lay helpless, fighting against a disease that was quickly breaking her body down. Why were the most beautiful so often the ones taken?

Wei would never know if the DNA solution helped her. He could only pray now that it would. If it did, he hoped that she would one day learn the truth about why her father took his own life. That it was an act of a man who had sacrificed everything to give her one last chance.

From the beginning, he knew it was unlikely they would be able to harvest the plants without someone finding out. He also knew that they might have to fight their way out to protect it. But when the Americans showed up, Wei knew his fate was sealed.

Nevertheless, a preemptive strike against the United States would only lead to trouble. Especially when they finally discovered it was a Chinese submarine that had destroyed the U.S. science vessel and not the Russians. And the most obvious solution to avoid the Americans' rage was to blame the attack on a rogue officer. Someone with both the authority and the mental deterioration to do it. After all, the man had lost both his wife and daughter. Once identified, his government would, of course, have to make him the example and the punishment severe.

However, Wei had other plans. Even in her critical condition, he had moved his daughter to a safe location. Some place his masters would never think to look. After the funeral service, he changed her name and enlisted the help of a truly honorable man: a rural doctor and a faithful man of God.

The doctor would care for Wei's daughter until her final day, whenever that would be. The rest of his satchel, packed full of money, would provide whatever resources the man needed to help his people. And one day, he might just be able to tell Wei's daughter the truth. That Wei was not mad. He was not insane. He was a man of morals who had seen too much in his life, and too much of the true state of humanity. He was not about to unleash the power of immortality upon a race whose only decent values came from the unavoidability of death. Left unchecked, with no earthly penance, he had little doubt that his fellow man's soul would become something truly terrible.

And yet, in the end, he was a father. A father who loved his daughter more than life itself. He could destroy the precious cargo of his masters, but he would *never* let his little girl go without doing everything he could to save her.

If she survived, perhaps her special DNA would one day in the future be discovered when the human soul had grown wiser. But the time was not now.

He only hoped that whoever was in charge of the discovery for the Americans, believed the same.

# 76

IT WAS HIS fault.

Admiral Langford stared down at Krogstad's headstone less than twenty feet away and struggled to maintain his composure. Giving orders that cost lives was not for the faint of heart. Nevertheless, no one could avoid the emotional agony when that person was a friend.

He had ordered Krogstad to stop the Chinese warship at all costs with a ship that had no ability to fight. But after the Russian torpedo attack, Krogstad was left powerless to do anything but delay the inevitable. He lost his life, along with several of his crew. And for what? The corvette had escaped with its cargo, protected by the Forel. It appeared the Russians and Chinese had been aligned the entire time.

The response from the United States would come soon enough, and Langford was quickly growing wary as to where it would end.

The Chinese now possessed one of the greatest discoveries in history, and the U.S. had nothing. The sample from aboard the Bowditch could not be found, which was not surprising considering the sheer damage to the ship and its science lab.

Langford glanced up forlornly at Krogstad's wife and family, still huddled in front of the marker. Commander Lawton stood next to her mother with an arm around her shoulders. All they would know was that Roger Krogstad was innocently attacked and that he still managed to save most of the lives aboard his ship. They didn't know that their husband and father was dead for a very simple reason. And that reason was standing only a few feet behind them.

Langford finally turned to go as the rain began to drizzle. He looked solemnly at Clay, who was standing nearby, waiting.

"It was a nice service."

Langford nodded. "Did you know that Roger and I entered the academy together?"

"Yes, sir."

"He was a hell of a captain."

"He was indeed."

Langford squinted up at the dark clouds and sighed. "The Russians are denying everything. Claiming they didn't have any knowledge of the Forel or its mission." He scoffed. "Next they'll tell us someone stole the damn thing." He looked back at Clay. "And Brazil is insisting that both the Forel and the Chinese corvette were sunk off their southern coast. So it appears the Chinese now have their 'deniability.'"

"Sunk by whom?"

"That's a good question."

"What happens now, sir?"

"Who knows?" He looked at Clay. "Go take some time off, John. You've earned it. I'll do my best to leave you alone this time."

# EPILOGUE

CAESARE WAS NEARLY finished typing his last report when Borger opened his office door and stepped inside. He closed it quietly behind him and stood, waiting until Caesare was done. While he waited, Borger scanned the room very carefully with his eyes.

"The room's clean, Will," Caesare said without looking up.

"Are you sure?"

"Would you like to bring your device back and scan it again?" When Borger paused to consider the question, Caesare looked at him. "What's up?"

Borger spoke in a hushed tone. "There's something I wanted to talk to you about. About...Guyana."

Caesare saved and closed his document then leaned forward. He watched as Borger grabbed the only other chair in the room and dragged it forward to the other side of the desk. "What is it?"

Borger didn't speak right away. Instead, he blinked twice before inhaling and spoke barely above a whisper.

"I've been thinking..."

"That was my first guess."

"About the mountain. About what we found." He paused again. "We both agree it came from somewhere else, right?"

"Right."

"And 'somewhere else' means pretty far away. Maybe *really* far."

"Okay."

"So…I've been thinking about something: *efficiency*."

"Efficiency?"

"Traveling through space takes energy, right? And if you want to do it quickly, it takes a lot of energy. We already know this. It's why even our spacecraft and probes are as small as possible."

"Correct."

"Traveling to Mars or Jupiter takes a while. And relatively speaking, they're not really that far away, right? So traveling a very long distance, like between stars, means you have to travel pretty fast if you want to arrive anytime in the foreseeable future. I mean, who's going to send something if they have to wait ten thousand years to get there?"

"Are we getting somewhere here, Will?"

"Yeah, sorry. What I'm really getting at, is that someone had to build that place inside the cliff, right?"

"Clearly."

"So, if they were going to travel here, to bring their tubes and DNA, they had to arrive in a relatively short amount of time. I mean, even *they* would have a finite lifespan, right?"

Caesare shook his head thoughtfully. "Presumably."

"Even if your body stopped aging, it doesn't mean you would survive forever. So, regardless, whoever brought those tubes here had to do it in a short enough timeframe that they could still finish the job."

"Which means fast travel."

"Exactly. And fast travel means a lot of power required. And that means efficiency."

"I see. In other words, you don't take what you don't need," Caesare said.

"Yes! You don't take what you don't need, so you can get here faster. It's no different from any other form of transportation."

"Very true."

"So whoever it was would have needed their cargo, food, and a host of other things. And the further away they came from, the more fuel they would need to achieve velocity. So my point is…that they would not only need all of this to get here, but they would need almost twice as much to get back!"

Caesare stared at him thoughtfully. "Which means if they had to get here and back within a lifespan, they would have to go even faster."

Borger nodded. "And that means doubling again the amount of fuel, and if you start nearing light speed, the energy needed begins to approach *infinite*."

Caesare leaned back in his chair and put two hands together in front of his mouth. "So, it was a one-way trip."

"It was a one-way trip," Borger repeated triumphantly. "It's possible it was round trip, but the probabilities and physics are hugely against it. Regardless of what kind of propulsion system they used. That's assuming we're not talking about some make-believe technology like on TV. No energy source is free from mathematics or economics."

Borger continued. "And since they clearly had cargo to transport, they had to use some kind of vessel or ship. So my question is this…*where's the ship?!*"

Caesare was looking at him over the top of his hands now. "Well, if they hid their cargo, they could certainly hide a ship too."

Borger nodded agreement.

"So…I guess either they bury it or ditch it."

"That's basically what it boils down to."

"So where is it?" asked Caesare.

Borger took another deep breath. "I have absolutely no idea."

Caesare remained in his chair, thinking about it for a long time. Finally, he shook his head and stood up. "That's a damn good point, Will."

Once he was standing, Borger noticed a large black bag sitting on the floor behind Caesare. "Are you going somewhere?"

"I am." Caesare picked up the bag and winced from the pain in his side.

"But you're not even healed yet."

"I know, but I can't wait."

"Where are you going?"

Caesare grinned subtly. "To find Miguel Blanco."

"Does Clay know?"

"Clay's busy."

* * *

The Hercules C-130 transport plane was waiting for Caesare on the tarmac at Andrews Air Force Base. Its four turboprop engines were already idling smoothly when he climbed aboard. He smiled immediately, seeing the faces of a Ranger team lining each side of the fuselage.

The door was closed behind him as he sat down onto the metal bench next to one of the soldiers. He peered down the line with a look of admiration before leaning back carefully against the metal wall behind him.

It was Caesare's favorite way to fly. And his flight

to Brazil would give him plenty of time to think about Borger's lingering question.

Where was the ship?

–

Clay dropped the main sheet, letting it slide down to the boom where he began folding it accordion style. He then quickly wrapped the straps around, securing it in place. He paused and laid an arm over the folded sail, looking out over the horizon again with amazement.

"I've never seen anything like this."

Alison grinned, wrapping the last strap around the smaller end of the boom, and gazed out with him. "I doubt many have."

He turned to her as Alison suddenly cleared her throat.

"Can I…ask you something?"

"Of course."

"Okay." Alison tilted her head nervously. "So, I know this might not be the ideal time and place, but… it's been a year now. And I know we haven't exactly been able to spend a lot of time together over the last three or four months."

Clay listened as she continued.

"I mean, not as much as maybe we'd like." She stopped herself. "Not that I'm assuming how much time you want to spend with me…" She rolled her eyes. "This isn't coming out right."

She looked into Clay's blue eyes and quickly glanced away. "It's just that…I want to, um…spend more time together. And I don't know if you're seeing anyone else. I mean, why wouldn't you be? You're amazing. It's just that I really like you and I don't know-"

"Alison," Clay said calmly, cutting her off. She stopped with raised eyebrows. He smiled warmly at her and walked the length of the boom until he was just on the other side from her. "Alison, I need to be honest with you."

Her heart sank.

"I haven't been interested in anyone else since our first date."

Alison's expression melted. "Really?"

"Really." He wrapped his hand over hers. "You're the one who's amazing. You're incredibly intelligent, beautiful, and compassionate. There are so many wonderful things about you that it's hard to even count them all. Not to mention, you're awfully cute when you're nervous."

Her eyes softened and she pursed her lips. He suddenly ducked under the boom and came up close to her. From there, Clay wasted no time, squeezing Alison's shoulders and kissing her deeply.

*Come now, Come now.*

"Just a minute!" Alison sighed, then turned and frowned at Dirk's head, bobbing out of the water, excitedly.

In the cockpit, she took the face mask from Chris and pulled the straps carefully over her ponytail.

Chris waited a moment then asked, "Air?"

Alison gave him a thumbs-up."

Next to them, Lee was helping with the second mask. "How's that, Mr. Clay?"

Clay grinned. He'd given up trying to get Lee to call him by his first name. He wiggled the outside of the mask to make sure it had a secure seal. "Good."

He then added the waterproof earplugs and turned to look at Alison. "Can you hear me?"

"Loud and clear."

Together they wriggled the BCDs and tanks onto their shoulders. They slipped their arms through and then clipped the wide straps together.

Through her mask, Alison motioned to Clay. "You're going to love this."

"I'm sure I will."

As he followed Alison to the stern of the boat, Clay stopped and gazed out again over the ocean. He was still amazed. Tens of thousands of dolphins together at once and surrounding the boat for miles. What *was* this place?

Clay watched Alison jump into the water with a scissor kick, keeping her head above the surface. She rotated herself around and waited for him.

He hadn't worn this exact kind of a system before, but Clay was almost as comfortable in diving gear as he was in his own skin. He fell smoothly into the warm Caribbean water and popped up a few feet away.

Dirk and Sally both circled around from behind and popped their beaks out of the water.

*We go now. We go now.*

She looked at John. "Are you ready?"

"Yep."

With that, the dolphins disappeared below, and Alison and Clay rolled forward, kicking their fins.

It was a clear day which provided the most sunlight and brilliantly lit up the beautiful coral below them. They hadn't gone very far before Clay's voice came over the speaker.

"Wow, Alison!"

She turned her head as they descended. "I know, right?!"

He stared, transfixed on the scene below them. The deep colors and vibrancy of the coral were almost unimaginable. "I've never seen anything like this."

"Me either. This is what they pilgrimage to every year."

Clay remained in awe as they drifted lower still. The amount and the variety of sea life were incredible, and he'd never seen underwater vegetation so encompassing. "I've never even seen this on a postcard before."

Alison laughed.

* * *

Above them, Lee and Chris leaned over the small table together, trying to block enough sunshine to view the monitor clearly. The area was much tighter than their Prowler, but it was still a nice boat.

While they listened to Clay and Alison's exchange over the speakers, Lee turned to Chris. "Are you going down again?"

"Heck, yeah!"

Lee laughed and looked around the white fiberglass cockpit of the catamaran. "Mr. Clay has a nice sailboat, eh?"

"He sure does. He needs a coffee machine though."

* * *

Below the boat, Clay reached out and grabbed Alison's hand. He kicked hard and accelerated, pulling her along with him. Still following Dirk and Sally, they glided over a small falloff in the coral, giving them a brief sensation of flying.

Several hundred yards behind them, the largest plants swayed rhythmically in the gentle current. Beneath the vegetation was a small crack in the coral. Very gradually, and almost imperceptibly, something small emerged from the crack barely a millimeter across. It slowly floated free and rose just a few inches before the bright, glowing green bubble popped and dissolved into the swirling water.

And if Clay and Alison had been able to view the reef from the air, the two would have noticed a strangely symmetrical shape. As though something large were buried beneath it.

# CATALYST

## PROLOGUE

WITH A PAINFUL wince, Steve Caesare brushed back his shirt and slid a hand down over the handle of his gun. The hallway he stood in was richly decorated with white marble walls and thick beige carpeting, allowing him to approach the door with very little sound.

Caesare glanced up at one of the overhead chandeliers, scanning the ceiling and walls for cameras. Too well hidden. His hotel uniform was bulging at the seams, barely containing his broad frame beneath. Anyone taking even a passing glance at a monitor would notice something wrong with his appearance.

The Tivioli Mofarrej was one of the most elegant hotels in São Paulo, and certainly the most expensive. Used by the wealthiest clientele, the hotel emanated a raw sense of power and prestige, towering among the cityscape of Brazil's richest city.

It had taken him two weeks. Two weeks following the man he had now tracked to the room at the end of the hall. Miguel Blanco was living large off the money he had stolen from Mateus Alves, his previous employer and one of the richest men in South America. After killing his former boss, Blanco had successfully stolen nearly one hundred million Brazilian reales from Alves' various accounts and trusts. It was only a fraction of the old man's wealth, but it was more than enough — enough to become one of the very elites Blanco had spent much of his life protecting.

And it had been no easy task. Gaining access to Alves' accounts was one thing. Blanco already had help with that. The hard part was covering his tracks. For that he needed the help of several others, compadres who were discreet and also stood to gain handsomely from the disassembling of Alves' vast fortune.

Caesare, however, didn't care about the money. He was there for a very different reason. The old man had been as corrupt as his murderer and Caesare held no sympathy for either of them. He was here for one thing and one thing only: retribution.

He was there because if it had been up to Blanco, Caesare would have been just as dead, lying next to the old man on top of that mountain. But Blanco didn't know he had survived. And after two weeks of searching, Caesare was about to pay him the mother of all surprise visits.

The absence of anyone guarding the door left Caesare a bit wary as he crept closer. Guests staying in a presidential suite usually had a security detail. Where was Blanco's? The man had previously been an officer in the Brazilian Intelligence Agency, which typically left men overconfident or completely paranoid. *But if he was paranoid, where was his detail?*

Blanco was definitely in the room. At least he had been thirty minutes ago. They had zeroed in on the target's cell phone signal, and pinpointed it to thirty meters from where Caesare was now standing before it was abruptly switched off. Now, ten feet from the door, he silently slid the .40 caliber Glock out from its concealed holster and laid his index finger along the side, just above the trigger guard. He turned his head slightly, using his peripheral vision to check the hall behind him one last time.

When he reached the door, Caesare kept to the side and brought the gun around his right hip. He raised it smoothly and leaned in closer, listening. There was no sound at all. No voices. No television. Nothing.

Blanco hadn't left Rio de Janeiro with anyone except the one person Caesare knew would be with him: Alves' young and longtime personal assistant, Carolina Sosa. She was the one person who had access to many of the old man's accounts and other verifiable information. *She* was the gateway to Alves' riches.

Caesare withdrew a small magnetic card, a used but very valuable card. It came from the hotel, which took only a few hours to find in São Paulo. From a person who could encode a master keycard for almost any hotel in the city.

He held it in his left hand and twisted his wrist to peer at his watch, waiting.

*Anytime, Wil.*

When Caesare heard the phone finally ring inside the room, he moved quickly, simultaneously inserting the card into the door's lock and pulling it back out. The loud click was masked by the telephone's ring and Caesare immediately pushed the door ajar — just enough to prevent the lock from reengaging. In the same motion, he brought the tip of his left shoe forward to prop the door open by half an inch.

The phone rang again, echoing through the room. The third ring was the last, immediately plunging the room back into silence. With another quick glance over his shoulder, Caesare pressed his ear close to the cracked door. No footsteps. No movement at all that he could hear.

He pushed the door in further and was met by a cool draft of air escaping past him. The door opened further without any noise, allowing Caesare a look inside. Down the entrance hallway, he spotted a dark polished table with chairs perfectly arranged.

He stepped inside, keeping the gun low but in front. The pain in his ribs screamed as he twisted around to ease the door closed — a result of the near fatal wound Blanco had given him.

The door gave a muted click shut and Caesare eased forward over the spotless marble flooring. He stepped away from the wall and gradually edged himself around the corner.

Then he froze.

The scene before him was not what he was expecting. The room seemed pristine except for two dining room chairs positioned in the middle. In each chair sat a motionless figure, bound and bloodied. Both gagged, with their heads down upon their chests.

The first was a woman, barely recognizable through

the dark brunette hair dangling in front of her face. Carolina Sosa. The second was Miguel Blanco himself, his body slumping but held in place by the ropes around his waist.

Neither was moving.

Caesare immediately stepped back out of sight, leaving only the gun and half of his face exposed. The scene looked fresh enough that the murderer could still be inside the suite. After waiting a minute, he slowly eased himself back away from the wall and moved at a wedged angle, slowly peering back into the main room. He crept forward onto soft carpet. Caesare rounded the next doorway, staying well away from the corner, providing him maximum visibility.

It took several minutes to ensure the entire suite was clear, after which Caesare returned to the front room. He gazed at the two lifeless bodies.

Approaching the pair, he stared into Carolina's hair-strewn face. Beneath the dark strands, he could see her badly bruised skin. He passed by her and stopped in front of Blanco. The man's face was entirely black and blue, his gag now fallen halfway off.

He stared at Blanco for a long time, finally shaking his head. Living a life of deceit often ended abruptly, and sometimes violently. The small rubber tourniquet hanging from the man's arm told Caesare that whatever secrets Blanco had now belonged to someone else. They had literally beaten and drugged it out of him.

It was too bad Caesare hadn't gotten to him first. At least he would have lived. He scanned the room one last time before returning the gun smoothly to its holster.

Caesare began to turn for the door when something

suddenly caught his eye, startling him. His gun was back out before his brain even registered what it was.

Blanco had moved.

It was slight, but it was movement. Blanco's eyes remained closed, but the movement was more than just residual muscle twitching. Caesare waited with his gun lowered but gripped firmly between both hands. Then it happened again.

With one hand, he reached up and eased the Brazilian's head back before pulling the rest of the cloth gag out of his mouth. The swollen eyelids struggled, but finally managed to crack themselves open. Dark, unfocused eyes peered out.

"Blanco," Caesare whispered.

It took time for the eyes to focus on Caesare. When they did, the recognition came quickly. They opened wider in disbelief.

Caesare managed to refrain from smiling at Blanco and vindictively muttering the word "surpresa." Instead he rose and turned toward the phone. He had picked up the handset when Blanco blurted something behind him.

"Não!" A moment later he mumbled again, switching to English. "Don't call."

"I'm calling for help."

Blanco's eyes dropped to his arm, where a small drop of blood was drying over the remains of an insertion point. "There is…no help…for me," he said weakly.

Caesare knelt in front of him. "Who did it?"

"Otero," he whispered.

Caesare knelt down next to him. "What did he want?"

"Please." Blanco's voice grew fainter. "Please... save them."

Caesare glanced around the room. "Save who?"

Blanco was now struggling just to make his lips move. "My family."

# 1

ADMIRAL LANGFORD LOOKED up as John Clay opened the wide door to his office with Wil Borger standing behind him. The Admiral quickly waved them in as he pushed a button on his phone and dropped the handset back onto the cradle.

"Okay, Clay and Borger are here. Go ahead, Steve."

"Bom dia, gents," Caesare called through the speaker. "You're missing some beautiful weather down here. Sweltering and muggy."

Clay smiled. "Sounds lovely."

"Yeah, unfortunately it's not all sunshine and roses."

"Did you find Blanco?"

"Oh, I found him all right. But I'm afraid he's not in the best of moods. He's dead."

Clay and Borger looked at Langford with surprise.

"Dead?" Borger repeated, confused. "But we traced that call he made right before he turned his cell off just an hour ago."

"Yeah well, I don't think he was the one who turned it off. I found him in his room beaten to a pulp. The Sosa woman was already gone and Blanco was just minutes away. I couldn't do anything."

"Was he conscious?"

"Barely. I got a little out of him, but it was brief."

Clay noticed an echo in Caesare's voice. "Where are you?"

On the other end, Caesare scanned up and down the metal stairs, working quickly to get his stolen uniform off. "I'm in a stairwell, at the hotel."

Langford looked at the phone. "Any idea who did it?"

"Someone named Otero. Ring a bell with anyone?"

They all shook their heads. "No."

Caesare nodded on his end. "I suspect he was someone involved with Mateus Alves."

"What makes you say that?"

"Because that's what they were after," replied Caesare.

"What do you mean?"

"What I mean is, they weren't after the money. They wanted *answers*."

"What kind of answers?"

"As far as I can tell, answers about Alves. Whoever this Otero is, he was looking for something specific. Money is easy to trace, but Blanco and his girlfriend looked like they were subjected to some serious narco-interrogation, followed by a lethal cocktail. Either way, I'm sure Otero didn't expect someone like me to show up before Blanco was dead."

Langford's brows remained furrowed as he leaned in closer to the speakerphone. "So what did you get out of Blanco?"

"Not much," Caesare replied. "He was pretty far gone. But one of his last words was clear: *mamaco*."

"Mamaco?"

Caesare peeled off the last of the uniform. "It's Portuguese for monkey, Admiral. Otero knows about Alves' preserve in Brazil, and he knows about the monkey."

Langford watched Clay and Borger exchange looks. The monkey was a small capuchin discovered by a team of "researchers" who had been employed by the old man before he was murdered. In actuality, they were all poachers, except one. One was a genuine researcher and had stumbled upon a very special capuchin monkey almost entirely by accident — a monkey very different from the others they had caught.

This particular one was highly intelligent and while the average lifespan of most wild capuchins was roughly twenty-five years, this one was discovered to be profoundly older. So much older, in fact, that the billionaire Mateus Alves threw every resource he had into two goals: finding out where the monkey had come from and doing it as quietly as possible.

Langford could see the gears turning in Clay's head. "Clay?"

He glanced up at the Admiral before turning back to the speakerphone. "How did this Otero know about the monkey? Or even that Alves was searching for it?"

"Or why someone like Alves would voluntarily abandon a billion dollar empire and completely disappear from public view."

"Otero must have known something," Clay mused. "But how?"

"Blanco had been talking to a lot of people," said Caesare. "Maybe he was trying to capitalize on what Alves had already discovered. And maybe he finally found someone crazy enough to listen."

Clay nodded absently. It was certainly plausible. Except for the crazy part. They all knew that what Alves was after wasn't crazy at all. Tracing the origins of the capuchin was one thing, but what Alves really wanted was its DNA. Primate DNA was more than 99% identical to humans. If a primate could live more than four times its normal life span, it wasn't much of a stretch for that DNA to be isolated, and potentially applied to humans.

Alves was old, in his eighties, and wanted more than anything to extend his own life. And he believed he'd finally found just the miracle to help him do it.

Clay continued thinking. "But someone wouldn't just murder Blanco on a whim…over the word 'monkey.' They'd have to have gotten more. Maybe a lot more. And maybe enough to justify killing Blanco on the spot, to shut him up."

Langford rubbed his chin. "Then we have to assume that this Otero now knows everything." After a deep breath, he leaned forward again. "Let's table that for the moment. It seems we have an even bigger problem to deal with. I just received a report from the salvage team near Guyana. They have recovered fragments of the torpedo and enough of its Comp-B explosive signature for a positive identification." Langford paused, looking at Clay and Borger. "The Bowditch wasn't sunk by the Russians like we thought. It was sunk by the Chinese."

Clay and Borger may have been visibly surprised at the news over Blanco being dead, but now they were absolutely *stunned.*

Two weeks before, the sinking of one of the Navy's most modern research ships had seemed to be a completely separate event. But it wasn't. It was connected to the billionaire Alves' death in a way that none of them could have foreseen. The U.S.S. Bowditch was investigating a Chinese warship quietly docked along the northern coast of South America, in the small country of Guyana.

However, what they discovered next was a revelation. The ship's Chinese crew was making mysterious trips into the jungle under the cover of darkness. The Chinese had made a startling discovery on the very same mountain to which Mateus Alves had traced the capuchin monkey's origins.

Over the speaker, Caesare was the first to reply. "Admiral, did you say the Bowditch was sunk by the Chinese?"

"That's right."

"But the only sub in the area was Russian."

"The only one we were aware of."

"Wait a minute." Clay suddenly looked at Langford. "That means a Chinese sub may have been there all along."

"It looks that way."

"And it waited to attack the Bowditch until their warship was leaving with its cargo."

Langford nodded. Clay knew as well as anyone how the events unfolded. *He was onboard the Bowditch when it was struck.*

"So, that's it!" exclaimed Clay. "That's why the warship itself never attacked...because it couldn't. And that's why their sub was there. For protection. They were there to make sure the warship and its cargo made it out."

"So they gutted the thing."

Clay nodded, as the pieces fell into place. "They'd

been bringing those crates out of the jungle for months. But there was no way they could have fit it into just one warship. It's too small. Unless they gutted the ship. Removing everything inside gave them the storage they needed, which meant it also left the ship defenseless. Their submarine was simply waiting, ready to clear a path for it."

Langford watched the expression on Clay's face. The guy never forgot anything. Given enough time, he could figure damn near anything out.

"Well, that was clever," Caesare said.

Langford frowned. "The Russians were bad enough. But the Chinese are a whole new problem."

Clay was thinking the same thing. Russia's relationship with the U.S. had reached new lows over the fiasco in the Ukraine. And Washington's relationship with the Chinese was also deteriorating, assisted by the Chinese coming out publicly in support of Russia's position. Until then, China had remained a reluctant geopolitical partner of the U.S., primarily due to many decades of economic trading history. But in recent years China had been taking steps of their own, inching closer and closer to an adversarial position. When news leaked out that they'd actually attacked and sunk a large United States naval ship, things were bound to escalate, and badly.

"What happens now?" asked Clay.

Langford shook his head. "Nothing good. What the Chinese found on that mountain was worth starting a war over. But make no mistake, we would have done the same thing."

Langford rubbed his eyes. The U.S. State Department had already begun condemning Russia for the destruction of the Bowditch. Now they would have to downplay their previous remarks and redirect their accusations at China. Yet they could not risk the trade relationship with China. If it collapsed, all hell would break loose, and there would be no winner on either side. The best the Administration could manage would be to corral the issue and turn it into a more subtle and very strategic counterattack. Langford knew the U.S. politicians were not going to rest until they had their pound of flesh, no matter what the long term ramifications were. The unfortunate truth was that politicians started wars but relied on men like Langford to fight them.

Langford blinked and found himself staring at the phone. The room remained silent. He straightened in his chair. "For the time being, I want you three to find out what you can about Otero. Alves had his connections and I'm sure this thug does too. And the last thing we need is the Brazilian government finding out and getting involved."

"Yes, sir," all three answered almost simultaneously.

Langford promptly ended the call with Caesare. He then watched Clay and Borger open the door, stepping out of the room.

The situation was unraveling quickly.

Langford let out a quick sigh. Soon he would have to tell the men what had happened to the Chinese warship immediately after it escaped Guyana with its precious cargo. Something that made absolutely no sense at all.

# 2

CLAY FOLLOWED WIL Borger into his darkened office, which was a generous word to describe the space where Wil worked. Located on one of the subfloors of the Pentagon building, the room was in dire need of some windows and sunlight. And a maid. The room was filled with racks of computer and signaling equipment which few people would recognize. A few pieces looked to be as old as Borger himself, who would soon be pushing fifty.

Wil Borger approached his desk, with a screen that was three monitors wide. Clay closed the door behind them.

With a loud squeak from his chair, Borger sat down and reached out to pull another forward for Clay. "Have a seat."

"I could use the stretch."

Borger nodded and spun back around to the monitors. "I need to show you something. Something I haven't told anyone yet."

Clay watched him open a new window on the screen and begin typing. A moment later a map filled the center screen. He raised his hand and briefly tapped a large hard drive resting below the same monitor.

"This is the hard drive I had on the Bowditch. Fortunately, I had it in my backpack when we were ordered to abandon ship."

Clay peered at Borger. "The one with the video footage?"

"Correct." He motioned to the map and reached for

his mouse. It was a map of South America, with Guyana centered on the screen. Borger then double-clicked several times, zooming in on the area around Georgetown. "When we got back, I wanted to see what really happened to the Bowditch. So I downloaded the video from the ARGUS satellite before and after the impact."

Clay was leaning over his shoulder when Borger stopped zooming and let the image crystalize. A moment later, they could both clearly see the U.S.S. Bowditch from an aerial view.

"There she is," he said, under his breath.

The image was frozen, but the white wake behind the stern was clearly visible and showed the ship traveling full speed toward Georgetown's small harbor. It was heading directly at the Chinese warship, which was trying to leave.

Borger then zoomed back out slightly, doubling the viewing area. Both ships were now smaller, but a barely identifiable wake could be seen several hundred yards behind the Bowditch.

A torpedo.

Borger hit a button on his keyboard and the overhead images began to play as a video. He moved out of the way, giving Clay a clear view. It was only moments later when the bow of the ship could be seen beginning to move. Clay knew it was the moment Captain Krogstad had given the order to do the unthinkable. *To bring the ship around.*

"Geez," Clay muttered.

"It's hard to watch."

"It is."

Over the next few minutes, they watched in silence

at the agonizingly slow turn of the ship, finally coming about just moments before the torpedo's impact.

The Bowditch was a science vessel, which meant it had no real weapons to speak of — certainly nothing with which to fight off a torpedo attack. The only offensive capability lay in the Oceanhawk helicopter housed on the main deck. In the video, they watched the rotors of the chopper gaining speed, desperately trying to lift off in time. But the torpedo struck first. Even in the video, the explosion against the port side of the bow was breathtaking. Most of the forward deck was destroyed instantly. On what deck remained, the Oceanhawk's desperate attempt to escape came to an end. Clay and Borger watched in eerie silence as the blast caused the helicopter to roll and slice its spinning rotors into the deck's twisted metal. The fragments burst into dozens of giant pieces of shrapnel just seconds before the Oceanhawk fell over the side, engulfed in an orange ball of flame.

The rest of the video played out exactly as the two men remembered it. They could see everyone, including themselves, huddled on the stern of the ship where Krogstad had ordered them. If he couldn't outrun the torpedo, his only other option would be to save as many as he could. On the stern, survivors had the best chance of deploying the lifeboats. The rest of the ship was sacrificed to take as much of the blow as possible.

When it was over, Borger stopped the video and leaned back. "That's only the second time I've seen it."

Clay nodded, his eyes still on the screen. "I can see why."

With a deep breath, Borger turned back to him. "There's something else I wanted to show you."

Clay raised his eyebrows and waited.

Borger clasped his hands in front of his protruding stomach. "So, I've been picking through the rest of the satellite video. I'm not sure if you know this, but the attack was big enough that most commercial aircraft in the area was immediately grounded, even as far away as Venezuela."

"I didn't know that."

"Yep. Everything. Down. Kaput." Borger then began to grin. It was a look John Clay had come to know well.

"You found something."

"All aircraft was grounded," he repeated. "All *commercial* aircraft."

Clay raised an eyebrow. "But not..."

"But not *military* aircraft."

"Meaning what?"

"Meaning...," Borger replied, "military flights were not grounded. Or should I say...the *only* military flight." He began typing again in a new window, which brought up a second map. The second map was fixed on Georgetown. Borger pointed to one frame, then to the other. "This one is the international airport in Guyana. Note the timestamp on both screens."

"They're both the same."

"Exactly. Same time, in two places. The first picture is the Bowditch after it was struck. The second, the Georgetown airport."

Borger zoomed closer in on the airport and sped up the video. Both feeds accelerated, still in sync.

After almost a minute, he froze them both. "That's it. Right there."

Clay studied the image. An airplane could be seen taxiing onto one of the airport's runways.

"What is that?"

Borger zoomed in closer and waited a moment for the image to sharpen again at the new resolution. The turboprop engines were clear, jutting out beneath the craft's high wing. Borger zoomed in still further.

"It's a Y-12," Clay said, under his breath.

Borger nodded. "Correct. Chinese made, utility design, and able to carry upwards of twenty passengers."

"Was it there the whole time?"

"No. It flew in three days before the attack. At night."

Clay frowned. Of course it was at night. Nightfall seemed to be the preferred time for everything the Chinese were up to in Guyana.

Borger rolled the video again and they both watched as the plane paused briefly then accelerated down the runway and lifted into the air. As it climbed, the aircraft banked and headed due west.

Clay straightened behind Borger and folded his arms.

"Care to guess where it's headed?"

There was only one country to the west that was within the plane's range. And it was another country with whom the U.S. had a strained relationship. "Venezuela."

"Correct again." Borger continued typing on his keyboard and skipped to another location. "But not just any airport in Venezuela. It flew directly to El Libertador Air Force Base in Maracay and landed three hours and thirty-seven minutes later. Upon landing, a single person exited the plane and boarded another." He scrolled the map and stopped on another aircraft. One that was much bigger.

This time, Clay recognized the plane without having to enlarge the picture again. Both its design and enormous size were unmistakable. It was a Xian Y-20. One of the largest aircraft in the Chinese Air Force.

"I'm guessing that's a transport."

"It sure is," nodded Clay. "But it's still in development. That one is a prototype they revealed a couple years ago."

"A prototype?"

"Yes."

Clay's frown was deepening. The El Libertador base in Venezuela was infamous for the coup attempt in 1992 when General Visconti seized control of the base and launched an aerial attack on the capitol city. But it wasn't the reputation that concerned Clay. It was the fact that the Chinese planes had landed at a military base and not a commercial airport. It meant the Venezuelan government was partially involved, or at the very least, aware of the activities of the Chinese. Having the Xian Y-20 there most likely meant the Venezuelan government already knew more than they would ever admit.

"Did it fly straight back?" Clay asked.

"It did. It refueled once in Hawaii before continuing on to Beijing." Borger peered at Clay. "But why would they send a prototype all the way to South America? That's risky."

"The Y-20 has the longest range of any of their transport planes. Sending an armed aircraft would have attracted far more attention. But they still needed something *secure* that could fly back almost nonstop."

"For one person? That's one hell of an expensive trip."

"Which means it was either a very important person," he looked at Borger, still seated in front of him, "or the person was carrying something important."

"Or both."

Clay nodded. "Or both."

Together, the two continued staring at the frozen screen where a tiny figure could be seen crossing the tarmac to the larger plane.

Clay's phone suddenly rang, snapping them out of it. He looked at it and answered, putting the call on speakerphone. "Where are you, Steve?"

"Outside, near Santos. Where are you?"

"We're in Borger's office."

"Good. I hope you're helping him clean it."

Clay grinned while Borger pretended to look offended.

"You two alone?"

"Yes."

On the other end, Caesare looked out at the ocean from a shaded spot beneath a large Brazilian rosewood tree. The beach was less than two blocks away and he stood scanning the area as he spoke, looking for anyone paying too much attention to him.

By the time Langford had ended their call, Caesare had already reached the first floor of the hotel and was off the property entirely inside of three minutes. It wouldn't be long before someone discovered the bodies of Blanco and Sosa, and Caesare had no intention of being nearby.

"So what did I miss?"

Clay glanced again at the monitors on Borger's desk. "It looks like Wil may have found something."

"Your voice doesn't exactly sound exuberant."

"I'll try harder next time."

"I bet. I'm going to guess there's bad news coming."

"Maybe. It seems someone got clearance and flew out of Georgetown just after the Bowditch was hit. On a Chinese turbo-prop to Venezuela, and from there a transport straight back to Beijing."

"You're kidding."

"I wish we were." Clay leaned in, peering closer at the screen. "Just one person. Carrying some kind of a case."

Caesare sighed. "That's not good."

"Now who's not exuberant?"

"I say we blame Borger."

Wil Borger's eyes opened wide with surprise, and then narrowed.

"We were actually getting ready to blame you."

In spite of the jokes, they all knew how serious it was. If Borger was right, then it looked like something had been taken off that ship before it departed. Something important enough to fly directly to Beijing, the political epicenter of China. Clay already had a guess as to what the man was carrying.

"Any idea who the person was, Wil?"

"Not yet. But I'll find out."

From under the tree, Caesare nodded, absently watching an attractive woman cross the street. "Well, I'm afraid my news isn't much better. There's something I didn't mention on the phone with Langford."

Without moving his head, Clay exchanged a curious look with Borger. "What's that?"

"I got a little more out of Blanco before he took his long ride into the sunset. He told me about Otero, and that he knows about the monkey. But it seems he knows more than that. Blanco managed to spit out what Otero was asking him about. He said *Acarai*. The name of the mountain."

Clay sighed. "Crap."

"Yeah. How much he knows, I'm not sure. But it's a lot more than just the monkey."

"If that's true," Borger said, "then he's gonna be going back up there."

"Exactly. And if he pokes around long enough, he may just stumble across something he's not supposed to find."

Without a word, Clay stepped forward and sat down in the chair next to Borger. "That means we need to get there before he does." He stopped to think. "And we're going to need help."

"I was thinking the same thing."

"How would you like to make a stopover during your flight back?"

From under the giant rosewood, Caesare couldn't help but smile. "Are you kidding? I love Puerto Rico."

Next to Clay, Borger raised an eyebrow and spoke loud enough for Caesare to hear. "You do understand we actually need DeeAnn *on our side*."

"Piece of cake."

Clay wasn't so sure it would be that easy. "All right then. Borger and I will see what else we can find out on this end. When are you leaving?"

"I'm not sure," Caesare replied. He wiped a bead of sweat from his forehead. With the phone still to his ear, he turned back to face the glimmering skyscrapers of São Paulo in the distance. "I need something first. I need to know where Miguel Blanco's family is."

From his chair, Borger stared at Clay's phone with a puzzled look. "You want to know where Blanco's family lives?"

"No," he replied dryly. "I need to know where they are right now."

## 3

THE BRIGHT PUERTO Rican sun shimmered over the top of the salt water tank, creating a curtain of glistening sunlight waving gently through the water.

On the other side of the thick glass stood Alison Shaw, watching as the two dolphins, Dirk and Sally, occupied the far end of the tank. A group of children stood packed together there. Both dolphins floated close, playfully bumping their noses against the glass at the spots where the children were pressing their hands. They screamed with excitement when Dirk impulsively turned sideways, placing one of his flippers against the glass.

Alison was happy. Really happy. She looked down and gently rubbed the bandage wrapped around her wrist. They had returned from their harrowing trip through the Caribbean, all in one piece, with only scrapes and bruises. Chris Ramirez and Lee Kenwood had taken the worst of it, but they were home and healing quickly.

Dirk and Sally had returned with them, even though they were free to come and go as they pleased. Dirk was especially eager to return to the lab in Puerto Rico, which surprised Alison. She was sure it had something to do with how much he was fed. Without having to spend any effort hunting for fish, she suspected her lab was becoming something akin to a vacation for Dirk.

Best of all, Alison was in love. She had found the man of her dreams. John Clay was the most amazing man she'd ever met, even if the men she previously dated had set that bar fairly low. But John was nothing short of a phenomenon. Handsome, strong, smart, and a man who could really communicate. He was every woman's dream.

"It's almost feeding time," came Chris's voice from behind her. "Which means it's time for us to start arguing about lunch."

Alison turned and eyed the mug in his hand. "Isn't getting a little late for coffee?"

Chris smiled. Most of the bruising along the left side of his face was gone. "It's never too late for coffee." His obsession had now become an ongoing joke between them. It stuck from the early days of their working together, sometimes spending all night at work. Like her, Chris's specialty was marine biology and he'd joined her team early in its formation.

Chris emptied the rest of the cup and set it down on his cluttered desk. "I'll see if the IT boys want to go. Are you in?"

"No, you guys go ahead."

Alison watched him cross the room and climb the wide stairs up to the second floor. When he disappeared around the corner, she turned back to the tank. The children were waving now, saying their goodbyes and being pulled gently away from the glass by their teachers. Another class visit was scheduled for that afternoon.

She took a deep breath and let it out slowly. There was only one thing that kept her from full contentment. And Alison was trying to remain in denial about it for as long as she could.

She glanced at the far end of the room where their massive, and now infamous, IMIS computer system covered the entire wall. Short for "Inter Mammal Interpretive System," the original version was what allowed for the incredible breakthrough back in their Miami research center. Since relocating to Puerto Rico, and closer to Dirk and Sally's natural habitat, the IMIS system had been radically improved. What that improvement led to next was a leap forward that not even they were prepared for. It not only expanded IMIS's translation capabilities beyond dolphins to primates, but it had done so in a way that surprised even their computer experts, Lee and Juan. And on top of it all, during a near crisis, IMIS had successfully translated pieces of language in a way that none of them had ever anticipated, or even programmed for.

She stared at the massive wall of servers, humming quietly with its hundreds of green lights blinking away. The system was silently crunching data and looking for more relationships between already established language patterns.

Alison looked away as she spotted a familiar face

entering from the long hallway which connected the lab to their outdoor habitat. DeeAnn Draper smiled and looked curiously around the silent room.

"Must be lunch time."

Alison grinned. "How'd you guess?"

"I love predictable men." DeeAnn smiled and watched the last of the children wave goodbye to the dolphins at the other end of the tank.

Alison's face took on a worried expression. She frowned and lowered her voice. "Are you still sure?"

"Yes," DeeAnn nodded. "I talked to Penny again this morning. They're getting things ready at the Foundation."

Alison sighed. She understood why DeeAnn was leaving. The last month had been devastating for her, both emotionally and physically. She had embarked on a trip that began as a cause to help find a friend, only to end up nearly perishing herself. If it weren't for Steve Caesare single-handedly saving her, she wouldn't have been standing in front of Alison now.

A serious brush with death had a habit of changing people. Alison understood that. And DeeAnn was one of them. She was alive and grateful, but she was done with adventure. She wanted nothing now but to live a simple life and to keep a single person safe. At least to her it was a person. And now, thanks to the IMIS system, she was absolutely sure about that.

"So…"

DeeAnn answered the question before she could finish. "We leave a week from Friday."

Alison pressed her lips together and nodded. She reached out and hugged DeeAnn. Over the last several months, the woman had become her mentor. An amazing woman in so many ways, who also had changed the world as much as Alison and her team ever had. The world just didn't know it yet.

"When are you going to tell the guys?"

DeeAnn cleared her throat. "Today or tomorrow." She managed another smile and glanced over Alison's shoulder to see Dirk and Sally approaching. They glided smoothly up to the glass, watching the two women.

*Hello D Ann.*

She blinked a tear away and turned her smile to them. "Hi, Sally. Hi, Dirk."

Dirk stared at her, quizzically. *D Ann sad.*

"A little." DeeAnn still couldn't quite get used to the way IMIS pronounced her name during a translation. According to Lee, the computers seemed to have trouble resolving a double "e" following the letter "d." He didn't understand it either, but the resulting pronunciation sounded more like "D-an" with a stutter. It wasn't a big deal, but it always reminded her that a machine was ultimately behind the translations.

*Why sad.*

DeeAnn looked at Alison. "It's a long story."

A loud buzz sounded from a monitor on the main desk. On the screen, a red error message displayed "unable to translate – story."

"It's all right," Alison said. She changed the subject. "Are you ready for food?"

Dirk became noticeably excited once Alison's words were translated into a series of clicks and whistles. *Yes, food now.*

Alison turned to Sally, who was hovering slightly

closer than Dirk. "How about you, Sally? Are you hungry?"

The women heard their translation emitted from the underwater speaker, but Sally did not answer. Instead, she simply stared at them with her dolphin's perpetual smile.

"Sally?"

Again the speaker sounded. After a long silence Sally finally replied.

*You leaving.*

Both Alison and DeeAnn's eyes widened in surprise.

"That's...right, Sally." DeeAnn answered. "How did you know that?"

*Why you leave?*

She frowned. *How could she explain human emotion to a dolphin?* It was a lot of things. Depression. Grief. Fear. Fear of somehow losing the purest thing she had ever known. And the love of finally feeling like a mother.

"It's...complicated."

The translation system buzzed again, unable to translate "complicated."

DeeAnn tried again. "It's hard to tell you."

Her response was successful, but Sally didn't answer. DeeAnn wasn't sure whether that meant Sally was satisfied with the answer or not. Dolphins were not human, but even with her limited time speaking with Dirk and Sally, she was surprised at how human-like some of the communication felt. She wondered if much of what we considered unique human communication actually had more underlying commonalities with other forms than we knew.

*How you Alison?*

"I'm good," she smiled. "How are you?"

*How you hurt?*

Alison glanced down at her bandage. "I'm getting better. Thank you." Since they had returned, both Dirk and Sally were surprisingly curious of their injuries, including those of Chris and Lee. In fact, curious wasn't quite the right term. They were more "attentive." She was very touched by their concern and wondered if they were somehow feeling responsible. They may have been there when it happened, but they certainly were in no way responsible. Still, at times it left her with a distinct feeling of not only sympathy from the dolphins but a sense of *empathy*. It prompted her to ask them on multiple occasions if they had been hurt by the explosion. They insisted they hadn't, but she wasn't so sure.

*Where man?*

Alison gave Sally a sly grin. The dolphin was asking about John. He had spent a few days with her on the island after their return and spent some time talking to Dirk and Sally. Being an expert in technology, he continued to marvel at what they had done with IMIS. He was particularly impressed with the vests Lee and Juan designed. Clay warned her that it was just a matter of time before the world truly understood what she and her team had achieved. He warned her to prepare for that. The wave of publicity they'd received in Miami after the first breakthrough would be nothing compared to what was coming.

Alison brushed her dark brown hair back behind an ear and answered Sally with a girlish chuckle. "John had to leave. He had to go home."

Sally made the familiar sound that IMIS had long ago identified as laughter. *He come back.*

Alison sure hoped so. And maybe one day he'd be back to stay.

* * *

Upstairs, Chris was sitting with Lee Kenwood and Juan Diaz in the computer lab. It was comfortably sized and well organized with metal tables along the wall. Neatly stacked shelves hung above them, filled with books, a wide range of computer parts, and mounds of magnetic backup tapes. Another larger table rested in the center of the room, illuminated by a bright lamp overhead. On the table lay a new vest with various cables strung to a nearby computer.

Positioned in the middle of the vest was a large speaker with a much smaller microphone and digital camera embedded just a few inches above it. It was a replacement for the damaged unit that DeeAnn had brought back from South America. The system data had still been intact, but the small motherboard and processor were not worth salvaging.

Chris watched Lee and Juan, patiently waiting for an answer on lunch. Both were distracted and staring intently at the monitor atop Lee's desk.

"I take it you're still looking for the ghost in the system."

"It's not a ghost," Lee mumbled, moving the mouse and scrolling down.

"Sorry, I mean "anomaly."

"It's not an anomaly either."

"Riddle?"

Juan turned and rolled his eyes while Lee, still facing forward, shook his head.

"Come on! I'm joking." Chris reached down and picked up a thick textbook from Lee's desk. He thumbed through it. It advertised itself as the bible of computer algorithms. He believed it. The contents looked completely unreadable. "So what's wrong exactly?"

Lee took a break and turned his chair around. "It's not that something is necessarily wrong. It's more that something isn't right."

"Is it part of the log problem?"

"I think so."

The log problem to which Chris referred had in fact been a serious problem. Before their harrowing trip to the Caribbean, Lee discovered that the IMIS translations and the related video feeds were falling increasingly out of sync. The logs on the servers showed the frequency of errors to be increasing rapidly, leaving Lee worrying that thousands of new lines of computer code had seriously broken something.

But after several sleepless nights, they discovered that IMIS was actually picking up on very subtle cues outside commonly recognized audible patterns. In other words, IMIS, a machine, was literally learning "nonverbal" communication.

However, Lee and Juan couldn't figure out how it was doing it. The vests were working almost *too* well.

Chris listened as Lee explained what they were looking for. "So, you're saying IMIS shouldn't be as effective as it is?"

"More or less." Lee walked over to the table and held up their new vest. "When IMIS detects speech patterns from Dirk and Sally, it digitizes the signal and compares it to the database of words it has identified. When it has a match, it sends those translated words back through the speaker."

"And then in reverse order when *we* speak, right?"

"Exactly. It works as expected with the dolphins because their language is mostly verbal. But that changes with a primate. Remember, DeeAnn says primate communication involves a lot of nonverbal communication like gestures and facial expressions."

"Right."

"Well, that's where it's not making sense," Lee shrugged, looking at Juan. "IMIS is now picking up on nonverbal cues — we've already established that. We're not exactly sure on how that's happening. But the more obvious problem is that while IMIS is picking up on those nonverbal cues, it has no way to *convey* them."

"That we can see," corrected Juan.

Chris squinted. "I'm not sure I'm following."

Lee thought for a moment. "Let's say, for example, that a nonverbal cue IMIS picks up from Dulce is a shrug. It sees that from the video feed and matches it with the audio. But how does it convey that?"

Now Chris understood. "I see. So while IMIS can *observe* a shrug, it has no way to actually transmit that gesture through the vest's speaker."

"Bingo!"

"Wow. That *is* weird."

"It shouldn't be able to translate gestures in both directions, but it does. And we don't know how."

Chris thought it over. He didn't know the answer either. He had a suspicion but nothing concrete. It was a topic that Alison and he had discussed several times over the last couple years and were sure others had too. After years in the field, working with different creatures, they had eventually come to the same conclusion; there was something deeper and unknown happening when it came to communication. Especially in less cognizant brains. It was something many people had wondered about at one time or another. How animals knew so much instinctively, even things they had never been taught by a parent.

Communication was the means to knowledge. But Chris and Alison, as well as other researchers, even veterinarians, were sure there was something else happening at a deeper level. A level that humans could not yet understand or measure.

But maybe IMIS was doing just that.

# CATALYST

The story continues.
And the world is about to change.
Forever.

*(Available on Amazon)*

# ABOUT THE AUTHOR

Michael Grumley lives in Northern California with his wife and two young daughters. His email address is michael@michaelgrumley.com and his web site is www.michaelgrumley.com where you can also find a supplemental Q&A page for this story.

# ABOUT DEEANN DRAPER

You might be interested to know, that while a fictional character in this story, DeeAnn Draper, is in fact, a real person. And much like the character she has inspired, the *real* DeeAnn is also very intriguing. Her education covers everything from science, math, and chemistry, to psychology and English. She spent over seven years working with Koko at the Gorilla Foundation in southern California.

Over the years, DeeAnn has enjoyed SCUBA diving, riding motorcycles, exercising and fixing up houses. She served as the subject matter expert for Dulce and much of the primate related elements of LEAP.

The few factual liberties I've taken were for story line reasons.

# MESSAGE FROM THE AUTHOR

Thank you for taking the time to read *LEAP.* I hope you enjoyed it. As some of you may know, I'm a part-time, self-published author, with the hope of one day being able to write full-time. I still have more Breakthrough stories stuck in my head. Not surprisingly, a self-published writer's only real means for accomplishing this is through reviews and referrals. I know leaving a review can be a bit of a pain, but if you could please spare two minutes to leave a review for LEAP, I would be very grateful.

Thank you,
Michael

## BOOKS BY MICHAEL C. GRUMLEY

BREAKTHROUGH

LEAP

CATALYST

AMID THE SHADOWS

THROUGH THE FOG

THE UNEXPECTED HERO

Made in United States
Orlando, FL
20 December 2022

27197059R00290